‖‖‖‖‖‖‖‖‖‖‖‖‖‖‖‖‖‖‖‖‖‖‖
✍ **W9-BED-125**

PANDORA'S BLACK BOX

"Don't you think we should investigate a little more before getting Headquarters in a tizzy? It could just be a simple mistake."

Dykes stopped pacing and faced Castor. "How? Think about it, Charlie. How could it possibly be just a simple mistake?" Dykes ticked off points on his fingers. "A module the exact size and weight of a legitimate package gets substituted on a shuttle flight. The module has the correct number stenciled on it. It must have even had an inspection tag on it, now that I think about it, otherwise the packing crew wouldn't have loaded it. The launch manifest lists the package for that flight, on that date, when the real module is not scheduled to go up for another nine days. The mission manifest, which is a duplicate copy of the launch manifest, is generated by the same person at the same time, yet the copy Kennedy has is different from what we have. The real module wasn't even in Inspection then, it was in the warehouse. The warehouse didn't pull it, Inspection didn't inspect it, no other package is missing and we can't find it in orbit, but we sure as hell put something up there."

Realization dawned in Castor's eyes, and his face blanched. "You're thinking some kind of terrorism, aren't you? My God, Joe! What could it be?"

"Not yet. Whatever they want, they know our launch make-ready procedures, and our launch schedule,

OPERATION DAMOCLES

OSCAR L. FELLOWS

OPERATION DAMOCLES

This is a work of fiction. All the characters and events portrayed in this book are fictional, and any resemblance to real people or incidents is purely coincidental.

Copyright © 1998 by Oscar L. Fellows

All rights reserved, including the right to reproduce this book or portions thereof in any form.

A Baen Books Original

Baen Publishing Enterprises
P.O. Box 1403
Riverdale, NY 10471

ISBN: 0-671-57771-9

Cover art by Gary Ruddell

First printing, October 1998

Distributed by Simon & Schuster
1230 Avenue of the Americas
New York, NY 10020

Typeset by Windhaven Press, Auburn, NH
Printed in the United States of America

To the times and the country of my
father—an America of conservative
values, individual liberty, common
courtesy, public decency and respect
for the rights of others.

Printed by Windhaven Press, Auburn, NH
Printed in the United States of America

For Mission Control, this flight, like a human

1

Columbia sat on the launch pad, nose to the blue-white Florida sky, vapor from her tank vents drifting and dissipating on the light, intermittent breeze. Her crew was aboard, and the gantry elevator had just been secured in preparation for launch. Inside her instrument panels and bulkheads, signals raced through electronic pathways of printed wiring as circuit diagnostic programs searched for faults.

From a bird's vantage point, technicians in white coveralls appeared like ants as they moved around the base of the gantry and the huge spacecraft. The temperature was rising on another humid June day, and the low-lying mist was burning off the backwaters of the inland, marshy estuary known as Mosquito Lagoon.

To the west, occasional palmettos, moss-laden oaks and windrows of salt-cedar trees interrupted the flat, hazy horizon of low scrub that was Merritt Island Wildlife Refuge. There, alligators, snakes, armadillos and marsh hawks were wrapping up a night of foraging, and settling into their cooler nests and burrows in anticipation of the sluggish heat.

On the eastern side of the launch complex, along the Atlantic shore, the surf frothed and gurgled among the gently lapping waves and low rollers that marked the transition between tides. It was a peaceful summer morning at Kennedy Space Center. The scent of the sea rode the easterly breeze, and the shuttle launch preparation in progress was unremarkable.

For Mission Control, this flight, like a hundred

previous ones, would be a routine, even humdrum mission, entailing three onboard science experiments, deployment of an ultraviolet astrophysics research satellite, and two term experiments that would be inserted into a decaying orbit—an orbit calculated to assure destruction upon reentry. "Term packages" were neat, clean—no additional space junk. They did their thing and disappeared, and they did not require the extensive application process required to secure a permanent orbit assignment.

"Fifty-seven minutes to ignition sequence," echoed the gantry loudspeakers. The gantry technicians continued their tasks with no apparent notice.

Inside Launch Control, launch team personnel were just as cool and professional, running through the diagnostic routines in methodical, workmanlike fashion. Launch Director Gene Obermiller walked between rows of technicians and engineers seated at computer monitors. He looked over their shoulders at their CRT displays, stopping occasionally to listen to the two-way conversation between a member of the shuttle crew on board *Columbia* and one of the technicians as they ran through the prelaunch systems checklist.

An hour from now, most of the people in Launch Control would leave, and Mission Control in Houston would take over flight operations. In nine days, assuming no technical difficulties or inclement weather, they would do it all over again for *Atlantis*.

"Launch telemetry ready."

"Goldstone, do you copy?"

"Are you gonna catch the game tonight?"

"Three is vented, you can disconnect," went the drone of quiet conversation across the room.

"Minus forty-three and counting at oh nine oh five," the annunciator echoed.

The sky and sea seemed quietly expectant today. In a few minutes, the fuming vehicle on the pad would ride a coruscated column of water vapor and white-hot flame into those boundless vaults of air, pirouetting gracefully as she performed her dance with destiny, and Merritt Island and the Cape Canaveral peninsula would vibrate to the crackling thunder of her engines.

Obermiller looked at the ceiling monitor that displayed the downrange horizon, ran his fingers through the dark hair that was beginning to gray above his temples, and massaged the knotted muscles in the back of his neck.

Taciturn by nature, Obermiller was unusually quiet and introspective this morning. His colleagues liked his poker face and unfailing dependability. They respected him as only one veteran can respect another. In engineering vernacular, Gene was positive-displacement. You knew what you were getting and you always got it.

Long ago, someone had laminated a newspaper cartoon and pinned it to the corkboard inside the glass-covered bulletin board in the lobby of the Launch Control complex. The person who had clipped it and penned in "Gene" with an arrow pointing to one of the characters was long forgotten, but the sentiment lived on in the minds of NASA old-timers. The labeled golfer in the cartoon leaned casually on a golf club, watching an atomic mushroom rise above a nearby city skyline, and said to the other golfer, "Go ahead and putt, Ralph, it'll take a few seconds for the shockwave to reach us."

That was Obermiller. The consensus was, if Gene ever got nervous, you might as well bend over and kiss your nether region good-bye, because you were about to witness the Second Coming. It wasn't that evident on the surface, but today Gene was nervous.

Forty-seven minutes later, "SRB separation at oh nine fifty-two," came the voice of the controller. "She's seventy-five miles downrange and five-by-five. Seven minutes of burn remaining."

A seated technician looked at Obermiller, who stood watching the overhead monitor. "Bermuda has com and telemetry, Gene, and Sydney is standing by for the handoff."

"Fine, It looks like a good one," Obermiller replied.

❖   ❖   ❖

Two days later, *Columbia* orbited the Earth belly down, her bay doors open to eject her payload toward a higher orbit. Two mission specialists worked in the cargo bay, intent on their task, oblivious to the black, yawning void above them and the majestic, blue-white, marbled planet turning below. The rest of the crew was busy inside *Columbia*'s cabin.

When the research satellite was away, controllers on the ground would fire thrusters on the "bird" to maneuver it into geosynchronous orbit 22,300 miles above Earth. Once her payload had been deployed, *Columbia* would roll over on her back, open bay toward the Earth, for her remaining days in orbit.

The important payload, the ultraviolet research satellite, was gently guided onto the spring-driven expulsion platform by the two mission specialists, and when the moment was right, ejected in a slowly spinning trajectory, like a rifle slug, toward the deep. The two remaining orbital experiments followed, lifted from the shuttle bay and released in *Columbia*'s wake by the robot arm, with just enough rearward momentum to assure they cleared the shuttle's vicinity, where engine and thruster maneuvers might affect them. As the astronauts watched past the tail of the ship, the instruments shrank to specks of light, and finally winked out in the distance.

"Payload insertion complete," radioed the mission specialist to the shuttle commander.

"Good! Secure for maneuvering," came the reply.

At two days into the mission, everything was going fine. *Columbia* would spend three more days in low earth orbit (LEO) as the crew completed the onboard experiments and other studies that comprised this mission's program, then, due to impending weather at Kennedy, she would land at Edwards Air Force Base in California. There, she would be mounted on the back of a 747 jetliner for transport back to Kennedy.

II

Mission Control at Johnson Space Center was located in building #30, one of a hundred or so buildings that comprised the 1600-acre Houston site. Most of the JSC installation consisted of administrative space and laboratories, with only a few core facilities actually dedicated to astronaut training and mission operations. As a senior NASA official once remarked, "NASA could put the giant fifty-story Vehicle Assembly Building at Kennedy Space Center on the moon if it wanted to, but there were no rocket engines made that could lift the paperwork required for the project."

Building #30 was a sprawling structure surrounded by grass, walks and a few trees. Large picture windows in the outer offices looked out over a flat, hazy vista that stretched eastward toward Galveston Bay, and southward toward League City and the Highway 45 expressway. Structures and trees cast sharp, contrasting shadows in the glaring, afternoon sun of a Texas summer day.

Inside, the chief of Mission Control was in the midst of receiving an unsettling piece of information. Big and craggy-visaged, Joe Dykes sat with customary ease behind the wide, executive desk in his fourth-floor office, his back to the expanse of plate-glass window that looked out on the courtyard, the horizon and the cloudless blue vault of the sky. Cool-white fluorescent lighting lent a supporting ambiance to the gray carpet and white walls which were intermittently demarcated by beige metal furniture, potted plants and framed commemorative

5

plaques. It was a pleasant, air-conditioned haven from the sweltering outdoor heat.

Across the oak-grain expanse of his desk, with its neatly organized stacks of paper, Dykes regarded Mark Miller, the Flight Operations Chief from Mission Control, with a quizzical expression. Both men were dressed in shirt sleeves and ties, and looked a bit lost sitting in Dykes' spacious, but spartanly-furnished office.

"What do you mean, *lost it*?" asked Dykes.

"Exactly that. Two term packages were placed in orbit; now one is there, and the other has vanished. We rechecked the record tapes from the shuttle. Insertion acceleration moments are within a couple of gram-seconds of one another. Unless one got hit by a piece of orbital debris, it ought to be there."

"Think that could have happened?"

"I don't know what to think. If it got hit by something, it should be spinning on an erratic path, or at least have left bits and pieces that would be easy to find. So far, not a thing. We haven't given up. We're still scanning the orbital track, but I thought you ought to know, just in case the customer calls up and wants to know what's going on."

"Whose was it, do you know?"

"No. No names on my paperwork, just the package numbers, vectors, insertion times, etc. We're just trying to do our routine confirmation of deployed payload. Found the first one right away, right where it's supposed to be, but we've been looking for the other one for twenty hours now. Nothing. Not even gas." Miller rose to go. "I don't know what else to tell you at the moment, Joe. I'll let you know if it turns up."

"I'd appreciate it, Mark. Thanks!"

"Sure thing," said Miller as he turned and left through the open doorway.

Dykes picked up the phone. "Denise, get me Bobbie-Jo Hendricks in Customer Relations, please." A moment later, "BJ, I may have a problem. We lofted two term packages last week, mission twenty-eight, *Columbia*. One has gone missing. Can you find out whose they were, and points of contact with phone numbers? Yeah, as soon as possible. Thanks!"

An hour later, Dykes sat mystified. He had learned that the missing experiment was officially listed by Kennedy as a pyrolytic metals experiment from the mechanical engineering department at Stanford University. However, Mission Control hadn't communicated with Stanford, as they ordinarily would have, in order to notify them when insertion was completed and transfer of responsibility had taken place. The reason for the glitch was that there was no mention of the experiment in Houston's flight operations plan. In fact, it turned out that Stanford's package hadn't flown on *Columbia*, and according to the university, was scheduled aboard *Atlantis*, slated to launch the following day.

The packing crew at Kennedy had a manifest which indicated they had loaded the Stanford module aboard *Columbia*, but the Kennedy Payload Inspector, whose signature was on the manifest, said that he had inspected only one term experiment for the Columbia mission, a module belonging to Argonne National Laboratory, and denied having signed a manifest for the Stanford package. He was aware of the module from Stanford, confirmed that it was scheduled for *Atlantis*, and that it was presently being inspected.

The following day, Dykes spoke with Charles Castor from Customer Relations, who had been investigating the incident.

"If it's an alloying experiment, why is it a term package," asked Dykes. "Don't they want the finished melt back for study?"

Castor was a slight, middle-aged man who had the natural ability to look comfortable in a suit. He resembled the rumpled college professors in Walt Disney films who always look at home wearing tweed jackets with elbow patches, a sort of born-to-it, casual look. He always seemed to go through a kind of physical ritual before he said something, as if talking somehow required a particular body position. Dykes thought that perhaps he just used the time to collect his thoughts.

Castor adjusted his glasses, crossed his legs, laced his hands together around his knee, adopted a serious mien, and responded, "The project description states that the hydrogen torch that fires the kiln, and the attendant outgassing from the metals, make it potentially unsafe to perform this particular experiment on board the shuttle. The design parameters for the experiment were all set up through NASA engineering. Because of that, the standard volume limit for experimental modules was extended to two cubic meters so that cameras, telemetry antennae, a spectrometer, a gas chromatograph and a heavy testing machine for hardness, malleability and other final properties could be included. It has much larger gas bottles, and an attitude control system. It has a CO_2 inventory for propellant, and a guidance system of sorts. Telemetry and transceiver frequencies have been cleared; everything is copacetic.

"Dr. Haas at Stanford is ticked off about all the questions. He says that all the preparations were done months ago, and whatever foul-up *we* have made, it has nothing to do with his package. He wants to know if his schedule is going to slip because of this."

Dykes waved his hand dismissively, got up and paced the room. "Tell him no. Tell him that the package we launched was simply misidentified somehow, and that his experiment can go as scheduled. The big questions now are, what did we launch, and why can't we identify whom it belongs to? It apparently fit the Stanford module dimensions closely enough that the packing crew loaded it without a bleep. All other scheduled payload has been inventoried and accounted for. Nothing is missing. Surely someone didn't just package a couple of empty oil drums in a payload module, and risk losing a job for a practical joke. It just doesn't make any sense."

"Whatever it was, it wasn't empty drums. It massed at four hundred and eight kilos."

"Why didn't they catch that? Isn't that a lot for an experiment package?"

"Yes, but like I said, special clearance was obtained."

Dykes' face showed surprise, doubt. "You mean, the Stanford experiment weighs the same?"

"To the kilo."

"Isn't that just the weight shown on the manifest?"

"No, Joe, the packing crew weighs all payload before stowing it for launch. That is the mass the crew chief logged at the time the package was loaded."

Dykes simply stared for a moment, then said, "A chill just went up my spine. It's beginning to sound like this was a very deliberate, well-planned substitution. The odds of two random packages having exactly the same weight and dimensions are astronomical." Dykes thought a moment. "I'm going to call Clarence Patterson."

"Don't you think we should investigate a little more before getting headquarters in a tizzy? It could just be a simple mistake."

Dykes stopped pacing and faced Castor. "How? Think about it, Charlie. How could it possibly be just a simple mistake?" Dykes ticked off points on his fingers. "A module the exact size and weight of a legitimate package gets substituted on a shuttle flight. The module has the correct number stenciled on it. It must have even had an inspection tag on it, now that I think about it, otherwise the packing crew wouldn't have loaded it. The launch manifest lists the package for that flight, on that date, when the real module is not scheduled to go for another nine days. The mission manifest, which is a duplicate copy of the launch manifest, is generated by the same person at the same time, yet the copy Kennedy has is different from what we have. The real module wasn't even in Inspection then, it was in the warehouse. The warehouse didn't pull it, Inspection didn't inspect it, no other package is missing and we can't find it in orbit, but we sure as hell put something up there."

Realization dawned in Castor's eyes, and his face

blanched, "You're thinking some kind of terrorism, aren't you? My God, Joe! What could it be?"

"Shoe-box nuke maybe, or some kind of bio-weapon. Either one could kill a couple of million people if placed just right. Maybe nothing more harmful than half a ton of propaganda leaflets. Lord, what a coup that would be for one of these lunatic outfits. I just can't think of a practical reason for doing something like that from space, unless the main intent is to embarrass NASA and the U.S. government."

Dykes picked up the phone. "I hope I'm wrong about all this, but I'm calling Patterson. Get all tracking stations busy trying to find that thing. Notify NORAD and the Air Force Space Command that we need their assistance in finding an experiment module that strayed off course. Give them dimensions, trajectory and last known coordinates. Do not tell anyone, there or here, what we have been talking about, okay? Not even your wife. If the media gets wind of this, the agency will be crucified, even if nothing bad ever comes of it."

III

Dr. Clarence "Butch" Patterson sat in his office looking through a water-streaked, plate-glass window at the Washington, DC, skyline. It had been raining, and right now it looked as bleak and overcast as a winter day. It matched his frame of mind.

Patterson looked the part of the distinguished scientist and administrator that he was. He fit the public image. In some part, that fact had aided him in his rise through the National Office of Science and Technology, and through NASA. Not that he wasn't a good scientist, he was, and a good administrator too, but he had learned long ago that he had a flair for office politics. His was a natural, untrained charm—an easygoing personality that instilled confidence and trust. The crinkle at the corner of his eyes when he smiled, the automatic conspiratorial wink he unthinkingly injected into every conversation with peers and subordinates alike—these were habitual traits that made people feel warm and personal with him, as if they were his closest confidants. He was well-liked by most of his staff and associates, and worshipped by the secretary of ten years whom he had taken with him in his last two promotions. He was generally known for his honesty, ready smile and laid-back nature. He wasn't smiling now though, and the unusually-accentuated lines of his face made him look considerably older than his fifty-five years.

To Patterson, the position he had attained this past January, as Director of the National Aeronautics and Space Administration, was the epitome of career achieve-

11

ment. It was his life's ambition, and it had come true. It meant that his name would be added to the annals of human history. His life had mattered. He had helped to shape the world and left a legacy that people of future generations would read about. He loved the stature, but God, he hated the social scene in today's Washington.

Nothing he had ever done had prepared him for the life of a Washington bureaucrat. It was insane. Interoffice spying was routine. It was like a pack of rats, scrabbling for an advantage, and woe unto him who let his guard down. Not even your own staff could be trusted beyond a certain point, he thought. You certainly didn't build intimate confidences.

The work he had trained for and loved all his life— agency business—was suddenly of secondary importance to everyone but him. Petty incidentals were all that mattered. His calendar was filled with important meetings about trivial stuff—protocol alerts concerning visits from minor VIPs and foreign dignitaries, and innumerable state functions with which he had nothing to do— and it seemed that the only thing ever accomplished at those meetings was establishing the time and date of the next meeting.

He was learning that, unlike science, nothing in cabinet-level politics was straightforward. Politics, to Patterson, was an elemental thing. It was making people like you. It was an emotional thing that worked best when it was a natural gift, as it was with him. A kind of subliminal cajolery that swayed most people, and if applied over time, eventually got you what you wanted. He knew what he was doing, and when he was doing it; it wasn't totally unconscious. He picked his targets, people who could give him a leg up on his career ladder, and he knew that he wasn't quite the sincere and caring man he pretended to be. The inner man wasn't particularly proud of himself, but he also knew he didn't belong among the blatant brotherhood of thieves that made up the woof and warp of Washington's social fabric.

Washington was a place of grand buildings and edifices, monuments to great ideals, but these days, it was peopled with all the utterly selfish of the land. Here, the only aspect of government business that mattered was who profited from it. Office politics consisted of getting the dirt on other people, even amplifying on their minor mistakes, while keeping one's own transgressions safely hidden.

In a way, he felt ashamed of his ingratitude. The newly-installed President Vanderbilt had personally appointed Patterson, lifted him above his equally-deserving colleagues and peers in the space sciences community, and set his name down in history. Lately though, the first flush of pride and pleasure in the appointment was waning, and he had begun wondering, *why me*. He had been director of the Johnson Space Center at Houston, and as such, certainly in line for the position, but somehow it just didn't feel right. In the past few months, he had come to understand that everything done in Washington, was done for a reason other than the one publicly expressed. If someone benefited, a payback of some sort was generally taken for granted. Vanderbilt had shown no reticence in pointing it out.

Patterson hadn't "known" anyone in particular. He knew that Vice-President Joseph Miller had lobbied for his appointment, but he didn't know why. He had never met the man. Why had Miller championed him? Why had Vanderbilt acceded? Had he just slipped through the cracks? Was his appointment an accident, a decision made by a man who was tired of thinking about all the minutiae of moving into his office, and who momentarily had no better candidate in mind? If not, if there was a hidden motive, what payback was expected?

It had begun to haunt him. A niggling doubt that hovered always on the fringe of consciousness, clouded his perspective, pulled his thoughts aside, inhibited the clear, free-flowing logistical thoughts of mission, people, tools and money that he was used to. His dream had begun turning sour.

And now this! Only six months into his administration, and out of nowhere, Joe Dykes had handed him a political hot-potato to top them all. His dream of a long and productive tenure was rapidly becoming a nightmare of being the first NASA chief to be fired in disgrace.

"God, let it be just another paperwork foul-up," he prayed, "just another innocent package that got coded wrong and pulled by mistake."

He didn't believe it, even as he thought it. As Dykes had said, there were too many matching factors for it to be coincidental. What would his historical legacy read if NASA had unwittingly orbited a weapon of some sort, someone else's weapon, to be used against the United States? And how to react?

In a normal environment, it was his duty to tell the President. The Commander in Chief should be informed of any potential threat to national security. But these days, it wasn't a normal environment in Washington. He had seen enough heads fall in the past six months to know that if he told the White House, it would be on the evening news. Not even a ghost of a doubt. The first thing they would do is wash their hands and make him the sacrificial goat. Even if it turned out to be some sort of innocent error, he would be painted a fool, at the very least, and his career finished.

If he was a heartless bastard, he could "uncover" the foul-up himself, and destroy the lives of a few select people in the agency to save himself. He couldn't bring himself to do it. NASA and its people had been his life, and he loved it too much to subject it to that kind of fallout. Security would get so tight that a person wouldn't be able to visit the bathroom alone, and the already paper-mired process would become so impossible that NASA couldn't launch a paper clip. It would filter out into all the support contractors and research groups until nothing substantive would get done. The agency would become just another budgetary black hole, and might even end up as part of another agency consolidation as Congress put on one of its shows of austerity for the

American public. They might even put it under military command. It was already regulated by the military to some degree.

He had admonished Dykes not to let the news leak, and he thought he could rely on him. With that thought, his resolve hardened. He would keep it quiet until the issue went away, or blew up. He would be no worse off in any event. He wasn't about to carry an ax over to the White House and bare his neck.

IV

Harold Tanner, newly appointed Secretary of Defense, was similarly preoccupied in the headquarters building at Langley Air Force Base. He had just come out of one of the strangest and most depressing meetings of his career, and now stood at a window in the spacious, third-floor officers' lounge.

Against government edict, he was smoking a cigarette indoors. He stood in a habitual attitude of military parade-rest, his feet apart and firmly planted, his hands locked behind his waist, cigarette between his fingers. He surveyed the pedestrians in their glistening plastic raincoats, their umbrellas bobbing along the sidewalks, and watched the metronome beat of windshield wipers in the slowly moving traffic along the main base boulevard.

His crew-cut hair, humorless gray eyes and weathered face, along with the posture of his spare military frame, looked out of place in the tailored gray suit. Though he did not move, there was no mistaking the anger and agitation in him. His rigid stance, the nervous flicking of the cigarette and the scowl on his countenance forewarned anyone who might have contemplated speaking to him.

Tanner had just carried out an order to reassign two highly experienced and successful commanders from the U.S. Air Force Air-Combat Command, to assignments that were an insult to their skills and abilities. He hadn't realized what was happening until he met and talked with the two officers. As a former War College professor,

16

he couldn't fathom the reason for such a move, and as the new kid on the block, he knew he would get the blame for it among the services.

The Vanderbilt administration had jumped into Washington politics with both feet, and the walls inside the Beltway were still reverberating. The deal-making and back-room bargaining had gotten under way with a vengeance that shocked even the jaded insiders of Washington society. Government programs and agendas were changing in ways that seemed mysterious, unconnected and illogical. Agency heads were toppling like dominoes, and bureau reorganizations were becoming commonplace.

People connected with government business, from defense contractors to those in financial institutions, were wondering at the surprising trends in corporate America. In New York City, key industry and financial managers were retiring, and second-string media people were quietly vanishing into other pursuits—even into other countries. Tanner knew that the public wasn't aware of these behind-the-scenes happenings, but he assumed they had noted the replacement of the odd network newscaster and television news-show host. It was as if Vanderbilt was assembling a team that encompassed far more than just the Oval Office.

And so many deaths! Vanderbilt had attended more state funerals in the first six months of his administration than any previous president. Two of the Joint Chiefs were dead. Admiral Poindexter and General Thompson had died together in a freak automobile accident in February. Patrick Monahan, Under-Secretary of Commerce, was killed by a guerrilla missile that downed his plane during a visit to Nicaragua, in March. Susan Kawalski, U.S. Deputy Attorney-General, had died of a seizure in May, and later that month, Victor Matsu, Deputy Director of the Federal Bureau of Investigation, died suddenly of a virulent strain of hepatitis.

The new agency chiefs were all Vanderbilt appointees, and while each expressed eloquent grief over the demise of their seconds-in-command, the deaths somehow seemed fortuitous in light of the fact that there had been friction between the new chiefs and their career deputies, and the vacancies created by the deaths could now be filled by more agreeable people.

Almost as remarkable as the chain of deaths, was how little coverage they received. A year or two ago, such a chain of events would have kept the media mill going for weeks. Even designation of the newly-promoted replacements had gotten very limited mention.

Tanner sighed, some of the tension leaving his body as resignation set in. He absently put his hand against the moisture-fogged window, feeling the cold seep into his palm. Not for the first time, he wondered where in hell Vanderbilt had come from. In one moment it seemed, he was an obscure and somewhat colloquial senator from New Hampshire, to whom no one had paid much attention. In the next, he was the most powerful public figure in the world.

The Vice-President, Joseph Miller, was a former U.S. advisor to the European Economic Council. Tall and dark, with dispassionate, questioning brown eyes that seldom blinked—eyes that seemed to bore right into your mind—Miller was another enigma. Somehow, in his quiet, dark way, Miller seemed to evoke trust. Tanner could not say why.

Vanderbilt was another matter. Tanner's little, old-fashioned mother had a term for people like Vanderbilt. He was "vulgar," she would have said. Vanderbilt had an habitual lewd and arrogant way in which he looked at people. Not when he was in the public eye of course, but in meetings with his staff, and in private, he made no effort to disguise his contempt for others.

Oddly, for someone who was not an old-timer on the Washington scene, Vanderbilt swept aside resistance as no predecessor had ever done before. By that alone, Tanner knew that there was some heavy-duty money behind him. All the media had taken on the Vanderbilt tincture, and Washington and New York society life seemed to take on a vaguely different nuance. It seemed strained.

Tanner observed that Washington had become overt in its corruption. The rhetoric was still the same; the politicians were still "serving" their country, but the "hidden agenda" wasn't really hidden anymore. It had become the wallpaper of Washington society. The politicians and power brokers didn't really seem to care whether or not the public knew what they were doing. Most of them flouted their arrogant confidence that there was nothing the public could do about it. Washington had lost even the semblance of being about representative government. It was openly about power. Power and money, other people's money, the "golden fleece" of legend.

The nation of sheep that provided the fleece might occasionally object to being sheared, and the unstated Washington objective was to apply just the right balance of threat and propaganda to keep them producing and in check. To create enough doubt and confusion to prevent open rebellion. People handling. Manipulating the masses. It took a special talent, and Washington was a magnet for such talent. Tanner knew that it had always been that way to some degree, but suddenly it was obvious to all but the utterly blind, and supported by a ubiquitous media. All the carnivores were stepping out of the tall grass, licking their lips and openly observing the dozing flock.

Tanner took a last drag from the cigarette and smiled grimly at the metaphor. It was a literal fact. He had been in and out of Washington for years, and knew a lot of people, but lately, new faces were everywhere. Foreign faces with attitude. Disdainful Arabs. Contemptuous Orientals. Haughty Europeans. Multinational faces. Cold-eyed faces that appeared in hallways and lobby corners, often in earnest conversation with nervous-looking congresspeople and agency heads. Cloistered meetings for unknown purposes were becoming daily occurrences.

The federal workers who ran the day-to-day business of the government didn't know a great deal of course, and neither, it seemed, did some of the newly appointed cabinet officials, including himself. The individual agencies were comprised of people who for the most part were innocent cogs in a machine. They weren't privy to the inner workings and high-level meetings.

They probably wondered at all the new changes, but there was nothing anyone could put a finger on. In their world, things went on pretty much as before, but for senior and mid-level managers in the executive branch, politics had become brutal. It was obvious that people who couldn't adapt to whatever the hell was going on, were being coerced to resign. People who had made even minor political mistakes, such as publicly espousing a point of view that was antipathetic to the regime, were being encouraged to quietly retire. If you were part of the secret circle, it seemed, or possessed some sort of necessary knowledge, you were judged useful. If someone had some misinformed idea of what was important, he or she was not useful, and when no longer useful, one way or another, that person went away.

The few of his peers that Tanner had enjoyed anything resembling an intimate conversation with appeared to be as ignorant as he was about the nature of the secret substratum. By its very nature the exclusionary climate bred suspicion, and he wondered if those peers were actually ignorant, or if they just viewed him as one who was not yet an initiate to the circle. Some of them seemed reluctant to talk, not merely ignorant.

It was almost as if the briefings and unstructured meetings with the president and department heads had been scripted, glossy charades—superfluous get-acquainted meetings with an undercurrent of knowledge that not everyone was privy to—a "sizing-up" of human resources. Tanner knew that somewhere, somebody big was pulling the strings.

Unlike Patterson, Tanner thought he knew why he had been appointed. Of those with the knowledge to run the Defense Department, he was the most agreeable. Vanderbilt had made it plain that he didn't want a figurehead in charge of Defense. Neither did he want a headstrong type with rigid ideas. He wanted someone who knew the department inside-out. Someone who knew the key people and, as Vanderbilt had put it, "knew where the bones were buried." Above all, Vanderbilt wanted someone malleable; someone who could be molded into an extension of his own will.

Tanner thought back to a time just six weeks after his appointment, when he had sat with Vanderbilt and Miller, going over the classified personnel files of the various base and unit commanders in all the services, and of those members of congress who were connected in any way with military operations and procurements. On the surface, it seemed natural enough that a new president would want to know all about his key people, but it had seemed to Tanner at the time, that Vanderbilt's questions had an odd slant. Tanner was only now beginning to realize that, in the power shuffle that was taking place, it appeared that the ones being taken out of key commands were those who were the most dedicated and loyal. Commanders with exemplary war records. Older veterans with a lifetime of military honor ingrained in their makeup.

Realization suddenly dawned, and Tanner's eyes went wide. *The entire top of the military command structure was being systematically replaced.* Tanner had identified many of those people, thinking that the most diligent commanders would be the ones Vanderbilt would turn to in a crisis. Instead, they were the ones being removed and, if some of the prior appointments were any indication, they were being replaced by incompetent upstarts who had little, if any, military accolades, and the ethics of ferrets.

Tanner was too weak to challenge the President, and realized now that Vanderbilt had counted on that. The knowledge made him angry, angry with himself, and with those who recognized his weakness and used it for their own ends. Like Patterson, he had enjoyed the first flush of pride in his appointment, and had looked forward to earning the respect of his agency—to accomplishing great things and leaving his mark. Instead, he was to be Vanderbilt's hatchet man and errand boy. He knew now that he would be despised in the memory of the armed services.

The thought rekindled his anger. Silently fuming, he ground out his cigarette on the polished tile floor and walked away, paying no attention to the glaring looks of two Air Force officers seated at a nearby table. He was ready to take the head off the first person to offer a petty criticism.

V

On June 18, six days after the missing experiment had been noticed by NASA, a very exclusive meeting was held in the Flight Operations Conference Room at Johnson Space Center. Present were NASA Director Clarence Patterson, Joe Dykes and Charles Castor, as well as the Chief of Engineering at JSC, Natividad "Zeke" Maldenado, and Dr. Thelma Richards, Chief of Astrophysics at the Jet Propulsion Laboratory in Pasadena, California, where much of the telemetry and data gathering for NASA missions was done.

Zeke Maldenado had earned his Ph.D. in mechanical engineering from the University of Texas at Houston, and had been at JSC since his undergraduate days. He had worked for Clarence Patterson during the Apollo program, when Patterson was director of Design Engineering. Maldenado had worked hard, gradually climbing the career ladder toward engineering management, and he knew more about spacecraft propulsion and airframe design than Robert Goddard, the father of modern rocketry, could have dreamed of in his day. At the moment, his cultured Tejano accent and reassuring tone was helping to calm the tension in Patterson's face. Patterson knew him and his family well, had worked long hours during grueling times with the man, and he trusted him.

Thelma Richards was another long-time friend. Tall for a woman, she had always reminded Patterson of a schoolteacher. Her no-nonsense gray eyes, wire-framed glasses, and eternal pageboy haircut might have something to do with it, he thought, smiling to himself in spite of his troubles.

Richards had been a mission analyst during the Viking missions to Mars, and had gotten to know Patterson during the initial mission planning meetings in Houston, back in the early seventies. They, too, had worked shoulder-to-shoulder, through many long nights. They had even been intimate for a few months, but their shared dreams and consuming fascination with space-flight and discovery had bound their souls together in a way that somehow made sex between them distracting and uninteresting. They had remained close friends over the years, even after marrying other people. They enjoyed their occasional get-togethers at agency functions and planning meetings, and still had frequent telephone conversations.

Because her section at JPL was a locus of flight operations for so many Defense Department and civilian missions, Richards had solid contacts throughout the space sciences community, from the military to academia. She had developed most of the exobiology test protocols for deep space and planetary missions, and had earned her stripes the hard way, by genius of mind and an unrelenting hard-headedness that would brook no bureaucratic B.S. if it stood between her and what she wanted to accomplish.

Something of a hippie and activist in her younger days, and contemptuous of authority and politics, she was still a bit amazed, after all the intervening years, to know that she had made a lot of friends during her career, and that she, herself, had become a scientific authority and political power of national significance.

Patterson liked and trusted these people. They were his old teammates, people he knew he could depend on to give him good advice, and to keep it among themselves.

"How do you suppose it evaded radar detection?" Richards asked Maldenado. "We couldn't track it as it boosted into higher orbit, and we can't find it now."

"State of the art stealth technology," answered Maldenado. "It was meant to be undetectable." He leaned forward in his chair, forearms on the table, fingers laced together, and surveyed the ring of worried faces.

"Best guess scenario," he said, "three hours after the package was released by *Columbia*, the container module separated. The gas bottles and accouterments, supposedly the workings of a hydrogen torch and kiln, actually comprised an engine. Same for the rest of it. The test equipment listed in the package nomenclature is probably navigational stuff and controls. The main body of the device was inside a contamination-proof housing, and engineering only has the visual record of the outer casing to go by. The plans we have are of the Stanford experiment, which may have no resemblance whatever to the package we lofted.

"The Air Force Space Command imaged the orbital-transition burn, three hours and eighteen minutes after deployment into LEO, and assumed that it was a part of our planned activity. The Air Force thought that the burn was just an attitude-correction maneuver within the planned orbit, and didn't pay any attention to it. Why should they? It was a NASA launch, not an incoming, hostile missile . . . right?

"They didn't track anything in a tangential path, just the container parts, as they swung along in the original, twenty-eight-degree track. Incidentally, those parts were lined with aluminum foil to give them a higher-than-normal radar albedo, just to keep the Air Force thinking that it was where it was supposed to be, until final maneuvers were accomplished.

"Anyway, we enhanced the image of the engine flare. The computed trajectory of the burn path could possibly put it in a geostationary orbit, but exactly where is hard to tell. It was headed out, though. We know the bird's mass and the duration of the burn, but we don't know what the fuel or oxidizer was, or the thrust of the engine. Spectral analysis of the engine flare gives a strong hydrogen line, but it could be pure Hydrogen and LOX [liquid oxygen], or something like Aerozine 50 with a Nitro-Tet oxidizer, even kerosene and peroxide. Projecting where it ended up depends a great deal on knowing the energy of the burn, and we don't. From the size and spectral temperature of the flare, though, it looks like it had more than enough energy for geosynchronous insertion. It may even be headed for Jupiter, for all we know. If it boosted to a higher transfer orbit, nobody saw an apogee burn that would have parked it in a station-keeping orbit. It just disappeared.

"So that's about the size of it. Unless the bird emits radiant energy of some sort—RF, microwave or something—we are going to have a hard time finding it."

"There's no chance of the orbit decaying, and it falling back to Earth? You're certain about that, Zeke?" asked Patterson.

Richards answered, "Not unless it makes a U-turn, Butch, and we know it hasn't yet. If it fired retros, it would eventually decay and fall back, but the chances of it surviving reentry are slim to none. What would be the point, anyway? Why go geostationary, twenty-two thousand miles out, only to drop out later. It wouldn't make any sense."

"What does?" remarked Dykes, absently contemplating the paperclip he turned round and round in his fingers.

"Well, at least this means that it is not a reentry vehicle for a weapon," said Patterson, his worried frown visibly relaxing. "It's certainly not big enough to be a missile launch platform, and geostationary orbit rather limits its potential applications to communications or surveillance, wouldn't you say, Joe?"

"Yes," Dykes answered with a sigh, tossing the paperclip on the table and leaning back in his chair with fingers laced across his stomach, "and I haven't breathed this easy in days. I think that, at worst, someone has hoodwinked us out of a free satellite-insertion job. A few million bucks in lost revenue is nothing to what this could have cost the agency in appropriations cuts, and loss of agency and personal prestige, not to mention the potential harm to the population, if it had been a weapon. If it is some sort of propaganda hoax, we can always deny that we helped to put it up, even if they claim we did. In fact, I suggest that we *do* deny it, emphatically. I don't like lying, but it wouldn't do anyone any good now, to admit to such a thing. If we did admit to it, we as individuals might eventually live it down, but it would do irreparable harm to this agency."

"A lot of other countries have launch capability," Castor interjected. "Even the Russian satellite countries. There's no way to prove that one of the European countries didn't do it, and I vote we play it that way. If some terrorist faction in the Middle East wanted to put one up, there isn't anything to stop them from buying a ride on an Ariane or Soyuz booster."

"That's true," Patterson said, gazing at the tabletop reflectively, "so why use NASA?"

"Good question," Castor responded. "It must mean that it's a U.S.-based group that did it. Someone without access to other countries' spaceflight communities. Perhaps it's as simple as someone who just wanted to get an experiment into space, but couldn't afford the freight. We're looking into past applications for experiment transport—you know, university science projects, small business research initiatives we've sponsored, that sort of thing. We get a thousand applications for every one that we accept. It seems like a stretch, but weirder things have happened."

Richards commented, "Whatever the case, I have an idea we'll know something before too long. Whether it's an experiment, a com satellite or just some sort of thumbing-us-off gesture, in order to be useful, it has to do something. When it does, we'll know what it's all about."

"Still no idea how they did it, Joe?" Patterson addressed Dykes.

"Not yet. Whoever they were, they knew our launch make-ready procedures, and our launch schedule, including particulars about our cargo. It had to be planned meticulously, months in advance, and skillfully carried out. We're checking employees, both those currently employed, and those who were dismissed 'for cause' as far back as two years. It's difficult, when you can't say why you want the information, especially with contract personnel."

"The Stanford group is particularly sensitive," said Castor. "You can imagine what would happen with something like this if it leaked at a university. They had the best opportunity, based on knowledge of payload specifics, but as far as we can tell, none of them have had any in-depth experience with the workings inside Kennedy Space Center, or with NASA in general. Everything—individual backgrounds, politics, work history—they all check out. Too obvious anyway."

Dykes observed thoughtfully, "Somebody currently working within the agency may have helped the perpetrators, but it would still be possible for someone on the outside, if they knew our operation well enough, and if there was enough money involved to buy information from a loose-lipped employee. Hell, it's even possible that an employee in Inspection or Packing gave out enough information to do the job over a few beers, and doesn't even realize it."

"We had better devise new security procedures for launch," said Patterson. "I would rather we did it than some heavy-handed zealots from the military and the National Security Agency."

"Amen!" said Dykes.

VI

Three weeks later, the *Columbia* incident was almost forgotten. It was a quiet, moonlit night on July 10, at the Twentynine Palms Marine Corps Base, in the heart of the Mojave Desert region of southern California. Near the south perimeter of the Marine Corps reservation was an old, all-but-forgotten World War II, B-17 airfield that once was known as the Eidermann Army Air Corps Heavy Bomber Maintenance Depot.

The full moon and the clear desert sky combined to make it a scene of ethereal beauty. Bright moonlight on wind-rippled hillocks of sand contrasted with stark shadows, as though a divine paintbrush had lightly touched the tops of dunes, sagebrush and stones, leaving a dappled reflection of ghostly silver on a canvas of blackest velvet. Moonlight on the roofs of hangars and the tops of crated equipment cast inky wells of darkness under building eaves, and on the leeward sides of equipment and containers. In the new, frugal Marine Corps, there were no sentries walking guard duty, not at remote, low-security places like Eidermann. Only surveillance cameras witnessed the silent, ghostly magic of the desert night.

At 0200 hours, Eidermann erupted skyward in a cataclysmic flash of energy, followed instantly by a pounding concussion and blast wave that shattered windows ten miles away in the small town of Twentynine Palms. Electricity crackled and arced within a blinding, incandescent hemisphere of expanding plasma, hotter than the surface of the sun. The growing fireball dimmed

29

from a painful white glare to red boiling blood, and
finally, to a black, ominous cloud, rising to obscure the
moon.

People in Twentynine Palms and all over the Marine
base were thrown from their beds by the ground-shock,
a seismic wave that spread outward from the point of
impact in an expanding circle, like a ripple from a stone
tossed into still water. A pool table in one of the local
bars bounced two feet into the air, and broke in half
when it landed. The two players standing near it, along
with the few other patrons of the bar, were thrown
sprawling to the floor amid spilled drinks and broken
glass.

Half the Marine base went dark as one of its two
electrical substations tripped off-line, and the town power
system blinked out completely. A mighty, thrumming
drone ran through the earth, so heavy in timbre and
powerful in amplitude that it hurt the teeth; it seemed
to vibrate the very bones of one's body. The acrid,
stinging smell of ozone permeated the air. St. Elmo's
fire danced along those overhead utility lines still
standing, the ghostly electrical flames eventually melting
away into the wires.

Water mains broke and geysers of water shot from
the middle of flooding roads. Streets and parking lots
resembled a battlefield that had been cratered by bombs
and artillery, with buckled sidewalks and pavements
everywhere. Here a pushed-up mound, there a gaping
pit.

The small county fire and sheriff's departments of
Twentynine Palms were inundated by frantic callers
demanding information. Half-dressed people milled in
the streets, looking toward the Marine base and the
rising pall of darkness that drifted on the high-altitude
air currents, blotting out the stars and dimming the
moon. Clusters of excited, gawking neighbors impeded
authorities who were trying to reach and assess affected
areas, repeatedly asking the same questions.

"Was it a plane crash?"

"Did the Marines explode a bomb?"

"I nearly bit my tongue off; I'm gonna sue somebody!"

"When will the power come back on?"

"My trailer house is tilted off its blocks, and the water pipes are broken. Everything I have will be ruined."

Similar chaos erupted on the Marine base as bugle calls pierced the night and cursing marines hurriedly dressed for formation.

Except for a few portable units, emergency generators had to be jacked back onto concrete mounting pads before they could be started. In many cases, electrical distribution transformers and broken utility poles lay scattered along streets and highways like ninepins, and restoration of power to some areas would take days. The base and town were a pandemonium of activity as engineering and maintenance personnel in trucks and heavy equipment scattered over their respective areas of responsibility, tackling the highest priority problems first, trying to restore power and communications, and isolate broken water mains.

The flash was recorded by Defense Department Milstar satellites, NASA Observer and NOAA weather satellites over half the northern hemisphere. Seismic stations as far north as Fairbanks, Alaska, and as far west as the University of Hawaii, recorded the thump of the solitary blow.

The Eidermann site had consisted of seventy or eighty abandoned buildings, mostly decaying, Quonset-type barracks, storehouses, workshops and hangars, and a cracked and weed-grown runway that was still occasionally used by Marine and National Guard personnel for "staging" exercises. The Eidermann post proper, including buildings, ammo bunkers, streets and utility works, and an old, rusting tank farm that had once stored aviation fuel, covered about ten square miles. It had lately served as an equipment storage depot for the California National Guard, and had been home to a couple of thousand pieces of moldering equipment— old "deuce-and-a-half" trucks, "water buffalo" trailers,

World War II and Korean War howitzers, tanks, crates of shelter-halves, field tents and other miscellaneous gear. These items, along with the buildings, facilities, scrub brush, cactus and anything else aboveground, now comprised six thousand acres of smoldering ash.

The Marine Corps personnel and the invited city and county officials from Twentynine Palms who were picking over the area the following day, save for a few pieces of exposed underground piping, could not positively identify a single artifact. Molten metal from the armored tanks and equipment had exploded like pellets from a shotgun, to dot the area with solidified slag. Rubber, wood, cloth and paper had been vaporized without a trace. Concrete, glass and stone had exploded into fragments. The very ground itself, to a mean depth of half a meter, had exploded from the sudden thermal expansion, as the meager moisture in the desert soil flashed to steam. Clumps of shiny, vitrified sand covered the site. The result looked like the earth had been turned over by a gigantic garden tiller and scorched by flames, and all outlines of buildings and streets were gone.

Two days after the Eidermann incident, a Los Angeles television station came forward with a cassette tape which had been delivered the week before. They had thought the message on the tape to be from "just another nut" trying to attract attention. They received such things daily, ranging from UFO sightings and encounters with extraterrestrials to out-and-out threats of one kind or another.

The station manager had listened to the tape, and it had held his attention for a few minutes, at least until it began listing demands, whereupon he labeled it and tossed it into the junk drawer where they kept such threats and crank calls. They kept such items for a few months, just in case something happened and the police had a need for them as evidence. The mention of Twentynine Palms called the tape to the station manager's mind, and he contacted the FBI.

The *San Francisco Chronicle*, *Washington Post*, *New York Times* and *Chicago Tribune*, among other newspapers and TV stations across the nation, now confirmed that they, too, had received copies of the tape. A few still had them. The FBI had taken possession of the Los Angeles tape, and five days after the Eidermann incident, the tape and the author of the message it contained were the subjects of an emergency congressional subcommittee hearing in Washington, DC. On the tape was what FBI voice analysis had determined to be the voice of a middle-aged, Caucasian male. Although he sounded calm, coherent and technically educated, what he threatened to do seemed impossible for a lone man, and probably beyond most nuclear powers in the world.

The hearing, currently in progress, was being chaired by Senator William Harford, Democrat from Delaware, and extant Chairman of the Senate Armed Services Committee. It was closed to television cameras, but a dozen journalists, and three dozen people from military and federal agencies, crowded near the front of the large, oak-paneled hearing room, leaving most of the auditorium vacant.

A wine-red carpet with a kingly black-and-gold castellated pattern covered the floor and the dais. Matching swivel chairs of rich brown leatherette lined the facing sides of polished oak tables. The tables were ornately inlaid with obsidian. A center aisle divided the rows of tables, like a small theater.

Running the length of its periphery was a long, enclosed desk that faced the room. Built-in microphones marked the desk and tables at regularly spaced intervals on the dais, and along the first two rows of tables that faced the dais from the floor.

The Vice-President of the United States, Joseph Miller, occupied a chair near one wall, behind and to one side of the dais where the congressional investigators sat, and quietly observed the participants of the hearing. Secretary of Defense Harold Tanner sat on his right, with CIA Director Casper Franklin, and FBI Director

Jack Mota, sitting on his left. Senator Harford was flanked on both sides by Senator Roth, Democrat from South Carolina, and Senator Isley, Republican from Idaho.

Harford, in top form this morning, was known for his ability to bluster and rail with the best of them. He was a short, heavyset man, with a round, balding, bulldog head. His face was habitually red, supported at the collar by multiple chins, and his expression was usually downturned. His ill temper and matching scowl were focused this morning on the military contingent in the front row.

"Well, Dr. Stickle, what the hell are we up against? Does the fruitcake on this tape really represent a power that has the capability to blow up an entire friggin' military base, or is this just a cover-up for something your screwball organization did? If the military is trying to cover up some sort of accident, the Joint Chiefs are going to regret it. What the hell kind of weapon is this supposed to be, anyway?" He waggled the cassette tape at Stickle. "We already know there isn't any residual radiation; that's the first thing anybody thought about. If it wasn't a nuke, what was it? It sounds to me like somebody had chemicals or explosives stored out there. Or maybe, just maybe, one of your harebrained, experimental weapons blew up in your faces."

Tall and thin, wearing a gray three-piece suit and wire-framed glasses, Dr. Gene Stickle looked more like an accountant than a scientist. Despite his appearance, he was one of the leading experts in strategic missile systems in the world. He was the chief physicist of the Air Force Office of Science and Technology, and currently assigned to Peterson Air Force Base in Colorado.

He sat with another scientist and two colonels from the United States Air Force Space Command, at the nearest table facing the dais and the congressional panel. Stickle was the primary target of Senator Harford's ire today, and to his credit, he responded with calm and deliberate speech.

"The destruction at Twentynine Palms was accomplished by a directed-energy weapon system in Earth orbit, Senator."

An audible hush passed over the room. Silence reigned for a moment as the gravity of Stickle's words sank in.

"You mean a laser weapon, out in space?" Harford was momentarily stunned.

"Yes. Or an advanced, particle-beam system."

"Are you serious? How is that possible? A laser or particle beam diverges, spreads out, dissipates its energy in the atmosphere. I know that much from the Star Wars hearings I've sat on. It would take an energy plant the size of a mountain to produce a pulse with enough energy to start a grass fire, let alone wipe out an entire airfield."

Harford's bluster had momentarily gone, and he appeared genuinely confused and concerned. It seemed almost as if he were trying to reason Stickle out of some preposterous stand.

"It was not a single pulse, Senator Harford," continued Stickle, calmly. "That's the one thing we do know about it, and the weapon is all the more formidable because of it.

"An Air Force satellite was looking at the southern California area when the base was hit. The satellite is designed to image radiant energy in the IR—infrared—spectrum, and couldn't image the beam itself, but it could image the impact point, or thermal bloom, as the instantaneous temperatures of things on the ground suddenly increased."

Stickle stood up and began to pace the aisle as he talked, his left hand in his pocket, his right hand casually emphasizing his words. "The beam is a CW—continuous wave—beam, which makes us think it is a laser or laserlike form of energy. Particle-beam weapons are, by nature of their power requirements, at least in our experience, pulsed energy packets. Relatively low-powered generators charge up energy storage capacitors, and the capacitors release the stored energy in a short-duration burst. This is necessary to obtain momentary energy levels in a contained plasma sufficient to create a destructive pulse. The same is true of lasers to some extent. Only low-power devices can usually operate in the CW mode. We will know more when we have the results of the material analyses that are being done."

Stickle stopped pacing, and stared meditatively at his fingers for a moment, gathering his thoughts. The room was silent except for the hushed sounds of breathing, and the muffled stutter of weight being shifted in vinyl-covered chairseats. All faces looked expectantly at Stickle, waiting for him to proceed. He resumed pacing.

"This weapon sweeps the target area with a sharply focused beam," he said, finally raising his eyes to meet Harford's frowning, confused countenance. "It traces a path back and forth across the target, like a child coloring in a picture with crayons, until the target area has been covered," Stickle illustrated a zigzag, painting motion in the air with his free hand.

"A television set or computer monitor re-creates images in much the same way. An electron beam sweeps across the CRT screen from side-to-side, working its way down the screen from top to bottom in a zigzag path. It only takes a fraction of a second, about fifteen milliseconds—fifteen thousandths of a second—for the beam to traverse the screen from top to bottom, but to human senses, it appears as an instantaneous event. One doesn't see the trace, only the completed image.

"This weapon does the same thing, and with enough precision that it could burn a picture onto the ground. As we've seen in the aerial slides presented earlier, the target area is sharply defined. The weapon has incredible power, perhaps forty trillion kilowatts in the beam. At least a hundred kilojoules per square centimeter at the Eidermann site."

"How do you know all this?" asked Harford.

"By analyzing the satellite pictures, and by cursory

examination of the site, Senator. The recorded satellite imagery can be slowed down, and transitory events measured against a precision oscillator, or computer clock. The satellite isn't equipped for very high-speed recording, so we can't actually see the trace sweep, but we can slow down the recorded signal enough to approximate a slow-motion film. In slow motion we can see the advance of the destruction as it traverses the length of the target area. It looks like the ground is erupting along a moving, parallel front. It took approximately half a second to traverse five miles. To those in the area, it seemed like just one colossal explosion."

Stickle motioned to his fellow scientist, who began taking papers from a briefcase. Stickle returned to his seat, but remained standing, taking various papers as his colleague handed them to him. He continued speaking as he shuffled through the documents.

"Metals, such as the steel of the armored vehicles and the aluminum in the electrical power lines that cross the area, have specific melting temperatures, vaporization energies, et cetera."

He studied a paper briefly, then read an excerpt from the report. "The metallic aluminum from the power lines was found in a condition of melted slag, with approximately thirty percent of the expected mass missing." He looked at Harford briefly.

"Vaporized, in other words. Based on the estimated beam diameter and sweep rate, any given object was in the beam for a period of about two microseconds— millionths of a second. The duration of exposure and the enthalpic energy necessary to vaporize the missing aluminum, along with other factors, gives us an approximation of the energy in the beam.

"Regarding the frequency of the energy beam, the penetration of the earth and the anomalous magnetic fields in some of the affected materials give us a few clues, also. The Marines who reached the site almost immediately after the blast reported burning throats and eyes from high concentrations of ozone, meaning the air was strongly ionized to the point that high-voltage, high-amperage electric currents had flowed through it. Given all that, we believe the beam is in the X-ray, or hard ultraviolet portion of the electromagnetic spectrum."

"How could they accomplish such a weapon system when we couldn't do it?" Harford demanded. "We spent billions on research. If it's feasible, why don't we have the damn thing?"

"We don't have it, Senator, because you, among others, cut the funding for the research, even before the breakup of the Soviet Union and the end of the Cold War. Even worse, what funds were put into directed-energy weapons research were mostly given to favored defense contractors with heavy political clout, rather than to innovative companies that might have solved some of the problems. Space sciences and defensive weapons systems have all suffered tremendous cutbacks since 1988."

"I'll ignore your insolence, Doctor. The important question now is, can you defend against it?"

"Possibly, in time."

Harford persisted. "Can you shield buildings from it . . . erect some sort of heat shield?"

"We don't yet know the specific frequency of the beam, Senator, or its exact makeup, but laser energy can be defeated by reflective and ablative coatings. Reflective coatings act to reflect the energy away, as a mirror reflects sunlight. Ablative coatings are surface films which absorb the energy of the beam and flash into vapor, thus dissipating the energy and leaving the coated object intact.

"Trouble is, we don't know how much control they have of the weapon. They can potentially sweep the target area repeatedly, several times per second. Ablative coatings would be gone after the first sweep. Reflective surfaces require highly precise coating techniques, especially in the higher-frequency end of the spectrum; it's not simply a paint job. At X-ray and hard UV frequencies, some solid objects are transparent, which further baffles everyone about the Eidermann site. Many of the objects at the depot should not have absorbed the energy of the beam at those frequencies, yet they did."

Stickle regarded Senator Harford, his look indecipherable. "Even if a protective coating was simply a matter of applying a coat of paint, how do you propose to paint every city in America? We could conceivably minimize the damage to some things by using conventional site-hardening techniques, such as covering exposed sites with rammed earth or foamed concrete, but we don't have the time. Assuming they keep their word, and use the weapon again within thirty days of the Eidermann warning shot, the deadline is now only twenty-five days away. Even if we had enough deep basements and caves, how could we possibly get several million people into them, and equip and provision them, in three weeks' time? Who would dig them out afterward? If these people have the power they claim, then they have the power to do any damned thing they want, and the government has no option but to give them whatever they demand."

"I can't accept that," said Harford, his assurance returning. "You said that in time, it might be possible to defend against it. What did you mean?"

"I mean that we need time to learn. We have no information to work with yet. Neither the Defense Department nor NASA can locate the weapon. We've been searching for it with everything we've got, for the past five days. We've found nothing. It possesses advanced, stealth, cloaking technology. We don't know how it works, what its fuel and energy limits are, how it is controlled, or where it is controlled from.

"If it has finite resources—for example, if its power plant is chemically fueled—it could literally run out of gas. It may already be out of fuel. For all we know, it could be a one-shot device designed to throw a scare into the United States government. We don't believe that's the case though.

"We've found no trace of an energy-emissions signature in space—a cloud of hydrocarbon gas such as a chemically fueled generator would produce. If it does have extended operating capability, such as a nuclear power supply, then our defensive best bet is to identify the control signals, and either interfere with them or take control of the weapon ourselves, and neutralize it in that way. If we can locate it, it may be possible to destroy it with a missile.

"In the meantime, we need to negotiate, to buy some time. If we knew who we are dealing with, it would help. It could be a terrorist organization in the Middle East . . . maybe even an old-guard Soviet or Red Chinese splinter faction that hasn't yet given up the idea of destroying us in a decisive global engagement. Whoever they are, they have access to state-of-the-art military technology, and the funds to acquire it. They also have the technical know-how to use it. If we knew who they are, we would at least know something about their motivations.

"If I were to make a guess, based strictly on the demands on the tape, I would suspect some domestic militia group. The technological sophistication makes that impossible. This weapon took advanced scientific knowledge, high-tech manufacturing facilities and cutting-edge engineering, not to mention expensive, exotic materials and other uncommon resources. It wasn't cobbled together in a barn, with off-the-shelf parts from a hardware store.

"As things stand, we are unable to plan a military solution. Diplomacy is the only card we have."

Stickle sat down.

"That is our assessment of the situation, Senator."

Harford blustered with indignation, "This government is not going to negotiate with a bunch of ignorant terrorists." He held up the cassette tape and shook it. "This asshole wants to dictate the Constitution to us— wants to dictate tax laws. Hell, he even wants to dictate education policy, for God's sake. You people had better get on the ball and resolve this situation, Stickle, and stop your cover-your-ass tactics. We didn't give you billions of dollars for research and fancy gadgets just to hear you cop out with a 'We can't plan a military solution,' the first time some yahoo blows up one of your ammo dumps. You're the Defense Department, so defend. Find the bastards and shoot them down like dogs.

"For your information, I'm not buying this 'space weapon' business, either. You always try to bullshit your way out of any responsibility before this body, Stickle, usually by trying to do a scientific-sounding snow job on the committee. I am here to clue you in, Dr. Stickle, that I am not easily snowed. I also head the Defense Appropriations Committee, and if you and your people want to exist next year, you had better lay off your techno-speak jargon and come up with something better than 'buying time.' I hope I'm getting through to you."

Stickle glared at Harford for a moment, struggled for self-control, and finally said quietly, "Senator Harford, you still don't seem to understand what has happened here. The Eidermann Depot was literally vaporized in the blink of an eye. Thousands of tons of equipment and structural material vanished as if they had never existed. Any explosives expert will tell you that nothing short of a thermonuclear bomb could produce that effect and, even then, it would only completely vaporize those objects within a few hundred yards of ground-zero, not five miles away. Furthermore, no bomb ever made burns a sharply-defined rectangular pattern on the ground. You saw the aerial photographs of the site at the beginning of the hearing."

Stickle sighed. "If there is a way to neutralize the weapon, we will find it, given time; but I'm telling you as plainly as I know how, that at this moment, from what we know, acceptance or rejection of their terms is not an option that you have. They can potentially snuff out the entire population of this city in a heartbeat.

"I may not be here next year, Senator Harford, but

I'm advising you to treat this business with caution. You know nothing about the mentality of these people. Whoever they are, they are not 'ignorant terrorists.' They have a superior technology; that much is apparent. We cannot do what they have done, not if we had years to do it in. They also have consummate planning ability, which should also be apparent, even to someone as dense as you. They put up a sophisticated weapon, at some time within the past two or three years, without anyone knowing about it. That took a heavy-lift launch vehicle with high-orbit capability. We have nothing on record during that period that is not currently accounted for.

"What we don't know about them is critical to mounting any kind of defense. How far are they willing to go, or how long are they willing to negotiate, or what does it take to piss them off to the point that they are willing to annihilate several million people."

Stickle's volume increased as he warmed to his inner feelings of contempt for Harford. He rose from his chair and leaned forward, knuckles on the table, staring into Harford's flushed face a few feet away, his face and body language emphasizing his loathing for the other man.

"You don't get into a chest-shoving contest with an insane person who has a gun, Senator. You swallow your pride and do as he says. You play up to him and kiss his ass, and you buy time until you have a chance to escape from him, or until you can gain the advantage and subdue him.

"What these people are demanding is not that impossible to do. The demands are not even unreasonable . . . at least not yet. What they want changed are policies that the majority of the nation have been complaining about for years. They want less government control over people. Only your bureaucratic pride and your personal power is at stake here, and as a technical expert, I'm telling you that they have the ability, as of this moment, to make you eat your pride. I hope *I'm* getting through to *you*," this last with a jab of his finger toward the senator.

With that, Dr. Stickle grabbed up his briefcase and stalked out of the hearing room amid winking flash cameras and a rising babble of voices.

VII

On July 15, Joseph Miller, Harold Tanner, Casper Franklin, Jack Mota and White House Chief of Security Lloyd Dahner sat with President Robert Vanderbilt in the ready room just off his day office. Vanderbilt sat at a large, ornate desk, legs crossed, absently running his finger around the rim of a drinking glass that sat on his blotter.

Vanderbilt was a big-boned man in his late fifties, with archaic, mutton-chop sideburns and thinning, curly, brown hair that was graying at the temples. With the exception of a slight belly, he was in generally good physical shape. He had a callous sense of humor, and often used it at the expense of those around him.

"So, you don't think they can fire again, Harold?" he was asking Tanner.

"Of course, we don't know for sure, Mr. President," replied Tanner, his face a worried frown, "but we've been unable to detect any sign of a thermal-energy signature in space. If the generator that powers the thing is chemically fueled, there should be one. Even if it uses a fission pile, it must have a heat radiator of some sort in order to get rid of the waste heat from the energy conversion system. No machine is one hundred percent efficient, so all heat engines must radiate some excess heat.

"According to Stickle and his experts, an orbital laser weapon would have to either generate power as it needs it, feeding it directly to the laser cavity during the firing sequence, or else generate the power prior to firing, in order to charge up an energy storage system, which would then supply the energy to the laser when called for. In either case, we should be able to detect waste heat being emitted as radiant energy, and so far, there is none.

"This leads us to believe that it was sent up with a one-shot charge already stored in some sort of energy storage capacitor. Since there was no fuel to be burned, there was no detectable heat signature when the thing fired.

"But, if it has no fuel, it can't recharge itself, either. A solar energy array could supply energy to such a weapon, but it would be slow to recharge, and due to the power requirements, the array would be very large, and certainly visible to our radar.

"Based on the lack of a heat signature, and the absence of a solar generator, we think it was a one-shot device, designed to get our attention."

"I'd say they accomplished that, all right," said Vanderbilt, absently studying the whiskey glass. "But what about fuel cells, that kind of thing?"

"Same argument. They generate heat."

"What about the energy beam itself? Can't your satellites detect it, and trace it back to the weapon?"

"We're working on it, Mr. President," said Tanner. "The scientists all agree that if the beam frequency is in the high-energy part of the spectrum, it must ionize gas particles as it passes through the atmosphere, leaving an electrically-charged path that exists just for an instant, something like a lightning stroke. The problem is, the area of space that it can be within is enormous. It is literally like looking for a needle of light in hundreds of thousands of cubic miles of atmosphere, a needle which may only exist for a few thousandths of a second, at best.

"As for our satellites, they're in the same orbital plane as the weapon, twenty-two thousand three hundred miles up, and either looking down at the surface of the planet, or out into space at other stellar objects, not across the orbital plane. Our defensive ground stations are generally tuned to detect radio-frequency and infrared wavelength energy, not stuff in the ultraviolet or X-ray spectrum.

"The few terrestrial-based, scientific sampling instruments that operate within those frequencies are not set up to image a point-source of energy in a wide-field area of outer space. Even if they were, the odds against someone looking at a particular area of the sky during the fraction of a second when the weapon is firing are enormous."

Tanner rose and walked across the room, obviously nervous in Vanderbilt's presence. Vanderbilt was aware of Tanner's unease, but he did not outwardly show it. The twitch at the corner of his mouth may have been an amused smile trying to form, but if it was, he controlled it well.

"We are taking steps now to correct that, though," Tanner continued. "We're setting up long-range Doppler-radar ground stations here at Langley Air Force Base; at Patrick Air Force Base at the Cape; and at several airports and other sites that have the necessary equipment. Falcon Air Force Base in Colorado is working with NOAA to enhance weather satellite imagery of lightning strokes, in the interest of detecting and logging all ionizing radiation emissions in the atmosphere over the U.S.

"The CIA is running the Langley site," he acknowledged Franklin with a nod, "but the Patrick operation is a joint NASA/military operation. The Air Force's 45th Space Wing is stationed there. The physics department at the University of Miami will do the actual monitoring.

"Caltech is contracted to do the monitoring at the Space Warfare Center at Falcon Air Force Base, and for NASA at the Jet Propulsion Laboratory in Pasadena. We hope to be ready if they fire it again. We won't have any satellite surveillance across the orbital plane—the beam wouldn't be visible in space, anyway—but the ground stations should be able to see the beam path through the atmosphere and triangulate the orbital position of the weapon platform."

"Do you think we should evacuate senior government staff from Washington, just on the off-chance that these freaks make good on their promise?" Vanderbilt asked, studying Tanner.

Tanner resumed his chair, and looked Vanderbilt in the eye, a neutral expression on his face. "None of your political advisors think so, Sir," he responded, deftly avoiding giving his own opinion. "They feel that it would only lend credence to the terrorists, and would really piss off the people who were evacuated, especially if nothing happened. It could do a lot of damage to your public image, too."

Tanner studied his fingernails a moment before continuing. "Tactically, the consensus is that chances are next to none that they have the stored energy to fire again. Of course, the Secret Service insists that you, and the senior White House staff and their families, be evacuated for a few days in early August, just to be on the safe side."

"Speaking of image, won't that look a bit strange to the public, not to say cowardly, if we just happen to vacate the White House around that date?" Vanderbilt asked.

"You can minimize it, Mr. President. Your security chief and press secretary can arrange for the Travel Office to schedule some sort of routine business engagements for you and the Vice-President, and the rest of the cabinet can find excuses to be elsewhere. If you stagger the dates so that it isn't obvious, and insist that you are just going about business as usual—attending prearranged events, and making it appear that you give no significance whatever to the terrorist threat—it should be believable to the mainstream public."

"Have our intelligence people had any success in getting a lead on who these people are?" Vanderbilt asked Franklin, as he resumed toying with his glass.

"Not yet, Sir, but they're working on it," Franklin

responded. "We're scanning all foreign and domestic launch records as far back as ten years, trying to determine the most probable launch sites. It's probably a waste of effort. It could be almost anywhere. Could be in the Russian Ukraine, India, southeast Asia, China, the Middle East, damned near anywhere. There's no telling when it was put up. It could have been anytime in the last couple of years, maybe longer. Other nations do a lot of experimental stuff, just as we do. We can correlate and verify those launches and payloads where the payload is still functional and we know what it is— a communications satellite, for example—but science experiments are generally term packages, and we have no way of verifying that they all burned up.

"It's also possible that a missile carried two separate satellites into orbit, while claiming only one—a MIRVed payload. Unless someone admits to it, I doubt we can find them by detective work alone. So far, no one is taking credit."

"You seriously think it might be a Russian or Chinese operation?" Vanderbilt studied Franklin's face.

"I know it sounds ridiculous, Mr. President." Franklin rose and paced the room. "Everything does. It's just that we can't rule it out, based on any concrete information. In my opinion, though, it's unlikely they would pull something like this. Certainly not the official Russian or Chinese military. Those nations have nothing to gain anymore. We are all partners in business, now. Anyway, why would they make demands concerning our tax system or our education policies?"

"What do you think, Jack?" Vanderbilt asked Mota.

Mota's brow furrowed, and his dark eyes looked toward some distant image in his own mind. "The sophistication of their science notwithstanding," he said, "I think it has to be some civilian faction, headquartered here in the States. Nothing else makes sense. Even that doesn't make sense. Assuming some militia could come up with enough money to buy a launch vehicle and the personnel to put it up, where did they get the scientific know-how and manufacturing technology to build the payload—that's the real mystery—and where is the paper trail? We're talking real money, a billion or two at the very least, for a launch vehicle, and the technical personnel to carry out launch and mission operations. You don't spend that kind of money without leaving a trail a mile wide, especially if it's a domestic operation. It has to come out of bank accounts and go into bank accounts. It has to buy lots of electronics and other exotic parts. So far, there isn't a trace.

"A very large institution might be able to hide such a sum in its routine expenditures over a period of several years, or several large institutions might manage it in one year, but it would require an extensive conspiracy in either case. I would rather believe that a foreign power is behind it than to believe that something of that magnitude could take place under our noses, without our knowing about it."

"That brings us back, full circle," said Franklin. "Why would any foreign government care about those specific domestic policy reforms? What government anywhere wants to *increase* democratic civil control of government? It's an absolute mystery. It doesn't make any sense."

Vanderbilt stood. "All right. It sounds like you've got all the questions in hand. See if you can find me some answers. Keep me up to speed on it. I want a daily progress report through regular channels."

He swallowed the contents of the glass, and replaced it on the blotter. "If something significant breaks, you can get me or Joe through the national priority net at any time. I want field commanders informed—they are to call me if anything important happens and they can't reach their superiors. I want the Chiefs of NORAD and Space Command to issue orders that nobody is to be punished for circumventing their chain of command in an emergency."

"Do you think that's wise, sir?" Tanner frowned. "It will piss off a lot of command people."

"I don't give a damn who it pisses off," said Vanderbilt,

bluntly. "If those people sneeze, I want to know about it the instant after it happens, and I don't want it filtered through a bunch of prima donnas who have to weigh the personal benefits of every bit of information that they pass up the chain. Make it plain to them, Harold. They had better play ball with me on this. I can't afford to fumble, especially not if those bastards actually do knock out a city. A few hundred thousand dead voters won't get me any roses, and if it looks like a bunch of inept bunglers in my administration let it happen, I'm going to come looking for some sacrificial goats. I'll let you guess where I'm going to look. Do you read me?"

"Loud and clear, Mr. President," Tanner said, frowning at the floor.

"Thank you for coming, gentlemen," Vanderbilt said dismissively, walking away. "I'll expect your first progress reports by ten o'clock tomorrow morning." He smiled over his shoulder at the troubled countenances of his bureau chiefs. He enjoyed making them worry.

VIII

On July 20, in Indianapolis, on the local, late-evening TV talk show *Perspective*, Dr. Harrison Taylor, a local college professor of psychology, was being interviewed regarding the Eidermann incident. Nothing more had happened during the ten days following the destruction of the base, and this interview mimicked dozens of others across the United States, and perhaps hundreds around the world, ostensibly trying to make sense of the event.

In reality, as was to be expected, the media was capitalizing on it to boost viewer ratings and ratings-share. During the first week following the incident, one couldn't turn on a TV set without seeing the same aerial video images of the destruction at Eidermann, or hearing someone, in every conceivable show format, discussing the event. The residents of Twentynine Palms were questioned about every nuance— remembered or imagined—from personal injuries to the psychological trauma to their pets, while TV news cameramen irritated the at-home viewers as usual, by panning full-frame nostril shots and eyeball views of tears rolling down the cheeks of the discomfited.

In spite of the obvious pandering by the media, the public was eager to hear each tidbit of speculation, and to hear the demands from the terrorist tape reiterated and reevaluated, again and again, from every possible perspective. There was no shortage of self-proclaimed experts willing to go on television and theorize, or make profound assertions.

Once the pool of "expert" guests dried up, news-casters resorted to interviewing each other, repeatedly analyzing the message on the tape for the viewers who had just heard it for themselves, by talking to one another in the standard formula. "Well Wally, what do you think they meant by that?" "Well Don, I think . . . blah, blah, blah."

"There you have it, ladies and gentlemen, from the Twentynine Palms Marine Corps Base and the Eidermann storage depot, or what's left of it, I'm Don Wallingford, JGN World News."

The tabloid shows had had everybody on, from defense experts to flying saucer proponents and end-of-the-world religious fanatics. The daily torrent of irrationalities ranged from the sublime to the utterly stupid; from meek acceptance to hysterical, impotent rage. The initial public shock had dulled somewhat, the novelty guests were becoming rare, and in an effort to lure the channel surfers to their spot, shows were beginning to drift into the realm of the "my boyfriend left me because of differences over the terrorists' cause" sort of thing. *Perspective* was of a more serious vein.

Beverly Watkins, host of the show, was a serious woman in her early thirties. She had shoulder-length blond hair, blue eyes and a voluptuous figure. She was attractive and, outwardly, the typical female-model-cum-newscaster-cum-talk-show host of the 2000s.

To her credit, she believed in what she did. Inwardly, she really wasn't a cookie-cutter model of the stock media "info babe," and genuinely tried to be of service to the people of her community by keeping her show on a high level, and by focusing on local and national issues that affected them. She didn't simply try to fill up an hour's air time.

She was also the programming manager for her station and, within certain constraints, she had a broad latitude of authority in deciding what was aired. At the moment her station manager was vacationing in Bermuda and, as usual, when he was away she was in charge.

She was saying to her guest, "The message on the tape dictates ten commandments that must happen within three weeks or, according to the terrorist, government installations and business centers along the Eastern Seaboard of the United States will be destroyed, including Washington, New York, and other major cities. We've had several people on the show who have talked about the scientific and technical feasibility of such a threat, and about the possibility of underlying reasons behind the threats, other than those expressed in the taped message. Though the person on the tape mentions no co-conspirators, most people think that a fair-sized organization was necessary to accomplish the enormous technological feat of constructing and putting such a weapon system in orbit. No independent organization known has such a capability. All nations with the capability of launching the weapon deny having any knowledge of it.

"Regarding the possible motives behind such an obviously expensive venture, the terrorist, or patriot, whichever label one chooses to apply, claims to be interested only in saving the United States. Can you cast any light on the psychological makeup of the man, Dr. Taylor?"

Taylor was a middle-aged, slightly heavy individual with pale eyes and horn-rimmed glasses. He wore a brown, three-piece suit which dated him as eighties-era fashionable, and played with a pipe which Watkins could see had never been smoked, and which she surmised was bought specifically for his appearance on her show. He and Watkins sat in armless swivel-chairs on an elevated coffee table set. Camera technicians operated two dolly cameras in the darkened foreground of the studio.

"Yes, Beverly. He obviously is an antisocial individual, a loner, a person with limited intelligence, possibly even a disgruntled Defense Department employee who was fired for some reason." Taylor smiled as if he had just announced the formula for eternal youth.

Watkins studied Taylor for a moment, only long practice at maintaining a poker face preventing her from showing her surprise. "Are you serious?" she asked, her voice flat and cold.

She realized, and in the realization felt angry and used, that he was just another brainless publicity seeker who had used the issue and her show to gratify his ego. She considered for a moment, then came to a decision.

"You know, Dr. Taylor, that seems to be the standard description the law-enforcement agencies always use to describe anyone who cracks up and shoots a bunch of people; he was a *loner*, *antisocial*, *disgruntled*, *paranoid*. Did they get that from you, or are you aping them?"

Taylor looked at her, bewildered. "I don't understand what you mean," he said, adjusting the bridge of his glasses with his finger.

"That doesn't surprise me," Watkins said, staring deadpan at him. "Aren't those words simply labels that the authorities use when they don't care to address the real causes? Can't you think of something original, Dr. Taylor? What about the frustrations of life that cause someone to eventually snap? The claptrap you just spouted is the rhetoric the government uses to describe people when they are trying to color public opinion. It's called *spin-doctoring*. They characterize everyone that disagrees with them as antisocial or extremist, or a group of people as a *cult*, just to bias public opinion. You're simply mouthing those standard phrases, Dr. Taylor, and avoiding discussing specifics. Do you even have a glimmer of what a real cause might be?"

Taylor recovered his composure, and smiled condescendingly. "Beverly, it may sound like standard phrases, but someone has to be mentally maladjusted to take out their petty grievances on society by random killing. These people can appear like normal individuals on the surface, but it's just a face they don for others. They truly are paranoid inside. They behave like normal, social individuals on the surface. Phrases like *government conspiracy*, *peoples' revolution* and other holy cause jargon are keys to the deep, underlying mental aberrations of these kooks. They tend to group together, like scared vermin backed into a corner. They're eaten up with the belief that the world is out to get them."

Watkins gazed at Taylor a moment before responding. "First of all, they haven't killed anyone, randomly or otherwise, Dr. Taylor. Second, they are threatening a very specific action, the destruction of the business and political centers of the nation. They haven't used any of the phrases you've mentioned. The individual on the tape doesn't mention affiliation with any group, paranoid or otherwise. Assuming there is a *group*, how can they be classified as loners, or antisocial, and what exactly do you mean by your use of the term paranoid?"

Taylor shifted in his chair, leaning forward and bringing hand gestures into play, warming to his live audience of one, and visualizing himself in the headlines tomorrow as an authority who had mesmerized his unseen TV audience with his sagacity. "Generally speaking," he said, "people are paranoid when they falsely believe that there is a collaborative effort by others, a *conspiracy* if you will, to 'get them'." Taylor emphasized quotation marks in the air with the two fingers of each hand. "These people really are loners, they just pretend to be sociable in public. In other words, they generally don't have any real friends, Beverly, they simply band together out of fear." He smiled. "The psychosis begins to develop in childhood and gradually gets worse as the individual matures, until eventually, they can't function within the framework of normal society at all."

Watkins leaned back in her chair casually, studying Taylor, and said, "I take it then that you do not believe in temporary insanity, *per se*?"

Taylor's expression grew serious and he said, guardedly, "What makes you say that?"

"In generalizing, you have just stated that anyone who commits a violent act against society has a cleverly concealed, chronic mental aberration that started in childhood. Nobody just 'loses it' spontaneously. Nobody is ever mad or frustrated with good reason. Let me ask you then . . . when factions of congress and local business get together and say they want to raise taxes on the American people so that they can buy a few votes with some pork-barrel project, can that be classified as a conspiracy?"

"Not really, Beverly, it's just routine government business. We have to have taxes and government. Unfortunately, some misuse of authority goes with the territory. Human beings are corruptible."

"So taxpayers who believe they are being robbed by a sneaky, insidious government that has become an institution of crooks that aid and abet one another for personal gain, are actually just paranoid kooks?"

Taylor's regard was no longer condescending; he answered cautiously, "I think that's a bit extreme, and a bit far afield, Ms. Watkins."

"My point, Dr. Taylor, is that I don't believe that everyone who reacts violently is suffering from a common psychosis. I believe that the only people who fit into categories are people who have been brainwashed into irrational, *mainstream* attitudes. If they all think alike, there can be no individuality or personality, and therefore they *must* have an implanted psychosis. That's when I question the motives of those who implanted the psychosis, not those of the people who resist it."

"I don't see what this has to do with the issue," Taylor said, backing away from verbal quicksand.

"All right, Dr. Taylor, to return to the issue, what does a citizenry do when the morons they elect simply brush their concerns aside? I don't think that taking more of my hard-earned money is 'just government business'. That statement, in itself, is a conditioned response. Taking a large portion of what I earn, by threat of force, deprives me of what I have worked for and diminishes my life. It's called robbery when anyone other than the government does it."

"Such conditioning points up the purposeful

selectivity of these labels. They apply to whoever you want them to apply to at the moment. What is the difference between the Mafia and the Internal Revenue Service if both of them demand half of everything I earn, and threaten to send armed men to destroy my life if I don't pay up? Why is one labeled organized crime, and considered bad, and the other labeled government, and my acquiescence is considered public duty?"

"That's not really a good analogy though, Ms., Mrs., uh, Beverly," Taylor smiled, trying to recover. "I don't understand where you are going with this," Taylor grinned at the camera, shook his head as if the audience shared his mystification.

"I'm trying to get an answer from a self-proclaimed expert, Dr. Taylor, on what the size limit is for a group of people to be paranoid kooks, and to discover what discriminates between a conspiracy and just plain business or politics as usual. I'm trying to pin you down to something specific and definitive, rather than listen to you babble generic labels and stock platitudes. I'm asking you to provide my viewers with a psychological assessment of the mentality of the players involved in a specific example of typical government behavior and the resulting typical social backlash. How about an answer?"

By now, the camera crew and set director were so riveted by the sparks flying on the set that they forgot to break for commercials.

"I can't see that this has anything to do with a gang of criminals who threaten to kill innocent people if the government doesn't give them what they want," Taylor responded heatedly. "They are not mainstream society, so by virtue of elimination, that makes them deviants."

Watkins pounced like a mongoose playing with a snake, "So by your implication, enclaves of native populations with localized interests are *deviants*? Does that mean that African-Americans and other ethnic minorities with a non-government agenda are deviants?

What about businesses with specific economic concerns?"

"No!" Taylor was exasperated. "We are not talking about subcultures or markets here, for Christ's sake. We are talking about individuals who do not fit into the mainstream beliefs of society. They distrust others. They keep quiet about their personal convictions in order to get by."

"Aren't 'mainstream beliefs' simply a product of whichever faction currently dominates the culture of a society, Dr. Taylor? Don't businesses distrust their competitors? If you and I went to live in a highly ethnic culture, say Sweden for example, and tried to fit in with the native culture despite our philosophical and cultural differences over sex, religion and social customs, wouldn't we be deviants by your definition? I mean, if we felt socially isolated, and sought out the society of other displaced Americans who shared our beliefs and customs, just as the Jews, Latinos, Blacks, Vietnamese, Chinese, Cubans, Italians and Poles do in America, wouldn't we be resented by the indigenous population, and treated as enclaves or cults of deviants?"

"Not in the true meaning of the word, Beverly, no. These criminals think that the government is persecuting them. They are retaliating against mainstream society because they think that is the only way to change the government."

"I want to change the government, too, Dr. Taylor. I want the public to take back control of it from the civil servants. For all I know, you may secretly feel the same way, and just be putting on a pro-government act in order to ease the government's suspicions about you. Does that mean you could do something like that—kill a bunch of people? I mean, could you, Dr. Taylor, be a closet paranoid who is just putting on an act to appear as a normal, mainstream member of society?"

Taylor eyed her defensively, trying to recover himself, subdue his anger. "Of course not. Maladjusted people have typical behavior patterns that identify them to the trained professional." He lost control momentarily, throwing up his hands. "Why are you attacking me? You sound as if you are defending these people."

Watkins, coolly, "I'm certainly not defending the killing of innocent people, I'm simply trying to find out what the underlying causes are. Why do you feel that I'm attacking you? Do you feel that I'm out to get you in some way, Dr. Taylor?"

Taylor eyed her warily before responding. "I don't know. Are you?"

"Are you paranoid, Dr. Taylor?"

"This is ridiculous." Taylor was beginning to bluster, his face red.

Watkins, still calm and studious in her regard, "Are you becoming disgruntled with me, Dr. Taylor?"

"Look, I didn't come on your program to be publicly humiliated."

Said Watkins, straight-faced, "I know you didn't, Dr. Taylor, you came on my show under false pretenses. You claimed to have some useful insight regarding an event of national concern, and what I'm hearing is dogmatic, biased drivel.

"I already have an opinion as to why this event has taken place. It is retaliation for the increasing unbridled attacks by police and federal agents on citizens who have committed no crimes against society. Citizens whose property has been confiscated and whose lives have been ruined without so much as a chance to be heard. It is because of policies that encumber and restrict and tax a population that has no other recourse. Freedom is under siege by our government. The rights of the individual are being stripped away in the name of 'saving the children,' 'anti-terrorism' and the ever-popular 'war on drugs.'

"Though the official stance is that these are the acts of terrorist kooks, we all know why this is happening. I'm trying to ascertain why, at this specific time and place, someone feels that change is so urgently needed that they are willing to kill millions of people in order to bring it about overnight. The weapon is here, now, but even the government acknowledges that it could have been put up months, or even years ago. Aside from the technology of the weapon, there is a sense of timing—an underlying knowledge that the public is not privy to. The new federal administration seems to be in some kind of internal upheaval. Agency heads are dropping like flies, and whispers are everywhere, but no one seems to know what is going on. All these events evoke the suspicion that something critical is about to happen. What do you think it is?"

"That's what I'm telling you," Taylor expostulated in frustration, pounding his fist into his hand to the beat of his words. "It's insanity! There are secret forces at work. They want to overthrow the government. They want to start a civil war. They want a revolution and a return to some mythical nirvana of the 1950s."

"Why, Dr. Taylor, you sound like a conspiracy nut," said Watkins, her chin resting in her hand, eyes wide in mock amazement.

Taylor fumed. "They don't realize that you can't force people to change their way of thinking at gunpoint. Americans like to gripe and complain, but when it comes down to it, they want someone in authority to tell them what to do. You cannot stir up patriotic ire by threatening to destroy part of the population. No one has ever tried that."

"I don't know about that," Watkins responded disdainfully. "Hitler did it in Germany in the 1930s; the United States did it in Europe and Japan in the 1940s, Korea in the 1950s, Viet Nam in the 1970s and Iraq in the 1990s. Russia did it in Afghanistan in the 1960s through the 1980s, and in Chechnya in the 1990s. The Serbs and Croats did it in Bosnia in the 1990s. The Israelis, Egyptians and Jordanians have been doing it continually since before the dawn of history. Those are just a few of the thousands of examples. It would take more air time than we have just to name all the wars, great and small, of the past two centuries, let alone in the history of the world, that have started because a population became divided over issues just like those we face today. They all must have had some reasons other than just mass psychosis and mass paranoia, Dr. Taylor."

"Those were wars, Beverly. This is at most a handful of people."

"How many does it take to make a war, Dr. Taylor?"

"Are you serious?"

"Never more so."

"It takes more than a few psychotic whackos, I can tell you that, Ms. Watkins."

"Since these 'psychotic whackos' aren't just randomly killing people for the fun of it, and actually seem to be pleading with people to change the country in their own best interests, I can't see them as disgruntled government employees that kill a bunch of innocent people just because they got fired, or because their wives left them. They appear to exhibit the same kind of nationalism and ideological purpose that all these other wars of mass destruction have been fought over. What if they're just *madder than hell, and aren't going to take it anymore*, to borrow a phrase?"

There was a pregnant pause, during which Watkins and Taylor simply eyed one another balefully.

"When people get mad, Dr. Taylor, occasionally it's for a reason. Like the first American colonists, they revolt when they feel mistreated by an insensitive government that not only pays them no attention, but taxes them, dictates to them and harasses them at will. They rebel. They threaten and demand. They strike back at their tormentors, and the violence of their outcry is a measure of how strongly they feel and how frustrated they are in trying to do something about it."

Taylor stood up, his face angry and flushed, and glared down on an unperturbed woman who appeared even at her lower angle, to be looking down her nose at him. "No sane person believes he can change the world by force, Mrs. Watkins. These people are psychotics who invent causes to kill and die for. They can hire people with brains to build a weapon, and to put it into orbit."

"It's certainly news to me, Dr. Taylor, that sane people don't believe in the use of force. It happens every day and is advocated by parents, employers, the police, the courts and the government. Even lovers use some form of coercion on a regular basis. In fact, force—and the threat of force—is behind everything organized society does. Everybody seems intent on bending someone else to their will by threat of some penalty or punishment. Throughout history, a lot of people, mainly revolutionaries and established governments, have effectively changed the world for better or worse through use of force. Every turning point in history is marked by a war. In fact, force seems to be the most common instrument of social change."

"That doesn't mean that a few dissatisfied individuals have the right to take the law into their own hands," stuttered Taylor. "That is anarchy, and in the end, it's idiotic martyrdom. They cannot win."

Watkins sighed and shook her head, unbelievingly. "Dr. Taylor, you've called these people stupid, vainglorious martyrs, loners, antisocial misfits, and applied every other label you can think of, but the military and scientific communities believe that these are some very daring, intelligent, organized people, with a technology far superior to that of anyone else in the world. How can you of all people, a trained psychologist, make from that a portrait of twisted, withdrawn, obsessive zealots, hiding in dark corners, casting furtive glances at each other and jumping at every little noise? For a supposedly educated man, you don't even seem to have a grasp of elementary history or basic human psychology. I think that if anyone is idiotic, it's you. I bid you goodnight, Dr. Taylor."

"Ladies and gentlemen," —a spotlight isolated Watkins, and on her cue the camera zoomed in on her, excluding Professor Taylor who strode, red-faced and muttering, into the darkened background of the set. "We have just heard from another self-proclaimed expert on the motivations and psychotic characteristics of terrorists in general, and he lumps the current event in with terrorist bombings, post office shootings, street muggings and all the rest.

"Contrary to Dr. Taylor's opinion, I find something uniquely different about this. First, the voice on the tape does not claim credit for any militant organization. Second, it does not ask for the release of political prisoners, espouse any radical political causes or demand any kind of ransom. Once again, the ten demands it makes are as follows:

"One: All tax-supported colleges and universities will immediately begin teaching evening classes for adults, at cost, in all disciplines, including the sciences and engineering, and these will be fully accredited, compressed schedule, degree-earning curriculums to provide the people of America with the opportunity to obtain a higher education even after they are married and hold full-time jobs. It is time that the people who pay the bills get some of the benefits.

"Two: The American Constitution and Bill of Rights shall be enforced to the letter, and enforcement of all victimless crimes shall cease. People shall not be treated like a common herd. They shall have the individual freedom to do as they please so long as they do not inflict their beliefs on others, harm others or destroy property. Law enforcement does not have the right to anticipate crime at the expense of liberty, and government does not have the right to dictate individual morals.

"No civil servant or group thereof may controvert the United States Constitution or Bill of Rights in any way, or make, or waive, the law of the land. Only the citizenry for which the civil servant works may introduce petition for change.

"No law may be passed without a majority vote by the affected population. Civil servants shall only enforce the laws, they shall not introduce them. No government employees, no matter what their agency or rank, shall use tax dollars to fund political propaganda or support special-interest groups, or cast any public opinions in such matters. That is a clear conflict of interest. This includes all civilian authorities and military forces.

"There shall be no impromptu use of martial law except in the case of civil emergency, and even then it shall be limited in scope to invasion by foreign nationals or armies, or to prevent looting in the wake of disaster.

"The justice system shall be streamlined to limit appeals to two, and to exact swift, just punishment of those who bring harm to others. Sentences shall be literal and shall be carried out exactly as handed down. All crimes against people or property shall carry standard, mandatory sentences without dispensation. No one shall have privilege in this respect.

"Three: The total parasitic load on society shall be reduced to no more than twenty percent of the gross domestic product. That includes all government—local, state and national. It includes the criminal-justice industry, the largest industry in the nation. It includes the combined military forces. In short, the public burden for all expenses for services supported directly or indirectly by taxes shall be reduced to less than twenty percent of GDP.

"To prevent hidden taxes, there shall be no income tax, inheritance tax, property tax, capital gains tax or corporate tax. The Internal Revenue Service shall be dismantled. The only tax permitted shall be a uniform sales tax, levied on everything except food, clothing, shelter, fuel and medical care, evenly applied to every individual without deductibles. The tax shall be collected by each state, and twenty percent passed on to the federal government for the national defense, and for the national regulation of health standards, interstate highways, public safety, quality of food, pharmaceuticals, air and water. There shall be no federally-supported endowments. Artistic expression and other such endeavors are not the purview of the government.

"Four: Parents shall have ultimate authority over

their minor children unless it can be proved that they are unfit or cruel. They shall have the fundamental right to discipline and teach their offspring as they see fit, including the limited exercise of corporal punishment, so long as such discipline is not cruel or unjust beyond reason, and such teachings do not engender disrespect for the life, liberty and property of others."

Watkins paused, "There are six more commandments or dictates, ten in all," she said, "and the content is lengthy. Just to summarize the main points, number five does not permit foreign ownership of United States real property or natural resources, or the exercise of political influence in the United States by foreign business or foreign nationals; number six restricts the terms of senior federal executives and makes conduct not in keeping with the interests of the American people treasonous; number seven establishes a mandatory life sentence without parole for the act of treason by a public official; number eight addresses conflict of interest by government employees; number nine restricts government involvement in the affairs of foreign nations; and number ten limits government interference in private enterprise to consumer safety, and to public protections against monopolistic advantage and profligate behavior."

Watkins continued, "The preamble of the taped message states: 'If the government fails in any respect to enact and enforce these laws, factories and businesses, military installations, even major population centers shall be destroyed. Such destruction shall continue until the people rally together, take responsibility and force their governing officials to comply. These commandments are not negotiable.'"

"I don't know about you folks," Watkins addressed her listeners, "but these demands do not seem insane to me, and are in fact the very things most of us claim to want. I don't understand why, with so much at stake, these things can't simply be done. If the people are willing to meet these demands, even desire the changes, then who are these civil servants to say no? For most of the demands, it would only take the stroke of a pen to change the law. Our elected officials are posturing and breast-beating and protecting their own perks, but there are millions of our lives at stake.

"Congress and the President claim that if they give in to these demands, no matter how innocuous they seem, that further, more impossible demands will be made in the future. In my personal opinion, I think that we should meet the demands until something impossible is actually demanded. What if these people are exactly what they say they are? Almost two weeks have passed since the tape was sent, and nothing has been done.

"I have interviewed five people, including Dr. Taylor, and I'm appalled at the moronic way this is being exploited. As with any big news item, the self-promoters like Dr. Taylor are coming out of the woodwork to get on television. The incumbent politicians are posing and acting defiant, while the ones who want to take their places are ridiculing the incumbents and offering asinine solutions, or no solutions at all.

"The military is speculating on whether or not this weapon is capable of the threatened destruction. No one seems to be considering the potential loss of life if it is, and if these people do exactly what they say they will do.

"There have been no attempts at negotiation, primarily because the terrorists have said there will be none. No one even knows how to communicate with them. They have been absolutely silent since the destruction at the Marine base in California. One assumes that they are listening to television broadcasts, and if they are, I hope that they will reconsider, and not destroy all those innocent lives. There must be another way to bring about change. We all know that our government is out of our control and we don't know how to fix it, but the massacre of innocent people can't be the solution.

"If you are listening, I appeal to you, sincerely, with

all my heart, whoever you are, please don't do what you have threatened. There has to be a better way.

"Once again, according to the warning, on August 11, residents of the East Coast need to be west of a line that runs roughly north-south along the Eastern Seaboard between Harrisburg, Pennsylvania, and Concord, Massachusetts. If what is threatened comes to pass, anyone who is east of that line on that day, is risking death. My instincts tell me to err on the side of safety. Take your most precious belongings and your pets, and move to safety. The man on the tape pleads with you to heed the warning. The only alternative is complete compliance with his demands, and as of this moment, that doesn't seem likely.

"I want to thank you ladies and gentlemen in the audience, and our viewers for tuning in. We are out of time. I'm Beverly Watkins for *Perspective*. Good night."

IX

On July 25, the White House held a press conference. The reporters present clapped sporadically as President Vanderbilt took the podium. Lack of the usual enthusiasm was a gauge of their concern, and Vanderbilt noted it.

"Ladies and gentlemen of the press," he said, surveying the quiet, serious faces that regarded him, "and my fellow Americans, I'm glad of this opportunity to lay your fears to rest, and to cast some light on this situation. I will make a statement, then take a limited number of questions from the press."

Vanderbilt glanced at his notes for a brief instant, his jaw working in a way that had become a noted characteristic, an unconscious manifestation of his thought processes when he was weighing which approach to take. He decided on his "comforting father" demeanor, rather than the "shaking his fist in the face of his antagonists" routine. Both were becoming the trademarks of his persona, and both were still fresh enough to garner a satisfactory response from the public when appropriately applied. Throughout his election campaign and his subsequent months in office, he had almost always used the comforting approach when he addressed concerns of policy that would affect jobs and similar domestic issues, such as economic matters of general interest to the nation. His damn the torpedoes approach was generally reserved for those small, sovereign nations, who for one reason or another, resisted U.S.-enforced United Nations edicts that dictated policy to them. Conflicts of those sort were generally only an immediate threat to the small nation and its neighbors, posed no real problem to the safety of American citizens, and so were not of great concern to the voting public, but his courageous image would be imprinted on the public psyche.

In the present situation, Vanderbilt had still debated, up until this moment, which tack to take. He decided that should his advice prove wrong, it would be safer not to be remembered as having dared the terrorists to "shoot and be damned." He could further shift potential public ire toward the military, by laying his advice before the people as the collective wisdom of his military advisors.

He looked up and addressed the unseen audience of millions, focusing past the camera lens into the imagined living rooms of the nation. "I realize that many of you are concerned about the televised warnings, and the hysterics-inducing rhetoric that certain irresponsible media people have used to improve their audience share." His disdainful eye drifted briefly over the assembled press contingent.

"Experts in the United States military, and the best scientific minds in our nation, do not believe that these terrorist threats have any real merit. This kind of communications-age goad is the greatest weapon in the arsenal of a modern terrorist, and he could not use it without the use of an information media that has instant access to millions of people. His actual power over people is magnified a millionfold by his ability to amplify the public's perception of it.

"His principal method is to engender fear into the minds of the timid so that they become disorganized and at odds with the authorities, and behave in a way that disrupts organized efforts to combat him. That is where the term *terrorism* comes from. He seeks to create panic and distrust of the government. I ask you all to understand this, and to regain your sense of perspective.

"Ask yourselves, how could a nation, let alone a single man, destroy such a vast area as the Eastern Seaboard? Such a feat would require dozens of nuclear missiles, and the greatest nuclear powers on earth could not hope to do it with impunity. Let's defeat this barbarous act of terrorism in the only way that it can be defeated . . . by ignoring it.

"If you will do this, these impotent threats will subside. The damage reported at Eidermann Air Force Base was greatly exaggerated by the sensation seekers. This was an old, almost abandoned, World War II airfield, in the middle of nowhere, which for the past thirty or forty years has been used only for the storage of obsolete equipment and war materiel. It was easily possible for some sensation-seeking whackos to plant explosives all over the place, and set them off with an ordinary timing device. Senator Bill Harford, Chairman of the Armed Services Committee, has conducted an in-depth investigation of the Eidermann incident, and he believes that it was accomplished in just that way.

"The United States Air Force Space Command and the United States Army Strategic Defense Command cannot confirm the initial idea that this was some kind of threat from space—an orbital weapon system of some sort. I don't know who proposed such a thing, but experts assure me that such a weapon would be of considerable size, if it were possible at all, and that they can find no such weapon anywhere in the vicinity of Earth.

"Let me assure you that the Space Command keeps very close tabs on all objects in orbit about the Earth, and knows the position of every last fragment that might interfere with planned satellite launches. They can find no unlisted objects there.

"The authorities conclude that this is an empty threat by some demented faction that wants to have some sick fun at your expense. Let's not give credence to these people, or even dignify such perversions by worrying about them. The authorities have things well in hand,

and are seeking the perpetrators as we speak. I have no doubt that we will eventually find and arrest these people."

Vanderbilt turned to his live audience: "Ladies and gentlemen, I'll take a few questions at this time. I'm due at a Commerce briefing in thirty minutes, but I can grant a moment or two if you will keep your questions brief and to the point. Yes, Martha . . ."

X

Richard Calvin Broderick occupied a secluded, corner office on the third floor of "G" Building, at CIA headquarters in Langley, Virginia. He and his small section consisted of twenty-two field operatives and a secretary. Broderick did not have a job description. If he had, under "Duties" it would probably have read, "Uses psychological terrorism and murder to manipulate public behavior . . ."

He did things to make sure that public thinking followed the path that Washington marked out for it. His job included drawing public attention away from embarrassing issues by creating diversions, or steering public opinion in a preferred direction, or just by instilling the fear of God into a particular group of people. Sometimes it just required a bit of S&M—smoke and mirrors. He was an inventive man.

Barely five feet seven, Broderick carried a big chip on his shoulder. Unsmiling and hard-eyed, he was never sociable and never made small talk. Few people outside those in mail distribution even knew his name, save for his secretary and perhaps a few in the other sections in the immediate vicinity of his office. He came and went with little notice. The people he passed in the hall really had no idea of what he did. When he did talk, it was to one of his staff or his immediate superior, and it was curt, to the point, and never friendly.

A certain faction in the CIA community had recruited Broderick three years earlier, in an under-the-table fashion, from the *Cosa Nostra*. The agency had need of his intimate knowledge of the underworld, and all his useful connections. It just so happened that it was also a good deal, and good timing, for Broderick. He knew a little too much about his former "family," and a few of his "relatives" were at the point of "punching his ticket" when the agency brought him inside. He was intelligent and ruthless. In short, he was as ugly a piece of work as ever came out of Brooklyn, and he was well suited for what he did.

Broderick was a domestic "mole," an underground operative with broad latitude and a hidden budget, secret even within the intelligence community. Like the few others of his kind, he served the hidden leadership of the nation, the underground power structure that really dictates federal policy—the anonymous money and power that makes and breaks politicians and industries.

Even he did not know who the ultimate powers were, but he knew they had vast resources, and he knew they manipulated governments as the hidden puppeteer manipulates wooden dolls. The public had no knowledge of this conspiracy that starts and stops wars, and controls world resources and markets.

Broderick and his kind were secret from the public because what they did was illegal; it was outside the scope and authority of the CIA charter and every other legal tenet. The CIA wasn't supposed to meddle in the internal affairs of the United States, and indeed, only a very few within the agency were aware of internal, isolated groups like Broderick's. His orders originated outside normal agency channels, from the White House itself, and sometimes even closer to the elusive aura of power that controlled everything.

On the morning of July 26, Broderick opened his office door to admit one of his operatives. James Reed was an experienced field agent, a communications expert, and had only recently become a member of Broderick's very exclusive staff. At six-two, Reed stood head and shoulders above Broderick, had a broad-shouldered, athletic build, and as with all bigger men,

Broderick had disliked him from the moment they had met.

Reed had been screened for Broderick's team because he had worked as a foreign operative for the National Security Agency in the Middle East during the Iran/ Contra days, and had been someone "in the know." He had been loyal and reliable, and had worked hard to mitigate the damage to the NSA. He had helped to cover the agency's tracks by destroying incriminating evidence and sending congressional investigators down blind alleys. He had also performed a few damage-control missions in the past, missions that required more than normal discretion. He was considered a "good soldier."

A farm boy from Kansas, Reed had been inducted into the community during his fourth year in the Marines. He was twenty-one when he became an agent, and after seventeen years, the agency was his home. He was loyal to it—believed in it.

Broderick didn't respect Reed, or anyone else for that matter, regardless of their loyalty, ethics or dependability. He considered people to be no more than tools, and he treated his tools with disdain.

Without inviting Reed to sit, he asked: "What about this TV news broad, Reed, the one in Indiana? Why couldn't we kill the broadcast over the networks? Those satellite-communications geeks in Central Communications Services are supposed to see that crap like that gets filtered out. The international wire services picked it up."

Reed walked into the office casually and, turning, faced Broderick as the smaller man closed the door and walked back to his desk. "They have a satellite link with an unlisted translator frequency," Reed replied calmly to Broderick. "No one knew it until CCS tried to kill the signal during the downlink delay. Even the TV station thought the frequency was registered. They have an approved frequency assignment. It was just a paper-work foul-up. We can't cover every little, podunk TV and radio station in America without ever missing a single detail somewhere."

"What about the opinionated broad?"

"Her name is Beverly Watkins. We got her fired. She won't work in broadcasting again."

Broderick turned livid. "You brainless fool," he flared. "Do you have any idea what you've done? You don't get them fired. At least not right away, and not over the real issue."

He sighed, shook his head, and explained as if to a child, ticking off each point on his fingers. "Get with the program, Reed. You have their management people counsel them against using antigovernment rhetoric. If they don't straighten up, you have their management fire them over job performance issues, such as being habitually late for work, or having a drinking problem, or even over artistic temperament. Those things will effectively blacklist them within the industry.

"If they actually have any suspicions that they are being isolated from the public, and get vocal about it, you have the IRS apply pressure to their families, their adult children if they have any, or their friends. It's more effective that way than applying pressure directly to them. They can feel self-sacrificing, instead of ashamed, for not retaliating.

"You shut them up, Reed, you don't give them ammunition and motive to use it. Because of your bungling, she'll file a suit, as sure as I'm standing here. Suits like that attract citizen watchdog groups like a carcass attracts flies. It makes a mess, Reed. Important people have to answer questions. My question to you is, how are you going to clean this mess up?"

"I don't understand why it was necessary to shut her up in the first place," Reed responded calmly. "It's not as if she were on a crusade against the government. It was an isolated incident, and with all the other media circuses this thing is producing, it would have faded from public consciousness within a few days. Even if a few people took notice, what does the opinion of one ordinary person matter?"

"*Why* is not your worry, Reed. She's not an ordinary person. She's a public figure. A newscaster . . . even if a minor one. We can't have wild-card revolutionaries in the communications industry, if we are going to keep order. As long as they are not directly challenged, Americans will grumble and complain, but they will remain passive. We can't have someone in the media stirring them up. It would be an authoritative voice confirming their deepest suspicions. Because of your bungling, we're going to have to find a way to silence her."

Reed looked at Broderick as if he had just turned over a rock and found something disgusting. Broderick glanced at Reed, noted the look, and glared back at him, black eyes filled with hate.

"What made you pick me for this outfit, Broderick?" Reed asked. "I've done things for God and country that would turn even your stomach, and I haven't questioned much, even when I felt like scum for doing it. I took it for granted that wiser heads than mine had weighed the need, understood the gravity of what we were doing, and had decided that no matter how terrible it was, it was necessary and justified. Now, you're talking about doing it to American citizens. I can't see how that can be called protecting America. Not by any stretch of the imagination. It's not even legal, according to our charter. Does your chain of command approve of what you're doing, Broderick?"

Broderick stood, keeping the desk between himself and Reed. "You have your orders, Reed. Clean up the Watkins thing. You'll do whatever I order you to do, or you'll become a GS-3 orderly at the Pentagon. You will get increasingly poor performance ratings for the next six months, and then you'll be fired. With that in your Official Personnel File, you couldn't get hired to clean restrooms in a national park. You'll lose your pension, and you'll be blacklisted everywhere."

Reed looked at Broderick for a long moment, as if

absorbing a new idea. Finally, "What do you want me to do?"

Broderick studied Reed's face. "I think you had better arrange an accident," he said. "Maybe she surprises a burglar, and he panics and kills her. It's the only thing we can do, now. We don't have complete control of the municipal courts. If we wait till she files suit, she'll be in the public eye. If we try to talk her out of it, she'll know for a fact that something shady is going on. We can't afford any more public suspicions that the media is being controlled. Not for a few more months, at least. You have the resources and the people, Reed. Make it happen, and don't screw it up."

"You're insane, Broderick," Reed said quietly. "You have no reason to kill her. There are many ways to discredit her. She's an American citizen, and she's not really a threat to anyone in government, or to the security of this nation."

Broderick stood, tense, eyes glittering with inner hate. "We're going to make an example of her, Reed, to the industry. If we don't punish her, radicals in the networks will get bolder. If the networks start letting rebel newscasters be heard by the public, they will raise issues we don't want raised. The news media has to be kept in line . . . and so do you, Reed.

"This isn't the Cold War—us against a foreign enemy. This is the beginning of the new world order. National boundaries don't exist anymore. Business and politics are global. If you can't adjust your thinking . . . if you insist on acting like a patriotic fool . . . you will regret it. I can promise you that."

The two men stared at each other, each a ruthless killer in his own right, but with a difference in philosophy that was miles apart.

"Are you going to do your job, Reed?" Broderick asked directly, outwardly calm.

"I'll have to think about that," Reed said. He looked at Broderick, as if speculating, then turned on his heel and left, closing the door behind him.

After a moment of thought, Broderick picked up the phone and dialed. He stared at the door through which Reed had just left, and after a brief wait, said into the phone, "I think we've got a problem."

XI

The congressional debate started on July 29, and raged for six days. The western politicians were willing to adopt a wait-and-see posture, while some of those from the east had constituents who were understandably frantic for someone to do something. No further word was forthcoming from the people wielding the space weapon. Television talk shows were counting down the hours until the threatened calamity—milking viewer fear to increase audience share.

The repeated assurances of government leaders had swayed the majority of citizens in the designated disaster zone and most were staying put, but no amount of assurances and scoffing could allay the fears of everyone, and some were leaving, taking household effects and all. The two-lane roads throughout much of the rural northeast were choked with overburdened cars and U-Haul trailers, kids and pets hanging out the windows, the roofs bending under the weight of furniture and appliances.

The fact that public officials from the "zone" suddenly seemed as rare as winter corn helped to convince the more astute that this wasn't just a drill. Some reasoned, and justifiably so, that if even the con men were leaving, then the threat might not really be just a terrorist bluff, as Washington insisted.

If it takes one to know one, it was understandable that many in Congress and state government had learned not to put too much faith in anything that came out of the Vanderbilt White House. As the deadline drew near, many of the politicians and the well-to-do were finding it a good time to vacation, or take a business trip to Europe, Hawaii or points west, with the family. The President and most of his cabinet just happened to be out of town on various and sundry missions before the scheduled date arrived.

Congressman Harford put on a defiant show, stating that he would not alter his schedule in the least, and would laugh at the "yellow-bellied reactionaries" among his colleagues after the thing had blown over.

Sporadic fights erupted in a few communities as angry citizens tried, some successfully, to evict stubborn civil officeholders from their nests. Some citizens and a few law-enforcement personnel were killed or wounded. National Guard units, and strategic and tactical military bases were on alert everywhere. Some states had called up National Guardsmen to protect government offices from rioters.

Many of the smaller cities and towns in the rural areas tried to comply with the conditions set forth in the taped message, at least as far as setting up adult education curriculums in their schools, striking victimless crimes off the books, and adjusting their payrolls and administrative budgets. Small-town politicians and civil servants tended to be closer to the people they served, and did not put up the arrogant resistance to eviction that their career brethren in the larger cities did.

Within the federal government, the executive and judicial branches refused to consider meeting any demands whatsoever. Congressional committees debated endlessly, and every representative that took the floor offered some provisional willingness to "look into" some of the terrorists' stipulations, which "might be possible if substantially amended."

Government agencies downplayed the warning, following the administration's lead, trying to get the public back into a calm and tractable state of mind. The official word was that if anything did happen, and that was considered doubtful, the military, the FBI and the other federal authorities were ready for it and would make short work of the terrorists. None of the demanded actions were taken at the federal level, and the few small-town attempts to comply were not consequential enough to merit serious media coverage. All in all, it was a wash.

Unknown to the public, terrestrial and orbital eyes were scanning the heavens incessantly, looking for any clue to the location of the weapon that the President had all but denied existed.

On August 6, five days before the threatened destruction, at 02:15 A.M., a tremor ran up the length of the east coast of North America like a giant, rumbling freight train passing in the night. The jarring vibrations were accompanied by staccato claps of thunder that wakened sleeping neighborhoods and knocked out power in isolated utility substations at approximately twenty-mile intervals, from Washington to Maine.

That evening, the news reported that an overload had caused power outages up and down the east coast, and that power grids were rerouting trunk lines as quickly as possible. Local news stations warned that further short interruptions might occur as workers made repairs. Utility company public-relations people and police went door-to-door in the affected areas, distributing hurricane lanterns and explaining that residents should buy ice and Styrofoam coolers to preserve perishable foods, because the power might be off for another twenty-four hours or so.

No one told the public that all the electrical substations affected had been reduced to smoking slag. No one mentioned the taped message that expressed one last plea, and a final warning. The Vanderbilt administration had decided to take direct control of the dissemination of information to the public, and by doing so, draw the fang from the terrorist's mouth.

Harold Tanner sat at a breakfast table in the presidential suite with President Vanderbilt and Vice-President

Miller. Vanderbilt was eating breakfast while the others drank coffee. It was the morning of August 8.

"They knocked out twenty-two electrical distribution stations," Tanner was saying, "along an almost straight line from Washington to Boston. Nobody hurt that we know of. The stations were mostly minor residential distribution points that could be easily rerouted. Nothing was hit that would seriously impact anything; no hospitals were deprived of critical power—nothing major at all."

Vanderbilt smiled. "And why do you think that is, Harold?" he asked, his eyes crinkling in merriment as he cut his eggs.

"Obviously, they didn't want to hurt anyone," he said, "but they did demonstrate that they have the capability to fire again, Mr. President. In light of this, I think we had better assume they can do what they say."

"You're missing the most obvious point, Harold," Vanderbilt said while spreading lemon marmalade on toasted English muffins. "They demonstrated two things. They demonstrated that they can fire, and they also showed me that they haven't got the guts to make good on their threat.

"If they wanted to really throw a scare into the government, they would have obliterated Washington, or Hackensack, or Newport News. We've got the idealistic bastards by the short hairs, now. Ha! Mark my words, on the eleventh, those simpering, gutless *patriots* will chew up some more unoccupied turf somewhere, if they do anything at all, then their bluff will fizzle. It's a stand-off, Harold, and we're holding all the cards worth having. A weapon is worthless if you haven't got the balls to use it."

"I take it you're going to stay here and defy them," said Tanner.

"Not on your tintype," said Vanderbilt. "The one target they might hit, if they can work up the gumption, is the capitol."

"What about warning the public?" Tanner asked.

Vanderbilt paused with a strip of bacon halfway to his mouth and looked hard at Tanner. "Don't be a damned fool. What have I been saying, Tanner? If you start a panic, they've won. We can't encourage them. As long as we ignore them, they're impotent. The presence of the public is what insures that they won't fire on a city."

Vanderbilt resumed his ministrations with his food and said, more calmly, "No! They've just about run out of gas, both literally and figuratively," he chuckled. "Now, if you will excuse me . . . Oh, on your way out, tell Dahner to come in. I'm going to leave for Palm Beach this evening. You boys can do as you like. Just no public leaks. I'll be back on the fifteenth."

Tanner exchanged a look with Miller. Miller's face was as passive as ever, but Tanner noted a hard glint in his eyes. They got up and left together. When they reached the outer foyer at the end of the wing, Tanner stopped a moment and looked at Miller.

"Well, Joe, what happens now?"

Miller returned the look for a long moment, as if weighing his next words. "Don't be in Washington on the eleventh," he said. He turned and left.

XII

Joseph Miller left Harold Tanner standing in thought just outside the White House, and got into his dark-blue Lincoln sedan. He instructed his driver to take him home, and sinking back into the plushly upholstered seat, he wistfully observed people on the tree-shaded streets, going about their affairs, seemingly without any cares. Tourists in shorts and colorful tops, with Washington monuments and patriotic slogans emblazoned on them, gawking and taking photos. Kids in multihued recreation-wear laughing and playing, or trailing along, bored, as they tagged after their parents. Happy people on vacation, seemingly without a care in the world.

He knew their lives were not that simple, but in relation to the burden of foreknowledge that he carried, he envied them their blissful ignorance.

Miller had worked for years with the economic leaders of the world as a United States emissary to the European Economic Council. Most Americans, if they had heard of the EEC at all, had no idea what it actually was, or what its aims were.

Ostensibly, the objective of the EEC was to standardize currency and business practices between European states, and to further regional European interests in world commerce. By necessity, to some degree, they were involved in the control of the World Bank and the International Monetary Fund, which of course included the United States and other western hemisphere countries. Over the years, they, too, had been infiltrated by wealthy corporate stockholders and bought advisors.

One of their stated objectives was the institution of a cashless society. The subject had already been broached in magazine "feeler" articles in the U.S. and elsewhere, just to gauge public reaction. As usual, there wasn't much of one. There wouldn't be until legislation began to be enacted, and too late, people became aware of what was happening.

The advantages of a cashless society that were touted to consumers included the convenience of paying bills and store purchases with one debit card and allowing the government to keep track of individual bank balances, interest accruals, etc. Miller smiled. *Big Brother* taking care of all that nasty, old bookkeeping for us.

Another benefit was the savings in government expenditures for the cost of printing currency. A few billions saved here and there added up to a good bit of pork that could be spent profitably, someplace else.

The unspoken downside was that the economic coalition espousing the "new world order" would then control world economic exchange. Individuals would not be able to sequester wealth in any significant amounts, and would be totally dependent on government regulators to keep a tally of their electronic capital.

It meant absolute economic control, since the government could freeze an individual bank account at any moment, and even feign "computer error," if they wanted to do it without legal sanction. What tangible proof would there be? Everything would be based on electronic records, including property transactions, inventories of goods, home mortgages—everything but grass-roots barter would be regulated. Even that would be discouraged in the end, by force, if it became substantial enough to permit a large underground economy.

It was possibly the largest conspiracy in the history of the world. It was certainly the most ambitious criminal enterprise ever undertaken. Its goal was nothing less than total world domination.

Miller reflected back to a day in his office in Geneva, three years before. He had considered resigning his position, outraged by the discovery of their agenda, but then he had decided it would be better to play along. Announcing the plot to the world would only have confirmed what many intelligent insiders already suspected. It might have made a side-bar article in a few papers and news magazines, but it would have been downplayed by the respective governments and forgotten in a week. He would have been forgotten in a month. Position and stature were extremely tenuous these days. Accidents were so easily arranged.

No, if anything was to be done about it, it had to be done from the inside, or at least done by people with access to inside knowledge. Miller had decided to be that man. He had made himself invaluable to those within the circle. He had become an indispensable part of their plan by becoming the information filter, the nexus of communications and negotiations within the international economic brotherhood. He had even suggested a few ingenious methods for achieving their goals, in order to ingratiate himself to them.

And to that end, he had divorced the woman he loved dearly, his wife of four years. He thanked God that they had been unable to have children. He had distanced himself from her and her relations in order to protect them, to let them become anonymous again.

Miller remade himself into a man without a past, erasing official records of family, friends, acquaintances, school. He substituted a faultless history of an imaginary life, a life that might have been led by another Joseph Miller, if he had not died in an auto accident shortly after leaving military service in the 1970s. Birth records had been traded, along with social security accounts and early financial histories.

His low-profile, but powerful, position had been perfect to accomplish his ends. He had high-level access, without the surveillance incurred by public prominence.

When he was selected as Vanderbilt's running mate, the false history had become concrete in the records of the world. There was no reason for anyone to doubt it, no need to probe into it. People he had never met remembered what he was like as a child—his girlfriends, his college pranks, his wonderful alter-ego parents that now rested under tombstones in Sadalia, Missouri.

Those innocent references had been told of secret military missions, of plastic surgery and a falsified death for their childhood chum, all for the sake of national security. It explained away their questions and substituted a mythic hero, someone they would immediately embrace with territorial pride and unreasoned defense.

As an only child, his other relations were either distant or dead, and easily handled by people passing as FBI agents. The hometown city fathers expressed regret that they hadn't known him better, but one or two remembered his folks with fondness. His war record showed commendable service in the Desert Storm action during the early nineties. He was a hometown hero.

His cover was not only solid, but unquestionable because of its prominence and open simplicity. Nothing flashy, just a good, solid background. He hoped it would hold up for another few months, at any rate.

Miller sighed and looked inward, barely conscious of the light-and-shadow play of the trees and buildings on the windows of his passing car, and the humming rhythm of the tires on the brick-paved streets. He crossed the Potomac and headed toward Arlington. Bad times were coming.

XIII

At 10:00 P.M. Pacific Time, on the evening of August 10, an encrypted telephone conversation took place between two of the conspirators involved in the subjugation of the United States government.

"Well, my boy, I'm afraid we're finished. I halfway expected it to end this way. I guess, deep down, I just hoped that the bastards would have enough compassion that they would capitulate, rather than risk the lives of millions."

"Hector, I'm amazed at you," the other voice responded. "You of all people should know that the only lives those bastards care about are their own." The speaker sighed.

"We can't quit. After all this time working together, I thought I knew you. I'm disappointed, not so much in you, as in myself. I guess I was just wishing for your convictions and philosophy to mirror my own, and I made myself believe it. I suppose I need accomplices to reassure me that I'm not a lone lunatic. Nobody else seems to give a damn, so why am I beating myself up over them?"

"Why are you, son? I know you believe in what you're trying to do. You want to save the world. If that makes you a lunatic, I guess all of us are crazy. There are ten of us, all supposedly intelligent people, who have worked right along with you these last two years. I've been proud of your accomplishments. We all have. The problem is, the world doesn't want to be saved. So why torture yourself over them?"

"Hector, I treasure all my friends, and I've been blessed with many good ones, but out of all of them, including even Paul, you are the one that I thought really understood what this was all about, the absolute necessity of it. You are one of the few people that I thought would really stick by his convictions to the bitter end. You're the closest thing to a father I've ever known. Save Paul, there hasn't been anyone closer since Judy died. What you're saying makes me feel incredibly alone and hopeless right now, and a damned fool to boot."

"Hell, son, you're not alone. We tried. No one can do more than that. We held out a life preserver to the public. They're just too timid to reach for it. They won't fight city hall. Either that, or they actually believe the propaganda they're being constantly subjected to. I'm sure some of them do. You figure those under twenty, by and large, don't have the experience to weigh what they're being told, and those over forty are so frustrated with the futility of trying to change things by the vote, that they've given up and don't participate anymore. We may as well face it. Democracy has failed . . . failed for lack of interest."

"Not yet, it hasn't."

"Come on, Leland, what more can we do? It's time to give it up and get on with our lives."

There was a pause, as if by mutual agreement, where neither man spoke. After a time, the one called Leland broke the silence. His voice was resigned, determined. "I won't let it happen, Hector. If they win, progress comes to a halt. We will sink into a dark age that will make life in Russia during the Iron Curtain era—even Germany under Hitler—look like the good old days. All the arts and finer things will vanish. Whole technologies will be lost. We can't let it happen.

"If we don't strive to evolve, and to become something more than bloody, scrabbling vermin, the whole species has no reason to exist. If mankind is going to make it to the stars, and become a mature species, they have to have liberty. Maybe they just don't have it in them. Maybe what we do won't matter in the end. Maybe I'll go down in history as the greatest monster of all time. All I know is that I am going to do what I can to keep the bastards from taking over. Whatever chance there is, mankind is going to have it."

"But what can you do? They've called our bluff. Our *big stick* has failed. There is nothing left but to cover our tracks and—"

Angrily, "Does everyone feel like you do, Hector? Are they all ready to throw in the towel?"

"Don't get upset, my boy. The committee met this morning. We don't like it any better than you do, but there just isn't any use. If we go on destroying deserted bases and utility systems, and making a nuisance of ourselves, it will only prejudice people against us. God forbid, even if we fired on a small town somewhere, even Washington, and killed thousands of people, we would be branded as criminals and murderers. It would only turn them further away from us, and make the government agenda easier. They'll think of us just as if we were any two-bit, foreign terrorists, and they would be right. It's a no-win situation."

When he answered, the one called Leland was calmer. "I knew the others would cave in, Hector, but I never thought you would. For the record, I agree. We can't continue just being an irritant, and I won't destroy a bunch of innocents in a small town as another warning. I won't escalate this thing incrementally, till we become the tyrants. If we don't carry out our threat, we'll just become ridiculous. That's why we're going to go through with it."

"You can't be serious? Millions would die."

"Nothing else is going to move them. If they have a choice between passivity and a fight, they aren't going to fight. We knew that starting out. I intend to remove all their options."

"The committee will never agree to it, son. Never. They've decided to destroy the weapon system. In fact, it is to be done at midnight tonight. It's over, my boy."

"No, Hector, it isn't. As I said, I knew the others would fall apart in the eleventh hour. So, after the last warning shot, I changed the control codes."

"What do you mean? For God's sake, Leland, you can't really mean to fire that thing at inhabited areas. It was supposed to scare them into action, not kill them. We trusted you, above all people. We all agreed it would take three of us to initiate the firing sequence. Everything we do requires agreement by all the leaders. Do you realize what you're doing? It's like the plot of a bad science fiction movie—one man having the power to destroy the world. It's monstrous. It's insane."

"Maybe, but just a few weeks ago, we all agreed that our society is insane, because it has permitted it to come to this. Regardless of what you and the others may think, that's the way it is, and you may as well accept it. I don't intend to argue. We have to have the guts to stop them, or we may as well give up and just eradicate ourselves. I don't believe it has to be that way. If I did, I wouldn't be doing this. What would be the use?"

"For so many to die, so many innocents. They didn't make things this way."

"Didn't they? The ones who bow and scrape when one of the hired hands comes to town? The silly women that vote for someone because of his looks, or his stand on 'women's issues'? The stupid men who vote for someone because he espouses an agenda that will make them money, without regard for their impact on anything or anybody else? The exploiters of racial bias that swing the minority vote simply because they appeal to minority interests? The chronic complainers that always bitch about conditions, but don't ever do anything to change things? *They* gave power to the civil servants. They entrusted them with their very lives, and refused to exercise the controls that might have kept them in check.

"We are all to blame. God did not ordain that some people shall have the right to rule over others. We did that, by our apathy. We permit it. Rats and politicians simply get bolder if they get away with something, and we have allowed them to get away with damned near anything. Well, not any more, Hector. Not any more."

Later that night, another encrypted call went through, this time to Geneva, Switzerland.

"Conrad, I'm sorry to get you up in the middle of the night; I'm afraid I have news."

"Hello, my friend. You forget the time difference. It's early afternoon here. I'm lounging about the house today. No point in working, now. Nikoli is off making calls, dismantling everything."

"Well, you had better tell him to stop. That's what I'm calling about. It's not yet over, after all."

"You didn't destroy the machine? But we all agreed."

"Leland didn't. I assumed that he would follow our lead, whatever we decided. Apparently, he knew us better than we knew ourselves. He took sole control of the system a few days ago. He fully intends to go through with it, Conrad."

"What do you mean, he's taken sole control?" The voice carried astonishment.

Resigned, the other replied, "Exactly that. He anticipated that we would waffle when it came down to it. He changed the control codes."

"Gott im Himmell. Where, Hector? Where will he strike?"

"The primary corridor of power in the United States. All the nerve centers and support networks are head-quartered along the eastern seaboard, from Washington to New York. Government, business, insurance, banking—all the controls and the people with the know-how to reestablish them are there. He intends to wipe the slate clean."

"What can we do?"

"It's my opinion, as clear as that can be after being up half the night, that we have to support him. We have to proceed with our preparations, just as we planned. As he said, we have no other options."

"Can we reacquire control of the device?"

"How? It's a trillion-bit encryption key. It would take months just to break down the repetitive sequences and begin testing probabilities. The control system has four completely different base vernaculars, one each for targeting, navigation, propulsion and system security. Leland designed the thing. The security system has a dead man's switch. If we start mucking around, we could even trigger it accidentally. The answer is no, not in your lifetime."

"Then we *must* stop work on the other systems. We can't add to his arsenal."

"I'm afraid that he insists we complete the work, Conrad. He anticipated that argument, too. It's logical that he would."

"What if I refuse?"

"He said that if you should refuse, he will translate the weapon across the Atlantic and begin systematically destroying Europe, one country at a time. If the weapons are not ready to launch, on schedule, he will destroy your home country—Germany. Each week thereafter, until the weapons are in place and he has assured himself that they are functional, he will destroy another country."

"My God, Hector, we've given a madman the power to destroy humanity."

"He's not mad, Conrad."

"No? You think of him as your own, Hector. You would defend him, no matter what. Can't you do something? Reason with him."

"I've tried, and as hypocritical as I feel, I'll ask you the same question he asked me: Why did you help him do it if you never intended to go through with it? And I'll tell you the answer: It was an adventure. We wanted to see if we could do it. We talked, and we planned, just as though we were all committed to going through with it, but we secretly knew, even if it was just in our subconscious, that we could always back out at the last minute. Now, we're horrified to find out that we can't.

"God, we are hypocrites. Hypocrites of the worst kind. We spent a fortune getting this far. If we weren't going to do it, the money could have helped thousands of sick and starving people. We believed this would ultimately do them more good."

"I can't believe it," said Conrad. "Forget what I said before. I like Leland, too. It's just that he is the most level-headed person I have ever known. I cannot imagine him doing this."

"He's also the most pragmatic person you've ever known. All these months, we've been operating from an emotional perspective, in spite of being supposedly objective people. Leland wasn't, and from a strictly objective viewpoint, he's right. People are not going to take action unless forced to. It's a matter of historical fact that populations never rebel until life is so miserable for everyone that the risk of death is preferable to living in slavery. It's stupid, but that's the human condition."

"I know you're right. I know we've been lying to ourselves, but Hector, in the end, we are scientists, not killers."

"You're using the same arguments I used to Leland, and again, I'll ask you what he asked me: Weren't you at Los Alamos during the 1950s, Conrad? Didn't you collaborate on the H-bomb?"

"That was different."

"Was it? Who created the neurotoxins and other chemical agents that the military has stored around the world? Remember Agent Orange, and mustard gas? We scientists have killed a lot of people over the years, Conrad, we just haven't taken credit for it. Anyway, it's pointless fretting and arguing. We can't prevent it. He won't bend. We can wash our hands and condemn him, or we can get busy implementing the plans we've spent so much time on. There are no other options."

"But, Hector, the horizontal beam deflection circuit is still too wide. Minimum deviation is eighteen seconds of arc. Almost two miles. It will kill thousands unnecessarily. Can't you dissuade him, Hector? He respects you."

"I just tried. I pleaded until I was blue in the face, but he's determined to go through with it, and he's right.

In order to succeed, he must fire now. The military is setting up a triangulation network using weather satellites to detect ionized particulates and water molecules as the beam penetrates the atmosphere. We're delaying them by sidetracking parts shipments, minor sabotage and the like, but we can't hold them up for long. We must fire before they complete their preparations. We can't risk the weapon being found too soon. If it is, the plan will fail. Leland's going to fire on the announced date, ready or not. In a way, I pity him."

"Pity him? Why?"

"Because he is absolving us of guilt. He is taking the sin on his own head. He feels deserted by us, and terribly alone. Soldiers kill people in wars, but they are absolved of guilt by their country, their peers. Leland has no one, now. We chickened out."

"But Hector, what about all those poor people? Millions of them. Women and children."

The one named Hector cried out, "Damn you, Conrad! My heart is like a stone in my chest. I can barely breathe, thinking about it. What do you expect me to do? I don't even know how to reach Leland." He screamed into the phone, "What do you expect me to do? We all set this in motion. If Leland goes through with it, in five hours, millions are going to die, and there is nothing on God's Earth that I can do to stop it." The connection went dead.

XIV

At 8:00 A.M., Eastern Standard Time, on August 11, a peaceful Virginia countryside was beginning to warm under a reddish, rising sun. Dairy cattle were being turned out to pasture, fresh from the milking barns. Birds twittered and searched the field grasses for insects. Urban workers were just arriving at work, and beginning their daily routine. Lights and office computers were being turned on, coffee made, phones beginning to ring. The whine of motors started up in factories as supervisors and shop foremen began organizing the production tasks. Farmers were just coming in for breakfast, from their morning milking and feeding chores. The distant hum of traffic was beginning to pick up as the interstate highways filled with trucks hauling freight, and cars began plying the city streets.

Suddenly, across the tranquil Virginia countryside, a brilliant line of light appeared on the ground. A peal of thunder like the crack of doom shook the air, followed by a heavy, hollow drone that obliterated all other sound and feeling, immersing all living things in a sea of sonic pain. The earth quaked, and a curtain of dirt geysered skyward along a two-mile line that bisected Virginia from east to west, just north of and roughly parallel with Highway 64. The gigantic wall of erupting earth, jetting fire and smoke thousands of feet into the air, began advancing northward through the eastern United States at 1600 meters per second.

As the invisible, ravening beam of energy advanced, lakes and rivers flashed explosively to steam. Concrete bridges and highways exploded into fragments as the moisture within their substance turned to steam and expanded, seeking a way out. Trees, grass, houses and other combustibles flashed into fiery gas and ash instantaneously. Superheated air near ground level expanded with an unimaginable thunderclap, followed by the deafening roar that trailed the racing path of destruction, sounding like a thousand gigantic jet planes breaking the sound barrier, then roaring away, the huge barrels of their jet exhausts resonating with the thrumming earth. A continuous concatenation of whip-cracking reports punctuated the deafening din, as electrical discharges flashed back and forth in the ionized, particle-laden atmosphere.

Outside the immediate burn zone, the fiery wind, created by air expanding away from the hellish heat of the beam, stripped the skeletons of buildings clean, like a child blows the down off a thistle. The earth heaved, and a shock wave traveled away in both directions—east toward Europe and west toward California—chasing the screaming wind. People actually saw it as it sped across the land, an uplifted, moving ridge, for all the world like a wave traveling through water, moving through the earth, buckling bridges and highways, shattering buildings twenty miles from the burn zone. Cars, trucks, buildings and people were bounced into the air. When they landed, some survived, and some were broken wrecks. It was as if a giant hammer had struck the elastic earth a single, prolonged, horrific blow. It left in its wake a wrecked landscape of broken trees, cracked highways and shifted rivers.

Sixty seconds after initiation, as the beam approached Alexandria, the weapon had measured orbital perturbation and map coordinates, and locked target coordinates into its fire control system. The beam began dancing across the heavily populated urban landscape, blasting selected buildings and installations into brilliant flashes of incandescent gas that turned to rising palls of black smoke. The smoke diffused into ragged curtains of gray as high altitude winds spread the dark clouds into tattered funereal shrouds, hanging above the land.

People over half the North American continent felt the tremor, though most of the serious damage was within ten miles of the burn zone. Fifty miles away from the path of the beam, the thundering roar was heard as a crackling sound, something like static on a radio, or the rattling gunfire of distant armies. McMurdo Station in Antarctica recorded the sustained seismic tremor that reverberated through the earth's core.

From space, the event looked as if someone had scribed a pencil line in fire, across the eastern edge of the United States from Fredericksburg, Virginia to Boston, Massachusetts; a line that immediately turned dark except for spots of fire here and there, where ruptured gas mains and underground fuel storage tanks continued to burn for hours afterward.

In seven and a half minutes, it traversed a zigzag path four hundred and fifty miles from Virginia to Massachusetts, a dotted line running through the government and financial sectors of Washington, Baltimore, Philadelphia, Trenton, New York City, Hartford and Boston; skipping the smaller cities, towns and countryside in between. Gone were the great landmark federal buildings of Alexandria, Arlington, Washington, Gaithersburg, Rockville and Silver Springs. Gone, the wealthy enclaves of Georgetown, Long Island and Boston, and the military industries in New Haven, Bridgeport and Portsmouth. Gone, the Pentagon in Washington, the Marine base and the FBI academy at Quantico, gone the Philadelphia Naval Yard, the Army base at Fort Belvoir and CIA headquarters at Langley. The great towered canyons of Manhattan were hills of smoking rubble. Nothing remained of the Manhattan peninsula but a blackened finger of land extending south from Harlem, to the confluence of the Hudson and East Rivers at Battery Park. Wall Street, the Stock Exchange and the Federal Reserve, the offices of the television communications and news broadcasting giants, the great banking and insurance empires—all gone.

Except for the Whitestone and Throgs Neck bridges, pocked and pitted Long Island was no longer connected to the mainland. Even the tunnels were collapsed. Save for the southern half of Staten Island, all five boroughs were without water and power. Newark and Jersey City were infernos, along with the refineries and industrial districts stretching up both sides of the Hudson River channel to Yonkers and beyond.

The actual burn swath was only two miles wide, but where the beam had touched, the line of heavy devastation was more than ten miles across. A million people died without knowing what hit them, vaporized in an instant, not even their bones remaining. Another three million lay maimed and injured in the shock zone on either side of the beam's path.

Even though they had been warned, the stunned silence that characterized public reaction to the news was mute testimony to the utter disbelief that had existed across the nation. No one had believed it could actually happen.

East of the lakes and the St. Lawrence Seaway, fear was a palpable thing. These people had felt the mighty blow close at hand, staggered over the heaving, thrumming ground, felt the fiery breath of Hell's own furnace, and now stared at skies dark with thick, roiling clouds of dust and ash. Electrical storms bubbled and frothed in the ionized atmosphere, lightning laced the black, tormented sky, and as the hours passed, the rising gases cooled and condensed, and muddy rain fell in torrents, flooding low-lying areas over forty thousand square miles. The destruction was complete. For all intents and purposes, the eastern seaboard was dead, from North Carolina to Maine.

Within hours, Army, Air Force and National Guard helicopters and troops were aiding local police and firefighters to evacuate casualties from the wrecked cities and towns along the edge of the burn zone. As the injured were brought out, victims in fifteen states

overflowed into hospital emergency wards and temporary
shelters. Medical teams directed the least critical patients
to hastily-erected field hospitals, comprised of army tents
and house trailers.

The nature of the injuries were limited in range,
which made the work of triage simpler. There were few
cases of severe burns, and most of these were the
secondary results of flammable materials igniting, not
the direct energy of the beam. Those poor unfortunates
directly in its path were no more. Vapors on the wind.

The preponderance of injuries were contusions and
fractures, and those closest to the burn zone were
naturally the most serious. Flying debris and falling
structures had accounted for most of the critically
injured. The blast wave had crushed and maimed,
leaving many cases of internal hemorrhage and shattered
ribs and limbs. Some were blind and deaf from the
overpressure, bleeding from the eyes, ears and nose.

Within the burn zone, there simply was no life, and
the vast area affected required response on a scale never
before experienced. There were no rescuers to spare to
search the rubble and torn earth within the zone on the
remote chance of finding someone alive.

Within forty-eight hours, all the states west of the
burn zone had mobilized rescuers and emergency
medical teams, and the roads and highways leading into
the midwestern towns and cities were jammed with
traffic. Airports and railway stations were crowded
beyond capacity with incoming volunteers and those
trying to leave.

News reporters descended like vultures to carrion,
harassing the stricken crowds, shoving microphones into
the faces of mind-numbed, floundering people. They
haunted airports and railway stations, TV crews and
equipment often impeding the flood of people trying
to exit or gain entrance.

Surprisingly, there were relatively few people fleeing
the area. If there had been more, total confusion would
have prevented the aid from getting through. It was as

though they were stunned too senseless even to flee,
or else assumed that the danger was over. Some of them
later said that they were in such a state of shock, or
so caught up in the rescue efforts, that the thought of
running away never occurred to them.

The major broadcast television networks were off the
air for an hour and twenty minutes after the strike, as
customary uplinks were rerouted to affiliates in Atlanta
and Chicago. These cities became the news centers of
the nation in the days that followed, and Atlanta, because
of its hub airport, warmer climate and convention
facilities, became the *pro tempore* seat of federal
government. Almost a third of the U.S. Congress was
missing and presumed dead, and some agencies' headquarters staffs were completely wiped out.

Government offices were being set up in crowded
federal, state and city buildings, and in rented hotel
suites and commercial offices across Atlanta. Some
were even put in conscripted warehouses and industrial space. School auditoriums, university conference
rooms, ballrooms and public theaters were being used
as impromptu meeting places for working committees
and conferences of federal, state and city officials.
Federal law-enforcement and military personnel were
arriving hourly to replace missing Justice Department
and Pentagon commanders.

One week after the holocaust, a third tape was
delivered to the Los Angeles television station that had
received the first tape. Needless to say, it was taken
seriously this time, and it was broadcast. The voice was
the same, and the message was short: "You have thirty
days. If you do not comply by September eighteenth,
I shall begin destroying strategic target areas all across
the United States. I shall not identify those targets, lest
you lose sight of what you must do, in your efforts to
flee. Flight is pointless. What I demand is simple, and
easily done. I had hoped that you would listen, but knew
in my heart that you would not. You have your proof.

If you do as I tell you, you will be all right. If you do not, heaven help us all, for I shall not stop until you submit. Not if every living thing has to die."

The public went insane. Public officials were attacked and killed on the street. Some were dragged from their homes, along with their families, and put on buses going anywhere, with nothing but the clothes on their backs. In Atlanta, 2,500 people were killed—police, congresspeople, national guardsmen and civilians—and thousands more were injured in city riots. L.A., Chicago, Houston, San Francisco, Denver and St. Louis were crippled by chaos as federal buildings were ransacked and burned, and their inner cities became war zones. State capitols fared much the same.

Within three days, amid a nationwide clamor from the public, a working group among the remaining members of the House of Representatives had drafted a bill titled "The Governmental and Educational Reform Act," which reiterated, almost word-for-word, the ten commandments laid down, and four days after the taped message, they passed it unanimously. The Senate passed it the same day, and the following morning, an embittered but silent President Vanderbilt signed it, without ceremony, into law. It was later rumored that he had broken the pen he used, and thrown the pieces on the floor.

State and city governments reluctantly followed suit, and public buildings were awash with people bustling to and fro, cleaning out desks and destroying records, a skeleton staff watching as others dumped the memorabilia of their careers into trash cans, and left the buildings forever.

XV

It was the second week in September, and the remains of Broderick's group now consisted of seven operatives. They were currently encamped in a Miami Beach hotel. His secretary and the other agents, in fact everyone stationed at Langley, Virginia, who hadn't been away on assignment or vacation when the weapon vaporized it, were presumed dead.

His operation was still being funded, although the routing of the funds had changed. New payroll accounts had been established by the White House, on some bank in the Cayman Islands, and they were being paid via letters of credit that established individual trust accounts at a Miami bank.

It was 11:30 P.M. on a rainy, overcast evening. Broderick sat on a sofa, smoking a cigarette and surveying the second-floor room they were using as a ready room. It was littered with dirty Styrofoam coffee cups and overflowing ashtrays. Telephone and electrical cables ran across the beige-colored carpet in all directions, connecting four telephones, three computers and two printers.

A copier stood against the wall where another sectional sofa, a chair and two end tables had been pushed, clearing the center of the room for two long, tubular-steel folding tables that were pushed together in a "T" arrangement. Two of the computers sat on opposite sides of one of the tables, and the rest of the surface area was covered with papers, maps, and litter from vending-machine coffee and takeout meals.

A half-dozen straight-backed chairs stood in disordered array around the tables.

James Reed was in Indianapolis. His assignment there was to kill Beverly Watkins, and through her death, to send a warning tremor through the media grapevine. An attention-getter to let them know that things hadn't changed where it counted.

Broderick's mouth tightened, as it did every time his mind turned to Reed. Reed was a dangerous bastard. The easy stride, slow drawl and laid-back mannerisms were a learned subterfuge, meant to throw people off—make them underestimate him. Broderick wasn't having any. He was an experienced judge of men, and he could see it in the way Reed moved. He was lithe, and strong, and fast.

It irritated Broderick that he was nervous in Reed's presence. Broderick had known some cold-blooded killers in his time, and wasn't easily intimidated, but Reed was something else again. Some people killed out of rage, some out of contempt. Even experienced hitmen had to give themselves a reason, to mentally gear up for what they were about to do. With Reed, it was different.

Something inside Reed changed when he focused in on you. He had the weird ability to turn off every trace of humanity. You could see it in his eyes. His normal look was remote, skeptical, but human. When you hit his button, he looked at you with a look of intense curiosity, then his face sort of went rigid, his eyes closed partway, the black pupils opened wide, and it suddenly felt like you were alone in the night, and you knew that something deadly was staring at you from the darkness. No, Broderick corrected himself, it was worse than that. It was like the man went away, and suddenly you were facing a merciless, fucking machine, and it was going to kill you, and that was all there was to it. In spite of himself, Broderick shivered.

When Reed left that morning, Broderick had felt like a mouse looking into the eyes of a hungry snake. He knew that everything in the big man's being had longed to twist his head off. If he'd had to endure that look a moment longer, he would have panicked and pulled the Colt in his armpit. He wondered if he would have made it. He shook his head. God, he was beginning to make Reed sound like Superman. All the same, he was glad he hadn't had to find out. In the end, Reed had obeyed Broderick's orders.

Years of training and habitual acceptance of authority had made Reed a company man. He didn't know how to be anything else. Broderick had counted on it. In the past three years, Broderick had met dozens of people like Reed. America's army of patriotic, secret soldiers. Take away their holy nationalistic icons, and their mantra of patriotism, and they were like a bunch of confused Boy Scouts without a leader.

Like so many of them, Reed was adrift in a sea of uncertainty. His whole reason for being, everything he had believed all his working life, was being ripped out by the roots. His "family" was changing into something unfamiliar. Broderick laughed. He had nothing but contempt for the government agencies and their militaristic culture.

Reed had been on foreign assignment for years, and hadn't had the gradual induction into the global government ideology that most other federal employees had been subject to. With Reed, no matter how it was understated, it was a radical change in company culture, and even though he consciously rebelled against the notion, it was beginning to come home to him that he was being used as a subversive agent against his own nation.

Some of the younger ones had delighted in the opportunity to disgrace their oaths; to turn on their fellow Americans; to experience a sense of power. Some of the older agents, like Reed, were ingrained patriots, with American nationalism in their bones. They were hard to turn. Many of them were granted early retirement, or reassigned to other agencies, just to avoid the

problems they posed. They should've done that with
Reed, thought Broderick.

He walked out the open door of the motel room, out
onto the shadowy balcony walkway, and flipped his
cigarette toward the dark, wet parking lot below. The
rain had stopped. The night air was cool, and a faint
breeze stirred his sweaty hair. Broderick missed the
cooler northern climate and the ethnic variety of New
York. The fall was sultry and humid in Miami. He missed
the womblike feeling of New York. The great city had
been like a world of its own—a closed world. Leaving
there had been like going outside. Long vistas of open,
uninhabited country made Broderick feel exposed.

He turned and went back inside, his thoughts turning
back to his immediate assignment. He smiled. First, he
would settle with Reed—make him pay for that moment
of fear. Reed would find out who was really the bigger
man. After that major irritation was handled, he would
get on to better things.

Broderick's operatives almost never did their own dirty
work, but he had insisted that Reed handle the Watkins
affair himself. It was meant to be a lesson in humility.
He had implied that Reed's willing and efficient cooperation would atone for past ineptitude, and return him
to a state of good standing. Reed had been defiant, but
in the end he had caught a flight to Indianapolis.

Three agents were still at the hotel. Two were in their
rooms, sleeping off the effects of too many cigarettes
and cups of coffee, and too many long hours of working
into the night. The other was preparing to depart for
the airport and a rendezvous with a Chicago "contractor"
in Indianapolis. His assignment was to secure a hired
hit on Beverly Watkins and James Reed. Broderick and
his company supervisor had decided, on the strength of
Broderick's judgment, to eliminate the potential threat
that Reed had become. Broderick wanted to close this
chapter out cleanly, with no undependable agent left to
create future problems.

Tomorrow, Broderick and the remnants of his team

would begin a new initiative. They were going to exercise the prerogatives that other government agencies couldn't even dream about. They were going to organize a bloody crime. They were going to turn the tide of public opinion against the wielders of the weapon. In a few days, he would relocate his people to a point further up the east coast, near, but not too near, Atlanta.

In order to turn the public against the nationalists, it would have to be made to appear that they were bent on random destruction of life, murdering innocent populations without cause, and making intolerable demands. Broderick's bosses had decided to fight fire with fire. How could the patriots react to mass destruction of people? They couldn't very well retaliate against those very people. Anything they did, when compounded by the damage that the government would also inflict on the masses, would just make the population blame them for everything.

For Broderick, it was an assignment made in heaven. It was his opportunity to put together the biggest scam in history—to really exercise his talents. And, he was up to it.

XVI

The nationally syndicated, late-night TV talk show, *The Midnight Show*, now hosted by a recently-installed David Balcher, did a segment of man-in-the-street interviews one night outside their new Atlanta studios. The government-approved topic was the "Doomsday Weapon."

Despite Balcher's leading questions, the participants weren't letting themselves be maneuvered, and Balcher was losing control. Opinions were still erratic, but there seemed to be a new, outspoken quality affecting the public mind. One Atlanta native epitomized the new attitude.

Balcher: "Sir, can I ask you your opinion on the terrorist situation? I'm David Balcher, host of *The Midnight Show*, and I would like to know how you feel about the murderers who killed millions of your fellow Americans."

Guest: "My thoughts are that the government had better give them whatever the hell they want."

Balcher: "What kind of dictatorial role do you think they ultimately want to play?"

Guest: "In my opinion, they've told us exactly what they want. They are in a position to demand anything, aren't they? If they told you to bend over and kiss your *bleep* on television, and the alternative was that there would be a vacant lot tomorrow where your house is standing, you would do it, wouldn't you?"

Balcher: "I see your point."

Guest: "I don't care what anyone says, I don't believe they're crazy. What they demanded sounded kind of foolish and idealistic at first, because we've all gotten used to hearing grand words and never seeing any results. Everyone has come to accept that politicians and businesses always lie, and that everything idealistic is impossible. They have shown us that these things aren't impossible at all, you just have to get rid of the organized, self-interested resistance. When you think about it, the things they want done are really necessary if we're going to save this country. The only hysterical people I've noticed are you lunatics on TV talk shows, and those damned, good-for-nothing politicians. If you ask me, the taxpayers ought to thank those people for putting you guys in your place. I'm sorry people had to die, but they warned everyone. They told them exactly what they were going to do, and they kept their word."

Balcher: "Do you think you would feel the same way if they had destroyed Atlanta? What if they had destroyed the South?"

Guest: "It's that kind of intelligent question that makes you television people so lovable. You'll do anything to stir up hatred between people, won't you? If the banking, insurance and political centers of the country had been in the South, it would have been the South that got destroyed. Now, you can go to hell, dirtball, and you know what you can do with that microphone, too."

The man walked away.

Balcher: "Wow! Ha ha! Somebody is not a happy camper. A little bit gruffsky, huh? Well, even cherries have pits, don't they? Ha ha!"

Balcher zeroed in on another passer-by.

Balcher: "How about you, ma'am? I'm David Balcher with *The Midnight Show*. Could I get your reaction to the terrorist situation?"

Guest, in tears: "I think those murdering monsters ought to be shot, and those slimy politicians along with them. My sister and her children lived in Maryland. They said it couldn't happen. Damn them! Damn you, you sensation-seeking bastard!" She covered her streaming eyes with one hand and shoved the microphone away with the other as she hurried away.

Balcher: "Wow! We're really hitting the sore spots today." He brushed his fingers against his lapel, feigning insult. "Good old Uncle seems to be taking it in the shorts tonight."

Balcher singled out a black man in a heavy overcoat who was striding past.

Balcher: "You, sir. What do you think about . . . ?"

Guest: "You bettah get dat microphone outta my face if you don't wants ta eat it, suckah!" The man kept walking.

Balcher: "Well, Ha, ha! I've had enough. Everybody seems a bit testy today. I guess that's what happens when the gun whackos and militias take over and start committing mass murder and dictating everybody's lives. Can you believe that first guy. He actually likes 'em. Weird, huh? Well, back to the studio. We'll be right back after these messages."

On a morning show in Chicago, the hostess, Loni Bardowski, had as her first guest the Reverend Jimmy Slatney.

Bardowski: "Reverend Slatney, if I understand correctly, you believe that this doomsday weapon is the Sword of God, and is the fiery doom that is prophesied in Revelations in the Holy Bible. Is that correct?"

Rev. Slatney: "We believe it could be, Loni. All the signs and portents mentioned in Revelations can be found today. Christians the world over are preparing for the Second Coming. We think it could be near at hand."

Bardowski: "We haven't heard anything from the Vatican or the mainstream religious leaders, Reverend Slatney. Have you had any communications with them that would lead you to believe that they endorse your views?"

Rev. Slatney: "No Loni, but that doesn't mean anything. They are always slow to adopt a position, and very conservative in the language that they use when they do respond. I believe that the majority of the faithful, by and large, agree with me, though."

Bardowski: "What you're saying, then, is that the end of the world is almost here?"

Rev. Slatney: "It's beginning to look that way, Loni. People have been arrogant, and strayed from the teachings of the Lord. We think that the ten commandments handed down by the Lord's Instrument are significant. They number the same as those that Moses received, and in context, they attack the same sins of greed and avarice. Destruction has been visited on the heart of the errant people, and shall likely be visited again. In the end, the almost total annihilation of mankind shall come to pass. Only the faithful shall survive."

Bardowski: "What do you mean by 'the Lord's Instrument'?"

Rev. Slatney: "Why, the voice on the tape, of course. He is the Instrument of the Lord, perhaps even His Angel of Death. In the beginning, God gave us ten commandments to live by. Now He gives us ten more to forestall the day of doom. He wants us to have a last opportunity to repent, and to become the honorable children He meant us to be. His Instrument is carrying out His will, and is tasking His children. His Instrument shall destroy the earth if man does not accede to His will."

Bardowski: "When do you think this will happen?"

Rev. Slatney: "We believe that it will happen either on Rosh Hashanah, the Jewish New Year, or during Christmas."

Bardowski: "So, you think that we have, at best, only a few months to live?"

Rev. Slatney: "Yes, Loni. We are praying for the salvation of mankind, in the eternity of the hereafter. Everyone should prepare themselves in their hearts— make peace with themselves. Ere long, His Sword shall fall again, and earthly cares shall be no more. Peace shall reign foreverafter for the faithful, and the wicked shall be punished."

XVII

Reed sat in an unmarked car, parked at the curb of a winding, tree-shaded street, watching the front of Beverly Watkins' house. It was an older neighborhood with wide streets, well-kept lawns, large houses set back from the street, with porches and gabled roofs—houses with character, like those from his youth. Homey, warm, family places on large lots, and big, venerable old trees and shaded backyards.

The birds were settling in for the evening, and the cares of the day were waning for the people in those houses. If not for his distasteful assignment, Reed could have enjoyed his evening vigil. It was 7:30 P.M., and the dusky daylight was fading into evening shadows. Reed was waiting for Watkins to come home. She had taken a job with an advertising agency, and he supposed her hours were irregular. It must be quite a comedown for her, he thought.

Her driveway ran alongside the house to a garage that was attached to the rear of the house. A connecting door led into the house through a mudroom off the laundry. The drive was empty, as was the garage which Reed had scouted earlier. When she arrived, if she was alone, he would walk up to her front door, ring the bell, and when she answered the door, he would shoot her with the silenced 9-mm Walther in his pocket, close the door, and walk away. If she wasn't alone, he would do it in the parking lot where she worked, when she arrived there tomorrow morning, or come back here tomorrow evening. It was only a matter of time till the opportunity came. That was the way it would be. Just another human life.

Reed had not often questioned his orders. He had done this sort of thing before, but always to other dedicated agents who would have done the same to him, and always with the conviction that what he did was necessary to protect his country and its way of life. Now he wasn't so sure.

Hell, he knew this wasn't right. This was a flagrant denial of everything his country stood for. He had viewed a tape of her broadcast, and the woman hadn't done anything except question the political stance of the current administration, and ridicule the mind-wash that the government routinely used to engender blind acceptance of police wisdom. That, after all, was what America stood for, the right of the individual to question the methods of all civil servants. "Government by the people" had to mean just that, literally, or America was nothing more than a sham—a pretense at democracy.

Was this Broderick's own agenda, Reed wondered for the hundredth time, or was it deeper than that? Reed wasn't blind to the goings-on in Washington of late, and his instinctive alarms had been ringing off the wall for months now. It had all the earmarks of a political coup, but in the USA? And who? Not a foreign power. At least, not in the old ideological sense. Most developed nations were pretty tolerant of other peoples' beliefs. What motive was there? They were all business buddies, these days. Business? It had to be. Did someone have the idea that he could enslave the golden goose without killing it? He had to admit that it was possible.

As for Broderick, Reed didn't think the little ferret had the authority to do something like this on his own. Someone higher up had to approve public executions. Broderick had some degree of latitude, but Reed didn't think it encompassed this. Someone big was sending a message, and James Reed was to be the messenger. End the life of a woman who hadn't harmed a soul, just to cow the hesitant news dogs who were considering changing sides.

Reed thought of his sister, Emily, who had died five years earlier. She had been his last worldly connection, their parents having died when they were teenagers. What if she had offended Broderick, and a brother agent was sent to snuff out her life? Beverly Watkins even reminded him a little bit of Emmy.

The doubts and blocked-out regrets for past deeds had grown over the past several days, and Reed knew that he would never again think of himself as a "company man." He was at the proverbial crossroads, and the question was, would he commit murder in the name of a "national security" cover that he knew was a lie, or would he take another course? And what course? If he didn't do as he was told, he would no longer have a job, at least not in the intelligence community.

Reed noticed movement in his rear-view mirror, and glanced up as a police cruiser pulled to the curb a block behind him. He had no reason to expect interference from them. There were other cars parked along the street, two between his car and the cruiser, and he was well dressed—not a suspicious looking character. Just an encyclopedia salesman, with a sample case to prove it. Not the most original cover, but plausible—even provable, if he elected to keep his identity from the local police.

He realized that something was wrong. The cops were just sitting there, waiting. Reed took stock. He was parked in a sort of pullout, near a culvert that crossed a drainage ditch. The spot was well shaded, even dark, and he didn't think the cops had seen him. It looked to Reed as though they, too, were watching the Watkins place. He decided to wait and see what happened.

A pair of headlights approached from Reed's front, and as the car turned in at the Watkins driveway, Reed could plainly see that it was Beverly Watkins driving a dark Mercedes sedan.

As usual, she didn't use the garage, but parked

halfway down the drive and entered through the front door. During the summer months, the car didn't need the protection of the garage, and she felt safer getting to and from her car in plain view of the street. She had often wished for a dog, a faithful, backyard sentry to keep the back of the house safe, but with their busy lives, a dog was an inconvenience neither she nor Nathaniel wanted to deal with.

Reed watched as she entered and closed the door, and glancing at his side-view mirror, saw the cops get out of their car and approach the house. He now knew definitely that something wasn't right. The cops were walking slowly, looking around in an almost furtive way, not walking directly and purposefully up to the door as if on official business. Suddenly Reed knew. They were contract killers, there for the same purpose he was. He knew it as surely as he knew his own name. Broderick didn't know Reed's specific plan, and he was uncertain, Reed now knew, that Reed would carry through. Broderick was making sure.

The cops walked up onto the porch, took another look up and down the street without seeing anyone, then pulled their weapons, opened the door and walked in, shutting it behind them.

Reed was undecided for a moment. He heard Beverly Watkins scream, and suddenly his resolve to carry out his orders vanished. All his pent-up doubts surfaced in a flood of regret and empathy for this woman he had never met—a woman who evoked memories of his little sister. He was running across her front lawn and up the porch steps almost before he realized what he was doing. He was responding instinctively to another human being's need, and after years of training and methodical thinking, no one was more surprised than he. He turned the knob and slammed through the door just in time to see one of the cops shoot Nathaniel Watkins in the chest.

As Reed learned later, Nathaniel's car was being repaired. The absence of a car in the driveway had led both Reed and the cops to think that Beverly was alone in the house. As Watkins fell, the woman tried to scream again, but it was muffled by the cop holding her. Reed shot the first cop, the one that had killed Nathaniel Watkins, in the back of the head.

The second cop released Beverly Watkins, pushing her aside and trying to bring his gun to bear on Reed. It was a fatal mistake, for as the woman fell to the floor, Reed had a clear shot, and pumped three slugs from the silenced Walther into the man. His eyes glazed over and he died as he fell to the floor.

Beverly Watkins crawled across the bloody floor to her husband, and collapsed sobbing across his chest as the last glimmer of life faded from his questioning eyes.

Reed stood still for a moment, scanning the interior of the house, gazing at the sobbing woman. Then he walked up the stairs. He walked straight to the end of the hallway, glancing in at the open doors of two small rooms as he passed them, until he reached what was obviously the master bedroom. He looked inside the closet, then searched the master bath. He found a linen cupboard there, took a sheet back to the bedroom, and spread it on the floor.

He intended to throw her clothes into it, but thought for a moment, then went back to one of the other bedrooms that he had passed in the hall. It was a guest room, and its closet served as storage. He found a nested set of luggage, and removed a clothes bag, a medium suitcase and a small travel case.

Taking them back to the master bedroom, he swept his hand along the closet rod, grabbed the hangers of a half dozen of her dresses, and strung them through the open clothing bag. He added three of her business suits, threw in two pairs of black pumps and a black belt, and zipped the bag shut. He opened the suitcase and, pulling out the bureau drawers, used both hands to scoop her flimsy underwear into it. He found a couple of pairs of folded jeans and sweatshirts which he added, then going back to the closet, found a pair of athletic shoes which he tossed in also.

He opened the small case and, holding it next to her

dressing table, swept her cosmetics and earring tray into it. He rifled the medicine chest in the bathroom and added a razor, a can of shaving cream, a bottle of peroxide and some headache tablets to the contents of the small case. He grabbed the towels off the rack and threw them in the suitcase for good measure. He looked at the contents of the open cases, glanced around the room, then closed the cases and took them and the garment bag downstairs. The whole thing had taken less than five minutes.

Beverly Watkins was sitting on the floor beside her dead husband, her shoulders shaking, tears and mucus streaming down her vacant face. Reed looked around, spotted a phone in the kitchen, dialed 911 and requested an ambulance. He went back to Watkins, and knelt down across her husband's body from her. He raised her chin with his left hand, and gave her a short, stinging slap with his right. Her eyes focused and she recoiled slightly, looked at him, frightened and bewildered, but with comprehension.

"Mrs. Watkins, I am with the C.I.A. Your husband is dead. The men who killed him were sent here to kill you. They didn't know your husband was at home. His being here saved your life. If you want to live, you must come with me. If you stay, you will die tomorrow or the next day. It will probably look like a suicide or an automobile accident. This would have looked like a burglary in all probability, if they had lived to complete the job." He indicated the two dead "cops."

"I know it's rough, but you've got to pull yourself away and come with me this instant. I've called an ambulance, and your husband will be taken care of. I've packed your clothes. We must leave now, before anyone gets here." He grasped her arms, and slowly lifted her up, still looking into her eyes.

She sighed, wiped her eyes and nose with the back of her hand, and looked down at her husband.

"I understand," she said.

Reed picked up the cases, told her to grab her purse

and open the door, and they went out together. She looked one last time at the body of her husband as she closed the door, and with a silent shaking sob, turned and followed Reed to his car.

Reed stowed the luggage in the trunk of his car, and got Beverly Watkins strapped into the front passenger seat. They drove off into the gathering darkness, heading south down Highway 65 toward Louisville, Kentucky.

Watkins sat dazed and uncommunicative, staring vacantly out the windshield at the lights of oncoming traffic. Occasionally her chin would tremble, and more tears would run silently down her cheeks. Reed was glad of her preoccupation. He needed time to think.

They had been driving for six hours, stopping only once for gas. Beverly Watkins had slept for two or three hours, exhausted with grief. They were a little south of Nashville, Tennessee, and heading toward Florida on Highway 75, when the radio station Reed was listening to, gave the announcement.

According to the radio, the Indianapolis police had discovered that Beverly Watkins, a former newscaster and militia sympathizer, and her husband Nathaniel, were somehow involved in a domestic terrorism operation. Two police officers had been sent to stake out the Watkins home until the F.B.I. could arrive. Unfortunately, their presence was discovered by the terrorists, and they were killed. Before he died, one of the officers had identified one James Reed, a former C.I.A. operative wanted for counterespionage and terrorism, as one of the ringleaders. Nathaniel Watkins had been killed in the struggle at the Watkins home.

Apparently, Beverly Watkins, James Reed and others had fled the Watkins house, which they knew was no longer safe for them. Several hundred pounds of high explosives and numerous assault weapons had been removed from the Watkins house. The F.B.I. estimated that there were more than two dozen members in the group, and that the government had thwarted the terrorists' plans only days—perhaps only hours—before an atrocity similar to the Oklahoma City and World Trade Center bombings was to take place. Watkins and Reed were wanted for murder, terrorism and espionage, and were considered armed and dangerous. A nation-wide manhunt was under way. Descriptions followed.

What had been a moral dilemma for Reed was now a much more basic question—that of survival. He wanted to kill Broderick, and he knew now that doing it would be doing something really worthwhile for humanity. With a word, Broderick had turned him from a loyal, federal employee into a public enemy with no choice but to run or die. If Reed stayed to challenge Broderick and his bosses, he would simply disappear in the federally controlled system, and never be heard from again.

Beverly Watkins brought him from his introspection with a single word. "Why?" she asked.

Reed turned his head, found her looking into his eyes, her face expressionless, her eyes dry. He told her everything, explaining Broderick's sanctioned, secret agenda.

She sat for some time after he had finished, watching the passing nightscape through the shadowed windows of the car, trying to absorb the idea of such a monstrous plot. It seemed absurd. This was the United States of America. Things like that didn't happen here. Government coups and enslaved populations were things that happened in Europe, in third-world countries, not the good old rock-solid republic of the United States.

The agony of her last look at Nathaniel welled up in her again, her throat constricting. She fought it down, and breathed deeply. Nathaniel was dead and she was a fugitive. She and the man who had originally been assigned to kill her. She shivered inside, glancing side-long at Reed. He had helped her. She had no doubt that he had saved her life. Her reason told her that she had no immediate cause to fear him, or to disbelieve him. He could certainly have made up a better story, if what he said was a lie. What would he gain by lying? Besides, the radio had confirmed it. Terrorists? The lying bastards! They were still around. They still had power. The weapon hadn't destroyed them, only driven them underground. They could still hurt people, still destroy lives to insure obedience in the media boardrooms. What would they do now? Where was Reed taking her?

XVIII

In Cocoa Beach, Reed took the car to a small wrecking yard and garage off Clearlake Road. Beverly sat in the car and watched as Reed had a few words with a rough, bearded man in dirty workclothes. The bearded man yelled to someone inside the garage. Reed returned to the car, collected Beverly and their luggage, and led her away down the rutted dirt and grass road toward the paved street. As they walked away, three young Hispanic men ran to the car, dragging hoses, jacks and air wrenches. By the time Reed and Watkins reached the street, the car was fast becoming used car parts.

They took a taxi to a Cocoa Beach marina, where Reed paid cash for an eighteen-foot open boat with a small outboard engine. They started down the Banana River, following the intercoastal waterway until it ended near Port Salerno. After leaving the mouth of the river for the open sea, they paralleled the coastline, keeping about a quarter mile off shore, taking their time, running along the outermost perimeter of light surf at trolling speed, putting in occasionally to buy gas and use a restroom.

Reed scanned the sea and shore constantly, expecting any minute to see a four-wheel-drive Bronco or minivan appear over the dunes, black-garbed agents with assault rifles swarming out of it, or a Coast Guard cutter growing out of the ocean horizon with klaxons blaring. If it happened, he knew the Walther in his pocket wouldn't be much of a defense in their exposed situation.

Throughout the long days that followed, Beverly remained distant and incommunicative, answering when spoken to, doing whatever he asked, never volunteering a thought or observation. Reed could see that she was withdrawing further into herself with each passing hour, but he couldn't think of anything to do about it. She spent most of the time lying in the bow of the boat, her head resting on the gunwale, a seat cushion for a pillow, staring out to sea with glazed eyes.

Their arms and legs were red and burned by noon of the second day, and they felt like they were growing maggots in their clothes. They took turns bathing in the sea, which turned out to be a mistake. The seawater dried, leaving crusted salt in their hair and under their clothes, causing them to itch and burn and chafe.

Reed finally bought a five-gallon can of fresh water, blankets, bathing suits, deck shoes for himself, and a bottle of suntan lotion at a marina. They changed out of their clothes in the restrooms. Reed used the fresh-water hose at the back of the baithouse to hose the salt and sweat off their bodies, then rinsed out their wet clothing and wrung it damp-dry. There were no public showers. They applied the suntan lotion liberally, to comfort their raw and tender skin, and put on loose shirts over their bathing suits. They were feeling better by the time they returned to their boat and left the harbor.

They camped on the beach the second night, sleeping fitfully in the cold and damp. When they arose in the early hours of the third day, a cold, wet mist was settling about them, and a fog lay over the sea. Beverly barely responded to Reed's quiet "Good morning," and didn't respond at all to his further attempts at conversation. Reed had to prompt her to get her up and moving. They ate a silent meal of lunchmeat and bread, and climbed back into the little open boat. Beverly had barely touched her food. They set out again, her face downcast and morose.

She sat awhile, a freshening wind from the sea blowing her hair and misting her face with airborne dew. Rivulets of condensate ran down her back as she stared out to sea. After a while, she resumed her reclining position of the previous day.

Reed was stiff and tired, and in a disinterested frame of mind, but even so, he abstractly admired her lush figure. She was a beautiful woman. Even now, with her hair stringy and pasted to her head and face by the wet mist, her long legs and soft curves aroused him. She was overflowing the bikini top of her bathing suit. He thought that she was far more desirable this way, than with her hair carefully coifed and in the professional business suit that until now, had been his only vision of her. The blankets were almost saturated with dew, but he spread one over her anyway, hoping to conserve her body heat and prevent her from catching a chill. They didn't have time to be sick. She didn't seem to notice his attentiveness.

Reed managed to pull a pair of fiberglass oars from beneath the seats and, cutting the sputtering outboard engine, he moved to the center of the boat, his back to Beverly, and began to row, trying to work out the kinks in his muscles. After a while, he felt better, and his mind began to function again. He rested occasionally, then resumed rowing, not expecting to get anywhere fast, just doing it for the rhythmic, calming activity.

As the sun began to climb, the heat made Reed's damp clothes itch and chafe, and the stagnant sea smell was the worse for his discomfort. Finally he removed the shirt he was wearing, and used it to blot his under-arms and face of the sweat he had worked up.

He stopped rowing, and turning around, rummaged in the suitcase for the undershirt he had worn under his suit. He looked at Beverly, noting that she still hadn't changed position. Aware that she had to be as uncom-fortable as he was, he decided to try to do something to bring her out of her vacant stupor and get her mind working again. He was beginning to fear she might withdraw from shock to the point that she would sink into a catatonic state and never awaken.

"Mrs. Watkins," he ventured, and got no response.

"We're surrounded by . . ." Sharks, he had started to say, then thought better of it. Don't be a childish ass, he thought to himself. I don't want to risk inciting her to panic. It might do her even more harm. He thought for a minute, then said, "Mrs. Watkins, tell me about your husband. What was he like?" Reed watched her face. She gave no indication that she had heard him. Her staring eyes hadn't flickered; her expression remained unaltered. What was his name, Reed wondered, Daniel? No, Nathan. No, Nathaniel. That was it, Nathaniel.

"Mrs. Watkins, tell me about Nathaniel," he shouted. "Where is Nathaniel?" Her eyes flickered briefly. Reed was beginning to worry, thinking he might already be too late. He nudged the sole of her foot with his toe, shouting, "Where is Nathaniel, Mrs. Watkins. Where is he?"

Finally, he shipped the oars and moved forward, crouching over her, shaking her arms, chafing her hands and legs vigorously between his palms. He raised her up until she sat limply upright in his arms, leaning into his chest. He rubbed her back and pinched her shoulders, working her muscles hard. He held her in the crook of his arm and splashed seawater in her face with his right hand, and slapped her cheeks lightly. "Who are you?" he repeated, over and over. "Where is Nathaniel?"

Finally, her brow furrowed, and her eyes blinked. She looked at him, searched his face, registered puzzlement.

"Who are you?" he asked again.

"Bev . . ." her dry mouth worked. She swallowed, trying to moisten her throat. "Beverly Watkins," she finally managed hoarsely.

"What do you do for a living?" he asked.

She stared at him quizzically, her throat working.

He reached around with his free hand and retrieved the thermos bottle of cold coffee he had bought the day before. He poured the cap half-full, and holding her in one arm and the cup to her lips, gave her a drink of the bitter liquid. She swallowed, choked a little, then took some more, and the color began returning to her cheeks.

"Do you know where you are?" he asked.

She looked at him, her face worried, then her eyes widened, and she glanced from side to side, toward the beach and the sea, panic rising in her face.

"Where is Nathaniel?" he asked relentlessly.

Her face froze, and she stared intently into his eyes. Suddenly, her eyes went wide, as comprehension flooded through her. Tears welled up, and her face contorted in anguish and rage. She began clawing and pushing to get away from him, and screaming, "He's dead! He's dead! They killed him! Oh, God, Nathaniel!"

She rolled out of Reed's arms, facedown across the seat, deep, racking sobs shaking her back.

Reed moved back to his seat, taking long breaths, shuddering with cold, emotionally spent. After a time her sobbing diminished, then began again, more quietly. Reed sat motionless for a while, staring unseeingly out to sea, his mouth a grim line. Finally, he took up the oars and began rowing again. After a while, he started the engine and picked up speed.

The cold, damp sea and monotonous shoreline had become a gray, netherworld limbo that sapped the brain of thoughts. He had decided that regardless of the risk, they needed to find a town and mix with the living. They needed to sit in a restaurant, among familiar sights and sounds, and eat a hot meal. After that, a warm motel room, a hot shower, a long sleep and some dry clothes. Familiar things the mind could deal with. Physical comfort. It was all he could do for her now.

It took them five days to drift down the Florida coast to Miami, stopping overnight in cheap motels at Fort Pierce and Boca Raton. Once in Miami, Reed felt both relieved and sad that the boat journey was over. It had been physical misery, but it had suspended the feeling of desperate flight for a time, and the sick feeling in his gut when he was reminded that there was no way back to his former life. Now he must become active. He must begin to plan.

Beverly was still distant and introspective much of the time, especially in the evenings. She still wept occasionally, quietly and to herself. He couldn't help her, so he quit worrying about her, telling himself she would eventually tire of grief, as the mind does, and slowly begin to put it behind her. In a couple of days, he thought, he would try to distract her, turn her attention to other things. Maybe take her to a nightclub and some of the more garish parts of the city. Give her a little color and excitement. Maybe it would draw her out of her shell. First, though, he had to get some of their immediate cares out of the way. At least she was coherent now, and there had been no further comatose lapses.

Reed finally came to terms with their situation, and the feeling of sick panic faded. He was a survivor. He accepted. He had spent his life in similar situations, fearing discovery and death, and his mind began following habitual paths, running through prospective travel plans, and weighing their chances of success. They needed identification documents and new personas. Those tasks came first, and were the easiest to accomplish. Secondly, they needed money. Fortunately, that, too, was not a problem.

Reed was single, and had worked in one remote hellhole after another for almost fifteen years. One day, ten years ago, he had been rummaging through his bureau drawer for something and discovered that he was pushing five payroll deposit slips out of his way, trying to find a spare apartment key among his jewelry. When on assignment, he lived on the other salary that he drew and banked under his cover occupation. His normal pay was sent automatically by electronic transfer to his personal bank account in Arlington, Virginia.

He decided to establish a secret account, just for future emergencies. He happened to be on assignment in Amsterdam at the time, and he had promptly opened an account in a bank, under a secret identity. He had drawn out alternate paychecks, once each month, and put them in the Amsterdam bank, half his annual salary after taxes, for the past ten years. He had $275,000 in savings and accumulated interest, and his agency had no knowledge of it. It would take a couple of days to transfer a few thousand dollars to a local bank, but then they would have a little breathing room. He decided then and there to take Beverly Watkins to California with him, if she would go, and to help her get established where he could help her and watch over her for a while. He felt responsible for her suffering, and wanted to at least help her to safety. He felt he owed her that much. That was the reason he gave himself, at any rate.

He rented connecting rooms on the second floor of a small motel, near a swim beach in south Miami. It was an older, two-story structure, built in the shape of a "C," with parking inside the center courtyard. It was run by a retired couple from Chicago, and while it was by no means a resort spot for the rich and famous, it was clean and well-managed. Tenants appeared to be passers-through. Reed noted that a preponderance of the cars were loaded down with luggage and beach paraphernalia, and sported out-of-state plates.

Reed bartered the boat near there, in a Cuban-run pawn shop-cum-gateway to the Miami black market, for new identity documents. His livelihood had depended on his having a great deal of arcane knowledge about the underbelly of society in a dozen countries. He knew where to find reliable "fix-it" shops in most of the major cities in America, Europe and the Middle East, where documents such as licenses, passports and birth certificates could be forged. That was why they were here. The shop in Miami was one he had used several times. They were completely professional.

Their birth certificates and other documents were put on quality counterfeit forms and letterhead stock, from county seats in Indiana and Oklahoma, near Beverly's and Reed's respective points of origin. The vendor had hundreds to choose from.

To be effective, new identities had to hold up under mild scrutiny, and Reed had long ago learned that it paid to keep the professed origins as factual as possible, so that accents of speech and colloquial vernacular were genuine, and knowledge of the area of origin was accurate.

The documents they received were "aged" to look convincing. They were dipped in mild acid and air-dried under an ultraviolet lamp, to fade the ink and fray the microscopic fibers of the paper, so that the documents looked as if they had been issued years ago. The driver's license photographs would have to wait a few days, until their appearances were sufficiently altered.

Reed bought new bathing suits and leisure clothing for Beverly and himself in a local department store. He bought a bottle of baby oil and three ounces of tincture of iodine in a supermarket pharmacy, and mixed them to make a tanning solution. They both dyed their hair black, and Beverly started wearing her shoulder-length hair in a pony tail, thus changing her appearance from that of a professional woman, to one with a more youthful, bohemian flair.

She wore contacts, so Reed took advantage of it. She was fitted with brown-tinted contact lenses to mask her blue-gray eyes. He stopped shaving his upper lip and let his mustache grow. They applied the tanning mixture liberally, and spent a great deal of the daylight hours on the beach, or walking around the casual resort section in bathing suits, shorts and tank tops to weather their exposed skin.

They lived in the brief clothing for the better part of two weeks, and at the end, the combination of sun and dyeing agents had darkened their complexions to the point that they could have passed for Cubans or Puerto Ricans easily. As they glimpsed their reflections in storefront windows and mirrors, they both agreed that their best friends wouldn't know them. Reed thought that asked unawares, they wouldn't even have recognized themselves in a photo. The time had come; they had their photos taken for their new driver's licenses.

A week after reaching Miami, Reed lay awake one night, thinking. His and Beverly's beds abutted the same wall, on opposite sides. The sound of someone weeping finally registered in his consciousness, and he realized it was coming from her room, again. It was a nightly ritual. His stomach sank from dread. He knew he must deal with it sometime, and he didn't have a clue as to how to go about it. He lay there for some time, listening, unsure of what to do. He wasn't certain that he should do anything.

He realized that he had been purposely distant from her, keeping his mind occupied with planning and replanning, and trying to sort out what resources he had in the Miami area; he had deliberately avoided thinking about her confusion and her still-fresh pain. Worse, he was beginning to treat her as an irritant. He admitted to himself that he had wanted to dodge the issue, hoping she would somehow come out of it on her own.

Her entire world had been destroyed in a twinkling, as if it had suddenly turned to sand and run through her fingers before her startled eyes. She had come home, weary from her day at work, and ten minutes later everything she had known was gone; her life had vanished before she had even had time to register what was happening. She had suffered a far greater loss than he had, and the realization of his own selfishness suddenly struck him. No wonder she's miserable, he thought. She's about as alone as she can be.

This was an ordinary woman, out of her depth, totally dependent on him for her very life. Like a child, she either asked outright, or looked at him questioningly before she did almost anything. The sudden awareness of this fact was like a blow. He felt inadequate for the first time since he had entered basic training in the Marine Corps.

Finally, reluctantly, he got out of bed and pulled his pants on. He trekked barefooted to the adjoining door, and knocked. There was a long delay, but she finally answered. She opened the door in response to his voice. Her face was streaked and her eyes were red from crying.

She was dressed in her green flannel nightshirt. It emphasized the points of her breasts and the curve of her hips. Reed was painfully aware of the fact that she was a beautiful woman, having seen her in a bathing suit and skimpy attire for days now. He had noticed the admiring glances that other men gave her, on the street and in restaurants, and noted with growing self-disgust his own feelings of jealousy.

At the moment, he was aroused, and yet sensitive to the fact that she was very vulnerable, and very confused. Not knowing what else to do, he took her in his arms and held her close, stroking her back and shoulders. At first, she looked confused, but didn't struggle. She had become accustomed to doing as he told her, accepting his actions without question, following his lead. After a moment, she pushed back gently, looking into his face.

He sighed. "I heard you crying," he said, "and I thought you needed comforting. I'm new at this—taking care of someone, I mean. I'm probably making a lot of mistakes that are obvious to you, but not to me. I've been preoccupied with arrangements, and I haven't been very conscious of your state of mind." He sighed again. "No, that's not true. Actually, I've been ducking it, hoping you would snap out of it. I don't mean to be callous; I just don't know how to help you. I don't know what you need, or what I can do to comfort you. You'll have to tell me. At this point, I don't even know if I should go on calling you Mrs. Watkins, or if we can be on a first-name basis."

He flushed, self-consciously holding and patting her hand. "I . . . I want to be your friend. Very much so. I'm not hitting on you. I mean . . . I want to, but I know it's not right, not just now. Oh God, what am I saying," he said, stepping back. "Look, Mrs. Watkins, I'm

sorry. I've made a mess of this. I just wanted to help.
Please just forget this ever happened."

He turned and left the room, embarrassed and in
haste. Beverly stood for some moments where he left
her, staring at the closed door, a blank expression on
her face. After a while, she got back into bed. She lay
for a long time, staring at the shadows cast on the wall
by the courtyard lights that shone dimly through the
curtains of her room. She listened to the sounds of traffic
in the street, hearing them for the first time. Finally,
her eyes closed and she slept. For the first time in
several days, she didn't have nightmares of her husband
being murdered.

After leaving her, Reed paced up and down in his
room for the better part of an hour, thinking tumul-
tuous thoughts, angry at himself. For once, he was
totally conscious of her, her alone, and the exigencies
of their flight were submerged beneath the passionate fire coursing through him. The memory of her
softness, of her breasts against him, of the curve of
her lower back as it sloped outward into the rounded
swell of her hips, hips that he had longed to touch,
was burned into the very fiber of his soul. The scent
of her lingered in his nostrils. He ached for her. Desire
sang through his blood like an exotic drug, so powerful in its urgency that it was almost a madness.
Raging adrenaline demanded action, and a new emotion, more powerful than any he had known, spurred
him to crash into her room and lose himself in her
soft flesh, her sweet scent.

At the same time, he feared the possible consequences. He wanted the same passionate response from
her, not just mechanical submission, and he wasn't at
all certain that she would submit. He knew that a self-
possessed woman still lurked within her, a spirit suppressed and submerged by shock, and by her forced
dependence on him, but still very much at the root of
her being. He felt guilty for his own role in her grief,
and thought that she might secretly despise him. He

feared to find out. He feared that if she were pushed, she might vanish out of his life forever.

He realized that, by degrees, he had become used to her being in his life and his thoughts, and he had just found out that he would miss her greatly if she decided to seek her own path.

His thoughts went round and round, always ending up with no satisfactory conclusions. He called himself a fool for going to her room in the first place. At the same time, he wished that he had kissed that soft, tremulous mouth, and attempted to make love to her. What would her response have been? What did she feel about him? Did she think anything at all about him? Finally, his racing heart subsided, sheer exhaustion set in, and he lay down in bed and fell asleep with the light still on.

The following morning began as usual. Reed knocked on her door and they went down to breakfast in the motel restaurant. Reed was his usual, businesslike self, laying out their schedule for the day. He was halfway through eating when he realized that she was just sitting there, silently listening to him and watching his face. He blushed, and sat looking at his plate, not knowing what to say.

"I would like you to call me Beverly," she said.

Reed looked up, surprised. She was smiling tentatively. He smiled back, then laughed, happy and relieved. He held out his hand across the intervening breakfast dishes.

"Hi Beverly," he said, "I'm Jim."

Later that day, she lounged on the sofa in his room, watching him and listening as he sat on the bed making innumerable phone calls. She wore jeans and a tank top. Reed was dressed in cut-off blue jeans and a T-shirt. They both wore tennis shoes. She had tied her hair up with a bright red piece of yarn, making a bow atop her head, and put on makeup for the first time since

Nathaniel's death. The TV was on—the volume turned so as to be barely audible.

Beverly took in Reed's long, muscular legs and broad frame. His face was ruggedly handsome. Not pretty, but with a masculine cast, and honest, expressive brown eyes. The female in her responded for the first time in a long while. She had been happily married—immersed in her career and the busy pace of her daily job. Suddenly, that had all been torn away, as if it had been only a dream. From that moment until now, Reed had been her only reference point in an unfamiliar world, a world in which she no longer had a place. Reed had been like someone giving her professional help—an expert guide who knew the streets and byways of a world gone dangerous and strange. She had seen him alternate from brief moments of being a big, happy boy to something incommunicative and dangerous.

When he was in that fey mood, he sometimes reminded her of a stalking panther, cautious and alert to their surroundings. At other times he seemed reckless and confident, as if he knew exactly where he was going, and their surroundings were of no concern at all.

Suddenly, he was showing his human side again, and she knew that he was smitten with her. She colored slightly, thinking about his awkwardness and discomfiture in the middle of the night. Her life had gone from a staid, predictable, planned existence to a concatenation of wild, new experiences, and she really didn't know how to respond to any of them. Something about his nocturnal visit had catalyzed all the mingled and suppressed emotions that had troubled her for days. Today was clearer. She felt alive and aware again. The numbness of the past ten days had receded a bit, and she was taking notice of her surroundings. A glimmer of hope had invaded her heart.

Reed was busily practicing his art, arranging all the minor details that would allow them to blend into the background of mainstream society once again, as new and different people. Like all successful agents, he had his own network of contacts around the globe—people known only to him, who were not the common hired hands of the agency.

He knew someone who worked in administration at the University of Central Florida in Orlando. The woman maintained a respectable life on the surface and was, at least to Reed, about as honorable as a mercenary gets. She was a computer specialist, and she made her living outside her cover life by selling and manipulating information to those with money and a need.

Reed had used her often to acquire records of a personal nature, such as financial transactions and personnel data. She had spent years developing routines that could gain entry into the most secure computer nets in the world. Reed had occasionally used her to sift through the intelligence networks of other federal and defense agencies in order to track the petty larceny and graft that covered serious intelligence leaks.

Many small bureaucrats and military officials knew things of national significance, but would not disclose them because it would require an admission of guilt in some petty dealings of their own. You had to weed through the minor graft to get to the pertinent information. On those occasions, the one being screened seldom knew it. The agency felt it was worth it to tolerate the petty graft, in order to maintain a useful source.

On this occasion, Reed was having her arrange for false scholastic records to be entered into the computer at the University of Miami in Coral Gables, and credit histories for their new names into the consumer credit network. He and Beverly had spent half the night working out the details of their scholastic and credit histories. They had stuck as close as possible to the truth regarding educational backgrounds.

When his contact had completed her task, the university's records showed that a man named Jack Townsend had a degree in communications engineering, and a woman named Eve Lawrence had a bachelor of science degree in television journalism, both having graduated from the University of Miami during the 1980s.

The mercenary had never known Reed's true name—to her, he was a man named Bennett, and he didn't think that she would connect him with the hunt for a rogue agent that had received a twenty-second mention on the evening news ten days ago. What he was having her do was no different than the things she had done for him many times in the past.

Occasionally, Reed would break his concentration on what he was doing, and catch Beverly's glance from across the room. He would smile, his eyes would light up, and she would smile instinctively in return, her heart skipping a beat and her ears burning slightly. She analyzed her reactions objectively, knowing she could not change them in the least. She was feeling the sexual response of a sensual woman to the attentions of an attractive man, and the conflicting guilt of a married woman. Her logical mind acknowledged that her husband was dead and gone, but her emotional mind rebelled at the betrayal of his memory. She finally decided to just take things as they came. At least she was thinking again, and some optimistic, irrepressible emotion was growing inside her.

Three weeks after arriving in Miami, Reed was satisfied they had accomplished everything there that they could. They packed their few things, checked out, and chartered a flight on a small commuter plane to Tampa.

After a day of prowling the hotels and the amusement park at Busch Gardens, they met a tourist doctor and his wife, and hitched a ride with them in their small plane to a private airfield near Houston. Reed was avoiding all conventional routes and means of travel, hoping to sever their trail as often as possible. He didn't want any connection, however remote, to lead from their new identities in California back to their old personas.

He hoped they had left no trail to Florida, but if they had, and if they were lucky, the authorities would assume they had used Miami as a jumping-off place to South America. It would have been a logical destination for people in their situation.

They stayed in Houston for four days while Reed found another private plane ride, this time with the president of a construction firm who took them to Tucson. From Tucson, they did the same thing again, this time with a preacher flying to San Diego. Reed concocted a different story and different names each time. Finally, on October 5, they arrived at their destination of Santa Cruz, California.

XIX

It was a quiet evening on December 20. Senator Isley was sitting in the large, comfortably-appointed living-room of his new combination home and office. It was an antebellum style house, with a pillared front entry, located in an older residential neighborhood on the outskirts of Atlanta. A fire crackled in the fireplace, while snow fell gently to earth outside. He occupied one of two overstuffed chairs that flanked a similarly proportioned sofa.

The chairs and sofa formed a cozy arrangement in front of a large, brick fireplace with an overhung mantle. A throw-rug with a pale-green oriental design graced the hardwood floor, and a huge painting of some 19th century, Victorian mansion, complete with giant, old Cypress or Willow trees and two girls in hoop-skirts and bonnets, hung above the mantle.

In the south wall of the spacious room, large floor-to-ceiling windows looked out on a snow-covered clearing. Bordering the clearing, a forest of fir trees looked like painted silhouettes against the muted light of the gray winter sky. Dark-red velvet drapes with gold brocade framed the windows.

Four grim-faced men sat with Isley, all but one holding brandy glasses in their hands. Dr. Stickle occupied the opposite chair and he was drinking coffee. Along with General Pat Hargety and Dr. Gene Stickle of the Air Force Space Command, sat Dr. Clarence Patterson of NASA and Joseph Miller, Vice-President of the United States. Miller paced slowly before the fireplace, sipping his brandy and listening to the other men talk.

Senator Isley had become, among other things, chairman of the Armed Services Budget Committee, taking the post of the late Congressman Harford. He was also the sole senator from his state, now that each state had only one senator and one member in the House of Representatives. Of his original staff of forty-odd, only three remained.

In many respects, Isley liked it much better this way. His office was quiet these days, and simplicity had brought about order. The flocks of lobbyists had finally faced reality, and most of them had faded away. Under the new rules, special treatment was not possible, and only a fool would risk it. Toward the end, military police had been required to eject the milling crowds of hangers-on from the public buildings, just so the government employees could begin to reorganize the shambles that remained. Influence peddling had diminished from a torrent to a trickle. To Isley, it felt almost log-cabinish—early Americana. He liked it a lot.

The purpose of this gathering was to discuss the weapon that had brought about such radical change. The military and civilian space authorities had continuously searched for it for the past eight months. Until now, without success. The present conversation was quiet and earnest, a welcome departure from the fencing bouts and blame-laying that Isley had enjoyed with Vanderbilt's appointed military incompetents during the past few weeks. Isley and some others had finally challenged Vanderbilt, threatening no further cooperation unless he replaced his yes-men idiots with people they could work with. It took a few weeks, but the military command structure had been reconfigured, with experienced officers in charge once again. Stickle had been recalled from a university post, and reinstated in his old position as Chief Scientist in AFSPACECOM. He had immediately been put to work trying to find the orbital weapon system.

"How can you be sure that what you have found is the weapon, Gene?" asked Miller. "The consequences are enormous if you're wrong."

Stickle stared into his cup as he spoke. "Ground-based optics have discovered a kind of shadow in geosynchronous orbit. It's only six milliseconds of arc across—about a meter. It doesn't reflect radar, but it eclipses stars and appears as a kind of dark spot to optical telescopes. We've plotted the likely angles of fire, backward from the two impact zones, and it's in the correct position to target them. It has to be the weapon."

"If it is . . . if we assume that we know where it is," said Miller, "what can we do about it?"

"We've had a lucky break in that respect, or at least we may have. During the mid-80s, the Strategic Defense Command put up a killer satellite, called Diana after the Roman or Greek goddess of the hunt. It is a kinetic weapon. Specifically, it shoots metal arrows—or projectiles made from spent uranium. They are hard, heavy material, and they have a lot of energy. They can puncture gas cylinders, smash electronics, in general wipe out a satellite's attitude control system and other systems—assuming they hit a critical element, of course.

"Diana's weapons complement includes eighteen uranium arrows, plus six explosive projectiles, four of them tipped with high-explosive fragmentation grenades, and two burst-shells filled with radioactive iodide. The burst-shells were designed to produce a large ionizing cloud around an enemy weapons platform, and blind its electronic targeting, navigation and communications systems. There are twenty-four projectiles in all.

"Diana is in a slightly lower orbit, and about ten degrees, roughly three thousand kilometers, behind the nationalist weapon. We are trying to find out now if she will respond to controls, and if she has the propellant gas to maneuver. She's been inoperative, simply powered down, for almost fifteen years. Our people are digging out the old command protocols and the computer operating instruction set. We should know something in the next two or three days."

"What are the odds?" asked Isley.

"Your guess is as good as mine, Senator. The big questions are batteries, controls and thrusters. The photovoltaics, or solar panels, are probably okay, but the batteries may be beyond redemption. Of course, if there is even the smallest pinhole anywhere in the thruster lines or connections, the maneuvering propellant has long since leaked away. Otherwise, the weapon system itself should be okay. All Diana's projectiles are driven by compressed gas, but each projectile has its own individual carbon dioxide propellant charge. The odds are that several, maybe all of them, are okay. The electronics are shielded, but twelve years in space means a lot of hard radiation and micrometeorite dust. Who knows?

"We have one other option as well. I may as well go into it while we're on the subject. We're acquiring a mobile launcher with a Soyuz intercontinental missile from a site near Minsk, in Russia. It has a five-megaton warhead. If Diana is inoperative, we will launch the warhead into the orbital track of the nationalist weapon at an accretion velocity. It's called a 'Trojan Horse,' for obvious reasons, in space warfare vernacular.

"We'll scrap the Soviet missile, and use a staged Ariane booster to lift the warhead into geosynchronous orbit. We'll launch from a site in Europe that's beyond the limb of the earth, and out of sight of the weapon. We think the element of risk is relatively low.

"Normal antisatellite surveillance systems aren't likely to detect the approaching weapon until it's too late, once insertion is accomplished. We don't know what kind of surveillance they have, and that's a chance we'll have to take. They may only have an aiming system, but I wouldn't want to bet on it—not with what's at stake. If they have a security envelope with a Doppler radar or laser autoranging system, we're sunk. If they have any kind of ground-support like a global, or even a hemispherical radar net, they'll see the launch vehicle during the boost phase, and it will arouse their suspicions.

"Assuming we can get it up without their noticing, the bomb will take a few days to slowly catch up to the weapon. Once in close proximity, it can be detonated. It will be disguised as something innocuous, like an old, mangled com satellite.

"A satellite?" asked Miller. "You think that will fool them?"

"We must assume that they will detect the approach of anything in the orbital track, once it gets close enough; but in that orbit, it would be more peculiar if they didn't see things like that. It may fool their instruments, or at least not elicit the immediate response that an approaching missile would. We'll also give it a high radar albedo—just the opposite of what anyone would expect of a sneak attack weapon.

"As a precaution, we will load the warhead envelope with radioactive iodide. Even if we miss it with the direct blast, the ionizing radiation and radioactive cloud of charged particles should hamper its target acquisition system's capability to fix on a target, at least for several hours. In case we only cripple it, we'll have an armed Titan ready to launch from the Cape, to follow through and finish the job—kill it while it's blind.

"In any case, the beauty of this approach is that if they don't recognize the bomb as a threat, we can get it close enough to destroy the weapon system. If they decide not to take any chances, and destroy our Trojan Horse just to be on the safe side, they still won't know for sure that it was an intentional threat. They would have no reason to retaliate."

"Why can't you just launch an atomic bomb right at it?" asked Isley. "Wouldn't a nuclear blast destroy it even from a long distance away?"

"Afraid it won't work. If we launch in a minimal elapsed-time trajectory, they can see the booster and kill it before it leaves the atmosphere, thousands of miles short of its target. The retaliation could be severe. If we use an accretion orbit, they may not be able to identify it as a threat until it is too late."

"Very well, gentlemen," said Miller, finishing his drink and rising. "Keep me posted on this Diana thing, and we'll go from there. The President wants a detailed briefing before any course of action is taken. I am your only point of contact. Understood?" Miller deposited his glass on the table, gathered his overcoat and umbrella at the door, and left. The others followed suit.

After they had gone, Isley sat looking out at the white-clad, forested beauty of the Georgia countryside. It was such a peaceful scene—the gently-falling snowflakes among the tall, gray fir trees, the overcast sky, the dim, white outline of the distant hills. He wondered, and not for the first time, if what they contemplated was really necessary.

Contrary to expectations, there had been no further demands from the people commanding the weapon—no self-serving dictates, no demands for riches or power—nothing. The world had held its collective breath for months after that terrible beam of energy had excised political arrogance from the federal government. They had waited for the other shoe to drop. Nothing had happened. After a time, the world had exhaled that collective breath, as a victim of fear will finally do, and breathed a tentative sigh of relief.

As more time had passed, people had begun to regain some of their confidence and laughter. Haunted looks in the faces of worried adults had eased; the glum countenances of the children, who of course sensed the strain that the adults felt, began to return to the roller coaster of gleeful, petulant, questioning, pouting, angelic assumption and naiveté that is their nature. Things were, in many ways, returning to normal.

It was true that to do nothing was to leave the country at the mercy of the weapon and its makers, but what would this country look like in a few weeks or months if the military failed in their attempt to destroy the weapon? Would those people controlling the weapon simply laugh at the failed attempt? Would they punish the United States and make an example to the rest of the world by destroying it utterly?

Dr. Stickle and his war-college experts had no doubts at all, that given sufficient fuel, the weapon could raze the entire surface of the planet. That thing was up there, in its cold and lonely orbit, looking down on humanity without compassion, or even interest. Its electronic brain cared nothing for humanity—had no biases, good or bad. It simply reacted to the conditions programmed into it. It waited, and watched with electronic eyes, a shadow against the starscape of heaven.

In a way, it could be romanticized as a sort of intelligent entity, since its instructions and nature were devised by intelligent creatures, but if such "inference by association" was granted, then its makers must take on the character it reflected. Cold, heartless intellect. But were they? What were these people like, who would kill millions as if chastising a child. No anger. No extortion. "This is for your own good, children. Do as I say, or I'll punish you. It hurts me to do this, but you must learn to obey." They were still a mystery. So was their weapon.

Some religious groups were calling it the Sword of God. Maybe it was. God could use people and technology as His instruments, Isley supposed. The military had code-named it "Damocles," after the Greek hero who had been forced to sit beneath a razor-sharp sword, suspended from the ceiling by a single, fragile hair. Damocles' sword now hung above the whole earth, and no one knew whither it would fall.

Isley's doubts were not born of cowardice; he could fight and die for a just cause, and he was no longer much impressed with the merits of humanity. His doubts sprang from the motives behind the proposed overthrow of the weapon. It was not for the people or the good of the country. Not one of those involved in the scheme even considered that a reasonable question. It was solely to win back control for the old power structure. The people would be dictated to in any case, but it was who did the dictating that mattered to them.

Isley had once had ideals. He had been a college preppie, and later a college activist, and still later an involved family man, active in the affairs of his community. He liked people, liked seeing them happy and embracing all the good aspects of life.

He thought about the men who had just left. Miller was a question mark. He seemed to have no opinions of his own. He just seemed to run errands for the President, and officiate at forgettable events. Isley smiled. Those were the merits of a perfect politician. The public couldn't pin anything on you if you were invisible. Miller was a "stealth" politician.

Patterson he knew and liked. He was direct and stuck to his guns over issues. He didn't think Patterson was really cut out for the Washington crowd, but then he didn't suppose that he, himself, was all that good a fit, either. Patterson wasn't happy about the military's scheme, but Isley knew that he would go along with the crowd. Patterson would defend his convictions, up to a point, but he wouldn't fall on his sword over anything that he couldn't hope to change. He was not one to buck the entire power structure in a public stand against the White House, simply as an act of principle.

Like himself, Patterson had given ground, bit by bit, over the breadth of his career in the federal government, ceding a little integrity here and a little there, until it was second nature to simply avoid conflict.

Hargety was Stickle's boss, but Stickle ran "science" in the Space Command, and in this day and age that was mostly what defense consisted of. Even the foot soldier was a walking cornucopia of technology nowadays, with night vision, com systems in his helmet, ground-to-ground and ground-to-air destructive capability that even the best field artillery and antiaircraft weaponry of two decades ago couldn't compete with.

If Americans had possessed such technology during

the Second World War, the war would have ended in a matter of weeks. Even the armor on today's tanks was "active" armor. In response to an impact, it exploded outward, countering and damping the shaped-charge explosion of the offensive shell before it could penetrate.

Now, though, America did not have the superior technology. It was in the same position that Hitler would have faced if the American technology of today could have been taken back in time to World War II, and used against the Nazis. There was no defense. Maybe it *was* American technology, orbiting overhead; who could say? The general consensus was that it was an American freedom militia, with a nationalistic agenda, that was behind it.

As he thought about it, he knew that it had to be Americans. He just couldn't believe that any foreign nation would hold the United States in such a defenseless position, without walking in and taking over. Not even some of the so-called allies. Nor would they uphold the U.S. Constitution, or care about individual opportunity, or taxes. It had to be Americans behind it. Somehow, they had found the money, the scientific expertise and the materials.

It was not only the United States that had changed. The rest of the world had paused also, waiting and wondering. Though they had not yet suffered directly, they seemed to act in unspoken unison, suspending regional hostilities and general saber rattling. It was almost like a noisy cocktail party that suddenly falls silent, and stands attentive and waiting when the police walk in.

He sighed. He was tired of months of useless speculation, and he just wished he could disengage from it all. He would have liked to sit it out on the sidelines, and simply wait and see what the foolishness of his fellow men would bring. He wondered why he didn't do that. Quit and go home. Probably because there were no "side-lines" anymore, he thought. The nationalists had seen to that; everyone was involved whether they liked it or not.

He didn't presume to know what was right anymore. He really didn't think that anything was. People were just out for themselves, and what was "right" depended on where you stood. Shakespeare had defined existence best: the world is just a stage where people play out their individual parts. "And," Isley added out loud, "when we disappear and are forgotten, the universe won't really give a damn."

XX

It was Christmas Eve in Menlo Park, California, and Jack and Eve Townsend—formerly James Reed and Beverly Watkins—were smiling at each other across a dinner table in the Steak Ranch restaurant. The remains of turkey and dressing dinners had been removed by the waiter, leaving a partial bottle of wine, their glasses, half a loaf of brown bread and a large wedge of Baby Swiss cheese.

Jack had taken a position as a project manager, for an engineering firm which was located just down the road in Mountain View. Prouss Engineering did contract work for the NASA-Ames Advanced Projects Laboratory, near Sunnyvale, as well as other, private-sector contracting.

The job had been arranged by an old friend named Edward Teller, who had retired from the "Community" several years before, and now lived in Santa Cruz.

Teller had also arranged for Townsend to meet a physics professor named Ortiz at Stanford University. Dr. Ortiz was head of the Coherent Radiation and Optical Science Department in the College of Electrical Engineering. Townsend had spoken to him earlier today, by phone. Their first meeting was to take place the day after Christmas.

Jack and Eve had returned from Las Vegas, Nevada, earlier in the day, where they had been married. Eating, sleeping and spending every waking moment together for three and a half months, they had endured what seemed an eternity of fear and privation.

During those long, fear-filled weeks, they had also developed the suspicious care and acute senses of the hunted, and become solely dependent upon each other. They were now a working team, almost reading each other's thoughts, anticipating the other's next action instinctively, before it took place.

They avoided the police as a matter of course, going out of their way to avoid potential encounters. The risk of being recognized was low, but the safest risk was the one not taken, and while the tension was less now, Townsend would not allow them to become unobservant and lax in their precautions. It had gotten so that they derived comfort only from each other, and were fidgety and fretful when they were apart.

Fear has a way of building a bond of loyalty and absolute trust in people dependent upon one another for survival. For Jack and Eve Townsend, that bond had developed into tempestuous love. The last ten weeks had been a time of small miracles, due principally to Edward Teller. Teller had taken them in from the cold, and helped them to be reborn into a new life. He had rented a house for them in a secluded canyon a few miles from town, bought them a car, and now, gotten Townsend a job.

Teller was retired from the federal government, but kept his hand in by applying his knowledge of federal procurement. He worked intermittently as a free-lance consultant to small companies and universities that did business with the government. He had worked closely with many small, high-tech businesses, and knew a number of their managers and CEOs very well.

For Eve, haunting memories and fears still lingered, and no doubt, would continue for some time. Eventually, they would fade. At the moment she was relatively happy—in a Christmas-time, melancholy kind of way.

Two weeks after they had arrived in California, she and Jack had come home to their new house from a late dinner at a restaurant. They were still sleeping in separate rooms, and up until that night, nothing of an intimate, romantic nature had passed between them since that memorable night in Miami, seemingly so long ago. Their relationship had changed, though. They were friends and allies now, beyond any reason or necessity, and they confided everything to each other. They felt totally at ease and secure with each other.

That evening, they were sitting together on a redwood glider that, aside from a small table of like construction, was the sole piece of furniture on a railed, wooden verandah that overlooked the rocky, cedar-covered canyon in back of the house. They sat in partial darkness, enjoying their after-dinner coffee and talking.

The late evening air was slightly damp and chilly, but not uncomfortable, and bore the faint fragrance of cedar, pine trees and juniper. The canyon was a dark well, falling away beneath the verandah, and the hill on the other side of the canyon was a black outline against the starry sky.

Eve had been job-hunting during the days, as had Townsend, and they had just been discussing the poor pickings so far. She had been feeling more resigned than depressed, at that point. Unexpectedly, he reached out and turned her chin toward him, and leaning over, he kissed her very gently on the mouth.

"Will you marry me, Bev?" he asked.

As close as they had become, she hadn't seen it coming. She knew that she loved him. She had hoped that he would stop being the methodical planner and the perfect gentleman someday soon, and begin treating her as a desirable woman, but so far, he had been exasperatingly noble and patient with her.

When he finally spoke, though, her mind was on all the endless job applications she had filled out during the past weeks, and she was just about to tell him that she wished they would pass a law making everybody in the world use the same employment application, so she could just hand in photocopies, when he caught her totally off-guard. She looked at him blankly for a moment, while it registered.

Thinking he understood her hesitation, Townsend tried to explain, in the logical, patient fashion that she had come to know.

"I know this is out of the blue," he said, "but you must have thought about us, too. I don't know when I actually started thinking about us staying together. I guess it was that night back in Miami. Now, I can't imagine leaving you somewhere, and never seeing you again. I don't even want to imagine it. I don't think I could do it, even if you wanted it that way. I don't want a life without you in it.

"You were married, and you had a life and a home with someone else. I never have. I've never loved anyone before. Honey, I'll wait as long as it takes, until you can begin to love again. I'll take care of you—make a life for us. Will you marry me?"

She smiled, and tears filled her eyes as she kissed him back, and she put her arms around his neck, drawing him close.

"I was beginning to think that you were never going to ask me," she said. "Lately, I've considered jumping you in the middle of the night, but I was afraid you would shoot me before you knew who it was."

"No danger of that," he grinned. "I've lain awake at night thinking about you, oh, for the last three months or so."

That was the first night they had slept together. Since that night, she had endured a strange mixture of bliss, melancholy and concern for the future.

Now sitting here together, married, and for the moment perfectly content, it was beginning to look like they had found a home and happiness together. Tomorrow they would spend Christmas Day with Edward Teller and some of his friends.

"It doesn't seem possible that only a few months ago we lived totally different lives—really lived in a different world," said Eve. "All that seems so very long ago. The craziest part of it all is that I'm beginning to get used to life being an unending, immediate crisis." She toyed with his collar, and put her hand on his face. "I think that you and Nathaniel would have liked each other. Do you think I can go back and visit his grave, someday? Just to say good-bye?"

Jack smiled sadly, and took her hand in his. "Of course, honey, in a year or so. It will take awhile for that connection to grow cold. In the meantime, I want you to do me a favor."

"What is it?"

"You called me Jim twice yesterday, and you have to put those names out of your mind. That's not us anymore. A trick I learned in the espionage business is to make your cover identity a fact in your own mind. I've had to assume a role on short notice, and I've learned the only way to avoid mistakes, such as inadvertent slips of the tongue, is to convince yourself that you *are* your new identity. That old identity was just a role that you played for a while, and now it's over.

"It really works," he responded to the beginning, small shake of her head. "You have to use my new name in your thoughts. Really think of me as Jack Townsend. In a few days you will fool your psyche into accepting it, and it will eventually become natural. You have to do the same with your own name, too. It's a serious concern for us, baby. The first time you run into someone you've met at a function, and reintroduce yourself as Beverly, and they look at you strangely and say, 'But I thought your name was Eve,' you will realize that you've made a mistake, and it's going to be difficult to make someone forget an incident like that. They will tell their friends. Pretty soon you're ducking invitations and staying indoors, and the more suspicious you act, the more suspicious people become.

"I've learned that it doesn't make a whit of difference to your cover whether you live as a lion or a mouse, as long as the cover is solid. People are only suspicious of someone whom they think they don't know enough about. If you are a loud-mouthed, blustering boor, or a sad little wretch, you will be accepted, but if you are the least bit mysterious, they get really curious. People love scandal, large or small, as long as they are not the focus of it.

"To avoid that kind of situation, we must play our roles to the hilt. Play it until we become the role. Believe me, honey, you can do it.

"Tell you what, say a sentence with my name in it ten times. Say it with your eyes closed, and while you're saying it, picture me doing whatever you're saying."

"Oh, Ji . . . oh, I'll feel silly."

"Please."

She mustered herself, closed her eyes. "Okay," she said, smiling self-consciously, "here goes. Jack be nimble, Jack be quick, Jack jumped over the candlestick . . ." She stopped, clamped her teeth together, opened her eyes wide a couple of times, then started laughing silently, shaking with mirth.

"What is it?" he asked, smiling in sympathy with her, his brow creasing in curiosity, and just a little worry for her.

She snuffled, blinked at him, red-faced with the effort of trying to contain herself. "Jack burned his balls," she whispered hoarsely, and broke down, laughing out loud. She tried desperately to curb herself, but broke down again. Tears of laughter ran down her cheeks.

The nearest other patron, a man sitting three tables away, grinned at Jack and looked away. He couldn't have heard what Eve said, but he responded naturally to her fit of laughter.

Jack realized that he had never seen her laugh before. Emotion welled up in his throat, constricting it painfully, and his eyes filled, too. He knew then, just how much he had come to love her, and suddenly, how happy she made him. His life had been so methodical, so stripped of emotion, that happiness was something new, something long forgotten. Now, she *was* his life.

He recovered himself, blew his nose, sat there with a twisted grin on his face as he waited for her to subside. She did for a moment, gathering herself, catching her breath. Then she looked at him and broke down again, her head on the table, holding her hurting stomach.

"I'm shocked, madam, truly shocked at your loose behavior," he said in his best imitation of Cary Grant. "I thought that you were a respectable woman. Now I find that you're just another little tart. Burned my balls, indeed!" He laughed.

She looked at him, tears streaming down her face, clutching her napkin to her mouth. "I pictured you jumping a flaming candelabra, just like you said. You had a sign around your neck with *Jack* written on it, and you were naked," she sobbed. "It just came into my mind . . ." And she broke down again, in spasms of laughter. This time, he joined in. The sparse clientele in the restaurant looked at them momentarily, then turned back to what they were doing, as if they assumed that the laughing couple were slightly off-kilter, but harmless.

XXI

Hector Ortiz was short, in his early sixties, had white hair with a small bald spot at the back of his head. He was a native Californian. He wore plastic-framed glasses with bifocals. He was habitually in a white lab coat when at work, and his colleagues thought he looked strange when they saw him in other clothes. He was outgoing and playful by nature, but outwardly sarcastic. You had to get to know him to realize that he wasn't the grouchy old curmudgeon that he pretended to be.

Despite the lab coat and the credential, Ortiz was more of an administrator than a scientist. He knew a lot of people throughout academia, and he could get things done. He obtained grants prolifically, and while he generally kept his secretary and the accounting department pulling their hair out by the way he applied appropriated funds in a helter-skelter fashion, he was generally well-liked, and kept harmony in his department.

He published one or two short, innocuous papers a year. He was also comfortably installed in a somewhat arcane niche and wasn't jousting with anyone for higher position. He had tenure, and he had one other outstanding quality; he thumbed his nose at bureaucratic authority. He also had a Hispanic friend on the Board of Regents, and because of the Board's unofficial emphasis on minority tenure, anyone would've had a hell of a time in ousting him.

It had worked well throughout the better part of two decades. No one had ever bothered trying. His resulting

154

sang froid bothered a few of his superiors, but not sufficiently to spark any real enmity. In short, he was pretty much bullet-proof, and he knew it.

His meeting with Jack Townsend was at the request of a mutual friend, a C.I.A. friend who had gotten him out of Cuba when the Batista government fell.

He had been a visiting graduate intern at the university there in 1959, when the proverbial excrement hit the fan. He had spent three days running and hiding, while fellow academics were rounded up. Those that were Cuban natives with families couldn't avoid capture—there was too much leverage over them. It had not gone as harshly with them as they had feared, but at the time everyone was in a panic of terror, thinking they were to be shot or imprisoned, and afraid for their families.

When he had stumbled into the big C.I.A. agent, he had never been so glad to see an Anglo face in his life. It was American, and he hoped, friendly. It turned out far better than he had hoped. The man was from the same area in California, and four hours later, Ortiz was with him on a small seaplane, bound for Miami.

Memories of those days were also a part of his personal armor. He had never been that afraid again. He and his savior, Edward Teller, had become close friends during the following years, and Ortiz had been involved in a number of C.I.A. community science projects. Both were bachelors, and after Teller retired, they became regular companions, fishing together on weekends, or watching sports on TV.

Ortiz was generally open to visitors and would have met with Townsend anyway, or almost anyone else for that matter, but Teller had introduced Townsend by phone and explained the special nature of this visit. Ortiz was very curious to meet the man. When he did meet him, in his office, on the afternoon of December 26, he suddenly remembered a forgotten feeling, a presence that he hadn't experienced in a long while. He already knew what the man was. His friend had told him, but he would have known anyway. He knew that look, that subliminal cast of the features, and his curiosity grew.

Before Townsend could speak, he advanced, shook hands and said, "I've been around enough spooks to know one when I see one, Mr. Townsend. I see Dr. Philips, the scientist in charge of your Community Affairs Office, once or twice a year at the odd convention or seminar. Know him?"

Townsend smiled guardedly, "Dr. Robert Emerson has been in charge of the Community Affairs Office for the past two years, Dr. Ortiz. Eddie said you were an 'irreverent old spic,' but he didn't tell me you were tricky, too."

"Did he call me that? Did that old, honky asshole call me a spic?" He pretended great offense. "What else did he say about me?"

"Just that he wouldn't trade you for all the oil in Alaska. I take it that you two have some sort of history together. Eddie didn't elaborate except to mention that he met you in Cuba during Castro's revolt. At any rate, he thinks a lot of you, and I trust him, so here we are."

Ortiz laughed. "Eddie and I go back to just about the fall of the Roman empire. We're keeping each other company while everything is slowly being overwhelmed by the Brave, New World. Or to put it crudely, we're watching everything go to hell in a handcart. What would a pair of old farts like us do, without someone our own age to commiserate with? You young dipsticks don't remember when cigarettes were a quarter, or when a hamburger or a gallon of gas was thirty-five cents. You've probably never even seen a drive-in movie.

"In my day, you could take your girl out for a hamburger and a beer, and go to a double feature with cartoons for five bucks. It was a magic age. A different way of thinking that no one can describe. Do you remember the Ventures? 'Walk Don't Run,' 'Pipeline,' 'Perfidy'? Or Roy Orbison, 'Pretty Woman,' 'Crying,'

'Blue Bayou'? Or 'La Bamba,' or Harry Belafonte, 'Banana Boat'? How about Herb Alpert and the Tiajuana Brass, or Peter, Paul and Mary?"

"I vaguely remember a few of those. I remember the Beatles."

"The Beatles sucked. They, and that whole tribe of gangly-legged, long-haired British hippies, ruined American music."

"I didn't say I liked them."

Ortiz considered him for a moment. They both laughed.

"I can see why you and Eddie get along," Townsend laughed. "You're a pair of crotchety old bastards."

"Well, it beats being pubescent young assholes," Ortiz said, sitting down at his desk, and gesturing Townsend toward a chair. "What's going on in spooksville, anyway?"

Townsend sobered, watching Ortiz' face narrowly. "This is not a company matter," he said, "and I wouldn't want it to get to them. There is some risk in associating with me. If that worries you, we'll end it there. I'm not about to get a friend involved unknowingly, or the friend of a friend. I need some scientific help, and Eddie seems to think that you can supply it."

Ortiz waved his hand dismissively. "Eddie told me all that. What is it you want?"

"I'm trying to find the people who made the weapon. I need someone who knows his way around in the physics community, someone who is familiar with what has been published and what hasn't, someone who's tied into the worldwide physics grapevine. It's inconceivable that something like that could be built, and nobody know anything about it, or how it was done. If I knew what kinds of parts were involved, I could trace parts and materials shipments.

"Somebody knows who they are, and more than a few somebodies suspect; but amazingly, no one in the physics community, outside the government anyway, is even making a guess. Why is that?"

It was Ortiz' turn to scrutinize Townsend. "Why do you want to find them?"

"I think I want to join them. Corny as it sounds, I want to fight for the rebirth of democracy in this country. I've been a part of the other side, and I know firsthand what this country is up against. I want to salvage humanity while it's still possible, and I don't believe there will ever be another opportunity like this one. It's a once-in-a-lifetime chance. We just can't let it slip by. If that weapon system fails, for whatever reason, we will have lost our only hope. They are too entrenched—too well established for us to gain control by any other means."

"Things seem to be pretty well in hand, in that respect. What makes you think that you can help?" asked Ortiz.

"I have the know-how to find the maggots buried under the flesh of this country. I know how the network is set up, and I know at least one individual who can get me started down the trail. I have personal reasons, too.

"If I have to operate alone, I will, but that way is too slow. I need help. That weapon gives humanity a fighting chance. We have to kill the puppet masters now, or we will never win this nation back. Those people are still with us, and they are not going to give up. If that weapon goes away, they will be back, big time."

"Could you identify and locate all these underworld kingpins?"

"I think so, but it would be much faster with help. I could ferret a few of them out, I'm sure, but this underground is worldwide. These people are part of the international set. They move around this nation and from country to country the way you walk across this campus. They live everywhere, but mostly on the coasts. New York and California are home to a lot of them—or New York was, before that weapon fired. They're in all the jet-set capitals of the world—Paris, London, Rio. It's going to take a lot of digging to find all the corporate connections, affiliations, history of buy-outs and mergers—almost like tracing family trees—and I haven't the resources to get very far alone. It's just too big a job for one man.

"It's one thing to suspect someone, but it's another to find the proof. I need the help of some dedicated researchers, and I no longer have a huge government budget with which to hire them. I need people who can manipulate computers, get into banking records and trace company pedigrees. Where the nationalists are concerned, I need specific information about the kinds of parts that would be required for such a weapon, so I can search for supply purchases and A&E firms that did unusual design and fabrication contracts."

"Don't you think that the government is already doing that?" asked Ortiz. "What makes you think you can succeed where they, with all their resources, haven't?"

Townsend smiled. "Partly, it's because I have faith in my own ability. I see things a little differently than most people—some indefinable difference in perspective, I guess. Whatever it is, a sixth sense, or subliminal knowledge, or some weird instinct—it has always found a way. Secondly, there is a lot of confusion about these people. What drives them—what their ultimate goals are. I have opinions about that too. You don't set a thief and scoundrel to fathom the motivations of a priest or a patriot. That's just an analogy, but you get my meaning. One can't fathom the thinking of the other, not in any real way.

"The government is looking at this in a military sense, like it was a militant faction, even a splinter force that broke off some army, somewhere, or like a rival mob that wants to take turf away from their gang. I think they're all wrong."

"Who do you think it is?" Ortiz asked.

"I think it's a group of scientists," Townsend replied, "or at least, a group composed mostly of scientists and engineers. Technical people, not military types. Their motives are altruistic, pure and simple. They have the physical institutions necessary to hide the acquisition of supplies and materials. The research could be broken up into a thousand pieces and piggybacked onto other, diverse research projects over a period of time, and no one would ever be the wiser."

Ortiz picked at his fingernails. "Sounds reasonable," he said.

"I'm convinced of it, Dr. Ortiz," Townsend said, studying the old scientist. "All that remains is to analyze past research projects for anomalies in parts, materials and services. I'll bet that these people used a lot of federal research grants as the piggyback vehicles to accomplish that weapon system. They probably laughed at the irony of it. Federal research grants require a lot of detailed record-keeping though, and I have access to those files."

"Well, I'll say this for you," said Ortiz, meeting Townsend's gaze, and smiling. "You've got the makings of a good detective yarn, or spy story. You're likely barking up the wrong tree, though. Scientists are fundamentally humanitarians and environmentalists— tree-huggers and fern-feelers. They don't make war, at least not directly."

"One thing I've learned about life," said Townsend, smiling back. "Given incentive, nature will produce a fluke. Man, animal or plant, if pressure is brought to bear, life will adapt, even if the adaptation is contrary to precedence.

"It's an irony and a pity," Townsend said, staring out the window introspectively, "every technological break-through has its yin and yang. Computers have revolutionized medicine, made space flight possible, helped us in a thousand ways, but they have also made a global, criminal network possible.

"The same holds true for this weapon. Right now, it appears to be a savior. If the Defense Department gets control of it, it will either be the ultimate whip to beat mankind into submission, or the ultimate shield of freedom. Whoever controls the Defense Department will decide which purpose it is put to."

"Do you think they will get control of it?" Ortiz asked.

"I don't know. I do know they intend to try. That's another area where I can be useful.

"A few weeks ago something happened that made up my mind. As a precaution, I wrote a computer program, just an algorithm really, but it enables me to gain access to several different secure computer nets in the intelligence community, including most of the affiliated agencies and their contractors. The complexity of the federal network is also its greatest weakness.

"Anyway, I had authorized access, but I suspected that authorization might be limited or revoked by my supervisor at any moment. We had a philosophical disagreement of sorts, you might say. I couldn't risk waiting until I was denied access, so I did it. As it turned out, it was none too soon; my department chief turned me out permanently. I'm a fugitive. Legitimate law-enforcement agencies are after me."

"Why are you trusting me with this?" Ortiz asked. "You don't know me."

"Eddie says you feel the same way that I do. You are not going to help me without knowing why, are you?"

"No, but it seems like an all-or-nothing gamble on your part. I could turn you in."

"Are you going to?"

Ortiz smiled, "Not today."

"Will you help?"

"I have a friend who has some theories. I'll let you talk to him on one condition. I want to know everything you intend to do, before you do it."

"Why?"

"I have my reasons. Uppermost is self-preservation. Only a little below that is concern for the lives of the people that I put you in touch with. I'm sorry, but I can't be as trusting as you. The Feds are well-known for entrapment schemes. There is too much at risk. For the moment, let's just say that philosophically I might agree with your political views to some extent. I will help you, insofar as helping you to do some computer research. I won't support any act of direct treason. That will have to suffice for now. Deal?" Ortiz extended his hand.

"Deal," said Townsend, shaking hands. "Thanks, Dr. Ortiz."

They stood up.

"Having someone like Eddie and you to talk to, makes me feel a little less alone," said Townsend. "Your help means a lot."

"Just call me Hector. I'll see what I can do. We'll meet somewhere else in the future, just to reduce the numbers of curious people watching us come and go, and to avoid the possibility of someone listening in, okay?"

"My thoughts exactly. Call you tomorrow."

XXII

Gene Stickle sat with three other physicists in a conference room at the U.S. Army Strategic Defense Command's headquarters in Huntsville, Alabama. Present were Able Johnson, a rangy, middle-aged Southerner from Georgia Tech University; Ted Wallace, a younger professor from Cal-Tech who, like Johnson, was a contract consultant to SDC; and Joe Mercer, a middle-aged government employee like Stickle, and past director of the SDC's now defunct Directed-Energy Weapons Program.

Johnson and Wallace had worked independently of one another to perform a contracted study for SDI. Their task had been to assimilate and correlate all the detailed data gathered about the effects of the weapon's beam and develop a theory regarding its operation and tactical weaknesses. Wallace had come up empty. Johnson was giving his report. Wallace doodled on a legal pad, listening, interjecting occasionally. Mercer and Stickle were attentive to Johnson, who was describing, in a rich, baritone drawl, his speculations on the technology of the weapon.

"I think it's safe to assume," he began, "that given the small size of the thing, that the energy beam is not just brute power. The weapon system's not big enough. The power plant required to deliver a forty terawatt beam to the earth's surface would be big enough to blot out a big part of the moon. The mirror itself would have to be twelve meters in diameter to deliver a focused beam with a three-meter aperture at the earth's surface.

It would stand out in orbit like a spotlight. Since we know the weapon platform is not much over a meter in diameter, they must have used a small superconducting magnet array to focus and modulate the beam. It simply can't handle that much power. Based on that assumption, I've tried a bit of computer modeling that leads me to believe that it must operate on the principle of resonance.

"The energy of the beam sets up a sympathetic vibration in materials, kind of like a microwave oven, at the molecular or atomic level. Maybe even the nuclear level. What was mystifying about the damn thing at first was that it seems to couple efficiently with a wide variety of materials. At any rate, resonant coupling could explain energy transfer ratios at sufficient amplitude to do what it does. The specific mechanism is not readily evident. I do have an hypothesis, though."

"You hinted earlier that you've eliminated infrared wavelengths, " said Wallace. "The bandwidth at IR frequencies is certainly sufficient for high frequency modulation. There are only ten elements in the periodic table with nuclear magnetic resonance frequencies over one hundred megahertz. Hydrogen is the highest at three hundred megahertz. Seems to me a carbon dioxide laser could do it."

"Ionization potential is too low at IR frequencies," interjected Stickle. "It's not simply a thermal effect."

"I agree," said Johnson. "It's in the UV or X-ray spectrum. It doesn't just heat things up until they melt or vaporize. You would be back to the objection of too big an energy requirement. No, this thing literally blasts things apart, and the thermal bloom we've seen in the satellite images is more of a side effect than a direct cause."

"You mean, the breakup of the target material creates an exothermic chemical reaction, right?" said Mercer.

"Exactly," responded Johnson. "I think it's a form of induced fission."

"Let's come back to that in a minute," said Stickle.

"What about the simple beam mechanics—control signals, feedback, and so on? Can we detect control signals, or targeting signals, and interfere with them? What kind of time do you think we have, from command initiation until it positions and fires?"

"Well, in my opinion, the uplink is as simple as shit, and there's not a hell of a lot that you can do to interfere with it. They have probably located a few simple, low-powered, modulated lasers at various sites around the country. These are set up as dumb terminals, or slaves. They can be controlled by modem, by telephone, by radio—a dozen different ways. I'd bet they're slaved to an active computer, somewhere.

"Multiple sites would insure that the weather can't block a signal, and more importantly, that a stratospheric rocket can't ionize the atmosphere with a seed chemical to disrupt ground-to-orbit communications. Any one of these lasers could send a hundred-nanosecond burst of digital data with target coordinates and a GO code. If you are them, and you've really been clever—and it seems to me that they have been, at every turn—you have several major firing events preprogrammed into the weapon's fire control system. You add a well-known little device called a dead-man's switch. The active computer I mentioned sends a signal pulse every so often to the weapon system's fire control, telling it to dump its current countdown, and start over again. The computer has to be manually reset at regular intervals.

"That way, if you are captured, all you have to do is threaten not to reset the computer that controls the switch. After a certain amount of elapsed time, the damn thing begins to acquire targets and fire automatically.

"A word of advice in that regard, gentlemen. If you do catch them, you had better not let anything happen to them until that weapon system is disabled. If you kill them, or if they refuse to tell you the control codes, that thing could kill every plant, animal and human being in the northern hemisphere. It could sterilize half the earth, and maybe as a side effect, kill the entire planet."

Johnson paused for effect. "Make no mistake about what you're up against, gentlemen. It may be literally the annihilation—utter and complete—of all surface life on this planet."

"Sweet Jesus," uttered Mercer, "it just gets worse and worse."

"No defense at all?" asked Stickle.

"The only survival possibility that holds any hope at all is deep undersea habitats with nuclear power systems," said Johnson. "Deep mine shafts and such might work for a while, but you've got to understand that the atmosphere is not going to be breathable for years— maybe decades. You would have to come up with some way to produce food, water and oxygen, and to handle wastes."

Johnson paused again, staring out the window into the distance. "God only knows what kind of weather patterns would eventually emerge. Look at what happened when it traced a thin line—a mere two miles wide—up the east coast. Think about that kind of energy and destruction crossing the breadth of the North American continent. It would probably sweep from east to west, like the shadow of a cloud passing over the earth. Everything the shadow touched would explode and burn. Even the bacteria in the soil would be destroyed. Dust and smoke in the stratosphere for ages, blocking sunlight. Nothing could grow. Onset of an ice age. The planet climatology might never recover."

"Maybe the Doomsdayers are right," said Mercer, despondently. "Maybe that damned thing really is the Sword of God."

"Maybe," said Johnson reflectively. "At any rate, living in the sea has the advantage that the water volume of the oceans provides an enormous buffer system. The food chain will suffer, and plankton and other life will be affected, but the polar caps are likely to suffer somewhat less. Fish, shellfish and various sea flora should be available for years, and breathing oxygen can be liberated from sea water by electrolysis or chemical reaction. Hydrogen too, for combustion processes, and for power production and light. The sea bottom can be farmed if you have light, and wastes are easily handled—they're even useful as fertilizer."

"I confess, I hadn't followed it out as far as you have, Dr. Johnson," said Stickle. "I guess we really are looking at a potential doomsday scenario. The people we work for certainly haven't thought that far ahead. They see this simply as a power struggle, a king-of-the-mountain game. I'm wondering what they will say when I present your findings."

"I doubt it will slow them up very much," said Wallace. "Most people don't know that many of the reputable scientists that built the first atomic bomb—the Manhattan Project at Los Alamos, during the Second World War—were afraid that it would set the atmosphere on fire and destroy the world. They wanted to stop the project. Maybe that's why they called it the Trinity Site, where it was tested. At any rate, they did it anyway. They took the chance, and risked all of humanity. That ought to tell you something about power-mad politicians."

"What else have you got, Dr. Johnson?" asked Stickle.

"Well, you asked about elapsed time for target acquisition and firing. From geostationary orbit, it takes light two hundred and forty milliseconds to go from a satellite to earth and back, round-trip. The destructive energy beam traverses across the surface of the target in microseconds, far too fast to acquire target analysis data and reflect it back to the satellite's fire control system, so that it can decide what the composition of the immediate object in its path is, and adjust the frequency of the beam accordingly. During the two-hundred-and-forty- millisecond delay, the beam will have traversed more than one-and-a-quarter-million meters.

"I've concluded that there are two possibilities. The possibility I believe the least is one in which the weapon sweeps the target with a mapping signal that analyzes the target footprint prior to firing the main laser. It

analyzes all the components that make up the target—
rocks, trees, highways, dirt—and their size, composition,
etc. It maps them into its fire-control system's memory
as Cartesian coordinates, then adjusts the resonance of
the energy beam as it traverses each mapped grid
reference during the firing sequence. It all takes place
in a few hundred milliseconds of course, but the
mapping sequence does require a finite amount of time,
depending on the area of the target. Figure a quarter
second for the mapping signal's round-trip transit, an
eighth of a second one-way for the main energy beam,
fifty-three milliseconds per square mile mapped—it
works out to about twelve square miles analyzed,
mapped and obliterated per second."

"My God!" said Mercer.

"Jesus," said Stickle.

"I'm still interested in your resonance theory, Dr.
Johnson," said Wallace. "Could you elaborate on that a
bit?"

"Well, as you are no doubt aware, one of the significant properties of a resonant signal is that it permits
maximum energy transfer between the signal—in this
case an energy beam—and the object or objects that
it is resonant with. This is the property engineers think
about most often, with regard to resonance. It's called
coupling efficiency, and is normally of primary importance to radio and television engineers. How far a
receiver will pick up a signal, its sensitivity in other
words, depends on its coupling efficiency. We couldn't
have radio or TV communications without resonant
circuitry.

"Another way to look at resonance though, is that it
allows a relatively small signal energy to pump up a very
large energy storage reservoir, until it self-destructs. Like
pumping up a balloon with a tire pump until it explodes.
To something the size of an atom, or even a molecule,
a few watts is a lot of power, and an energy pulse of
only a fraction of a watt becomes a lot of power when
the pulses come at a rate of three times ten to the

fifteenth power—three quadrillion pulses per second. To deliver forty terawatts to the surface of the Earth at that frequency, with an energy conversion efficiency of say, twenty percent, a sine wave coefficient of RMS power of 0.707, and an attenuation or loss factor of ninety-five percent of the beam energy in passing through the atmosphere, the power supply would still only have to generate a fraction of a watt. A few watts, at most. That's why your IR detectors couldn't find it, gentlemen; a coffeepot radiates more heat.

"Some of you may recall reading of instances where buildings, or bridges, were set in harmonic motion by the wind, or by traffic passing over them. They began oscillating, each oscillation stronger than the one before, increasing in amplitude as the resonant signal continued pumping the system, until they whipped themselves to pieces. That's why soldiers march in route step when crossing a bridge, to break up any repeating impulse. Even dogs, with their peculiar trotting gait, have been known to set a suspension bridge into violent motion. Those are classical, elementary examples. Neither the soldiers or the dog could knock down a bridge by kicking or stomping on it, but by simply walking across it in a synchronous step that matches the bridge's periodic chord, they can. Simple harmonic coupling."

Johnson continued, "Closer to our time and technology, laser cavities are commonly pumped with an extraneous energy source, at the resonant frequency of the cavity. The valence electrons in the lasing medium, usually a gas or dye, are pumped up with energy until they simply can't hold it any longer. When the electrons pass the threshold of their ability to absorb energy, they cascade to ground potential, giving up the trapped energy as a monochromatic burst of electromagnetic radiation, or simply put, an intense beam of colored light.

"All this happens in a few microseconds, of course. Not a lot of energy involved, overall, but look what it can do—burn through metal, or carry a TV picture to Mars.

"In the case of this weapon, though, that's where the similarity ends. The electrons in the target material aren't allowed to drop back to a neutral state. If the timing was uneven, and some electrons reached saturation before others, the result would be a mild electric current flow, as the free electrons traveled through the material and bumped other electrons off their parent atoms. Each atom that lost an electron would become a positively-charged ion for a few microseconds, until another stray electron came along and filled the void created by the missing one. The thermal effect of the electric heating might warm a metal object, but that's about all. The charge on the atoms would then be in balance again. The net effect would be a lot of random heat generated by sporadic electric currents, but nothing truly destructive.

"The factors that make the difference are time and uniformity of energy distribution in the target material. Electrons travel through matter at a finite speed. In a copper wire, it's about a hundred and forty thousand meters per second, much less than one percent of the speed of light. Now, for the sake of argument, let's say that an energy beam moving at the speed of light ionized almost all the atoms in a chunk of material—gave them a positive charge—all at once. Like-charges repel one another. Each resonant pump of the beam would force the atoms to a higher energy state. The energy beam would do this so fast that the electrons would not have time to flow between atoms; they would all be simultaneously repelled, and blown away completely. They would be forced away from the nucleus, out into the space normally occupied by the covalent electronic bonds—the shared electron orbits between associated atoms that hold matter together. It would make every atom in the matrix of the substance repel every other atom, and the substance would fly apart with tremendous energy."

"That brings up the problem of frequency," said Wallace, intent on Johnson. "How does the beam couple with all the different elements involved at the same time, in order to generate repulsion uniformly throughout the target?"

"There are a couple of possibilities there also," said Johnson. "First of all, one could select a fundamental, or even a harmonic that closely matches the resonant period of most of the elements in the target material. Another way would be to pick a specific frequency that is resonant with a single element that is common to most of the compounds that make up the target materials. For example, an element that is common to steel, plant life, soil, et cetera—even to fuels and lubricants—is carbon. It's the basis of all organic tissues, including animal life."

"But it flashes water into steam, Dr. Johnson," said Mercer, "and that's simply hydrogen and oxygen."

"If you'll reflect, Dr. Mercer," said Johnson. "I'm sure you'll agree that as far as we know, it flashes *groundwater* into steam. Groundwater is comprised of hydrogen and oxygen, just as is pure water, but it also has dissolved impurities—minerals, decomposed plant and animal life, acid chains—a true pot-luck stew of hydrated compounds and elements, including carbon. The energy released by the fissioning of carbon compounds would provide the exothermic energy to do the rest, and carbon is only one possibility. Hydrogen and oxygen are also good candidates for a key element. The problem with that is that coupling efficiency would not be maximum for every element or compound, and that grates on my bias toward symmetry."

"You said there were two possibilities," prompted Wallace.

"Yes. Well, the other is the most likely in my view, because it has symmetry. It permits efficient coupling with all the elements involved, and it also negates the need for a mapping signal to analyze the composition of the target. With the bandwidth available in an ultraviolet laser beam, there can be any number of modulator frequencies, all operating at once. Enough to cover all the elements in the periodic table, if need be. I favor this explanation because in complex compounds, such as any target is bound to consist of, the different ionization potentials of the integrated elements would cause low-energy substances to ionize before others, like in a distillation column, and the resulting currents flowing through the less volatile compounds would tend to damp the phase-sensitive reaction. The latent energy in the volatile elements would also sap the thermal energy of the beam. It would increase the energy demand on the beam, and make for a bigger power supply for the weapon.

"No, these people were efficient. They wouldn't get that far, and overlook something so obvious. It's so much easier to introduce multiple gating frequencies. That way, all the elemental atoms attain peak energy at nearly the same instant. With nowhere to go, the charged electrons can only drop back to ground state by disassociation or radiant emission. Some soil silicates have latent fusion energies exceeding eighteen hundred joules per gram. The beam acts as a catalyst to release the energy. The compounds fission.

"Once that happens, the electrons avalanche to ground potential, giving up all that stored energy as electromagnetic radiation, across the entire spectrum, from hard UV to radio waves. Almost everything in the target area dominoes into the reaction. Instantaneous temperatures and pressures inside solids would be incredible. Well, gentlemen, have I missed anything? Any flaws in my argument?"

"Nothing that is immediately evident," said Wallace. "You've been most thorough, Dr. Johnson."

"So what we have, assuming for the moment that your hypothesis is correct, is a laser disintegrator. Buck Rogers and Star Wars come to life," said Stickle.

"That's about it, I'm afraid," said Johnson.

"So how do you recommend we attack it, Dr. Johnson?" asked Wallace.

"I think that your only chance is at close range, from orbit," answered Johnson. "Anything else is too risky. If you make a mistake and shoot yourself in the foot on this one, it's really going to hurt. The whole human race might pay for it. Speaking as one human being to another, I don't want to see the Earth destroyed.

"Since I'm as much a pessimist as Dr. Wallace, I'm sure you're going to go through with the attempt, no matter what I say, so for the sake of humanity, gentlemen, please don't fuck it up."

XXIII

"Mr. Jack Townsend, this is Professor Theodore Wallace," said Dr. Ortiz, as he introduced the men. "Ted is the leading lasers and optics man in our neck of the woods. He hangs his hat over at Cal Tech. When he's home, that is. I've been trying to reach you for three days, Ted."

"I had to attend a meeting back at Huntsville," Wallace said. "I'd like to talk to you about it later. The graduate student taking my messages took ill while I was gone, and everyone else is off for the holidays. Was it urgent? Oh, excuse me, I'm glad to meet you, Mr. Townsend."

"Same here, Dr. Wallace," replied Townsend.

"No, it wasn't that urgent. I could have called your dean at home, but I thought I'd give it another day before I got worried. Jack has some technical questions concerning the space weapon, Ted. He's the friend of a mutual friend, a real good-old boy," Ortiz said. A look passed between Wallace and Ortiz. "I'd like you to help him if you can."

Wallace regarded Townsend curiously, as if assessing him. "I'll be happy to do what I can," he said.

Townsend hadn't survived as an undercover agent all his life without developing a keen sensitivity to subtle behavior in others. He didn't know what to make of the electric warning glance that had passed between the others, but he had noted it. He had been in Ortiz' office when his secretary unexpectedly announced Ted Wallace. He suspected that the two men would have some interesting things to say about him, after he was gone.

"Ted has two labs on our campus, Jack. He teaches an irregular graduate course here, one day a week. I've asked him to let you have some space, and a couple of graduate students. That should get you started. He'll need three computers, and internet and web connections. Will you see to it, Ted?"

"Of course," said Wallace.

"That's very kind of you, Dr. Wallace," said Townsend. "I'll try to be as little bother to you as possible."

"No bother, Mr. Townsend. I'll have everything set up by next Wednesday, barring the unforeseen."

"Thank you both," said Townsend, getting up. "I really do appreciate your help. I guess I'd better be getting home. I'll be back Wednesday afternoon, then." So saying, he left.

Though he didn't hear the conversation, his instincts were proven right a few minutes after he had taken his leave. Wallace signaled to Ortiz, and they took a slow stroll across campus, talking as they walked, pausing in their conversation occasionally, to let a student within hearing distance pass.

"Well, how close are they to working it out?" asked Ortiz.

"They surprised the hell out of me, actually. Whoever started the asinine rumor that Southerners were dumb, never met Able Johnson. He's a physicist at Georgia Tech. With the exception of a couple of minor points, he's right on target. He almost sounded like Leland, in describing system resonance. Come to think about it, Leland's from the South, too, isn't he? Would they know each other?"

"Leland's from Utah, but they still might know each other. I'll ask, next time I talk to him. He's got to know about this, anyway. What are the minor points they missed? They might be important to us."

"Just control details really. Johnson thought that several laser transmitters might be located around the country, as a contingency measure, to prevent the military from interrupting the control signals by seeding the stratosphere with an ionizing isotope. Not a bad guess, really, since we did anticipate that possibility. If I were in his shoes, it's a solution I might have thought of, too. The only other thing is the power supply. They don't have a clue, as of yet."

"I'm not sure it matters anymore," said Ortiz. "Their attack strategy is going to be based on the assumption that it has the capability to fire, and for as long as it has to. They can't afford to assume anything else."

"What do you think they will do?"

"Joe says the people at Peterson Air Force Base are trying to activate an old killer satellite called Diana. The Strategic Defense Command abandoned it in orbit some years back. He sent me the encrypted physical data via the mail drop in San Francisco. It's a kinetic launcher with spent uranium spears for projectiles. From the engineering data, it looks like the missiles and launchers are all independent systems. There is a good possibility some of them are intact, and can be fired. The big *if* is the satellite maneuvering and guidance systems. If those can be reactivated, they have a chance."

"Think we should offer to help?"

"No. They've got to do it on their own. If we get too involved, we might slip up and generate some suspicion. We don't want to have anything more to do with them than is absolutely necessary. We've got people inside their telemetry sites already, and that ought to be sufficient for now."

"What if it fails, or can't be reactivated?"

"Joe thinks their only backup plan is to try to launch a nuclear warhead into a catch-up orbit. It would have a small target cross-section, and with a little luck, could be mistaken for space debris until it's too late. It might also be disguised as an innocuous communications satellite, or a derelict booster shell. Paul and Leland both predicted it."

"What if they can't make coincidence?" asked Wallace.

"We'll help them in a roundabout way."

"Are we so certain that this is going to work, Hector? Can we really predict what they are going to do, with such certainty? It seems to me that we should just lay down the law to them, and get on with it. Things are going pretty well now, don't you think?"

"Yes, they are, but the minds of the American people have to be won; don't you see, my boy? They must understand, without a doubt, what kind of government they have. They must see them in action, all subterfuge stripped away."

"Don't you think that they might just return things to what they were before?"

"I don't think so. I think they will use the events of the past year as an excuse to impose totalitarian rule. They have to subdue us now, so that nothing like this weapon can happen again. They must remove any possibility of future interference by subjugating the planet."

"I guess you're right about everything," said Wallace. "You've managed to call the shots pretty accurately, so far."

"Well, at the risk of seeming a little too cocky, one does acquire a bit of wisdom simply by growing old. You can only hear the lies so often, before you begin to understand how things really work. Only the young can really be whipped into an idealistic fervor by the same old bullshit that's been used over and over again, since the days of Rome—probably since the dawn of man. Why do you think that the fighting military is made up of teen-age kids? Who else could you talk into charging into machine-gun fire and mine fields?"

"Your subtle point is, that us younger guys aren't too bright. Is that about it?"

"Well, I didn't exactly say that. Of course, I wouldn't argue with you, either."

XXIV

Paul Haas was a tall, rangy man of fifty-two. Abbott to Ortiz' Costello. He was dean of the Mechanical Engineering Department at Stanford. He and Hector Ortiz had known each other for thirty years.

Like Ortiz, he had a wry sense of humor, a presence that came from absolute confidence in himself, and a total absence of any sense of status or hierarchy, with regard to himself or anyone else.

Haas, his wife and oldest daughter had just returned from vacationing in Chile. On the afternoon of January 10, Ortiz walked into Haas' office.

"Well, Paul, how was Chile? Did you get to enjoy any of the Christmas and New Year's festivities?"

"Hector, good to see you," Haas' face lit up. "It was just great, and yes, we spent Christmas with Antonio Hernandez and his family in La Paz—had a wonderful time. We went back to Iquique over New Year's. The hotel bar had a New Years Eve party for the American guests, and it was plenty, as far as we were concerned. I caught a marlin—no record, but he gave me all the fight I ever want to experience. Almost three hours. I'm still sore all over from it.

"We took a camera safari into the mountains last week. I can't wait to show you some of the slides I took. The views are breathtaking. We looked at some twelfth-century middens, and a couple of mummies, circa 500 A.D. I just enjoyed the scenery. I love the tropics. I swear I lived in Mexico or South America in a former life. How have things been with you?"

"Same old, same old. I wanted to talk a bit. Care to take the air?"

"How about the cafeteria, instead? This time of day there's hardly anyone there. We can find a secluded corner. This fifty-degree weather is rough on my old bones, especially when I was in eighty-degree temperatures just two days ago."

"Fine with me."

The two men walked down the hall, talking campus trivia as they went, and took the elevator down to the first-floor cafeteria. In a few minutes they were seated at a table near a plate-glass window, with steaming cups of coffee before them.

"Is everything ready?" asked Ortiz, taking a sip of his coffee.

"Everything is set," responded Haas. "I rented an old church. It will sleep about fifty people, and we can set up a field kitchen in an army tent, next to it. We've got plenty of those big, forty-foot tents. I think we could bivouac about three hundred, if we had to. The antennas and other satellite comm equipment is on its way there now. I left two people there to supervise the Chilean contractor who's going to install the systems. A systems specialist from La Plata, Buenos Aires, and Tony Madragal, my Associate Professor.

"I also want to set up a dispensary, Hector. We can inoculate a thousand kids from the surrounding villages while we're there. I promised the local *jefe* that we would throw a little business his way, too. He runs the local liquor store in Aqua Dulce, the nearest town to the dig."

"What is the site like?"

"The main site is nothing remarkable, but decent. There was a sixteenth-century Spanish garrison there, with a churchyard cemetery and lots of foundation remains. I found a second site that I think is a pre-Columbian tomb. It looks really good—a wall of cut stone, exposed by the erosion of an embankment, beside an old dirt road that winds through the hills. We can make a small detour in the road to move traffic away from our excavation. Not much in the way of traffic anyway—just farmers.

"Between the two sites and a dispensary operation, we can spread out several dozen folks and keep them busy for three or four months. Hell, we might even find something."

"Good! Good!" said Ortiz. He sat silent for a moment, looking out the cafeteria window at students passing through the outer arcade.

"What's up?" asked Haas, sensing that something was troubling him.

"Well, nothing much. I just wanted to fill you in on a couple of developments. We have a wannabe recruit. Guy named Townsend. Showed up at Christmas. He's a friend of Eddie's, a former C.I.A. agent that claims to be out in the cold. It's official too, for what that's worth. He's wanted for murder.

"He claims it's a setup, that he refused to whack a woman newscaster—she's with him incidentally—and his section chief decided that he knew too much to live.

"I had Pete Yarborough, in Chicago, check her out. Her real name is Beverly Watkins. She was fired back in August or September. Her husband and two cops were found shot to death in the foyer of her house, and she's wanted in connection with it.

"Townsend claims it was for airing an interview live, that blasted the federal government. It was just a local show, and ordinarily, nothing would have come of it, but it was picked up by the wire services and broadcast worldwide. The lunatic in charge of Townsend's section decided to teach all errant newscasters a lesson by making an example of her.

"Most of the story checks out. Anyway, Townsend wants to join up."

"Think he's on the level?"

"Eddie trusts him, but suggests discretion. Even old friends can turn on you if they think it's in the holy name of national security. I've turned him over to Ted Wallace for a while. He'll keep him busy while we consider things. It's possible that he could be of use to us."

"How?"

"I don't know yet. He claims that he can infiltrate the American and European undergrounds, and eliminate some of the hidden players. He wants help in identifying them—research help."

"Hell, go for it, Hector. What have you got to lose? You don't have to involve him in anything else, or let him know anything else. Just give him a few computers and two or three grad students, and see what he comes up with. We need that data, too."

"He also wants to track down the 'makers of the weapon.' How do you feel about that? And what if I give him the help, and it's an entrapment scheme. He could accuse me of treason for helping him, and not reporting him to the government."

"I'm beginning to understand your dilemma. What are you going to do?"

"I did give him the computers and student helpers, just as you suggested, but I made it explicit that I wasn't helping him in any antigovernment scheme. I offered to humor him, more or less, that's all.

"I'm going to let Ted distract him for a few days. We'll give him the computers and the help, but then . . ." he shrugged, "I don't know. It would be a shame to waste him, or his help, if he's genuine. We can't risk everything on it, though. I've been trying to think of some way we can authenticate him. Is there a way we can influence him into some kind of test situation without appearing to do so? We don't want him to know that we are organized, or that we have any particular viewpoint, or that we are active in any way whatsoever."

Haas idly studied his half-full coffee cup for a moment before responding, "Let me think on it a day or two. Maybe Eddie would have some ideas. Have you thought to ask him? After all, he and this Townsend are a lot more familiar with sneaky tricks than you or I."

"No. I hadn't thought of that. It's a good idea. I'll drive down and see him tonight."

"Have you heard from Leland lately?" asked Haas, changing the subject.

"No. Not for about a week, now. He's been busy reconfiguring the control frequencies. He's being very careful. It's almost comical," Ortiz laughed. "He still loves us, but he doesn't trust us any farther than he can spit. Can't say I blame him, really."

Haas smiled, then frowned. "No one could usurp control anyway, could they? Even if they knew the operating frequencies? How could they, without knowing the pass codes?"

"I don't know. I just know that Leland thinks it must be done, so it's going to be done. You know him as well as I do."

Ortiz changed the subject. "Ted just got back from Alabama a few days ago. He was fortunate enough to be one of two contract consultants hired by Stickle's group to do an assessment on the weapon."

"They don't have a clue, do they?" Haas laughed gleefully.

"Surprisingly, and maybe unfortunately, they do. Ever hear of a guy named Able Johnson? He's a professor at Georgia Tech."

"As a matter of fact," Haas said, looking concerned, "I know him slightly. We met at an OTEC energy-physics seminar at the U. of Hawaii a few years ago. Ate and drank together a couple of nights, along with a few others. Seemed like a sharp guy, kind of introverted and thoughtful—not a party animal. We sat alone in the hotel lobby, late one night, and talked shop into the wee hours. I liked him."

"Did any of that talk concern molecular resonances, or anything related?"

"I'm not sure," said Haas. "God, I hadn't realized how long it's been. It's twenty-five years or more. Let me see, 1979 I think. I was into transient thermodynamic phenomena at the time—Stirling Cycle engines and thermoacoustics. We were investigating a variety of heat engines as candidates to power orbital weapons platforms, as a matter of fact.

"Joe Beatty and I went down together; he was doing shock-tube research at Livermore then, remember? I really don't think we discussed resonance, but who knows? I take it that Johnson is speculating that resonance is involved?"

"Damn near has it all worked out, according to Ted," said Ortiz. "He was the other consultant. Ted discreetly pumped him for as much detail as he could get, and he agrees with your assessment of him—he's sharp."

"So Stickle's bunch knows, then. What can they do with it?"

"I'm not sure. I told Leland about it. He didn't comment much, just asked questions. I don't see that it furthers their cause much at present. Given three or four years, they could have a similar weapon system."

"Who would they use it against? They are a lot more visible than we are. We could prevent them from ever putting it up."

"All true warriors are optimists, Paul. They really can't believe they'll ever lose, so they keep coming back, no matter what. They unconsciously believe that they will somehow overcome any obstacles. They have to keep trying, anyway. It's what makes life interesting for that personality type. War, business and sports—in-your-face competition—that's the way some people are made.

"And we scientists are just as bad in our own way. If we didn't lust so single-mindedly after nature's secrets, without regard for the uses that our discoveries are put to, the world wouldn't be in this fix."

"I've heard that argument before," said Haas, "and I don't buy it. Pick any time in history, and they were just as bad before the next technological advance came as they were afterward. They misuse whatever technology is at hand; it makes no difference what it is. When the technology was swords and armor, the rich guys had the swords and armor, and they used it to subjugate the weak and the poor."

"Well, maybe you're right, said Ortiz.

"Of course I'm right," grinned Haas. They both laughed.

"Is Leland okay?" asked Haas, sobering. "He seemed really down last month. I'm worried about him. I tried to get him to take a few days and go with us to Chile, but he wouldn't. He's under a lot of strain."

"I know. I feel sorry for him. He has suffered a great deal over all of this. I just can't bring myself to think of him as a heartless killer—knowing him as I do. He would have chosen another way, if it were possible. Now that it's done, it's like a dream. All those millions hurt. He broke down and cried, afterward. Begged my forgiveness. I felt ashamed. We didn't intend it to be that way, but in retrospect, we used Leland. He believes humanity is worth fighting for. I'm not sure I do, anymore. Maybe, deep down, we all knew he was idealistic enough to carry through with it, when we didn't have the guts. Like sending an impressionable, naive boy to lead the way into hostile country."

"Leland's not a boy, Hector, as much as you like to think of him that way. He's always been a realist. He's as human as anybody when it comes to needing approval and support, but he's always said that either something is real or it isn't. If an experiment doesn't turn out the way you hoped, it does no good to try to rationalize the results and defend your theory. You accept the result and you do what you have to do, even if it means dumping ideas you've clung to for years. We couldn't go through with it and he knew it, so he did what he had to do."

"It still doesn't absolve us. We still used him."

"Had to be, though." Haas wagged his head regretfully. "Had to be. I couldn't have done it; I know that now. Neither could you."

"I know," Ortiz sighed. "I just wish that we could find a way to exorcise the greed and perversity out of humankind altogether, while we're about this. It would make the whole, bloody business worthwhile, if we could just get rid of the megalomania that lusts for domination of others, once and for all. That would make it worth all the lives."

"You're talking about reinventing man," said Haas. "Never happen. The best we can do is try to instill principles. As to the rest, Thomas Jefferson said it best: 'Occasionally the tree of liberty must be watered with the blood of tyrants and patriots alike.' Every so often, it takes a bloody revolution to put things back on track for a while. History has confirmed it ten thousand times.

"Maybe someday we'll be able to save the actual memories of past generations, and feed those experiences and lifetimes of learning into the brains of newborns, so they won't have to keep repeating the same stupid acts throughout eternity—won't have to learn everything anew, every generation. God, what an evolutionary leap that would be.

"We've already reached the limits of the mind, to absorb information through sensory input and experience, and most of that is wasted nowadays on television bullshit. It takes forty years of learning and experience under the best of conditions before we begin to know anything, and by then our immune systems have started to decline and aging is progressing rapidly.

"What a leapfrog that would be, to be infused with a couple of centuries of direct scientific experience and reasoning while the body is young and vigorous. We could skip the twenty years of education that take up the first third of everyone's life. Hell, we'd be out of a job," Haas grinned gleefully.

"Funny. Townsend said something similar a few days ago," said Ortiz. "Actually, there are some people working on it."

"Really? Who?"

"Lots of folks, really. A company called Cyber-Biotics has been doing research on human memory mechanisms for the last fifteen years or so. Made some real progress, too. I think they've proven the concept of hereditary, conscious memory."

"What is hereditary, conscious memory?"

"Well, everyone in the biological and cognitive sciences will admit that we come preprogrammed with a set of basic assembly and operating instructions. These instructions determine what we look like, the color of our eyes and hair, how tall we will be, genetic tendencies such as obesity, cancer, mental disorders. All our autonomic functions are preset. Our hearts beat, our glands secrete hormones in the proper amounts at the proper times, throughout our lives. We also come with a programming set that permits us to learn, to weigh variables and make judgments, and to note and store information.

"The basic theory behind hereditary memory is that experience and learning alters our neural wiring, and as we age, the children we have are given attributes according to our *developed* cellular memory. Our cell DNA has not only carried forward the prior genetic information that determined the kinship peculiarities of our physical construction, such as getting our father's eyes, or our mother's cheeks, but some of the new experiences that we have collected have subtly altered the genetic information we were given by our parents, and so we pass along the original text to our children, plus some of our own unique, mental programming—an edited version of ourselves."

"Then wouldn't all late-born children be smarter than their older siblings?"

"If that were the only factor, they probably would. Unfortunately, the act of living also produces cellular damage via disease, accident, naturally-occurring background and cosmic radiation, etc., and for the past century, there has been an ever-increasing abundance of man-made things that are detrimental. Fossil fuel by-products, electromagnetic radiation, nuclear waste, asbestos—just a ton of environmental chemicals, dyes, food preservatives and so forth. Such things damage the reproductive system.

"Genetic development is so slow, anyway. Each generation gains an infinitesimal bit more, and up through the industrial revolution, it seemed to be working well. It's not dramatic evolutionary change, like the sudden appearance of Cro-Magnon man, and the subsequent disappearance of Neanderthal man, or Neandertal as some say now, but it was a gradual increase in height, brain volume, intrinsic intelligence.

"Now it seems that we're backsliding. Dirty air, dirty water, stupid politics, and as you mentioned, years of watching mindless, erroneous pap on television; a virtual bombardment of the human genetic memory bank by all those internal and external physical and environmental factors.

"Young minds have no experience by which to gauge incoming information and filter out the bullshit. The mind accepts it, especially if it comes from what most young people think of as an authoritative source, such as television and newspapers. Later on, as they gradually find out that literally thousands of things they have been told are outright lies, from manipulative social bullshit to the impossible physical stunts they see in every movie, they undergo a real, traumatic adjustment, and pretty soon, the mind distrusts all information. It's a societal syndrome brought about by the ignorant assholes that control the media.

"When the mind is lied to, and cruelly teased, with no cessation in sight, it is a form of mental torture. The psyche subconsciously rebels. The kids stay frustrated and angry. Maybe they turn to robbing and killing. Or to drugs. Deep-down psychologically, they want revenge on society, and they revert to basics because everything else that comes along may be just another pack of lies. It's all taking its toll on the physical equipment that forms the psyche. The codes that hand down the autonomic and physical programming are damaged by the worsening environmental factors, and the higher cognitive hand-me-downs are neuroses, frustrations, impotent rage—all the antitheses of contentment, happiness, and calm, speculative reasoning. It's no wonder that antacids and ulcer drugs are so common.

"The only inspiration these days has to do with crime. Fraud, political maneuvering, legal lying, fakery—anything shitty. It's all obvious, but in our society, not necessarily illegal. Even when it is, you have to have hard evidence to prove it, and even then, the crooked, because of their station in life, may be pardoned. The surprising thing is that even the dumb bastards that mismanage things in the first place, wonder why things seem to be getting worse? Aaagh! For the last twenty years, I've had a growing desire to live on a deserted island and be absolutely unconscious of the rest of humanity."

"That's just the hippie in you, Hector," grinned Haas. "You felt the same way when we were undergraduates. Our generation hated authority and social manipulation then, just as much as we do now."

"Maybe you're right," Ortiz laughed. He made a "V" with his fingers. "Peace," he said.

XXV

It was 5:30 P.M. the following Friday afternoon, and Townsend sat in a chair across from Ted Wallace. Townsend had just gotten off work in Mountain View and driven to Stanford.

Wallace's cluttered desk butted up against two of the painted cinderblock walls, and bookcases and shelves overflowed with papers, books and three-ring binders with arcane legends on their spines.

They were drinking coffee. Wallace had loaned Townsend two of his graduate students, a girl and a boy, and three PCs, and encamped them in one end of a laboratory where a laser was set up on an optical table. They had arranged steel wall lockers and storage cabinets to divide the lab and delineate a space for Townsend and his helpers to work. There were two lab tables and a desk with a telephone. Townsend had claimed the desk. The laser experiment was Wallace's own, so no students used that particular lab, and it was quiet.

"Making any headway?" asked Wallace.

"Some. I've laid out a detailed routine for the kids to follow, and they're hard at it. I've got them tracking down majority stockholders in a list of international corporations. We're looking for affiliates—subsidiaries and holding companies that have common stockholders and are in the top twenty percent of profit-takers in the world.

"We're also looking for signs of political access, whether obvious or just potential, and building something like a truth table to correlate our data. I hope it will

189

point up some promising candidates, and assuming it does, we'll begin in-depth background investigations.

"I have a few starting points already, but I'll keep them to myself and see what the kids come up with. If they identify some of those people that I know are involved, I'll know that my matrix is working and that the kids are being thorough."

"What did you tell the students?"

"That we are doing a geopolitical study on international commerce," said Townsend. "What did you tell them about me?"

Wallace sighed, wrinkling his brow and looking at his fingernails. "Just that you are with a private engineering firm that has a funded contract to perform a government study. Nothing more. I told them that you would look in on them evenings and weekends, if they wanted to work those hours, and they agreed."

"That's good," said Townsend, smiling. "You don't like me very much, do you, Dr. Wallace?"

Wallace looked startled, then smiled tightly in return. "You're given to bluntness, aren't you, Mr. Townsend. I'll be direct, too. I don't like government goons. I never have. Unfortunately, in my line of work, the government pays for most of the research that gets done. I won't give up my line of work, so I have to deal with them. This is the first time I've had to put up with one of you in my lab, though."

Townsend's gaze turned flat and cold, and somehow, without moving, his physical presence suddenly seemed to change, to dominate the small office. To Wallace, it was if he had suddenly realized he was in the presence of a living werewolf. The hackles rose involuntarily on the back of Wallace's neck, and a feeling of sick foreboding settled into his stomach like a lead weight. The blood drained from his face. The familiar room had suddenly become a close and confining place with no way out, and he felt in deadly peril.

Townsend's voice was soft. "I gave up my career, my security and my government paycheck when I found out that working for them conflicted with my moral code," he said. "Since you are willing to go on working for them, however indirectly, even though you hate what they stand for, then I guess that makes you a hypocrite and a whore, as well as a 'government goon,' Wallace."

He rose, and stood for a moment, gazing coldly down at Wallace—focused, calculating, restrained power—then turned and walked out of the office and down the tiled hallway, his footsteps echoing hollowly back to Wallace, who sat frozen in his chair for several minutes. Finally, Wallace took in a great, shuddering breath, and the blood rushed back into his face and hands, tingling. He took a drink of coffee, and his hand trembled. He had never been so afraid.

In telling Ortiz about it later that evening, Wallace described it as "A mask falling away from a human face to reveal a deadly, staring animal. An utter absence of mercy, coupled with deadly intent." He shivered when he said it, and Ortiz knew the man was deeply shaken.

"I know the feeling," he said. "Men like Townsend and Eddie Teller fought their secret war for a long time; they lived with imminent death for years. It changes them in a way that's impossible to describe. Oh, I suppose some psychologist could describe the mechanics of your reaction, and even profile the mental makeup of someone who is used to killing other men, but it doesn't begin to convey the emotional impact of a firsthand experience, when you are suddenly facing one of them. I've experienced it a couple of times in my life.

"Once, when I was a student, barely twenty-one, I went on a drinking spree in Tiajuana with some class-mates. We were in some smoke-filled dive watching some strippers, when I got sick. I found my way out back to an alley that smelled like a urinal. I threw up till my gut ached. All of a sudden, this black dude was standing there, looking at me, and looking up and down the alley. He had on one of those stocking hats, a dark sweatshirt and army fatigue pants.

"Funny, the things that run through your mind at a time like that. His hands were in his pockets, and I knew he had a knife. I'll never know the reason—money perhaps—but I knew he meant to kill me. I thought I was going to die in the dirt of that filthy alley, laying in that piss and vomit. I remember the cold night air against the back of my throat, and the taste of vomit in my mouth. I remember cold tears in my eyes. Neither of us said anything, but we looked into each other's eyes and knew each other's thoughts, and that rapport didn't make any difference at all in what was about to happen.

"Then, by the grace of God, three other guys came out the back door, laughing and staggering around drunkenly. They stopped there and lit cigarettes, and were laughing and talking, and the guy just turned and walked away. My legs almost gave way. I've never been back to Tiajuana, and I haven't frequented any rough bars since that night.

"We take certain things for granted in other human beings. Maybe it's one of those psychological curtains that we close to shut out fearful thoughts. Our minds won't admit that the world is not a warm and fuzzy place—at least, not on an emotional level. We couldn't stand the constant strain. When the curtain is suddenly pulled aside, we are shocked to find that the nightmares are real, after all. Yes, I do know the feeling."

"What should I do?" asked Wallace. "I hate myself for feeling like a coward, and I know I was wrong to insult him, and it's going to be hell if I have to deal with someone I'm afraid of. It's almost as if I were back in elementary school, and afraid of the school bully. I feel ashamed."

"I think you already know the answer," said Ortiz. "First, forget your ego for the moment, and make up with him. If it was someone that you had frightened, or behaved badly to, a student for example, I know you well enough to know that you would seek him out and apologize. You wouldn't feel any loss of face in that situation, and logically, you shouldn't in this situation.

You admitted that you shouldn't have insulted him. Just walk over there bearing an olive branch and say so.

"Second, you don't have to be a coward to be afraid of some things. It's a survival instinct. You wouldn't pick a fight with a prizefighter either, and Townsend is something much more dangerous. He's also human, and can be rather likable if you give him a chance. We don't know him well enough to let him in on certain things, but that doesn't automatically make him our enemy. My instincts tell me he's all right. Go shake hands."

The following morning, Wallace carried a box of warm donuts to the lab where Townsend and his team were working. As Wallace walked in, the two students looked up and greeted him. Townsend stopped his work at his computer keyboard and sat back in his chair, silently looking at Wallace. Wallace sat the donuts on the desk, glanced at the students, then back at Townsend.

"Peace offering," he said, indicating the donuts. "I apologize for the insult. I guess I always wanted to tell off some of the smug, government-program managers that I've had to deal with, and here you were, on my turf so to speak, and my resentment just boiled over. I'm sorry. I was unbelievably rude to you. I acted like an arrogant ass, and I had no call to take out my feelings on you. I would like to start over." Wallace held out his hand, "Friends?"

Townsend stood up and took the extended hand, but did not smile. "I'm willing to try," he said. "God knows, I don't need any enemies."

XXVI

A month later, on the tenth of February, Jack Townsend was ferrying underclothes from the chest of drawers in his and Eve's bedroom, to an open suitcase on the bed. She was trying to dissuade him from taking a trip to Atlanta.

They had not been apart since they met, and though she had been a very confident and independent woman in her former life, she had become very needful of his comforting presence. She was loving but not usually clinging, and he had noticed that her times of silence, her introspective moods, were getting to be less frequent. She was even playful much of the time, now.

He knew that eventually she would get over the trauma and her self-confidence would reassert itself. He secretly hoped that she would still love and want him when it happened. In the meantime, he didn't mind her wanting to be with him as much as possible; in fact, he enjoyed it. Their love was new, and even though they were mature adults, they liked the petting and making calf eyes at one another, and he knew they needed it for a while. There would probably come a time, he thought ruefully, when he would sorely miss it. There would be plenty of time for sobriety and dignified reserve in their old age.

"I don't understand why you have to go," Eve said, miserably.

Jack stopped packing for a moment and sat on the bed beside her, taking her hand between his. "I've got to make a presentation to a review panel at the Advanced Research

Projects Agency. It's called ARPA. My company does defense-related work for them, and for NASA and other federal agencies as well.

"We've got a contract to develop an automated warehousing and material handling system for the Department of Defense. It's all part of the downsizing of government. They are exploring ways to reduce personnel. Smart robot systems can control inventories, shift materiel, even qualify and select bidders to perform contract work. It's a matter of designing robot warehouses and handling equipment that can accurately take inventory, ship and receive supplies, and place orders.

"Prouss Engineering has the best proposal, and if we succeed in getting the award, we will develop a pilot project in Denver. It's one of several government supply hubs. If we get the contract, I may have to do this often.

"In any case, it couldn't have come about at a more opportune time. I need a security clearance in order to keep this job, and I can fix that if I can get into the C.I.A. computer center in Atlanta. I can access some secret C.I.A. and F.B.I. databases from here, by computer modem, and I can read files, but I don't have the access I need to *write* files into the databases.

"I recently contacted an old friend in the C.I.A. Office of Development and Engineering who was stationed at the CERN high-energy physics laboratory in Geneva. He's into all kinds of cutting-edge computer work and advanced systems design. Turns out that the agency has recalled a lot of people from overseas assignments to replace staff that were killed in Washington. Fred was one of them.

"He's in Atlanta now, and he can help me to install an in-depth history profile with a *secret* clearance in the F.B.I. files. All my references will be either the names of people killed in Washington, or dead of natural causes, and of course a few living people like Fred, who can vouch for me.

"Since it is an industrial contractor clearance rather than something for a government post, I'm counting on no one within the agencies affected paying very much attention to it." He paused a moment, then reluctantly, "I am also going to try to locate Broderick."

"Oh no," said Eve, pleading with her eyes. "Oh, honey, I would die if anything happened to you. Can't you just let it go; let them forget about us?"

"That's exactly why I need to find him, sweetheart. He's the only one that's driving the search for us. I don't believe that we are high on the list of any of the regular law-enforcement agencies, not even the regular federal boys—not with the reductions in force and everything else that's going on these days.

"It's a personal thing with Broderick, for some reason. No sane man would have ordered your death in the first place. It was for too petty a reason. Hell, the federal government undergoes far worse criticism every day, even from conservative talk-radio hosts. Your incident would have been forgotten in a week. No, Broderick believes he has a mission to control what the public sees and hears, and he enforces his edicts with gangster-style tactics. As the kids would say, he's a *bent dude.*"

He resumed packing. "When he's gone, his unit will disintegrate. We'll be able to fade out of everyone's memory and get on with our lives without constantly looking over our shoulders. In five years' time we'll be pillars of the community, Mrs. Townsend." He pulled her up off the bed, took her in his arms and kissed her, holding her close. "Don't worry about me, sweetheart," he whispered, "I used to do this sort of thing for a living, remember?"

Eve kissed him hard, and hugged him tightly, as if to imprint him with some spell that would keep him there, or insure his safe return. Finally, she relaxed and dropped her arms—began drying her wet eyes and runny nose with one of his T-shirts. "When will you be back?"

"In about a week if everything goes as planned. I'll call you every night. I know you can't help but worry. Just go on as usual. Try to occupy yourself; put your mind on other things.

"Watch out for strangers, though, and don't open the door to anyone you don't know. Use the intercom and the peephole. For instance, if a cop comes to the door, presumably for some routine reason, let him stand there while you call the police station and verify that he is who he says he is. If he isn't, tell them that someone impersonating an officer is at your door.

"Next, call Eddie. If he doesn't answer, call his beeper number. If he sees this number, he knows to come. Then go back to the door and tell the guy that you called the police.

"Keep the doors locked at all times. Stay away from the windows. The phone and power lines are buried where no one can easily get at them. The doors are heavy and the windows are barred. He's not going to spend the time necessary to break in, if he thinks the cops are on their way.

"After he leaves, wait for Eddie, then get in his car and go with him. He will know what to do. I'll pick you up at his place when I get back. I don't anticipate any trouble, but I want you to be prepared. You need to react just the way I've described. Can you do it?"

"Yes. I can do it," she said.

"Good. I know you can." He closed the suitcase and set it by the door. He kissed her again, lightly on the lips. "Let's try to get some sleep. I've got to be at the airport at 5:30 A.M."

XXVII

At midnight of February 14, Saint Valentine's Day, by prior arrangement, a man sitting in a darkened motel room in Titusville, Florida, received a telephone call. Next to the phone was a small electronic box, and the man reached over and threw a switch as soon as he heard the caller's voice.

He said hello, listened a moment, then said, "Yes, it's me. Turn on your encryptor. How are you?"

"It's on. I'm fine." The voice sounded sad, distant. The Titusville man said so.

"I'm okay," assured the second man, in a resigned tone. "I'm just tired, and in a mood today. I'm hopping time zones like a kid playing hopscotch, and working twenty-hour days. I can't stop thinking about the cost in lives. It's one thing to contemplate doing something of that enormity, to remotely rationalize the costs versus the long-term benefits to humanity, but it's such a horrible thing to know you have done it. I can't help thinking about the innocents—especially the children."

"I never thought it would really go that far," said the Titusville man, "when I agreed to help you. I thought I knew you well, and I didn't think you could go through with it—not all the way, I mean. I had no conception of how powerful that thing is. My God, it could dominate the world! And from what I'm hearing through the grapevine, that is one of several schemes being concocted in certain quarters. As we thought, the Air Force Space Command is planning to try to use Diana to find and destroy it, but there is another group in Washington that wants to gain control of it for their own ends. Can they do it?"

"No. Have no fear of that. It's equipped with a dead man's switch. It must be reset every so often, or a preset program takes over. It would destroy ninety-two hundred military and financial center targets—almost every major base and significant outpost in the world—then self-destruct. It would ruin the world economy for a while, but it would keep people busy putting things back together, and the world would recover. In the meantime, it would strip away most of the underworld's power, and render them incapable of global domination. If I am captured or killed, I want to leave the world with a fighting chance."

"Do you have a contingency plan for Diana?"

"Yes. Actually, Diana is crucial to our plans. We anticipated their reactivating it, as well as several other tactics they might try. I don't imagine for a moment that I've thought of every conceivable means of attack, but I spent years planning this. A lot of that time went toward keeping up with what is in orbit, and in exploring possible countermeasures they might try. In the end, I decided we were as ready as we would ever be, and time was running out. We had to move now, or lose the opportunity—perhaps forever."

Suddenly, the Titusville man started at the sound of a loud thud outside the door. The next moment, the door burst inward, and a squad of cursing, shouting men rushed into the darkened room. Spotlights beamed through the window, filling the room with glaring light and stark shadows.

Automatic rifles were trained on the seated figure as he sat holding the phone, the red spots of aiming lasers playing over his body. Blinding light filled the room as the lights were switched on.

"Freeze!" ordered an intent young man with a pistol trained on the seated man. The man did as he was told, sat with hands raised, elbows on the arms of the chair, the phone still in his hand. Another man walked around behind the seated man without getting in the line of fire, took the phone, listened into it, then placed it in the phone cradle. He looked at the first man—shook his head.

The first man stood slowly, holstering his gun. He addressed the seated man:

"Mr. Obermiller, I'm with the Federal Bureau of Investigation. You are under arrest for conspiracy to overthrow the government of the United States."

"No," Obermiller said quietly, a look of resignation on his face, "you overthrew it. You don't represent the country or the people. We are just trying to take it back."

"Well, isn't that patriotic?" the agent said sarcastically. "My country, 'tis of thee . . . ? You and your friends murdered a million helpless people. After we find out what we want from you, your government is going to see that you get about six feet of country for your very own, and the People will cheer when they stick the needle in you."

Turning away, he said to the others, "Cuff him and get him out of here. I want him strip-searched and printed as soon as you get back to base, and get me ten sets of photos ASAP. Make sure he can't harm himself. I want him in a straitjacket and under constant observation until further notice. If anything happens to him, it's going to be somebody's ass. Do it."

XXVIII

Captain Bill Robinson stood with Lieutenants Donald Phelps and Pete Goldman outside SATCOM, in the underground complex at Cheyenne Mountain, Wyoming. They were discussing the impending mission that the U.S. Air Force Space Command was calling Operation Damocles and having a final cigarette before relieving the current crew. Robinson was just finishing his tour of duty, and waiting for the new watch officer to relieve him.

Phelps and Goldman were young, brash and eager, and they were excited, as young military men always are on the eve of war. Robinson was a seasoned officer, and a bit less enthused by what he knew, which was a good deal more than the grapevine gossip that Phelps and Goldman were going on.

He had personal reservations about the wisdom of attacking the weapon, the Damocles of current interest, but wasn't about to communicate his feelings to the two junior officers.

Phelps also seemed more troubled than eager, but was unavoidably excited about the impending action. Everyone throughout the command felt the tension. Goldman was openly cocky, though. No reservations, there, thought Robinson.

"It's official. We've confirmed that it is the weapon," said Goldman, smiling.

Robinson already knew—had known for some days—what Goldman had just learned, but intended to keep his foreknowledge a secret. He didn't want to deflate the younger men by stealing their moment. No one in this command had thought of anything else for months. They were frustrated by the waiting, and the news was a much needed break in the monotony.

"Where? How?" he asked, pretending curiosity.

Phelps was the science technician. Without Goldman's exuberance, he responded, "At about twenty-five degrees above the plane of the ecliptic, something is blocking starlight as it passes between the stars and the earth. We can't image it. Their cloaking technology is truly amazing. Its shadow seems to be only about a square meter in area. There are ways to make sure, but if they have an antisurveillance system, they would notice a ranging laser or a radar pinging pulse. We can't risk assuming they wouldn't. We would alert them that we have found them, and our signal would direct them right to us. We can't take the chance. God knows what they would do."

"We, and this installation, would become a bubble of incandescent gas about ten milliseconds after our pinging signal hit them; that is what 'they' would do," said Robinson. "You guys had better wake up. This isn't a video game. If you don't watch your p's and q's, and operate by the book, twenty-first century technological warfare is going to jump up and bite you on the butt. That isn't a manned craft up there; you're not combating other human beings. It's a sophisticated machine, and if you screw up, you'll be dead in a heartbeat. We all will."

"Where is Diana in relation to it? Can we move her within range?" asked Goldman.

"She's actually only about ten degrees behind, and five degrees south longitude away from their orbital track," said Phelps. "She has gas thrusters, and enough gas inventory remaining to get her to coincidence."

"What about her weaponry? Can she kill it?"

"She has a kinetic launcher with twenty-four, three hundred gram, spent-uranium projectiles, each with seventy-four hundred Newton-meters of energy. Four are tipped with proximity-fused, high-explosive frag, and two are ion bombs."

"Why use the solid projectiles at all?" asked Goldman Why not just the explosive shells?"

"Because there's no point in not using them," said Robinson. "If one of the HE heads should have a defective fuse, and it's the only one to come within range . . . what then? One of the solids might be the one thing that gets through, especially if Damocles fires back. A slug of molten uranium could do a lot of damage. Even if Damocles doesn't fire, one of the solids may be the only thing that connects."

Phelps interjected, responding to Goldman, "Don't forget, Diana was made for this kind of job. If she can hit a solid section, she can hurt it bad, maybe kill it. Trouble is, we don't know how the thing is constructed. If we shoot through a thin membrane, such as a solar parasol, we won't hurt it, we'll just alert them, and because of the reaction moments of her weapons propellants, Diana must be repositioned after each shot."

"What kind of absolute range does Diana have?" asked Robinson, curious to see how far the men had been briefed.

Again, it was Phelps who had the technical knowledge. "She's theoretically accurate on a ten-square-meter target, out to about two kilometers, but she was meant for close-in work—destruction of surveillance and com satellites. She has a very narrow frontal aspect ratio, deliberately made that way because SDI was thinking of killer satellite counterdefense, and wanted a low profile. She's about ten centimeters wide, where the projectiles exit—kind of like a hatchet head.

"Because of her small radar cross-section, tactical operations thinks that she can get within one klick of Damocles without being discovered. If the terrorists used a common imaging radar system, it won't image much under half a square meter at that range.

"Ops thinks they may have used something of low discrimination, because Damocles is so damned small anyway. He's probably built for orbit-to-ground attack only, with very limited counter-satellite defensive systems and sensors—at least insofar as combating close-in objects that don't emit IR signatures from heat engines. The terrorists would probably rely on the stealth cloaking for defense, and use the bulk of the weapon's mass for power generation."

"What if it uses a high-discrimination laser interferometer?" asked Robinson, smiling slightly.

"Then we're screwed," said Phelps, returning the smile. "Diana's aiming system is the real worry," he continued, turning serious again. "She uses an old optical system with twenty-power magnification, and cross-hairs at point of aim. Her sights are mounted in the center of her weapons cluster, but even the four uranium solids closest to the sights are six centimeters away from line of sight."

"What's the optimum range at the point of zero parallax?" asked Robinson.

"There is no parallax problem. The Army had the right idea, there. Except for gravitational trajectory, the projectiles stay parallel to line of sight, all the way out. No divergence.

"The problem is that Damocles is so damned small. Or at least the cross-section that we can see is small. He may be a one-meter tube, twenty meters long, for all we know. Anyway, one minute of angle is twenty-eight centimeters at one kilometer. Add six centimeters of coincidence error, and you've got thirty-four centimeters of deviation to play with. Diana's mean aiming radius is four meters, so a minute of angle is one-point-one-six millimeters of rotation. Her weapons' phalanx, fired all at once, covers a bit over a square meter of area at the target. At one kilometer, if her optics or her point of aim is off dead center by half a millimeter, we're dead meat."

"Bottom line?" asked Robinson.

"She's going to have to get close enough to Damocles to mate with him, if we're going to be sure of a kill," Phelps said with as much drama as he could muster.

Robinson couldn't help but laugh. "What about his power system?" he asked, genuinely wondering whether or not the boy had heard anything new at the briefing. "Have they managed to pick up anything?"

"Not a glimmer. We still don't have a clue as to what powers that thing. There's not a half-degree Kelvin difference between Damocles' temperature and that of the deep space background. Disregarding heat from internal circuitry, and that's a lot to disregard, how in hell do you think they avoid solar heating? That thing has got to be the best insulator ever devised."

"Dr. Stickle thinks that it gets rid of waste heat by converting the IR energy into a higher frequency, and somehow radiating it away on the beam itself," Phelps responded, intent on his subject. "It makes a lot of sense, and conserves energy by adding it to the weapon's output."

Robinson reflected, with utterly no patronization, "The more we learn about this thing, the more I wonder if we're even bright enough to play in the same league with these guys. I'm almost ready to believe in the Big Brother-race-of-aliens theory—you know, protecting us from ourselves, for our own good."

"There's another danger that we mustn't forget," Phelps said. "If we damage its control system without deactivating its weapon system, it could potentially strafe the earth, out of control, and kill millions before it runs out of energy. We aren't going to be popular if we wing it, and it retaliates.

"People are worried about the threat it carries, but most of them like the way things have changed. They aren't going to want to go back, especially at the risk of destroying half the planet."

"They won't have any choice in the matter," Goldman answered smugly. "We will carry out our orders, and the civilians will fall in line."

Robinson looked disappointed at Goldman's arrogance, and glanced at the smoldering, rebellious face of Phelps. Phelps was considering Goldman, and looked disgusted.

Robinson said, "I'll leave it with you guys. I'm going to get some sleep."

He moved away, paused to pass his keys and sidearm to his relief, who had just walked up, and walked away down the corridor. The new officer of the day, Captain Cogdil, passed by the two lieutenants and entered the command center.

"Why haven't they got a choice, Pete?" Phelps confronted Goldman, speaking just above a whisper. "Why should we go back? Things are better now."

"Look," said Goldman, "I can sympathize with your feelings. Things are better for the average Joe Blow, but they aren't going to stay that way. Whoever controls that thing has a weakness. It may be money, or women, or just having power. Who knows? Sooner or later, they will become corrupt. Everyone does. You've heard the old adage, Absolute power corrupts absolutely, haven't you? Well, it's true. Power is intoxicating, and if we don't take them out, they will soon be making our lives miserable. That's the official stand, and it sounds right to me."

"What if you're wrong? What if, like the message said, we're throwing away the only chance we will ever have. I haven't noticed anyone asking our opinion about the way things are run. Have you?"

"That's the way the world is, my friend," Goldman said, putting out his cigarette. "Whether we like it or not."

"Goldman," Phelps said, putting a hand on Goldman's arm. "Give me a straight answer. Do you believe in the concept of democracy? Would you rather live under a dictatorship? I mean, I'm doing my hitch for my country, and I understand the need for a military, but I'm getting out after I serve my tour. The structured life may be okay for some, but it's not for me, and I sure as hell wouldn't want the whole country to be run by a military regime."

"Of course I believe in democracy," said Goldman disdainfully. "I have plans, too. My old man is as capitalistic as the next guy, and I'll be a VP in his company after my hitch is over. That has nothing to do with the here-and-now."

"I think it has everything to do with it," said Phelps, intent on Goldman's face. "My folks say the spirit of the country is better now than it has been in fifty years. All kinds of opportunities are springing up. People are getting back their independence. They're happier, and we can keep it that way. You and I. Right now, Diana is the only hope they have of destroying Damocles. What if we *accidentally* exhaust her propellant and put her in a decaying orbit? She would burn up, and then nothing could reach Damocles undetected."

Goldman looked at Phelps as if he had just discovered the man was a leper. "Are you saying you want to stay under the threat of that thing from now on?"

"Why not?" Phelps face went from belligerent to pleading. "Pete, if you'll get your head out of your ass for a minute, and look at commerce, education, everything—everyone is happier and more productive than they were before. Look at all the positive things that have come out of this. Fewer people are going hungry, disease is being treated, there is general peace worldwide for the first time in the history of the friggin' world. Don't you remember how it was? Half the leadership of the country was criminally suspect, from real estate swindles, to kickbacks, to murder, and everything in between. Everybody just looking for an excuse to hate everybody else. Kids killing each other. Half the country on dope, and the other half selling it. You hardly ever hear of any of that crap anymore.

"Who will benefit if Damocles is destroyed? Its destruction is only in the best interests of those scheming bastards who want to take power again. Why must we be robots and help them achieve it? Why can't we, for once, act in the interests of humanity?"

Phelps eyes were tearing from the intensity of his angry emotion. "Pete, if I have a choice of who dictates our lives, I opt for the present dictator."

"You have been thinking about this, haven't you?" asked Goldman, looking at Phelps curiously.

"I'm going to do it, Pete. If you won't help me, just don't try to stop me. If you blow the whistle on me, I'll tell the press what's going on. I swear it!"

Goldman smiled, clapped Phelps on the arm. "All right, Don. I guess I agree with you when you put it that way. What you say makes sense. What do you want me to do?"

Phelps face lit up with relief. He smiled, excited. "We begin maneuvering checks tomorrow. Connally will give me the control system telemetry codes so that I can program Diana's thruster firing sequence. You and I report for duty as planned. Once Connally gives me the codes, it will take me about ten minutes to get control of her attitude and propulsion telemetry. You distract Connally. He'll be supervising the telemetry programming. Just distract him from his master-terminal screen long enough for me to log in and initiate the control sequence. I'll program the thrusters for maximum burn, and punch in the initiate command. Once I've fired her thrusters, Diana will be in a tangential vector, falling inward, and even if Connally gets them shut down within ten seconds, it would still take more propellant than she has to get her back into higher orbit. I'll say it was a computer glitch—that the program initiated the firing sequence on its own."

"They'll never believe that."

"No, they won't, but they will believe that I just screwed up, and that I'm trying to save face by blaming it on a computer glitch. They won't suspect that I did it deliberately, and they won't suspect that you had anything to do with it. Will you help me?"

Goldman smiled, "Sure, buddy, I'm with you. Tomorrow, we do the deed. Right now, I guess we had better get in there."

"Thanks, Pete," Phelp's lip trembled with the emotion of his gratitude. As he turned his back, and started through the open door of the command center, Goldman hit him on the side of the neck with the edge of his hand. Phelps fell to his hands and knees, stunned. Goldman pulled a heavy instrument module from the rack near the door, and brought it down on Phelps' head.

Captain Cogdil, had just turned away from a printer, several folds of greenbar between his hands, when he glanced up through the door and witnessed Goldman's act. "What in God's name—" he yelled, springing toward them.

Goldman smiled, looking down at Phelp's bloody head, and tossed the instrument module on the floor. It hit with a heavy thud, and lay still. "Sir, I've just killed a lousy little traitor, that's what."

Cogdil drew his pistol and pointed it at Goldman. "On the floor," he said.

Goldman said angrily, "He was going to sabotage Diana, sir. He wanted me to help him."

"If you open your mouth again, I'm going to put a round in your knee. On the floor, mister. Now!"

Goldman complied, red-faced and silently fuming.

Cogdil stood over Goldman with his pistol pointing at the man's back. He called to a gawking lieutenant inside the command center, "Evans, call the A.P.'s. Tell them it's an emergency. You got that?"

"Yes, sir," yelled Evans, rushing to the desk phone.

In minutes, Goldman had been handcuffed and taken away. Within the hour, Cogdil was giving a preliminary statement to the provost marshall, and to Colonel Whitfield, the deputy base commander.

"I had just assumed the watch when it happened, sir," he told Whitfield. "I saw Phelps fall out of the corner of my eye, I guess. As I looked up, I saw Goldman pull an indicator module off the calibration rack and hit Phelps in the head with it."

"No idea what provoked the attack?" asked Whitfield.

"No, sir. I didn't pay any attention to them when I arrived. They were standing near the door talking. I relieved Captain Robinson. I think he was talking to them when I got here. He may know something about it. After Goldman hit Phelps, he said that he had killed him because he was a traitor."

"Do you know Phelps and Goldman?"

"Yes, sir. I haven't had much social contact with Goldman. I share the opinion of most of the staff, that he's an asshole. Phelps was a decent, likable, naive kid— never slacked, always ready to help, good at his job, always friendly, trusted everybody. I can't tell you, sir, how badly I wanted to shoot that grinning son of a bitch in the face."

"Think there was any truth in Goldman's accusation?"

"Sir, Phelps was a small-town boy from Iowa. He loved his mother and father; he had a pretty little thing waiting for him; he wanted to get married and start a computer sales and service shop when his hitch was over. They don't come any more American than him. I'd stake a year's pay on it.

"It wouldn't make any difference if he was a spy. The kid was down, on the deck, when Goldman caved his head in. The murdering bastard smiled, can you believe that? After doing something like that, he smiled!"

XXIX

Reed spent two days in Atlanta. The afternoon and evening of the second day, he spent several hours with his friend from the computer center at the new C.I.A. headquarters.

Frederick von Braun was a dark-haired, blue-eyed young man of medium height, who wore glasses and Armani suits. A yuppie, in eighties parlance. He also worshipped James Reed as the big, sophisticated, super-spy brother that he had never had.

Reed called him the evening he arrived, and asked Fred to meet him. When von Braun walked through the restaurant where they had arranged to meet, he walked right by Reed without recognizing the dark, Latin-looking gentleman in the window booth. Reed laughed, and as Von Braun gazed blankly around the room, he beckoned him over. He was aghast at the change in Reed, and it took him awhile to relax and resume a semblance of his normal, gregarious spirit. He kept looking at Reed, as if trying to confirm what his eyes were telling him, intermittently shaking his head and laughing.

Townsend/Reed decided not to tell him all the particulars of his new identity or location until some indefinite time in the future. Not for lack of trust, but as a precaution. Too many people were at risk, and you learned to place your organization and the lives of your comrades over one person's feelings. Fred understood, and believed in his hero's promise. He did tell him briefly about Broderick's unit and the falsified charges.

✧   ✧   ✧

Fred took him to an off-site office that served as a satellite communications center for the systems research unit Fred worked for. Fred got Reed through the security post—got him badged and through the inner security door and into the low-security installation. They walked through brightly lit corridors that were delineated by modular furniture—a rabbit warren of cubicles, each with a computer desk and hutch, computer terminal, office chair and horizontal file cabinet.

They found Fred's cubicle, and Townsend smiled at the personal memorabilia tacked up on the partition walls: photos of girls, old European inns and tourist sites in Switzerland and Austria, a picture of Fred with his graduating class from the academy.

Fred pulled in another chair from an unoccupied cubicle for Townsend, and turned his terminal on. Once it had booted up, he gave Townsend access into the mainframe computer system through his terminal, then went to a break room to get them some coffee from a vending machine.

By the time he returned, Townsend had inserted the 3.5-inch diskette that he had brought with him and loaded the history profile and security clearance information into the system. Fred had not seen the data.

Next, Fred keyed in the names and identity numbers that Townsend had provided. They were the employee locator numbers of Broderick and his remaining personnel. He also did a search for agency telephone traffic from the Miami area, filtered out the resident office and agents, and correlated the personnel data as a crosscheck.

Broderick had wisely moved to a location in South Carolina, just up the coast between Savannah and Charleston. There were dozens of barrier islands and miles of empty beaches, all within an hour's drive of main, arterial Highways 95 and 16.

From the volume of telephone traffic, Townsend concluded that Broderick was extremely busy with something.

Townsend surmised that he was probably using underworld contacts and petty criminals to establish a boiler room operation and computer net. It would take too much time to find and indoctrinate suitable people from other agency sources. It took a lot of arranging and legwork to organize the kind of propaganda that Broderick specialized in, and leaks could not be tolerated. Broderick could use a criminal record for leverage in exacting obedience from that type, and the proper lack of inhibitions and moral character were already in place. The media would not have supported, or even given air time, to anyone who decided to spill the beans, but it helped to use people who already had a healthy and ignoble interest in not doing so.

Broderick thought of himself as a creative genius when it came to his work. In reality, Townsend admitted, he did have a feral intelligence, but without the bias and collusion of the news media, and the use of an unaccounted-for federal budget, he would have been just another dirty little killer.

It looked to Townsend like Broderick was gearing up for something big, and he thought he knew what it was. Broderick had dropped hints of a plan to discredit the nationalists—to make their motives suspect. If the government underworld succeeded in overcoming the weapon, they would need to brand the patriot movement as the work of cultists and terrorists. The new regime was popular, and growing more so with each passing day, as greater numbers of people came to trust the promise that this was not enslavement, but a return to liberty and uniform justice. The seed of personal freedom had been planted in their minds. That trust had to be turned around.

In order to regain its former power, the government had to offer something in place of freedom. It had to offer the hope of warmth and security in a cold, insecure world, and they had to destroy that budding faith in the makers of the weapon. The only way was to make them think the nationalists were killing people without reason.

It was Broderick's favorite scheme, but on a much grander scale. To be convincing, thousands, perhaps hundreds of thousands of citizens would have to be sacrificed in order to simulate even a small sample of the destruction that the weapon was capable of. How were they planning to accomplish it?

The only thing that came to Townsend's mind was a napalm and incendiary bombing of a city. That would take time, and a lot of bombs. People would see the planes and the falling bombs. The destruction would hardly be sufficient to kill and silence every inhabitant—and they couldn't use a nuclear device because the space weapon did not leave radioactive residue.

Suddenly, it came to him. "Fred, see if you can find any unusual stockpiling of gasoline. I think I have an idea what the bastard is planning."

"Funny you should mention gasoline. Somebody in the community has recently been buying truckloads of gasoline and having it delivered to Miramar Naval Air Station, on the California coast. Almost a hundred and fifty thousand gallons. Nothing unusual, for the Navy, they have lots of vehicles—but why is the community buying it? A lot of this Broderick guy's phone traffic is going that way, too. What do you think it means?"

Townsend stared into space for a moment. "I can tell you exactly what it means. It figures that it would be a western city; they want to destroy the support for the movement that exists in the west.

"Unless I miss my guess, one of the major cities— L.A., San Diego or San Francisco—is Broderick's target. They are planning to kill a city. L.A. is my guess. Heavy industry, cross-section of ethnic backgrounds and races, center of shipping and overseas trade—it would hurt the country the most. Stir up the most hate."

Townsend thought a moment. "Los Angeles is ideal for another reason. The stagnant air patterns that cause much of L.A.'s smog problems are perfect for their purpose. Some night, several large tanker planes, KC-10s maybe, equipped with aerosol spray systems, will fly over the heart of the city spraying finely-atomized gasoline into the air at an altitude of about three thousand feet. If they pick a night with just enough wind to stir and mix the droplets, and spread the saturated air over a wide area, they can kill millions. When the planes clear the area, they will ignite the cloud. Short of a hydrogen bomb, nothing could possibly equal the destruction.

"With so much military air traffic in the area already, no one will give the tankers a second thought. At night, no one would see the spray. Survivors won't be able to point any fingers, or even guess where it came from. They will likely believe that the space weapon is responsible."

"Good Lord! Do you really think the community would do such a thing, Jimmy? To Americans?"

"Fred, this twisted son of a bitch is not the community. He's a mole, but he's a sanctioned mole, and he works for a hidden power structure. Where better to operate from, without discovery, than within an agency where no one knows anything about what anyone else is doing. The agency is busy looking outward, not auditing itself, and when the White House and others with clout get involved, even the agency heads don't ask too many questions. It's a perfect cover for an operation like Broderick's.

"Someone slipped up in screening me, and I ended up in Broderick's little cadre, much to my regret. Although, I'm almost glad now. If I didn't know about it, I couldn't do anything about it, and I do want to do something about it. To answer your question, yes, he would do it in a heartbeat, and never lose a minute's sleep over it. I've got to stop him. We've got to stop him, Fred. I need your help. Will you help me?"

"Jimmy, an industrial security clearance is one thing, but this sounds an awful lot like treason we're talking here. You know I believe in you, but you've got to admit, this destroying L.A. thing is pretty fuckin' incredible. What are you asking me to do?"

"Just to find out who in the community authorized the fuel, exactly where it's being stored, any connected business such as movement of tanker aircraft to Miramar or vicinity. Anything on tanker aircraft modifications. Anything connected with Broderick's operation that involves the west coast. Look, Fred, if I'm wrong, nothing will happen, and your conscience is clear. You're not being asked for state secrets or anything that would compromise normal agency business. Any problems with that?"

"No, I guess not, Jimmy, but I feel funny about all this. You know I want to help you, and I feel like I've let you down, man. I'm really feeling gut-sick over it. At the same time, I feel like a traitor. Please tell me something that will make me feel better."

Townsend smiled reassuringly. "Welcome to the spy business, Fred. It's not as glamorous in the trenches as you thought, is it?" He put a hand on his friend's arm, and forced Fred to meet his eyes. "Fred, the Cold War is as alive now as it ever was. The only difference is that the enemy has moved onshore. He has infiltrated our government, slowly, insidiously, for years. Nationality has lost its meaning, that's all.

"And we've all been looking the other way. It only became noticeable when the Soviet Union collapsed. Suddenly, the threat that had been the focus of our attention for the past forty years was gone. In spite of all their efforts to divert attention to the conflicts in other countries—some of which they may even be responsible for starting—Americans began to notice that a lot of crap was happening here at home.

"This administration has divided the country, singled out groups of dissenting people and with the help of the media, attached labels to them, in order to isolate and brand them bad, turn public opinion against them. Many of those groups are comprised of ordinary, patriotic people that were veterans and heroes of past wars. The National Rifle Association, and similar groups. They love this country, and they want to return it to the way it was. Now they are made out to be extremists, and right-wing radicals.

"There is a real push to unite the world under one big, incompetent government, irrespective of widely differing cultural beliefs, political systems and faiths. Almost no one in the world wants that. If the powers that be get their way, the people won't have any choice in the matter."

Fred's eyes searched Townsend's face, growing wider as he listened. Then they became furtive, began to avoid his, as if searching for a reason to suddenly be somewhere else. Townsend's heart sank. He knew that he had made a mistake by confiding too much to the young man, and he didn't know how to recover. He had overlooked the civil brainwashing that had molded Fred's life, and his lack of experience against which to weigh things.

Fred had never known personal warfare, or hunger, or lean times, or a time of real internal unrest in this country. Life was a TV adventure to him, and Townsend had suddenly lifted up the curtain and shown him the seamy life behind the screen. His hero worship was turning to fear and suspicion before Townsend's very eyes, and he was seeing Townsend in the light of his social conditioning. He was beginning to believe the agency line, that Reed had turned. Townsend couldn't do anything now but forge ahead, and try to win back the boy's confidence.

"Think about it, Fred," he pleaded. "Why, all of a sudden, is there so much domestic violence? And is it really as prevalent as they say? Ask yourself how crime statistics can be going down, and at the same time the media is trying to whip people into a frenzy of fear. Why are we continually moving toward martial law? Why the all-out attack on the Constitution? Why have the once-united people of this country been broken up into separate, distrustful factions that blame each other for all their misfortunes? The media are being used to incite the distrust—to destroy unity. Why, Fred?"

Townsend paused, waited while a woman carrying a printout passed Fred's cubicle.

"Fred, Kruschev once said that they would bury us without firing a shot. I don't know if there is a real connection or not, but it sure seems that our country is under attack by people espousing the same political doctrine of a supreme socialist state, and an unarmed, submissive populace. *You* tell *me* what it means, Fred.

"My fall from grace came when I refused to kill an *American citizen* for saying what she believed. You explain that to me in context with your idea of patriotism, Fred."

"I can't. I don't know what to think," said the boy, looking miserable.

Suddenly, pleadingly, he grabbed Townsend's arm. "Jimmy, let's talk to my section supervisor, Richard Phelps. He's a great guy. He'll know what to do about all this. He'll straighten it out, Jimmy. Honest. I'll vouch for you, and he'll get you reinstated. You've got to come in, man."

"I'm sorry Fred, honestly," said Townsend. "There comes a time in every person's life when they have to fish or cut bait. You can't always feel safe and righteous and above it all. Somebody has to get down in the ditch and fix the broken sewer. I guess it's my time. It's not yours, though. I'm letting you off the hook. All I ask is that you keep everything I've told you to yourself. Can I count on you to do that?"

Fred smiled sickly, his eyes meeting Townsend's briefly, then sliding away. "Sure, of course, Jimmy," he said.

"Well, let's get out of here, then. C'mon, I'll spring for dinner somewhere."

"Okay, Jimmy, just let me hit the head before we go, my teeth are floating."

Ten minutes later, Fred returned. He wouldn't meet Townsend's eyes, and Townsend knew that he had lost the battle. He felt sick inside for the loss of a friend, and for what he must do. He didn't have that many friends, and he held dear those that he did have. His heart was bitter with the irony of his position. Fred was loyal to the government of his country. Only a few months before, Townsend would have felt this same sickening loss, but he would have killed Fred if he had found out that he was a traitor to that government. Now, it was reversed. Townsend was the traitor in Fred's eyes.

He followed Fred out of the building. They had come in Fred's car, a blue Nissan sedan, and except for a half-dozen parked cars, the darkened parking lot was deserted.

As they approached the passenger side of the car, Townsend put his hand on Fred's shoulder, and Fred turned to face him. Townsend put both hands on Fred's shoulders, and looked at him sadly. "I am truly sorry I involved you, Fred. I would give anything if I could go back and undo it. Please God, forgive me." With a sudden move, he snapped Fred's neck. Fred's lolling face looked momentarily surprised, then his eyes clouded over as he fell dead in Townsend's arms.

Townsend dug the keys out of Fred's pocket, put his body in the front seat of the car, then went around to the driver's side and got in. His eyes were moist as he pulled out of the deserted parking lot and drove away. "I've been trying for the last fifteen minutes to think of some way to keep you from compromising me without killing you, boy. I just couldn't come up with anything. If you had told your section chief, he would have warned Broderick, and millions would have died. God help me, I couldn't do anything else."

He drove out of the city, passing through darkened, thinning suburbs until he found a long, sloping stretch of road bordered by pine forest. He slowed just at the crest of the hill and made a U-turn, stopping beside the road, just off the pavement. He waited for a couple of solitary cars to pass by, thankful that there wasn't much traffic this time of night.

He put Fred's body behind the steering wheel, and sat beside him on the passenger side. He lined up the wheel and put Fred's body against it to hold it. He waited till another car passed and was out of sight, then he put the car in drive, released the emergency brake and slid out the passenger door.

The car began to roll slowly at first, down the gentle incline, picking up speed gradually. It was only doing twenty-five or thirty miles an hour when it went off the road into the trees. Townsend heard a thud, a crunching jangle of sheet metal and glass, then silence. The police might puzzle at how such a minor crash could break a man's neck, but stranger things had happened.

Townsend began walking back toward town through the darkness of the cold Georgia night, ducking into the trees to avoid passing traffic when he could, and was back into the sparsely settled outskirts within half an hour. After that, he no longer tried to hide, since there was no cover anyway, and he was far enough removed from the scene that he was unlikely to evoke any connection in peoples' minds when the body was discovered in a day or two. To any passing motorist, he could have come from any of the nearby houses.

As he walked, he couldn't help but go over the evening's events—his conversation with Fred. Over and over again, he chastised himself for suddenly dumping his own, newly-acquired, bias on the boy, and expecting him to swallow it all in one sitting. He wouldn't have, in Fred's place.

It suddenly occurred to him—what if Fred had managed to contact someone, or leave a message for someone? He was gone to the bathroom a long time. He had trusted Fred out of habit, even when he knew the boy doubted him, and it hadn't occurred to him that Fred might give him up right away. *God,* Townsend thought, *when am I going to wake up and realize what I'm doing?*

He knew he had to get to Broderick soon, tomorrow if possible. He had entertained half-formed ideas of torturing information out of Broderick—information that would lead him to bigger fish. Now, that was unimportant. If Broderick learned of Townsend's efforts to find him, he would bring all the government's law-enforcement resources to bear on finding Reed, and all those who had helped him or been in any way connected to him. Eve, Eddie, Hector—maybe dozens of their innocent friends and acquaintances. It might already be too late.

The highway he was on became a main thoroughfare as it entered the city, with side streets branching away into affluent-looking neighborhoods of single-family homes. Eventually, he came to a corner convenience store, and called a cab.

XXX

Once back in his hotel, Townsend called the airport and the bus station. Greyhound had a bus going to Charleston, South Carolina, within the hour. He packed a single duffel bag with a change of underwear and some extra clothing, left the rest of his things in the room and took another cab to the bus station. He got a sandwich and coffee in the terminal restaurant, bought a Charleston paper and perused the classified ads as he ate, looking for a cheap used car for sale by an individual. He circled a few.

Later that night, he got off the bus in downtown Charleston, and walked a few blocks to a brick-front motel. He rang the night bell, and stood listening to the hissing neon sign, with its darkened NO and lighted VACANCY and its blinking arrow pointing toward the office where he stood.

After a few seconds, a porch light came on and an old man opened a screeching, screened door. Townsend registered under the name of Robert Hill and paid cash, explaining when asked, that he lived in New York City and didn't own a car, and had taken the bus down for a visit, but didn't want to wake his relatives in the middle of the night.

The next day, he paid a young black man $500 for an old Volkswagen Beetle with a rusted-out floorboard. A loose piece of gray-painted plywood barely covered the hole in the floor, and Townsend could see the passing road surface sliding by through the peripheral openings.

He took the car to a gas station and had one new tire put on, and the engine and transmission serviced. Then he drove to another private address that he had found in the classified ads, and bought a pump-action .22-caliber rifle from an older man who had several guns for sale. On his way south out of town, he stopped at a hardware store and bought a pair of binoculars and a hundred rounds of ammunition.

A few miles south of Charleston, he saw a narrow stretch of paved road cutting off into the trees. He took it, and was soon on a two-lane dirt road that wound through high marsh grass and swampy pools of water. About a quarter mile from the turnoff, he stopped and got out of the car. He leaned against the car and listened awhile.

Crickets and cicadas sawed away, sometimes loudly, and above their sounds and that of the saw grass rustling in the lightly moving air, he could barely hear the distant sounds of cars on the highway.

He extracted the rifle from the rear floorboard of the Volkswagen and loaded seventeen cartridges into its tubular magazine. He had carefully inspected the little rifle when he bought it. He was sure that the action was tight and worked smoothly, that the barrel was straight and the bore in good condition. He knew it would shoot well, but he wanted to test-fire it and adjust the sights.

He picked out the limb of a fallen, waterlogged tree sticking up out of the water about fifty feet away. He doubted that the sharp crack of the little gun could be heard at the highway.

After four rounds he had the rear sight elevated to the point that the bullets were hitting at the right elevation, but about three inches to the left.

He cursed himself for not buying a screwdriver and hammer at the hardware store he had stopped at earlier. He looked around and found a smooth rock a bit larger than a golf ball. He rested the end of the gun barrel across the top edge of the Volkswagen's bumper and used the rock to hammer the front sight a minute amount to the left in its dove-tailed slot. He tried the rifle again.

After two more adjustments, he was hitting the limb dead-on and holding a shot group that could be covered with his thumb.

Satisfied, he reloaded the rifle, put it back in the rear floorboard and returned to the highway. He headed south to find Broderick.

Broderick was in a rented beachfront house on Edisto Island, a charming mixture of modern beach resorts and old-world, antebellum culture that typified the southern cotton-plantation era.

Broderick liked remote places with lots of tourist attractions. They provided perfect cover. Strangers came and went continuously without provoking anyone's interest, and Broderick could hold meetings with any of his nefarious friends and contacts without fear of the neighbors noticing.

Since beginning his career with the government, Broderick was, in simple terms, a logistics man. He arranged for people and supplies to be in certain places at certain times. He choreographed a simple show here and there, from behind the curtains, then he was on to other things. Few people even knew of his existence, much less any connection between him and events that took place clear across the country. He pulled strings at a safe distance, and when satisfied with the misery that resulted, he moved on to the next event.

Townsend found the address, a typical two-story, beachfront house with first-floor garage, and stairs leading up to a wide, covered porch that wrapped around the house on the three sides overlooking the shore. The next nearest house was a half mile north along the beach. For almost a mile to the south it was open, public beach, deserted at this time of day in February.

A boardwalk with handrails led across the dunes to the beach a hundred yards away. The coastal road passed within fifty yards of the house. A driveway cut through the low, wide dune that paralleled the main road, and circled around to the side of the house. The dune obscured the lower part of the house from the road, otherwise the house had a clear field of view in all directions.

Townsend could see two eight-passenger vans parked near the corner of the house as he drove by the driveway entrance, and off to one side, a pair of satellite dishes were set up on a flat-bed trailer.

Sand roads tend to form ripples over a period of time that depend on the amount of traffic and, if not graded often, they become so rough that speed is reduced to a crawl in order to maintain control of the vehicle. From the way the little car's shocks were machine-gunning at twenty-five miles per hour, Townsend figured that the road grader was due again soon. He hoped he wouldn't need to make a fast getaway.

It was almost four o'clock in the afternoon. Townsend drove on past the house for another half mile, then turned around and went back toward town. He found a small restaurant, ate and gassed up the car. Afterward, he wandered around on foot, looking at streets and shops, noting the casual foot traffic. He changed clothes in a service-station restroom, from slacks and shirt to jeans and a dark blue jersey, and replaced his dress shoes with a pair of blue canvass athletic shoes. He put on two undershirts beneath the jersey. The February temperature had gotten to almost sixty degrees during the day, and it had been fairly comfortable inside the car with the sun heating up the interior. Now, the thermometer was falling rapidly as the sun went down.

By six-thirty, it was twilight and getting dark rapidly. Townsend drove back out the beachfront road, going on past Broderick's house for at least a mile without slowing. He encountered no traffic.

He returned to a roadside pullout where he had turned around earlier that afternoon, about a half mile south of the house, and parked the car. He didn't know if there was a regular beach patrol along this road, or even if Broderick had his people run an occasional check, but he had no choice but to risk discovery of the little car. If someone happened by, he reasoned, they might think it was just someone taking a walk along the beach, and not bother to investigate.

Unless Fred had gotten a message out, Townsend doubted that Broderick would feel the need for strict security. His work seldom required direct contact with anyone, and he had no reason to think that anyone outside his superiors knew where he was.

He didn't believe that Broderick had anticipated any retaliation from James Reed either, over the past months. He thought it likely that Broderick assumed that he and Beverly Watkins had left the country for parts unknown, or were too busy hiding to retaliate. He was a vindictive sort though, and he wanted Reed and Watkins dead just on general principles. Watkins because he had ordered it done and wanted his sentence carried out. Reed, because he feared and hated him.

Townsend didn't think that Broderick had put much effort into finding them. He had more immediate things to worry about, and it probably gave him pleasure to think that he had destroyed their lives and sent them into hiding. He had cut Reed off from agency resources, made him a fugitive, and if Reed showed his face or tried to come in, Reed would end up in a cell. He wouldn't consider Reed much of an immediate threat, if any at all. Of course, if he learned that Reed was hunting him, that attitude would change.

Townsend pulled on a pair of thin, latex-rubber gloves, the kind surgeons wore, and used his handkerchief to wipe the rifle clean of prints. He didn't intend to leave it behind, but he prepared for eventualities. He never left fingerprints at the scene. It was part of training and lifelong habit. He had handled the small .22 cartridges when he loaded the gun, but he had held each one by the lead tip of the bullet. The surface area was too small and irregular to retain a fingerprint, and as for those that were left at the scene—after they had passed through the gun barrel and impacted anything at a thousand feet per second—no fingerprint lab in the world could lift a print from them.

Pocketing the loose cartridges, he crossed over the dune to the beach, and keeping low and as close as possible to the irregular contour of the dune, he made his way toward the house.

An icy breeze was blowing in from the sea, and the rushing gurgle of the constantly ebbing and flowing surf muffled the sound of his progress as he trudged through the soft, sinking sand. The smells and sounds reminded him of the flight along the Florida coast to Miami. It seemed a thousand years ago.

It would have been easier walking out on the wet, packed surface of the beach, but the risk of being seen was too great to chance it. He slowed as he approached the house, gingerly creeping closer, staying in the darker shadow of the dune.

He was almost winded by the time he reached the house, from walking in the uneven, foot-dragging sand at the toe of the dune. He stopped within fifty feet of the house and stayed there, silent and motionless for a while, watching, listening, regaining his breath. The second-floor windows were lit, and an occasional, indistinct shadow would cross one or the other.

Once, someone came out a screened door onto the porch, lit a cigarette and paused for a few minutes in the shadows, smoking and looking out to sea. After a bit, the individual went back inside, the screen door slapping noisily behind him.

Townsend couldn't hear anything intelligible from inside, and had no idea how many were present. He eased up to the side of the house. The garage walls were of heavy, wooden piles covered with plywood and tar paper, and an outer layer of tongue-and-groove lumber painted white. He climbed the slope of the dune where it met the garage wall, easing up until he could see above the floor of the banistered porch. He hoped that the glossy, gray-painted, wooden flooring of the porch wasn't creaky.

He swung the arm that held the rifle and one leg up onto the porch, then rolled in under the banister, and kept rolling until he was up against the wall beneath the window. Again, he lay silent for a time, listening. The noises were indistinct. Easing up on his knees, he peered over the sill of the open window, through the screen and the edge of a gauzy curtain into a spacious living room, warmly lit by several incandescent table lamps.

He saw the partially-bald top of one man's head over the back of a sofa that faced the front door. He was reading a paper and smoking. Broderick sat at a table across the room, working on something that Townsend couldn't see from his low angle. He sat almost facing the window where Townsend kneeled. An arm came up in front of Townsend so suddenly that he flinched backward and almost fell. A third man was lying down on a sofa or window seat just under the window. His arm had come up when he changed position. When Townsend realized it, the relief made him want to curse. He hunkered there, not moving, until his pounding heart subsided. No one else had moved.

He backed away from the window and got down on one knee, slightly behind the side curtain, the gun to his shoulder. He took a breath and relaxed, got the sights up and level, then shifted his weight to the right as he straightened his knee beneath him, and into the center of the window.

He fired three shots into Broderick's head and face, as fast as he could work the pump. The man on the far sofa was trying to get up. Townsend shifted and shot him in the head. He crumpled to the floor like a loosely-filled sack.

The third man screamed, diving through Townsend's

field of vision and momentarily obstructing his view of the room, then he was through the screen door, leaving it banging against the door frame, and Townsend heard his feet on the steps of the stairs leading down from the porch. He didn't attempt to pursue. In a moment, he heard the engine of one of the vans roar to life, and the ping and rattle of sand and gravel hitting the house as the spinning tires threw it out. He heard the tires squeal as they hit the harder surface of the main road, and the sound of the vehicle faded into the night.

Townsend rose and looked in the window. He could see Broderick's face and upper torso, lying on the floor by the table legs. The other man was heavy, and lay where he had fallen, an oblong lump on the dirty floor.

Townsend walked around the corner of the porch and through the screened door. He looked at the wound in the fat man's head, and didn't touch him, passing on around the sofa to where Broderick lay beside the table. He was still, one eye gone, the other staring vacantly into eternity. Townsend put the gun barrel in Broderick's ear and shot him again.

He looked at the material on the table that Broderick had been working on. There was a soft briefcase and some papers. The mechanical pencil Broderick had been using lay on the linoleum floor near the wall. Townsend put the papers into the open briefcase, zipped it up and hurried down the front steps.

He stayed out on the harder wet beach this time, and ran the half mile to the car at a brisk jog, the briefcase in one hand, the gun in the other. He crossed the dune, and slowing, crept over the edge until he could see the car. It was as he had left it, with no one in sight.

He threw the case and rifle onto the passenger seat, started the car and drove straight through the island without incident. He looked for the van as he passed lighted convenience stores and fast-food places, thinking that the man might try to use a public phone to report the attack. He didn't see it again, anywhere.

He turned south on the Savannah highway, stopping only once along the way for a moment, where the marshes approached the highway. Leaving the car running, he took the rifle down near the water and threw it as far as he could into the tall swamp grass. He got back into the car and drove on to Savannah. There, he took Highway 16 west, back to Atlanta.

The next day, Jack Townsend checked out of his Atlanta hotel, and took his scheduled flight back to San Jose. He had left the little Volkswagen in the hotel parking lot, its VIN number removed and the registration papers destroyed. He had never registered the sale.

XXXI

"By God, something is finally beginning to break our way," said Teller.

Edward Nigel Teller was named after the great physicist (his father had given himself second billing) in his father's futile hope that it would direct Edward's destiny. It hadn't. At sixty, Eddie was active and incorrigible, a genuine colorful character who either rubbed off on people, or made them despise him. True to form, if you liked him, he liked you back, if you didn't, he didn't give a damn. His war-worn body was still as flat and hard as pavement, and he wasn't afraid of Satan himself.

Naturally outgoing and friendly, Teller was nonetheless a purposeful man, whose outward charm and submerged focus had made him an incomparably efficient and successful agent during the "bomb years," as he referred to the Cold War era.

At the moment, he was standing in front of his bookshelf, his hands working at eye level, trying to thread a Justin Wilson tape on his old reel-to-reel machine in order to rewind it. "One of these days, I got to get a machine with automatic rewind," he observed.

Ortiz and Townsend sat on the sofa, each with a Miller Lite in his hand.

"Why don't you get rid of that antique and get a cassette player?" asked Townsend.

"Ah! Those damn things don't give true sound," replied Teller, "don't have the bandwidth."

"Getting back to the issue, what are we going to do with this information?" asked Ortiz. "We really can't prove anything, so any kind of action through the civil authorities or news media is a wasted effort."

"Maybe not," said Teller, setting the tape reels in motion and resuming his seat in the adjacent chair. "If we could get the plot aired, even as an unconfirmed rumor, it would make the bastards more reluctant to go through with it. It would have to be carried nationwide, though. A local broadcast wouldn't do it."

"Who are we going to get to air it?" asked Townsend. "The conventional media wouldn't touch it."

"How about taking a hostage, and forcing them to air it?" asked Ortiz. "It could be the only way."

"Who do we get to sacrifice himself by holing up with a hostage?" responded Teller sarcastically.

"There is a way," said Townsend. "The hostage could be left alone—tied up with a fake radio-controlled bomb. That way, nobody gets caught."

"This is bullshit, guys, get serious," said Teller. "First, you would have to kidnap someone in the limelight in order for it to work. You kidnap some ordinary Joe, and you'll spent two days arguing with the local cops, and accomplish absolutely nothing. We don't even know if they will go through with it, now that Broderick has bought the farm, and we don't know what their timetable is. Who are we going to grab on short notice?" He waved his hand at the absurdity of it and took a pull on his beer.

Townsend got up and walked casually to the window, his hands in his pockets. He gazed absently at three boys playing in the street with their skateboards. "I keep remembering that trailer," he said.

"What trailer?" asked Ortiz.

Townsend turned back toward the room. "In South Carolina. Broderick had a small cargo trailer sitting by the house, with two satellite dishes on it. It was one of those ready-com kits, Eddie, with its own gas generator and everything you need to set up a quickie, satellite groundstation.

"I don't know why, but the image of it—sitting there with its wheels half-buried in the sand, and its dishes aimed at the sky—has stuck in my mind. Listen, could we tap into a commercial satellite transmission and broadcast our message—you know, interrupt the news or something?"

"No good," said Teller. "Everything is filtered; you know that, Jimmy."

"I thought you once told me that everything but sports is filtered," contributed Ortiz, looking at Teller.

Teller and Townsend looked at Ortiz, then at each other, their faces lighting up.

"Eureka!" said Teller, grinning maliciously and rubbing his hands together in the classic parody of the mad scientist. "You got the transponder codes, Jimmy?"

"That was my job in Broderick's outfit," grinned Townsend. "Ain't irony grand?"

"What are we going to say?" asked Ortiz. "We don't want to come off like a bunch of whackos."

"We'll set it up just like a news broadcast," said Townsend, returning to his seat. He leaned forward earnestly, "The community college has a closed-circuit TV studio. It's for their television communications courses. Has a news desk, studio and everything. It's attached to the drama club theater building. Has satellite dishes on the roof, tape equipment—the works. We could produce the tape and broadcast from there—and I just happen to know a trained newscaster. Eve can write the material and orchestrate the production."

"Will they let you use it?" asked Ortiz.

"I didn't intend to ask," responded Townsend. "We'll go in at night, do our thing, and leave without anyone knowing. We also need to get to the TV station transmitter that's going to carry the game. We have to install an uplink translator. We also have to rig things so that the transmitted signal can't be interrupted from a remote site," he explained for Ortiz' benefit. "We'll wire in a relay that switches all feed circuits directly to our translator, and run a direct auxiliary power circuit as well. We'll have to rig the station monitors so that the feed they see is strictly from their remote camera at the game.

We don't want them trying to pull the plug until we're through. Sixty seconds ought to be enough."

"Who's going to do all that?" asked Ortiz.

"Meet the guru of intelligence communications," said Townsend, extending an introductory hand toward Teller.

Teller put his thumbs in the armpits of his sportshirt, pushing outward in a parody of suspenders. He grinned at Ortiz with wide-open eyes, bobbed his eyebrows up and down several times in a Groucho Marx impersonation, and said, "You're a hell of straight man, Hector. We couldn't have done it without you."

Ortiz sneered in mock derision, "You're ten years out of date with the technology, you old dipstick. You're going to stick your fingers in an electrical circuit and fry your dumb ass. Or the both of you will get your dicks shot off by some security guard."

"Why Hector," Teller said in his most convincing Peter Lorre, "I never knew you could be so vulgar."

"You two old farts invented vulgar," laughed Townsend. "But seriously, Hector, the stuff Eddie was playing with ten years ago *is* today's technology. Back when TV cameras were too big to carry, he installed a miniature CCD camera in a shower head in one of the women's dressing rooms in the United Nations, and fed its output to one of the security monitors. It was there for almost a year before the security chief discovered it."

"Didn't the security guards know it was there?"

Teller winked at Ortiz, "Of course they did. Those guys still love me."

"And on that note, I'd better be leaving," said Townsend. "I've got to pick up Eve in town."

"How is she holding up?" asked Teller.

"She's fine. She's a tough little trooper underneath, and she'll spring back, once her life begins to return to normal. There is no way of knowing for sure what Broderick may have set in motion. I don't think he had a fix on us though, and I think it'll probably fade away now that he's dead. I can't continue to keep her cooped up like a prisoner, in any case. I can't help wondering what will happen to *us* when she doesn't need to depend on me anymore," he confided, gazing introspectively at the beer bottle in his hand. "I'm not exactly what she's used to."

Ortiz leaned over, put his hand on Townsend's knee. "Eve loves you, son. Anyone can see it. The only thing that's going to happen, when all this shit is over, is that the light we occasionally glimpse behind her face is going to brighten and burn steady. She's a keeper, my boy. If she was going to fold, she would have left you months ago."

Townsend smiled. "I hope you're right."

"Of course we are," said Ortiz. He patted Townsend's knee, rising from the sofa. "Tell her that Eddie and I both want her body, and we'll gladly kill you for your insurance and run away with her. All she has to do is give us the high sign, and you're history."

"I think she's fond enough of you two old goats that she might consider it," Townsend said ruefully, getting up. "But I'll tell her you said hi."

XXXII

"What are we going to do about Gene, Hector? We can't just leave him to their mercy, can we?" asked Paul Haas. He twirled the ice in his glass, regarding it absently. He and Ortiz sat smoking cigars and sipping bourbon in the warmly lit living room of Haas' Santa Clara home.

"No, but Leland thinks he'll be all right for a while. We don't know where they're holding him, and we can't very well start blasting away in order to save him. We'll have to go about it some other way. In any case, he'll have to wait. We've got more pressing business."

"This gas-bomb thing?"

"No. Leland has that under control, I think. I'm going to need your help with the telemetry on that ghost of yours. Diana is closing in."

"Do you think they can find it?"

"You've got to give them credit. Those boys really are pretty good."

"You sound like you admire them."

"It's wrong to downplay your opponent's ability, Paul. To win, you have to operate on facts, not prejudice. Besides, most of them are just young people that have been indoctrinated to think they are being patriotic—serving their country. We shouldn't lose sight of that."

"Bullshit, Hector! Those 'young people' know the difference between shooting at the soldiers of a foreign enemy, and shooting American citizens. Nobody is that fucking stupid."

"Well, obviously, some of them are. They've been taught a command structure that does not include civilians, except for the President and Secretary of Defense, and they've had it drilled into them to think that they are better than their civilian brothers and sisters. Also, they've been isolated demographically as much as possible from their own kind in the past few years. That alone shows you that it was coming; it was being planned."

"What do you mean, 'isolated demographically'?"

Ortiz looked at him curiously. "I thought you knew. Remember that Colonel Hayes that took over the Domestic Policy Office a few years ago? He gave a speech at the ROTC graduation in San Diego last year. No? Well, no matter. Anyway, he had almost all enlistees and junior officers in the military, with more than two years of service remaining, relocated. He established new recruiting and training policies. Kids from the southeast ended up being trained and stationed in the northwest, and vice-versa. Kids from L.A. ended up at Newport News or Fort Bragg, Kentucky. He wanted them to feel as little kinship with the local civilians as possible.

"He also intensified training in riot control. Didn't you hear David Goldstein's talk on this just before Christmas?"

"How could I? I was in Chile."

Ortiz nodded, "So you were; so you were."

"What did David suggest we do about the military mentality?"

"Well, he actually had a few good ideas for a change. I thought so, anyway. For one, he wanted to change the Pledge of Allegiance."

"That sounds like David," Haas said sarcastically, rolling his eyes at the ceiling.

"He has a point," said Ortiz, waving Haas down. "For example, he suggested that it be made mandatory, that every civil servant—from the lowliest private in the military to the President himself—formally stand at the beginning of the workday, and recite the Pledge of

Allegiance. He wants the police, the dogcatcher, the county clerk to do it. He also suggested the words be changed to: 'I pledge allegiance to the people of the United States of America, and to the Constitution I am sworn to uphold.' There's more, but you get the idea. It's the same thing that the women's movement has been trying to do—instill ideas and make people think about old, ingrained attitudes by making them sensitive to the meaning and appropriateness of words."

"You think it would work?"

"Can't hurt. We grew up pledging allegiance 'to the flag, and to the republic for which it stands.' Nothing wrong with that, in itself, but somewhere along the way, we came to subconsciously believe that the 'republic' was the people who run government—a few dozen civil servants—the hired help.

"It seems kind of crazy when you stop to think about it. It's a battle for minds. Human beings, for some indefinable reason, abhor logic. Otherwise, they couldn't be controlled. They like rituals, and chants, and symbols—all that mindless crap. It gets their blood pumping, and the adrenaline flowing, and they don't want to know if it makes sense. It's like the cereal commercials on TV; if they thought that it was good for them, or made sense, it would spoil it for them. They wouldn't eat it.

"Why do you think they like spectator sports so much? Why do people boogying around a dance floor suddenly feel foolish if someone turns the music off? Or the lights on? It's because no one would be caught dead acting like a spastic chimp with a corncob up his ass, except under certain, programmed as acceptable, conditions."

"You would have made a fair psychologist," said Haas.

"Comes from learning to live with prima-donna-scientist schleps like you, all my life." Ortiz gave him a Cheshire grin.

"Pity you didn't learn to psychoanalyze yourself. Maybe you wouldn't be such an asshole," retorted Haas, smiling back extravagantly.

"How about another whiskey?"

"Coming up," Haas said, rising to do the honors. "Where is Leland, anyway?"

"He's freezing his tail off in Zurich."

"What's he doing in Switzerland?"

"They're getting ready to put their system up. Sydney is almost ready, too. He'll be going there next."

"What about the Chinese? And the Russian military? Won't they see them?"

"It can't be helped. We could theorize for years on what their reaction might be, and still be wrong in the end. For my money, the sooner we get them in place, the better off we'll be, no matter what they do."

"Where are we going to be launching from?"

"Bonn, Germany, and a place near Woomera in Australia."

"Isn't the Space Command at Woomera?"

"Yes. We'll be launching from practically under their noses. There will be a small diversion to occupy the Air Force people at the site, but everyone else in the country will think its an official shot from Woomera AF Space Com."

"Pretty damned clever."

"I think so, too."

"How did they set it up without anybody knowing? How did they construct the rockets?"

"They didn't. They bought two ex-Soviet, truck-mounted ICBMs, and modified them with strap-on solid boosters and a bigger delivery capsule. Seems you can buy any kind of military hardware in the Balkan republics now. They broke the missiles down and shipped them out as sewage plant equipment, leaving the warheads behind. The one near Bonn was reconstructed in a barn."

"That's amazing. I guess, deep down, I never really thought we would be able to pull it off."

"It wasn't that hard—finding a way to get them up. Hell, we did it with NASA, twice in two weeks, but thanks to you and Leland, we had *something* to put up there. You're both very remarkable men. Tesla would have been proud of you. So would Einstein. I intend to hand you the Nobel, personally."

Haas smiled and colored at Ortiz' facetious flattery. The smile turned to a frown, and he said, "I feel like Leland does, Hector. We've paid a dear price for what we've done. I don't even want to kid about getting a prize for it. My only hope of consolation is that we succeed in what we're trying to do. I couldn't live with myself if all those people died for nothing."

XXXIII

President Vanderbilt paced the room thoughtfully, one hand holding a smoking cigar, from which he took an occasional puff, his other hand in his pocket.

The large Georgian manor house suited him. It wasn't as big as the White House had been, but it was big enough. In some ways, it was more palatial, with its sweeping staircases and interior columns that reached upwards thirty feet in the reception hall. The floor-to-ceiling windows of his new office looked out into a beautifully-manicured garden that was just beginning to bloom. Huge magnolias and fir trees formed shaded canopies and screened, open glens in a parklike vista of sculptured shrubbery and flower-bordered paths. In many ways, he liked the southern city much better than Washington. Parts of it, like the section he was in, reminded him of the great estates and houses of the landed English nobility of days gone by. It suited Vanderbilt's image of self.

"Are you telling me that the man who killed Broderick is one of our own agents?" he asked.

He spoke with the Director of the C.I.A., Orville Tomlinson, and his Deputy Chief of Operations for Internal Affairs, Frank Ketchum. Vice President Joseph Miller was present also.

Tomlinson and Ketchum were standard-issue Washington civil managers—medium height, gray suit, nondescript haircut. Seeing a crowd of them together made one think of a bunch of actors that all came out of clone-makeup at the same time.

Perhaps that's what they were, after all, Vanderbilt thought.

Ketchum was briefing him. "The man is a rogue, Mr. President, wanted by the agency. His name is James Reed. He was a computer and telecommunications expert who was recruited for Broderick's section from Covert Operations, just last year. He had a good record—maybe too good. He apparently didn't fit in at Special Ops. Broderick reported a problem with him when he was ordered to eliminate a woman newscaster in Indiana. Reed objected to killing an American citizen.

"He ended up wrecking the hit on the woman, then he disappeared. So did the woman. Broderick had an APB out on him, but couldn't get a whisper.

"From what we know of Reed, it's not surprising. He was a good field agent, as well as being a technical specialist. He worked the Middle East for eight years."

"Why didn't Broderick just have him reassigned to another section?" asked Vanderbilt, stopping his pacing to look at Ketchum and to take a puff on his cigar.

"You know . . . or rather you knew Broderick, sir. He tried to force Reed to go through with it. He was a size-conscious little tyrant, and he could never stand it when a big guy like Reed defied him. He wanted to break Reed—get a hold on him so he could bring him to his knees."

"Yes, I knew the little snake," said Vanderbilt. "Except for the fact that we're going to lose his contacts, I can't say I'm especially sorry that he's bought the farm. What are we going to do about that end of things?"

"We're on it. As secretive as Broderick was, we managed to discover some of his ties. It will take some time to make friends, but introductions are under way. We're spreading a little money where it will do the most good. The local fish are biting, but naturally, the international connections are cautious. It will take awhile, but it will happen."

"Are they that important to us?"

"It always helps to have the local talent on your side,

when you're doing something in a foreign country. It would make things a lot more difficult without it. It's awfully time consuming trying to recruit people to sell out their countrymen. Chancy, too. You never know if you'll recruit some citizen with ideas of patriotism, who will alert others and mess things up. Also, it's messy to clean up after amateurs, if anything goes wrong. No, it's always best to work with pros."

"Where is this Reed, now?"

"Working for a firm called Prouss Engineering in Mountain View, California. Going by the name of Townsend. Before he hit Broderick, he used an inside buddy named Fred von Braun in Atlanta, to gain access into the community computer, and load in a background file and an industrial security clearance. Von Braun got nervous when Reed told him that he was looking for Broderick and started preaching a lot of anti-government crap to him. He was able to get away from Reed long enough to leave a phone message for his section supervisor, but he wasn't very coherent. Really upset. Didn't really know what information Reed entered, but knew it was for a low-level industrial clearance.

"After that, it was easy. We just looked at all the files written to the system that were not on the previous day's backup tapes, found the one that fit the time period, and *voila!* Reed must have found out that von Braun gave him up, though. The kid was found dead in an engineered car accident, on the outskirts of Atlanta. Broken neck."

"Why do you suppose Reed wanted an industrial clearance?" asked Vanderbilt. "What good would that do him?"

Ketchum thought a minute. "In my opinion, he just wanted to disappear, Mr. President. He needed a clearance to work on federal defense contracts; that's his company's primary business. They don't do anything top secret, just civil and industrial engineering projects and the like. He's taken a new identity, and lists a wife. The physical address he gave is phony, we've already checked that out. We'll find that out in the next few days, though."

"Why bother?"

"I beg your pardon, sir?"

"Forget him. If he's not a threat, let it go. We've got more important things to worry about than to waste manpower trying to get revenge on some guy just because he fell out with Broderick. We know where to find him, if we decide we want him. If he's on the run, he's also watchful, and he's a trained agent. Why risk a potentially messy business? We may even want to bring him back in at some point in the future. Doesn't pay to waste resources, Ketchum."

"Aye, sir. Guess you're right."

"Of course I am. Let him keep his clearance, and his job. Let him get fat and comfortable. Hell, I feel like sending him a cigar for disposing of that arrogant, little bastard." Vanderbilt smiled, "I never liked him."

Everyone laughed.

"Let's get down to business," said Vanderbilt. "Who is going to do the L.A. job?"

Ketchum looked at Tomlinson, who returned his look and nodded. Ketchum spoke, "We have an Air Force major named Donahue, and two of our agents, both former pilots. They will each lead a crew of three. We have two KC-10's and a C-5 at China Lake, being outfitted with spray equipment. They'll fly into Miramar Naval Air Station and fuel up there. The fuel is already in storage tanks there. Between them, they can deliver almost a million pounds of fuel to L.A.

"The basic plan is for them to approach along the coast and cut inland near Long Beach. They'll follow the San Diego Freeway north, and begin spraying somewhere near Inglewood. They'll make a U-turn when they reach the San Fernando valley, and follow the Hollywood Freeway south until their tanks are empty. Then, they'll turn inland over the mountains and return to China Lake. We have an array of incendiary shells set up at a private residence just off Mulholland Drive.

They will be fired by remote control just as soon as the aircraft are clear."

"How many people know about this?" asked Vanderbilt.

"Just the pilots and the nine crewmen," said Ketchum. "To everyone else, it's just a training flight."

"Good!" said Vanderbilt. "It looks like you've done well. One slight change, though. I want you to fire the shells before the planes get clear."

"But, sir . . ." exclaimed Ketchum, his face aghast.

"You have a question, Frank?" Vanderbilt stood staring coldly at Ketchum.

Ketchum held his startled expression for another moment, then subsided. "No, sir," he said.

"Good. Is the camera coverage arranged?"

Tomlinson answered. "Yes, sir. We've arranged for a news crew to be shooting a late-evening, celebrity, memorial-dedication ceremony at Wildwood Canyon Park, just outside Burbank. We've arranged the camera angles and timed the ceremony so that the cameras will be aimed back toward Hollywood when the atmosphere is ignited. It will be a direct satellite feed. All the wire services will have it within seconds, and it will no doubt be aired within minutes."

"What is your estimate of the damage?" Vanderbilt stood before a window, his back to the room, looking out at a newly budding oleander screen that grew along a white picket fence. The fence abutted both sides of a gate that was surmounted by a white, latticework arbor. The arbor was covered with climbing roses, and framed a storybook path that led away into the trees.

He took a puff on the cigar clamped between his teeth; his hands were clasped behind his back.

"A million, minimum. Maybe two," answered Ketchum.

"That ought to do it," Vanderbilt said, and smiled.

XXXIV

It was mid-March. Eve Townsend, Hector Ortiz, Ted Wallace, and Wallace's wife Jenny sat at the Townsends' kitchen table playing a board game and talking. Teller and Townsend sat in front of the TV set in the adjacent living room. The sound was turned low on the TV, and the two men were absently sipping beer and watching a basketball game as they talked.

Eve moved a piece on the board, then got up and removed a swollen bag of popcorn from the beeping microwave oven. She took two bowls from the cupboard and prepared one for each group, adding a little salt and two sets of paper napkins.

"Would you take this to the boys, Hector?" Eve asked, handing him one of the bowls.

"Sure," he said, taking the bowl into the living room. "Hey, you spooks want some popcorn? The James Bond Code does allow popcorn, doesn't it?"

Townsend looked at Teller with a pained expression. "Why don't you get him fixed?"

Teller glanced up at Ortiz as the latter handed him the bowl and napkins. "Oh, no! You never want to castrate a Mexican. It's that Latin macho thing. They'll go weird on you. He'd probably get religion, and I'd have to shoot him. Then where would I be?"

"Dead in a ditch, you old gringo cocksucker. What're you two hatching up out here, anyway?" Ortiz responded, unperturbed.

"I think you two ought to get married," grinned

Townsend. "You've already got the adjustment period out of the way."

"I could never live with him," said Ortiz. "He has disgusting bathroom habits."

"Just a word of warning, Jimmy," said Teller, "never get drunk at his house and pee on his toilet seat. He'll never let you forget it."

"The toilet seat, the wall, the floor, the lavatory cabinet, the bathtub . . ." said Ortiz, walking back to the kitchen.

"See?" said Teller, shrugging helplessly at Townsend.

Townsend doubled over, laughing. Teller joined in, their laughter drawing mildly interested glances from those in the kitchen. Townsend finally caught his breath, and subsided with a sigh of weary pleasure. "I really envy you two," he said. "I've only ever had one friend that close. Someone I could share everything with." He told Teller about a high school chum he had grown up with named David Lebowitz. "When I went to the Middle East, we lost contact. Our lives went separate ways. Now, I can't even contact him without putting him in danger. I wish that I had made more of an effort to keep in touch with him. I really miss that rapport." He smiled, slightly shame-faced. "I am beginning to get something like that back, just being among you guys. I can't tell you how much it means to me, Eddie, your taking me in."

"Aw, pshaw," said Teller. "You're among friends, Jimmy. Things are going to get better. You just settle into that new job and make a life for yourself and Eve. Forget the political shit. That will take care of itself."

"What about what Broderick has set in motion? We can't let that happen," said Townsend.

"That's being handled. I've got a few active contacts yet," said Teller. "You can relax, as far as that is concerned. Believe me, I wouldn't say it if it wasn't true. You did your part by finding out about it."

"You mean you don't want to do the newscast thing?"

"We considered it. It's just not necessary, Jimmy.

People are so sick of hearing propaganda that it probably wouldn't accomplish much, anyway. Whether they did manage to take out a city or not, they would say that your 'newscast' was just a preplanned effort to shift the blame. How do John and Jane Q. Public separate the truth? That's the whole thing with these entrenched bastards and their bought-and-paid-for media: they can turn almost anything to their advantage. If the nationalists do something good, they find a way to take credit for it, then they turn around and kill a few civilians and say that nationalist radicals did it. Nature always favors the weeds, Jimmy, not the flowers. The only way to stop them from taking over the garden is to pluck them out."

Townsend shook his head, sadly. "I wish that I could come up with some way that I could prove myself to you guys. I think all of you know more than you're telling me. I understand your caution—I could be a plant, as far as you know. I really want to help, though, and of course, I'm curious to know a bigger part of the picture."

"We have shown you our trust, Jimmy. Hector and I have put our lives in your hands by not turning you in. You know that it wouldn't make a damn to the boys in power, that there is no concrete proof that we've done anything wrong. If you turned us in on suspicion of treason, we would either die in prison, being tortured, or killed outright when we resisted arrest. Hector and I made that decision, for ourselves. We don't have the right to put anyone else at risk. You're going to have to leave it at that, Jimmy."

"I understand," said Townsend. "I'll continue to do what I can, though, on my own. It's my fight, too."

Teller saluted him with a raised bottle of beer, saying, "A man's gotta do what a man's gotta do, Jimmy. Just so we don't stumble over each other, though, let's keep each other informed of our whereabouts, okay?"

Townsend lifted his bottle in return, and smiled. "You got it."

XXXV

Three massive planes lifted off the China Lake runway at 0400 on March 21. Like three huge vultures, they wheeled slowly in the night sky, until they were on a heading for Miramar NAS on the California coast.

Two of them were Air Force KC-10's—giant tanker planes used for refueling strategic bombers during flight. The other was a mammoth C-5 cargo plane which was normally used to transport troops, supplies and heavy equipment, such as tanks and armored fighting vehicles, into battle zones.

All three planes had been fitted with spray heads and piping under their wings, and high-volume pumps. A liner of Hypalon rubber had been cut to fit inside the huge cargo bay of the C-5, and seamed together with cement and a heat gun to create a liquid-tight bladder, in order to turn the plane into a tanker. Other engineering modifications had also been necessary, including honeycomb aluminum baffles inside the bladder to prevent sloshing and shifting of the fuel weight, and the unstable flight dynamics that could result.

The fleeting shadows of the three aircraft raced across the moonlit desert, following the fading roar of their engines. The flight was without incident, and they landed at Miramar NAS forty minutes after takeoff. The flight commander presented his orders and flight plan to the operations officer at Miramar. When they had been processed, the nine crewmen were taken to breakfast at the Officers' Mess, and then to a BOQ barracks where they could rest and get some sleep.

It took the Miramar POL crews twelve hours to fuel the three cavernous tanker aircraft, and because heat causes fuel to expand, and reduces carrying capacity, the refueling crew had to wait until the following evening to top off the tanks—after the sun had set and ambient temperatures had fallen.

The adaptation of the C-5's cargo hold, and the spray equipment under the wings of the planes had caused some comment among the POL crew members at Miramar. No explanation was forthcoming, though, so the crew had simply followed orders and fueled the planes.

At 21:30 hours that same day, as night was falling and lights began twinkling along the populous Pacific coast, the planes lifted ponderously off the runway at Miramar, and headed west, out over the ocean, climbing to their planned altitude. From a height of ten thousand feet, they could still see the afterglow of the sun, setting in the west.

Their "official" flight plan called for a bomber refueling exercise fifty miles off the California coast, near Los Angeles. Once they were out over the ocean, at the fifty-mile point, the planes turned north. After turning, Major Donahue, the Air Force officer who was in command of the flight, gave the order to pressurize the spray discharge systems. He wanted to run a visual check before they lost the daylight.

"TP Two; TP Three; turn on your accumulator pumps and pressurize your lines."

"TP One, this is TP Two. Pumps are running. We're holding 200 psi."

"TP One, this is TP Three. Pressure is steady at 205 psi."

"Good. I want to run a test. Station your crews so they can see the release nozzles, and release for five seconds on my mark."

There were a few moments of silence as the flight crews got into position, then:

"TP Three. Ready when you are."

"TP Two. Same here."

"Okay, on three. One, two, three, mark!"

A fog of atomized fuel filled the wakes of the aircraft for five seconds, then disappeared in the distance as the valves were closed.

"TP Two, all nozzles are working fine."

"TP Three, we're good, too."

"Fine. Mine are working, too. Looks like we're good to go."

Five minutes later, the planes were ten miles south-southeast of Santa Catalina Island, losing altitude as they approached Long Beach.

Then, for an instant, their shadows appeared starkly on the surface of the dark ocean, like figures in the beam of a flashlight casting their images on a wall. Then they were gone.

Observers along the southern end of Santa Catalina saw a brilliant flash in the star-studded sky, then an angry, red, fireball cloud that darkened and disappeared as they watched. A few seconds afterward, they heard a loud, popping concatenation of sound, like that of a distant fireworks display. They could not see in the darkness, as a waterspout formed out of an area of boiling sea, just where the fleeting images of the planes had been, nor note the twisting flume heading out to sea, calving a second waterspout, then another, as it went. Fortunately, storm warnings had been issued earlier that afternoon, for impending weather from the west, and no boats or ships were in the area.

The following day, the military reported the loss of three planes on a training exercise, just off the California coast. The names of the crewmen were being withheld, pending notification of next of kin. In the following days, no names were forthcoming, and the incident passed from the minds of the public and the press.

Obermiller stared dazedly at the acoustic tile of the ceiling. The drugs made it hard to focus his eyes. One eye was almost blind. It had a dark spot in it that almost completely obscured his vision. How many days had it been? He didn't know; the days had run together.

They had him strapped to a gurney, even his head was strapped in place. His gums were bleeding. The bleeding and blindness was probably caused by something in the mixture of drugs, he thought. A side effect. The CD changer paused and started over again. It played four rap-music chants, over and over. It never stopped. When they weren't grilling him, they woke him every two hours with a shot of something that made him burn and itch inside, all through his veins. He wondered how long it would take. He hadn't had solid food in three days, and his crotch was raw from his feces and urine. They had worked over him in shifts, all the first day and part of the second. Now, they were sleeping eight hours between trials. This was the fourth or fifth period of torture. Each lasted for a week to ten days, he thought, then was offset by a few days of recovery and decent food, and the freedom of his room. He was growing weaker. During the last intermission, he hadn't been able to get out of bed until almost the day before they started again. His joints ached with lack of movement, as with advanced arthritis. He knew that if he survived, he would likely be crippled for the rest of his life. His internal organs were failing, too. He was passing blood in his urine and bowel movements.

He had alternately cursed Leland for getting him into this mess, and prayed that he would fire the machine at his tormentors, and kill them all. He wanted them to die, even if half the world died with them. He hadn't said a word to his captors since his arrest. Hadn't responded to their taunts and torture. They had made lewd, profane remarks about his dead mother, and denigrating comments about his manhood, about his not having "the right stuff."

Now, he was resigned. Death would be a comfort. Please, God, let it come soon, he prayed. If only he could turn on his side, bring his knees up, move his arms and head, he would be glad to curl up and sleep forever.

XXXVI

Air Force Captain John Connally stood behind Lieutenant Lewis Pritchart, watching the monitor as the seated Pritchart fired the maneuvering thrusters to position Diana into Damocles' orbital track. The thrusters were powered with CO_2 gas, an inert substance that did not leave a detectable heat signature, as a burning rocket propellant would have.

Most defensive sensing devices were equipped to look for radiant heat energy emitted by engines or electrical equipment. Diana was in reality a fairly unsophisticated piece of hardware in comparison with most terrestrial weapons systems, but for her space-oriented stealth application, she was like her namesake who, in mythology, had hunted and stalked game in the forests of the gods—a well-endowed, silent, almost invisible killer.

"What's your propellant inventory?" Connally asked.

"She's showing a hundred and sixty kilograms. That Y-Y valve is still sticking. It's getting better, loosening up, but I'm still a little afraid to use it. It takes more gas, because you have to add moment, then reduce it, but I'd rather rotate around and bring another set of thrusters to bear, than risk losing all her propellant and spinning her out of orbit."

"What's your velocity and trajectory, now?"

"She's slowed to seventy-five hundred meters per second. She's increasing orbit radius by two meters per minute. She'll cross Damocles' orbital track in about four hours."

"That's close to the predicted vertical vector. What's the horizontal like?"

"She's on the money, now. If Damocles is in a really stable orbit, he'll run right into her on that plane. Like billiard balls. Is the plan of engagement still the same?"

"Yes," said Connally. "Diana will increase orbit radius twenty-five kilometers above Damocles' track, slowing so that he is accreting velocity with respect to her. As he swings around the limb of the earth at two hundred and forty degrees, she will begin firing thrusters, picking up velocity and falling inward into Damocles' path. She'll be waiting for him at a hundred and ten degrees west."

"What about her targeting system? And the firing sequence? What was decided?"

"Well, since we don't have anything to practice on, we've got to assume that her aiming optics are in alignment. As for the firing sequence, we won't have the luxury of repositioning after each shot, and trying it again. The brass have decided to manually fire all twenty-four projectiles at once. If we miss, the best we can hope for is a head-on collision. That's the reason her attitude is so critical when the projectiles are fired. We don't want the recoil moments to push her out of Damocles' path. Even if those missiles are dead-on, we still want Diana and Damocles to collide. Her braking thrusters are programmed to fire as soon as her armory is empty. She and Damocles should impact at almost sixty meters per second, relative."

"Unless Damocles sees her coming, and blows her out of the sky."

"Yes. There is always that possibility," said Connally, sighing loudly.

"Will people on the ground see it, you think?"

"If it's a clear night, people in Arizona might see a pinprick flare of light with the naked eye. Of course, if we miss, and Damocles retaliates, they will get a hell of a show."

"Yeah, I've been thinking about that, too. If we are one of the military targets programmed into his fire control system, we are likely to miss seeing that show. We will be the show."

Connally rolled his eyes, an expression of long-suffering patience on his face. "That's what I like about you, Pritchart. You're such a fucking optimist."

XXXVII

"I want to speak to Dr. Thelma Richards please," Ortiz said into the phone. "Yes, I'll hold."

He sat at his desk, played with the hem of his lab coat and stared at it introspectively, his mind far away. A greeting in the earpiece brought him back to the present.

"Hi, babe. How's my gal?"

"Hector, you old horse's ass, where are you?"

"I'm in my office; where else would I be?"

"Damn," she responded, "the way my secretary spoke, I thought you were nearby. I wanted to plant a big, sloppy kiss on your old, bald head."

"Hell, I'll come down there for that. I'd rather you scrubbed my back, though."

"Not that the thought isn't somewhat intriguing, but Charlie might object to that effusive of a greeting."

"That's silly. Charlie is my best compadre. We swore to share everything, years ago."

"Oh, yeah? Whom have you been sharing with him? Not that little Rosie-thing you were dating the last time I saw you, huh?"

"Oh, that reminds me, tell Charlie that Rosie asked about him. She especially wanted to know if his wife still doesn't understand him."

"You miserable old bastard. Did you just run out of people there to aggravate, or do you actually want something?"

"Well, really I just wanted to hear you talk dirty to me, but as an excuse to call, I thought I might ask you how Butch is doing."

"He's holding up. Between Zeke and Joe Dykes, and a weekly call from yours truly, he has a lot of support, and he's putting up a brave front. At least, to the world."

"Is he ready to come in with us?"

"I just don't know, Hector. I've never even hinted at it, you know? He doesn't know anything. It makes me feel like a traitorous bitch every time I talk to him. He's suffered a lot over all those deaths. We all have, but with him it's really bad. He feels responsible. You would think he was involved, the way he sits and stews over it, or that he did it all by himself.

"Anyway, it seems really rotten for me to know and not tell him, but I halfway worry that it'll push him over the edge if I do."

"I know how you feel, babe, and you have to be sure of his reaction before you tell him. It's still early days. We can't come out of the closet, yet. There is too much at stake."

"I know, I know. Not to worry. Tell me again, why he has to know at all. At least, why right now?"

"Well, it's not that urgent, but within a few months, when all this is over, he's going to have a hell of a lot of money to spend, and we want to hit the ground running. The economy is going to need the jobs in order to recover quickly and put these times behind us. He has a couple of years of planning to accomplish in a few months. The sooner he's on board, or out of the way if it comes to that, the better off we're going to be."

"You sound heartless, Hector."

"You know I don't mean to be. I've got to be pragmatic, though. We've been utterly callous with the lives of millions; we can't quit now, and know we spent those lives for nothing, just to spare the feelings of one of our own. That means I have to be an asshole to my friends, also. I don't like it, and it's not the real me. It's who I have to be, for now."

"I know, Hector. I didn't mean it." She sighed. "I'll find a way to break it to him, feel him out, talk him into it. I'll fly back to Atlanta this weekend, if he's free."

"Thanks, babe. If he joins up, he'll have the opportunity to accomplish more than any of his predecessors. The major emphasis is going to be on expansion of science and technology, and the creation of jobs in humanitarian enterprises. It will be a time of dreams come true for the entire world. I want him to be a part of it."

"You make it sound like heaven. I'll do my best to convey that idea to Butch."

"Okay. Come up and see me, if the opportunity arises. Bring Charlie. I want to see if I can talk him into conjugal rights."

"Why Hector, I thought you were straight."

"You know what I mean, you shameless hussy. Charlie is kind of cute, though, when you think about it."

Later that night, Hector Ortiz and Paul Haas sat in a deserted laboratory at Stanford University. It was early on a Tuesday morning, and they had been up most of the night. They had two computers and two large monitors set up side-by-side on a lab table, and both men sat on stools in front of them, watching the screen on Haas' monitor intently as two dots of light moved slowly across a fixed, glowing gridwork of lines. Ortiz' monitor showed a concentric circle with a cross-hair, and a single point of light in its center. A speakerphone and encryptor sat on the bench near the computer, and the red light showed an active circuit. A panel with a glowing, green indicator light and a push-button switch sat in front of Ortiz. The phone was tied into a satellite transponder and dish antenna on the roof.

"How is your signal now, Leland?" Haas said into the phone.

"Much better," came the reply. "I've got my gain at maximum, though. Something is interfering with the relay satellite. George is boosting that signal now. Ah! There it is now, strong and steady. I can reduce my gain now."

Haas and Ortiz listened to vague words and sounds as the people on the other end of the phone talked to one another in the background, then the man on the other end was addressing them directly again.

"What is your telemetry telling you, Paul? I want to cross-check the range with you as they close. Ready on my mark . . . one, two, three, mark. I'm reading 2870.1 meters. What have you got?"

"I've got exactly 2869.7 meters. Our calibration is pretty close. It will be only a few centimeters difference by the time they're within firing range."

"What is the velocity delta now?" asked the voice on the phone.

"Two meters per second, on the nose," Haas answered. "Diana will be within one kilometer in just under sixteen minutes. What do you show?"

"The same," came the answer. "All right, we're about as ready as we can get. Be sure and let me know if you see the least bit of drift out of alignment, Hector. If they miss with their weapons, we've got to make certain that impact takes place, or that our backup makes it appear so. Is the bomb armed?"

"Yes. We've got a green light," responded Ortiz. "If they miss, and if it looks like the recoil moments are pushing Diana out of alignment, I will detonate the explosive."

"Do it anyway, Hector," came the response. "If they even come close with their phalanx of missiles, detonate the bomb. If they miss by a wide margin, then we'll have to wait for collision, otherwise they might suspect."

"Will do," said Ortiz. "Not to change the subject, but how did the other launches go?"

"No problems, so far. We heterodyned a signal against their radar transmitters, shifting harmonics all across their bandwidths. We used directional signals with big dishes and lots of power. The receiver circuits weren't meant to cope with that kind of gain. It blew some circuits and effectively pulled the plug at Woomera, and shut down their radar systems for a few minutes while we launched. They don't have any suspicions, as far as our contacts have heard—put it down to a simple equipment failure. One civilian airport radar reported what they thought was a military launch, since they get them regularly from that direction, but the military doesn't know what to make of it. They are passing it off as a radar glitch. They had no means of interfering with it anyway, but it's important that they think they have only the one system to contend with. Both insertions are complete, and they are on station as of yesterday afternoon, one hundred and twenty degrees apart. We're doing the final ranging-systems calibration, now."

"That's a relief," said Haas.

"I know. I'm glad it's over, too. Now all we have left to do is to carry out this little production of ours, and if it works out the way we hope, it will all be over within a few months at most. Keep your fingers crossed."

"I've got everything that I've got two of crossed," said Ortiz.

"We're getting close, Leland," interrupted Haas.

"Okay, you guys have the ball. I'll just sit back and watch."

The seconds ticked by as Ortiz and Haas waited, eyes straining for any indication that the killer satellite had fired. The distance had narrowed to eight hundred meters.

"Six point seven minutes to impact," said Haas. "Why haven't they fired?"

"They've got balls," said Ortiz. "They're risking discovery and annihilation on getting close enough to make a sure kill."

"There it is!" exclaimed Haas excitedly.

A cluster of dots raced across the screen, right to left, between the two original blips. It took less than two seconds for the cluster to meet the second, oncoming blip.

"It's dead-on, Hector. Detonate!"

On Ortiz' monitor, the cluster of lights loomed toward his screen, like a bird's-eye view of a shotgun charge. The missiles were coming directly at the satellite's camera. The image transmission time was factored into Ortiz' actions; at this range, he barely had time to see whether the projectiles would be moving in the right direction before sending the return signal to detonate the explosive. Haas had said "detonate" as the speeding projectiles left Diana's armory. A fraction of a second later, they were crossing the halfway point when Ortiz closed the switch. Ortiz thought he saw the machine markings on the tip of a closing projectile, just before the image on his monitor blanked out.

"Well, that's that," he said.

The operations center at SATCOM in Cheyenne Mountain erupted in a bedlam of cheering, yelling personnel. Captain Connally raised a fist in the air and jerked it downward, signaling victory. Technical personnel were hugging each other. The base commander looked at his deputy.

"Well, that's that," he said. "I guess I'll go make a phone call."

XXXVIII

President Vanderbilt sat back in his chair, smiling expansively at the Secretary of Defense and the Vice-President. Orville Tomlinson and Frank Ketchum were there, also. With the exception of Joseph Miller, who seldom ever smiled, all faces were lit up with satisfaction. Vanderbilt grinned forgivingly at Ketchum.

"Well, Frank, you botched the L.A. job, but it looks like the Air Force hauled your chestnuts out of the fire. The bastards are out of business, anyway. Now, I want you to openly go after them. I want you to find those sons of bitches and bring them to me. I may decide to have a summary execution by firing squad, in a city park."

"I'm not so sure that's a good idea, sir," said Tomlinson. "There is a smattering of public support out there, now that the thing is destroyed, but only a smattering. If we are going to win them back, now is not the time to run roughshod over the law. We should work them up a bit—make them remember those who were killed by the terrorists. Give me a couple of months, and you'll have a sixty percent approval rating again. Then, a quick and emotional trial, followed by a swift execution."

The smile faded from Vanderbilt's face, and he regarded Tomlinson coldly.

"If I ever need your advice, I'll ask for it, Tomlinson."

Tomlinson blanched, said nothing.

"You may as well hear this now," said Vanderbilt, surveying the ring of faces. He smiled, gloating in anticipation of their reactions to what he was about to tell them. "We have decided it's time to clamp down. Soon, there will be no further pretense of seeking public approval. We are going to place the country under martial law and kick the shit out of dissenters until the rabble fall into line. The sooner they understand their place, the better.

"You people had better do as you're told, too, and you had better do it enthusiastically if you want to remain in your elevated positions. It won't be long before having a whole loaf of bread will be a status symbol.

"If you continue to prove your loyalty, you can enjoy the good life. If not, you'll live in alleys and eat garbage, like all the rest. Is any of this sinking in?"

Tomlinson sat cowed, eyes searching the floor for some ray of security, and finding none. Ketchum had a look of resignation. Harold Tanner gazed out the window, a silent tear rolling down his cheek. Miller's expression did not change, nor did his eyes waver.

"Now, get out of here, you sniveling cowards," said Vanderbilt. "I want an expensive bottle and a cheap whore. I'm going to celebrate. A new day is dawning. I suggest to you all, either get on board, or go find a quiet place to blow your brains out. Now, get the hell out."

XXXIX

Townsend sat at his desk in the offices of Prouss Engineering in Mountain View, his elbows on the desk, his chin resting on his hands. He couldn't concentrate on the engineering statement of work that he was trying to formulate as part of his company's proposal package to ARPA, the Advanced Research Projects Agency. If their bid was successful, it would mean a feather in his cap and a healthy income for Prouss.

ALS stood for Automated Logistics System, and it was his baby. He had described the rigors of federal procurement to his new boss shortly before Christmas, and persuaded him to let Townsend spend the time to respond to an RFP—request for proposals—from ARPA. He had been excited at the prospect of doing something creative that would help lower the cost of government and help the nation in a real, definitive way. He had developed the algorithms that would make a computer able to qualify bids, canvass inventories, order supplies, monitor the progress of contracts, record transactions, weigh orders and issues against standard parameters, and query when in doubt.

It would be a smart system, capable of learning and modifying its own instruction set within certain limits, and would, given certain specific input by a contracting officer, formulate draft specifications and spit out a contract, complete with boiler-plate, in minutes.

The federal acquisition regulation was programmed into its decision matrix. It would save every sizable military base and federal installation thousands of man-hours per year in procurement costs.

Now that he had this wonderful opportunity, all he could think about was Ortiz and Teller at their archaeological dig in Chile. The two scientists had taken a couple of dozen followers and established an operations base there under the guise of a scientific expedition. They would wait out the coming war there, directing operations and gathering information via their secret satellite net. In other countries, the underground forces were holing up in similar ways.

He had suspected, even before Ortiz finally told him, that Teller and the university people were involved with the patriots somehow; he just hadn't suspected how deeply. They were the masterminds behind the whole movement.

A part of him resented their not including him in their circle of conspirators, but he understood logically that they could not risk capture and death, and the failure of the last hope of the world, out of concern for his feelings. He wondered how they were making out. He almost regretted not going with them. A summer adventure in South America would have been good for him and Eve. He would have lost his job and his project, though.

Hell, he thought, that really wasn't the reason. If there was going to be a fight, he didn't want to be somewhere else. He wanted to personally make sure the enemy paid a price for every life they took.

Unable to think, he got up and went outside to the parking lot. It was midafternoon and the weather was mild. The cedars along the front of the building moved intermittently in a gentle, westerly breeze. He ambled across the parking lot, hands in his pockets, breathing deep and taking in the beauty of the surrounding hills.

Suddenly, he saw them. A thin, dark line of dots on the western horizon that stretched out for miles. The dots were growing larger, and now he could hear the faint drone of engines. Ortiz and Teller had been right.

They had better inside information than even the C.I.A. had, because the Vice President and who knew how many high-level federal officials, were reporting to them. He stood watching as hundreds of helicopter gunships loomed into view, followed by dozens of C-130 troop transports flying at a higher altitude. As they passed over, they darkened the sky.

Townsend saw other people stepping outside to see what was going on, saw them pointing at the vast numbers of aircraft that blanketed the sky, and talking to one another in wonderment.

Townsend told his boss that he was leaving, briefly explaining what he thought was happening. The office staff looked at him as though he were demented, as if they had just realized there was a lunatic in their midst. Townsend left his drop-jawed, wide-eyed colleagues standing in the reception office, staring after him.

He felt sorry for them, but as Ortiz had said, there was no other way to wake them up. America had to be reborn in that oft-quoted, ever-doomed-to-be-repeated crucible of death and destruction before it could reaffirm what freedom is, and discover again the value of participatory government.

Townsend smiled to himself as he steered his new Jeep Cherokee onto the freeway that would take him home. Sounds corny, he thought. "Corny is good, though. I can get into corny," he said aloud, and laughed.

Eve came through the kitchen to meet him as he entered the front door. He quickly explained what was happening.

"Come into the living room," she said, "the President is on TV."

He followed her into the room, where Vanderbilt's face filled the television screen. " . . . and I urge you all to remain calm. Now that we have destroyed the infernal machine, we have to root out this widespread conspiracy in order to bring peace and safety back to the American people. You are likely to see soldiers and police in your neighborhoods during the next few weeks. Remain calm. Stay indoors during the evening hours. If they come to search your homes, cooperate gladly. Remember, these seditionists murdered a million of your fellow Americans, and we must discover and apprehend them."

The camera dollied back to include the podium that Vanderbilt stood behind, and the presidential seal on its front. The shot also took in the Vice President and the speaker of the House of Representatives who were standing behind and to either side of Vanderbilt, and the large American flag behind them.

"If you see any suspicious behavior among your neighbors, be sure and call the authorities. Report anyone with weapons of any kind, or people who have made negative remarks about the government. These conspirators could be anyone, and it is likely that they are people you have known and liked for years. They may even be members of your own family.

"I know it hurts to think about such things, but you must remember your duty as Americans. Your duty to your country comes first, even above family loyalty. Help us to find these murderers and traitors . . ."

Townsend turned the set off, his face grim. "Just like Hitler," he said. "It's starting in exactly the same way. Divide and conquer. It's an old formula, but it always works. Are you ready, hon?"

Eve nodded, still staring at the blank screen, her face a stony mask.

They had prepared for this day, and had backpacks and duffel bags filled with tools, weapons and provisions. They had roamed the surrounding hills for a hideout, and found a spot near a hilltop water reservoir where they could shelter from the elements in the giant, concrete overflow pipes that protruded from the hillside, around the side of the hill from the dam.

The pipes emptied into a concrete-lined, erosion-prevention ditch that led down a brushy draw and fanned out at the base of the mountain. They were dry inside, seldom ever having an overflow from heavy rains that produced more than a trickle through them.

Jack and Eve had spent the past few weekends stashing canned goods, ammunition, batteries, fuel and supplies in rock cairns near the site. Jack had bought several big GI ammo cans from an Army surplus store. The cans had gasketed seals to keep their contents dry, and were ideal for keeping small animals from spoiling their caches.

They had also stashed propane lanterns and a camp stove, and a half-dozen twenty-five-pound cylinders of liquid propane at their campsite. They found a tent that would just fit inside the giant pipe when erected. Eve refused to sleep in the open pipe with nothing around her. Jack had constructed a floor foundation for the tent by sawing the cross-members of two large freight pallets so that they would match the curvature of the pipe and give them a level sleeping platform. They rested inside the pipe, raised a few inches in the middle to allow any water to trickle through underneath the tent without ruining their bedding or giving them a wet awakening in the middle of the night.

The location provided them a base camp with shelter, an ample supply of water and—unless they were caught out in the open by a reconnaissance aircraft— a safe, remote place to live that was unlikely to be discovered.

"Get our things together," he told her, "we're going to have to move to camp. I'll shut off the utilities and lock everything up. C'mon, baby, this is what we've been preparing for—get the lead out." He smiled and kissed her.

"*Oui, mon Capitan*," she snapped to attention and saluted.

"You're actually happy about this, aren't you?" he said.

"I'm scared to death, but at the same time I'm excited," she said. "For the first time since all this started, I can do something besides sit on my hands and worry. Who would have ever thought that someday little

Beverly Anderson would live in the woods and fight commies."

"Well, don't haul out your guns just yet, General Patton," he said, hugging her. "You're not going to go charging into fire with your guns ablazin' if I can help it. You're going to guard our camp while I do that. I'm the hero here, and don't you forget it. What will our kids think if they learn someday that their sweet mother wore combat boots?"

"If they are fortunate enough to turn out to be girls, they will probably be very proud that I fought by their father's side to win back our country," she responded, turning and walking toward the bedroom.

"Feminist!" he called at her retreating back, then he too, got busy. God, I love that woman, he thought.

It was near 6:00 P.M. when they arrived at the camp. Jack immediately stretched a camouflage net over the Cherokee and threw scrub brush around and over it.

He helped Eve erect the tent, their noises and voices echoing hollowly inside the pipe. It was cool and shady in there. They set up the tent forty feet back from the downslope opening.

There was only a slight grade to the floor. The downslope opening faced west, and was well-lit by the afternoon sun. The upslope end opened out through the concrete side of the reservoir, about sixty feet further in, and had a steel grate with six-inch openings between the heavy crossbars.

Jack surveyed the opening, as he had the preceding Saturday, and found the water level unchanged, about two feet below the lip of the pipe. He attached a dog-leash-collar clip to the end of a piece of nylon cord, and tied the other end of the cord to one of the steel bars. He needed a pail to get drinking water, and had an empty three-liter plastic soda bottle that he had brought for the purpose. He cut holes in each side of the neck, and threaded through a bent-wire clothes hanger. Using a pair of pliers, he twisted it together to make a bail. He cut a larger hole in the side of the bottle, just below the neck.

Using a screwdriver and a large sheet-metal screw, he attached a wire with two flat, fishing sinkers threaded onto it, to the tough bottom of the bottle. He clipped the nylon cord to the bail and dropped the bottle into the water. It filled and sank. He pulled it up to chest height, and tipped it over the bar, emptying it into an insulated plastic water cooler.

"Just like it was made for it," he said to himself, and continued bailing until he had filled the water cooler.

As Eve was sorting out the blankets and finding the wherewithall to prepare a meal, he took a pair of binoculars and climbed atop the earthen dike that ringed the reservoir.

They were surrounded on the south and west by hills, but he could see a section of Mountain View to the north, and in the hazy distance, a stretch of Highway 101. He could see two convoys of Army trucks moving north. There were several Highway Patrol cars among them. They were probably local troops, he thought, and the airborne units were incoming reinforcements.

We didn't get out any too soon, he thought. They will be setting up roadblocks before the night is over.

He knew that the shock troops would form up at the nearest bases, then home in on the bigger cities. San Francisco, Los Angeles, Sacramento, San Diego and similar high-density population centers would be first. Activity would be heaviest where military installations were the thickest. It might be a couple of months before the smaller towns and rural communities in Middle America saw troops, and even then it would probably just be a couple of platoons to reinforce the local law enforcement people that had aligned themselves with the conquering regime.

If they encountered much resistance, a mobile battalion would move in and put it down. They would make extreme examples at first, applying classic military tactics for suppressing civil rebellion. They would move in, blast the crap out of everything until the populace was impotent with fear, then establish neighborhood patrols to insure obedience.

They would call the tune and everyone would dance. If they didn't, they would die. They would haul rebellious citizens out into the street where their neighbors could watch, make them kneel in the street, and blow their brains out. Simple as that. Neighborhood by neighborhood the cities would capitulate. The smaller towns would follow suit.

As it had ten thousand times before, freedom would fall. The population might not know anything about history, but the dictators and would-be dictators knew it well, and because they knew it, they would win. At least, they would win in the short term. The people didn't believe it could happen here. They never did, until it was too late.

Later that night, the two of them sat at the mouth of the pipe, drinking coffee. Jack had built a small fire. He didn't think it would be a problem tonight. The mountain was between them and any built-up areas, and tonight everyone would be concentrating on what was happening within the cities and towns—not looking for holdouts in the mountains.

Eve sat staring thoughtfully into the fire. Jack watched the interplay of dancing lights and shadows that the fire made on his wife's face, her cheekbones standing out, her eyes shadowed except when she tipped her head to take a sip of coffee.

She wore jeans and a blue flannel shirt, and sat with her legs crossed under her, her forearms resting on the insides of her thighs, her hands clasped around the warm coffee mug. She seemed relaxed and introspective. How she had changed over the past few months. She could be playful and witty and cute and little-girlish, sometimes all at the same time. She was intelligent and insightful. She had grasped intuitively the working details of the ALS system he had been working on. She had even made helpful suggestions that had saved him time, and possibly even prevented a downstream problem, assuming it ever got built.

And God, she was warm and soft and delightful in bed. Both before and after making love, he liked to lay on his side with his face in her breasts and his arms around her soft hips and back, her arms holding his head snuggled against her, and just bask in the soft, warm cocoon of her sweet body. At times, she would almost break his ribs, squeezing him between her thighs in her passionate striving, hugging him so tight he thought they might melt together into one body.

He wondered sometimes if that was what she was trying to do, fuse them together so that nothing could part them. He used to watch her sit withdrawn and distant, gazing into some inner eternity where sadness dwelled. He knew at those times that she was thinking of Nathaniel, perhaps seeing his grave, and it wrenched his guts.

He felt sorry for her, and for her loss. He even pitied Nathaniel. For the most part, though, it made him feel lost, alone and unwanted. At those times, he felt that he would never be able to fill the void in her heart that Nathaniel had left. His misery was a tangible thing, a cold, hard knot inside his chest. He wanted all of her, her memories, her love, her very spirit. He knew that it was unrealistic and selfish, but he couldn't help it. He could only disguise it, push it down, keep it from her, and hope in time that it would fade.

Those times were fewer now, and at times she seemed completely happy. He often wished he could read her mind, and just as often, he was glad that he could not, fearing what he might find there.

Eve looked up, becoming aware of his gaze. Putting aside her coffee cup, she crawled over and sat between his legs with her back to him, and pulled his arms around her. She lay her head back on his shoulder and closed her eyes, smiling contentedly. He drew her into his chest, sinking his face in her hair, nuzzling her ear.

"What were you thinking about, just then," she said. "Are you worried about me?"

"Yes. I'm such a fool. I should have taken you to South America. We could be there now, sitting around a campfire with Hector and Eddie. I wanted my little war, and now that it's too late to leave, I realize that you are in danger. Nothing on earth is worth losing you. There are no words to tell you how much I love you. Before you, love was just another word. I had no idea that I could ever long for the touch of one person, to literally ache with want of you, and to hurt in my throat and deep down inside me when I see you sad. It's incredible. It's like a horrible sickness that you don't want to be cured of."

He pulled her tight against him. "I want to be with you until the end of time."

She turned in his arms and put her arms around his neck, kissing him long and tenderly. "You will be, my love. I promise," she whispered.

The following night, they sat up on the reservoir rim, looking at the distant pinpoints of light. Far to the north they could see silent flashes, sometimes red and lingering eruptions that slowly faded, sometimes brilliant flashes that happened and were gone in an instant. The distant sky was full of the moving lights of aircraft, circling around the ground glow of the city like moths around a lantern. Occasionally, some slight change in the wind would permit them to hear a faint, distant popping.

"It's really bad down there, isn't it?" said Eve.

"Yes. I'm afraid so, honey." He put his arm around her shoulders and pulled her close against his side. They watched for hours before finally going to bed, where they lay holding each other in silent thought until they drifted off.

XL

What followed in the next few weeks defied description. Police, soldiers and federal agents broke into private homes in the middle of the night, and ransacked them in search of firearms. Those who objected were shot dead. Whole families were murdered, some still in their beds. In some suburban neighborhoods and small adjacent towns, bands of citizens fought back. Helicopter gunships flew overhead, the thunderous chatter of their mini-guns chewing up stores, homes and streets, killing everything in sight. Whole communities were burned out by armored vehicles with machine guns and flame throwers.

The carnage went on for weeks. It was not only happening in the United States, but in other countries as well. Resistance groups, formed up too late by inexperienced citizenry, were cut to pieces in short order. Those that managed to hoard a few weapons and go underground were unprepared, and lived the existence of vermin, hiding by day, foraging for food at night, suspicious of everyone—almost totally ineffective against the well-armed, well-fed, well-trained government forces.

Military forces and civilian police on several continents were combined into mobile intercontinental peace-keepers with vast resources. They put down insurrections without mercy, coldly impersonal and passionless, as only foreign occupiers can be.

Abominations too vile to speak of were routinely visited upon women and children. Men were killed outright, without compunction.

Military pay trebled. Red-light districts sprang up on

military bases and in occupied districts all over the United States, filled with easy women and every intoxicant and hallucinogen known to man. Federal agents and local civilian law enforcement personnel were given huge pay increases, and bonuses based on numbers of arrests.

Jails and prisons became indoctrination camps. People were not held for court appearances or trials, just arrested, brutalized for a few days, and released. Some were killed.

Initially, some military and police personnel objected to the carnage, and refused to take part. They were shot by their fellows. Resistance disappeared.

Eight weeks after the purported fall of Damocles, the United States had been divided into nine military regions, each with a centralized base of operations, most of them headed by a foreign commander with his own personal cadre of guards and unit supervisors to distance him from the American troops. Other countries were undergoing similar strategic consolidations of power, some run by Americans.

By now, riots and firefights were sporadic. They were dealt with efficiently, by local response teams. Resistance was dying out. Five million people had died, worldwide.

Businesses and public works alike were conscripted and taken over by the federal government, military managers were assigned, and wide-area logistics control centers came into being. Work schedules were dictated and compulsory labor strictly enforced. Area populations were assigned to produce goods according to economic efficiency. Small businesses were assessed for their capabilities, and assigned quotas of different production items.

People in businesses that were no longer deemed necessary, such as some types of manufacturing and service companies that did not produce "necessities," along with other unneeded professions, became laborers, clearing away bodies and debris, and picking through demolished residential neighborhoods for salvageable goods and personal plunder.

Some people were shipped cross-country to agricultural work camps, and put to work picking cotton and harvesting sugar beets. Teachers, academics, administrators, sales people and service providers, all types of professions and vocations not presently needed, became mill workers, crematorium operators and grave-register clerks. Unnecessary people, such as the elderly and indigents, were taken to military reservations in Arizona, New Mexico, Nebraska, Georgia, Alabama and California.

Food and water were rationed with a system of allotment coupons. International trade devolved into conscripted shipping and distribution facilities, operated with forced labor. Currency exchange was eliminated, replaced by ration centers. There were checkpoints at intervals along all roads and highways, and gasoline issue required a government permit. So did clothing and utilities.

Robert Vanderbilt had fallen in stature in the new regime. He was now something of a minor deputy to one Barbara Morrison, the newly delegated authority over region three of what had been, just a short time ago, the United States of America. He didn't like his new position, but as Morrison frequently pointed out, he had been just a second-rate front for the government, and he had neither the intelligence nor the vital skills to recommend him in the new order. She suggested that he accomplish the errands that she assigned him with as much enthusiasm as he could muster or, to use his own words, find a quiet place to blow his brains out. Like most mid-level despots, he hadn't foreseen the possibility that after the dirty work was done, he would no longer serve a useful purpose.

Morrison was tall, brunette, attractive, intelligent, efficient and utterly ruthless. She descended from one of the monied families in Massachusetts—a family that had always had its hands on the political strings of the country. She had been bred to assume her place among the behind-the-scenes manipulators of mankind. Now, after generations of secret dealings and obscurity, the families were surfacing into the light of day, assuming their long-desired positions as totalitarian rulers who would direct the labors of mankind, and live off the fruits of their production.

Like many others, she had lost most of her family and East Coast estates to the Damocles machine, but she and other far-flung siblings had survived. They had many other holdings. Her European cousins were assuming like places of responsibility in the new Euro-American Alliance. Were in fact, the new regime.

It was the "coming out" of the world's monied aristocracy. Together, they would fashion islands of wealth and opulence in a sea of decay and misery. Absolute power. The thought caused giddy tingles to run through Morrison. How she loved to give orders to commoner scum like Vanderbilt.

They had served a purpose. They had carried out the schemes of their secret masters, and enjoyed the trappings of power for a while—tasted that which they were never bred for. She liked being despised and feared by them. She enjoyed forcing them to do things that belittled them, humiliated them.

As for the common herd, they were of no interest whatsoever. The only thing that might be classified as a regret, with regard to the new order, was that some of the challenge would be gone. Secretly controlling the public through their stupid, corrupt legal system, wheeling and dealing, playing dice with the fate of businesses through the stock market, playing factions of the population off against one another by using their pathetic fears and prejudices to manipulate them—it had been such fun. Absolute power didn't require exercising the wits.

But all things could be overcome when you had the world to amuse you. Morrison thought that she could invent a new diversion or two, if really put to the test. Say, pitting armies of slaves against one another? Yes!

She liked that. The ancient Roman emperors had enjoyed such sport. So had the Greek and Roman gods. Yes, it was fitting. The ghastly things did breed prolifically. It would do them good to thin them out occasionally. Life was going to be good.

XLI

Townsend crawled up the last ridge to the camp, and called. Eve answered, and he stood up and walked in. She was barely visible in the wan moonlight. She had been sitting just inside the dark interior of the pipe, invisible behind the edge of the deep shadow cast on the floor of the pipe by its upper circumference. It was almost 3:30 in the morning, and the night air was chill. They hugged each other tightly.

"What did you find out?" she asked.

Jack shucked out of several ammunition bandoliers, flak jackets and two M-16 rifles that were slung over his shoulder. He dropped a bundle of clothing—Eve could see they were camouflage military uniforms—and sat down on the ground near the lip of the pipe, while Eve sat on the edge of it.

"Any food left?" he asked.

She got up and walked back into the darkness of the pipe. In a few moments, she returned and handed him a slightly warm bundle of aluminum foil and one of the canned sodas that they kept inside the water cooler. He unwrapped the roast beef sandwiches. It was four days since they had moved up to their camp.

"Are you hungry?" he asked, offering her the crinkled foil bowl with its greasy, savory-smelling contents.

"No. You might as well finish that up. It won't keep much longer."

"They're patrolling the main streets," he said, as he began eating. "They've got a squad of men and a vehicle about every three blocks along the main street. The men are spread out along the street. Regular U.S. troops with M-16s.

"That's where I got the rifles. I waylaid a couple of soldiers patrolling through an alley. M-16s will be better for the kind of close-in work we'll be doing, than our civilian guns. They have larger magazine capacities and they can fire full-auto. Besides, it's the only way we'll be assured of the availability of ammo. They'll guard or destroy any gun shops.

"Squads of military and police are still going door to door, pushing their way in and collecting any available weapons, throwing them into a troop truck that follows along. I heard yells and screams, and shots were fired in some of the apartments and houses. Some of the troops are wearing blue helmets. At least they looked blue in the streetlights, and I heard some of them speaking Italian. I think they're U.N. troops. There are several other groups with insignia and uniforms that I don't recognize. The general haircuts and appearance of one bunch made me think that they were European, though. Maybe Czech. Some of them are Vietnamese."

"So it's happening just as Eddie and Hector said, isn't it?" she asked. "They have joined forces to destroy us."

"America is one of the last strongholds of the free," he said between bites. "One of the last armed nations. The U.S., Canada and Australia—perhaps a few others. Mainly the U.S. They will have to concentrate their strength here until they have disarmed us and nullified the threat we represent. They will want to get it done and over with in a hurry, so they can begin to consolidate control and organize the population."

"What will they do with us?"

"Slavery," he said. "They intend us to work for them. Eventually, they will probably establish some form of common currency, maybe some kind of credit-debit card, just for accounting simplicity, and the world will go on much as before, but what we will earn for our labor will be subsistence, nothing more."

"How do they think the world will be better for them? They already have everything, don't they? I mean, they were wealthy already."

"It won't be better. In fact, it will be much worse, at least, in my opinion. It wouldn't appeal to me to sit inside a rich house and look out my windows and see squalor everywhere. It will be much simpler, though.

"From a business point of view, they eliminate the need to advertise, to pay the labor costs required for safe working conditions, health insurance, unemployment, or worry about such nit-picking little things as human rights. And in a gross way, they can even benefit the ecology of the planet by thinning out the human herd whenever they feel like it. Castration, sterilization, all those things that any good herdsman does to control the economics of his business.

"Wealth is not the real reason for tyranny, anyway. The most important factor is ego. Like so many people, they believe in elitism. It's one of those human failings that is always with us in one form or another. It begins in small, basic ways. Everybody wants to be different, to belong to an exclusive group that most people are denied access to. Money, influence, credentials, licenses, degrees—that's what those things accomplish. They say it's to protect the public, but mostly it isn't. It's to keep the riff-raff out. All institutions are that way. Visit any university campus, military base or corporate head-quarters and you will see elitism everywhere. Personal prestige is the measure of personal worth, and human equality is simply an habitual expression, like, 'Hi, how are you?' No one takes it seriously.

"The difference is that these people don't make any bones about it. They truly believe that we are subhuman, and now, they won't have to put up with any resistance or back talk from us. They'll own us as chattel. That's probably the most important point as far as they are concerned."

"What are we going to do?" she asked.

"We only have two choices, honey. Fight or capitulate. That's all that's left."

"I know that, dear. I *am* here, aren't I? I mean, what are we going to *do* now?"

He grinned. "Well, I'm going to do what I can to throw a monkey wrench in their works."

"Great. What's the plan?"

"I hate to disappoint you, but I haven't actually got one, at least not yet. They only just arrived, you know. We need to give them a little time to get established, form routines, get organized.

"The way you hurt an army is by reducing its capability. There are two principal methods of accomplishing that. You destroy ammunition, armament, fuel stocks, equipment and supplies. In short, you destroy or limit the tools they need to operate with. Sooner or later, this reservoir will be important to someone. We will have to watch for that, and be ready to move. When they decide that it is a strategic resource, I'll dynamite the wall and release the water.

"The second thing you do is limit their human capability. Wound them, make them sick, demoralize them, knock out their leaders. You can never win by slowly picking off soldiers. Either you have the trained troops to inflict massive casualties and severely incapacitate your enemy, or you find the head of the snake and cut it off.

"The common soldier is just cannon fodder. Kill one, they send in another. It's only when war comes home to the movers and shakers that they feel any need to give it up. If you want to stop a big corporation, you go after the major shareholders, not the little guy working in the factory. He doesn't make any decisions.

"That's why Ortiz and the underground are doing it this way. You can never get rid of them unless you can find out who they are."

"When do you think that will be?"

"Your guess is as good as mine, baby. Better, probably. I think they will surface pretty soon, though. Somebody is controlling this mess, and it's back to that ego thing, again. It's no fun having power if you can't flaunt it. They have operated through figureheads for a long time. I'm betting they will come out of the woodwork as soon as they think that things are under control."

"Then aren't we delaying things if we resist?" she asked. "It would be better in the long run just to let them believe it's all over, wouldn't it?"

Jack looked at her, thinking for a moment. "You're right," he said. "It would be best. You're pretty smart, aren't you. I keep underestimating you."

"Aw, pshaw, as Eddie says," she waved his compliment away.

"I guess I really fouled things up by not taking you to Chile. I've risked your life for nothing," he said, looking remorseful.

She kneeled down in front of him, concern on her face, and put her hands on his shoulders. "You were just being you," she said, "reacting in the only way that you know. You're tired of running, tired of worrying about me, and you wanted to fight back. That's what you do. It's who you are. You're a strategist and a fighter. A man of action.

"You can't sit and wait for others to do things; you have to wade in yourself. You don't like the sidelines. You do think and plan, but you think best when you're moving. When you sit, you begin to stagnate. I guess that's why you were a good spy."

"I knew that someday I would feel like a second stringer next to you," he said. "You were in a daze, and now you're waking up. I've often wondered if you would want to stay with me when it happened."

"Now you're underestimating yourself. You are one of the most intelligent men I've ever known, and you're far more intuitive than most. Every woman wants a strong, supportive man, and I've been fortunate to have the love of two wonderful men.

"Like every woman, whether she admits it or not, I know what love can do to a man, especially when it's his first love, or if he's a bit shy with women. You lose your confidence, you feel clumsy, you worry about being masculine in your woman's eyes, your little brains turn to mush." She rubbed his head, playfully. "Eventually, you all come out of it.

"I hope I'm smarter than some women I've known. I'm not going to use your love to browbeat you or emasculate you while you're in this pitiful state. I'm going to love you with all my heart, and when you do come out of it, I hope you will still love me. I don't want to be a shrew, or make you hate me. I don't want to lose you in a few years."

"God, you really are one in a million," he said, kissing her and holding her tight. "Sometimes I feel so proud and so lucky that I'm afraid I can't contain it. I adore you."

"I know," she laughed. "You've got good taste, sugar." She kissed him and got to her feet. She walked toward the tent, swinging her hips suggestively. "And if you want a taste, you know where I'll be."

XLII

Jack and Eve followed the game trail down the mountain in the dim light, and crossed a shallow valley into the outskirts of town. The only noises were the crunching of the sandy soil beneath their feet, and their breathing. They talked little after starting out, Eve simply following Jack's lead. The stars were clear, and the air cool and damp.

It was almost a week since his first reconnaissance trip into Mountain View. The previous night he had gone into Palo Alto, and had killed two soldiers who had been escorting three civilians to a detention cell. The three men had turned out to be civilian militia. Their leader, a man named Robertson, had been captured that morning, and they had been trying to organize a rescue when they exited a building into an alley, and ran smack into the two patroling soldiers.

Townsend went with them to reconnoiter the compound where roughly three dozen prisoners were being held. Chain-link fence and barbed wired cordoned off an area about an acre in size. Sentries walked the perimeter fence. Tents and vehicles bordered the compound for about a third of its circumference. On the side opposite the tents, portable toilets were lined up inside the fence. The compound was open, and prisoners sat on the ground, singly and in small groups. Troops were housed in an apartment complex two hundred yards away, and sentries walked the adjacent street.

Townsend suggested a plan. He would provide a

diversion that would pull most of the troops away from the area. Fifteen militia members would surround the compound at 3:00 A.M. the following morning, each with a designated target. After Townsend drew the troops away, on signal they would kill the sentries and release the prisoners. The prisoners would be directed to scatter in all directions, bettering everyone's chances of escape.

Eve had refused to let him go alone. She had turned a corner emotionally, one that even Jack hadn't anticipated. She had retribution on her mind, and wasn't going to be denied.

She had grown up on an Indiana farm, and had some experience with guns. Jack had taught her to field-strip and reassemble the M-16, and to operate its firing mechanism. She knew how to use it.

He had stretched a wire across the mouth of one of the other concrete pipes, and hung a blanket over the opening to muffle the noise. They test-fired the guns he had collected, in there, shooting into a cardboard box he had filled with dirt and sand. He drew a bull's-eye on the side of the box with a marker pen. Once she became used to the gun and got the sights adjusted to suit her, she did well enough, managing to group her shots within a three-inch circle at a distance of fifty feet.

The body armor was adjustable and lightweight. Eve had gagged and turned green when, as she was trying on the body armor and uniform shirt the day before, she had noticed the crusty, brown blood on the shoulder straps of the armor and the collar of the G.I. shirt, and realized what Jack had done to get them. She had soaked them and scrubbed them clean before completing her adjustments.

Eve's uniform was too big and Jack's too small, but they were not uncomfortable. They both had black hiking boots that Jack had bought several weeks before, so footwear was not a problem. The trousers were worn bloused, so it didn't matter if they were a bit too short, and he had cut the sleeves off the cami shirts and rolled them up to their biceps, in the fashion that many soldiers wore them. All things considered, he felt that they would pass all but a close inspection, especially at night.

They approached town through a residential district and walked in brazenly, their rifles held ready. Jack thought that their most immediate danger was that some patriotic citizen might mistake them for the enemy, and take a shot at them from one of the nearby houses.

They made it into the center of town without incident. As they got within two blocks of Main Street, they began to see pairs of roving soldiers, as well as isolated guards posted on alternate street corners. They weren't challenged. Jack thought that it might be due to the international mix of troops. They couldn't know each other very well yet, if at all. The sentries were far enough apart that he knew he could kill one or two of them and still get away with Eve, if he had to. If someone stopped them, he would not wait to argue, he would kill every enemy in sight.

They made their way to the alley behind a three-story building, just a block from Main Street, and climbed to the flat roof via an iron fire escape. Once on top, they could see quite a bit of the activity. It was after 11:00 P.M., and there was no civilian traffic. Jack assumed that the occupation forces had established a curfew. Across town, Jack found what he was looking for. There was a brightly lit area, and as they watched, a helicopter landed there. Jack had reasoned that the military would establish a staging and supply area near one of the bay bridges for convenience, and assumed that either Palo Alto or Menlo Park would be selected. The troops in Mountain View and other outlying towns would be rotated and provisioned from there.

They climbed back down to the street and proceeded in the direction of the lights. Now the sky glare was evident, and the noise of men and equipment increased as they approached. They crossed a street and climbed over a low cinder-block fence into a wide, parklike embankment with trees and grass. They walked up the embankment and climbed a small, steep slope at the farther side. At the top, they immediately crouched down in the darkness near a palm tree.

They were on the verge of a well-lit parking area and playing field. Guards were everywhere, and troops were busy unloading two six-by-six trucks and a cargo trailer. Near at hand were fenced tennis courts, and just the other side of the trucks and parking area was a manicured track for field sports.

"It's a school," Eve said.

"Makes sense," said Jack. "Administrative offices, ready telephone and computer connections, a cafeteria, and classrooms that can be converted to barracks by just shoving the desks out of the way and installing field cots or bedrolls. C'mon, let's see if we can find where they're putting their supplies. We especially want to find their ammunition and ordnance stores."

"Where would they keep them?" Eve asked.

"Someplace protected, and easy to get to—a concrete building away from wherever the troops bed down, I would guess. Certainly nowhere near the administrative offices."

"See the guys unloading that truck on the other side of the playing field?" Eve said. "They're carrying heavy boxes into that big building with the round roof, two men to a box. I think that building is a gymnasium or indoor stadium. Could that be where the ammunition is?"

"We'll know in a minute," he said, unslinging a small pair of binoculars. He watched the men as they struggled to carry in ammo cans and heavy wooden crates with ropes on the ends.

"You're absolutely right. That is munitions. Some of it is mortar shells—probably tear gas and fragmentation for riot suppression, and maybe star shells for flares at night. Lots of small-arms ammo. I'd like to get a big can of .223 ammo, but it will be a pain to carry it all the way back to where we parked the Cherokee.

"Of course, we might find a vehicle we can use, too, but it will be risky. When that stuff goes up, we need to be back on the other side of town, or better yet, back in camp."

"What are we going to do?"

"We'll find somewhere to wait. After about one o'clock, everyone but a few sentries will be in the sack. Then we'll work our way into that gym. I'll have to see what kind of stuff is available. I would like to be able to rig a time delay of some sort, so we can get a little distance away before it goes up."

"Think the building could have an alarm?" Eve said, thinking out loud.

"It probably does, but I'm not so sure they would use it. They have sentries, and they think they are pretty secure. Those helicopter gunships ate this place up last week. There isn't going to be much fight left in these people."

"I just had a horrible thought, Jack. What if we do this and they retaliate by killing some of the townspeople? They might, don't you think?"

"Yes. It has occurred to me too, honey, but if we don't do anything, and Hector and friends fail, it's all over for everybody, from now on. We *have* to fight back. Obedience is not going to stop these bastards from killing people anyway, at least not in the long run. They are vastly outnumbered by the population. The only weapon they have that can prevent the citizenry from overthrowing them is fear. That's what domination of this sort depends on. They shoot a lot of people at first, really rub their noses in the dirt, then they don't have to deal with much resistance in the future. Everyone is too scared to fight back."

"If we blow up that ammunition, will it make any difference?"

"Not much. They'll resupply from Alameda Naval Air Station or one of the other bases. They're distributing just enough so that the occupation forces have a ready supply on hand, to deal with any contingencies."

"Then why are we doing it?" she asked, looking into his eyes.

"To create a diversion while the local underground rescues their leader. Robertson is a capable leader—a good organizer and strategist. The underground needs that kind of person. The reason I gave in to you and brought you along, is that I thought you wanted revenge for Nathaniel, and I thought a certain measure of it might be good for your peace of mind," Jack replied. He studied her face, the hint of a smile on his lips.

"I do," she said, "but I really want to hurt them. If we should get caught and die for nothing, the bastards will have won again." A tear rolled down her cheek. "And if they retaliate by killing innocent people, I want them to pay dearly for every life. This is not a joke to me, Jack."

"I know it's not," he said, wiping her tears away. "When that thing in orbit cuts loose, they will pay. If it should fail, then I figured you needed this basic training for what lies ahead. Years of war. Hit-and-run fighting. That's all that's left. There won't be anywhere in the world to go. It's the best I can do to assure your survival."

She dug her face into his neck, her arm around his shoulder, snuffling quietly. He held her until she felt better.

"The future is not that dismal, yet," he said when she pulled back, drying her eyes. "Let's build a surprise for these boys, then go home. Okay?" He slapped her bottom gently.

She smiled, "Okay," she said.

They skirted the parking lot, and approached the gymnasium through a service driveway that led between the gym and an adjacent utility building. As they crept up to the corner of the building, they heard voices. They flattened themselves against the wall of the utility building, and Jack peered cautiously around the corner. Two soldiers were slouching against the wall of the gym, smoking. One had his rifle in his hand, butt resting on the ground. The other's was slung over his shoulder.

Jack turned to Eve and whispered in her ear, "Two

sentries. I'll take care of them. After I do, I'll come back. Be quiet and stay down."

She responded with a nod, looking anxiously at him. He kissed her on the nose, and slinging his M-16 over his left shoulder, walked brazenly around the corner. The men were not more than fifteen feet away. The one with the slung rifle straightened up as Jack walked up, a questioning look on his face. The other was facing away from Jack, toward the other man, and had just started to turn when Jack put the silenced Walther within an inch of his head and fired. His pace never slackened, and his next step took him inches from the other soldier. Jack put the gun under his chin and fired. Neither man had time enough to realize what was happening before both were on the ground, dead, their lifeless limbs jerking and twitching as their last, scrambled nerve impulses caused rapidly weakening convulsions. In seconds, they were still. Jack never paused to check them. He knew with the sureness of long experience exactly what he had done.

He turned back to the corner of the building and retrieved Eve. He led her to the doorway of the small, utility building and tried the door. It opened. Inside was a large gas-fired boiler. Jack assumed that it provided heat and hot water for the gymnasium. The building also housed items of grounds-care equipment in the form of two riding mowers, and various wall-hung implements and garden hoses.

"Honey, I want you to crouch down in this doorway and keep watch on these two sides of the building. Someone may show up to check on the sentries. If someone does, shoot him before he has a chance to find those bodies and raise the alarm. A random shot is probably not that uncommon, and isn't likely to rouse as much attention as someone yelling for help. If nothing interferes, I'll be gone for about thirty minutes. If I hear you shoot, I'll come running out that door over there. Don't shoot me by mistake, okay?"

"I wouldn't think of it. I'll be okay. Go!"

He went, slipping out the door of the utility building, and into the back entrance of the gym. Eve heaved a restless sigh, her tension easing somewhat, and kneeled down in the shadowed doorway, sitting back on her heels, her rifle across her thighs. It was very dark now, the shadows of the buildings like inky wells of blackness.

Jack walked down a dark hallway for about thirty feet. Doors opened off the hall into two offices, men's and women's restrooms, an equipment room and a janitor's closet. He checked these as he went.

At the end of the hallway, he looked out cautiously into a big, open gymnasium with a hardwood floor and basketball hoops at either end. Polished wooden bleachers ran the length of the building on both sides. About half the length of the floor had been divided into square sections with cleared lanes criss-crossing between them. The square sections were comprised of pallets of ammunition, rations, sleeping bags and weapons.

An M-60 machine gun and two mortars sat among other stuff in the square nearest him. These drew him, and after a brief search he found mortar shells and several cans of 7.62-millimeter NATO ammunition for the M-60. It took a bit longer, and a search through three other blocks of supplies, before he found the hand grenades and boxed, two-pound bricks of C-4 plastic explosive.

He took two cans of .223 ammunition for their M-16s, and two twenty-pound boxes of fragmentation grenades. He wasn't sure how they would carry the ammo and grenades, but was willing to see if providence would provide a means. He carried them into the hallway, and left them by the exit door. Returning, he searched the piles of ordnance for fuses and timers, but didn't find any.

Going back along the hallway, he looked inside the equipment room and found the sprinkler controls. There was a workbench against one wall, and an upright metal locker with some tools and maintenance supplies inside. He found an electrician's test meter, a partial roll of

electrical tape and a spool of electrical lamp cord. He took
these items, along with a screwdriver and pliers back to
the sprinkler control box, which housed a clock timer with
adjustable switches to turn the electric zone valves on and
off. Having assured himself that the clock was working,
he loosened the "on" switch setting and moved it to the
three A.M. position. With the electrician's meter, he
checked the voltage across the switch. Satisfied, he dis-
connected the switch wires from the bussbar that fed
current to the zone valves and left the two wires hanging. Using the pliers, he stripped the insulation from the
ends of the two-conductor lamp cord, and twisted the
bare ends together with the switch wires. He took two
nails from a nail-and-screw bin, and carrying the reel of
wire, went back inside the gym, unreeling the lamp wire
as he went. At the pallet with the plastic explosives, he
emptied out four boxes of the paper-wrapped bricks and
made a pile of them. He cut the lamp wire and removed
the insulation from the ends as before. He twisted the
bared ends around the nails and jammed the nails down
into one of the bricks of C-4. The conductors of the lamp
wire were composed of dozens of very fine wires twisted
together into a single strand. Townsend separated out a
single thin strand of wire, and wrapped the ends around
the nails, completing the electrical circuit. When the timer
closed the switch, the tiny wire would short the circuit
and explode with a bang, setting off the explosive.

He paused to survey his work, and noticed that the
polished hardwood floor was gouged and scuffed where
equipment had been dragged across it, and he pitied
the school athletics director. He knew how dear such
things were to them. It made him feel a bit less badly
about blowing it up.

He piled mortar shells and ammunition on the pallet
above the plastic explosive. He went the length of the
gym looking for other munitions, and his heart leaped
when he found a crate of binary chemical explosives.
He quickly broke the coverings off a dozen of the
flexible, two-pound plastic packages, and ruptured the

internal membranes, allowing the two chemical compounds inside to mix. Once mixed, they were highly explosive. He dragged the crate of binary half the length of the gym, and parked it next to the wired C-4. To preclude some sentry arriving and spoiling the surprise before the timer went off, he tied a grenade under the pallet of explosives with electrical tape. He tied one end of the remaining lamp cord to the grenade pin and unreeled the wire down the hall to the door.

He cautiously opened the outer door, and seeing no one around, waved at the darkened doorway where Eve was crouched. He set the ammo and grenades down outside the door. Gingerly pulling the lamp wire taut, he stepped outside and allowed the door to almost close. Reaching inside, he looped the wire around the panic bar, tied it off, and gently closed the gym door behind him.

Jack gathered Eve back inside the utility building, carrying the ammunition and grenades inside with them. With the remainder of the electrical wire, he made a shoulder harness to carry the two cans of rifle ammo, one on his chest and one on his back. Slinging his rifle, he carried a box of grenades in one hand, and he and Eve carried another between them. It made creeping difficult, but he wanted the munitions.

They circled the parking lot again, going back the way they came. They had gotten as far as two blocks past the main thoroughfare with no problems, heading back toward the suburbs on their side of town, when two soldiers in an open Hummer turned a corner and approached them from behind. The headlights of the vehicle picked them out and cast their shadows, large and moving, on the walls of the buildings they were walking past. The vehicle pulled to the curb next to them and the officer in the passenger seat challenged them.

"Where are you two soldiers headed with that ordinance? Do you need a lift?" he asked.

Jack stopped, lowered the box of grenades in his right hand to the sidewalk, and turning across in front of Eve, approached the vehicle. The man asking the questions was a major, and Jack guessed that he was in command of one of the detachments stationed in the city. He knew that it was hopeless to attempt to fool him. He was white and obviously American. The driver was oriental, but didn't speak, and Jack couldn't tell from his unmarked battle fatigues if he was American or foreign military.

The major's eyes were scrutinizing Eve, noting the feminine shape that the fatigues couldn't hide, and roaming over Jack too, as he approached the vehicle. Jack could see doubts beginning to form behind the man's blue eyes and quizzical expression. Jack brought the Walther up and pointed it at the man's face, just inches from his nose.

"Tell him to kill the ignition," he said, indicating the driver with a motion of his head. The major frowned, then said, "Kill it, Li."

"Just sit still and keep your hands where they are," said Jack. "Put the grenades in the vehicle, hon," he said to Eve as he lifted his end of the box they carried between them, "and get in the back seat."

Eve did as he said, without comment, climbing in behind the driver and resting the barrel of her M-16 on the back of the driver's seat, muzzle pointed at the back of his neck. Jack climbed in beside her, keeping the pistol trained on the major's head.

"Drive in the direction you're headed," he told him. "Stay on this street until I tell you to turn. Make a wrong move and I'll kill you. Do you understand?"

The major glanced sidelong at Jack and nodded. He motioned to the driver. They pulled out, traveling unhampered and virtually unnoticed past occasional pairs of sentries walking the streets. They passed a truckload of soldiers under a corner streetlight, who were just being loaded aboard in preparation for going somewhere.

They reached the outskirts of town without incident. Jack was looking for a street or road that would take them out of sight of the developed neighborhoods, when just ahead he spotted a service road that led off to some sort of public works building. The timing was fortunate. Two blocks further on, there was a sentry-guarded roadblock at the edge of town, where the street they were traveling turned into a country lane.

They drove up to the cinder-block building with its chainlink-fenced compound, and Jack could see that they had found the sewage treatment plant. The plant was on a slight rise, and as they pulled into the lighted parking area, they could see four large, open lagoons spread out just below the rise, as the land sloped away from the city.

At Jack's direction, the driver pulled up next to the building and stopped. When the driver turned the ignition off, Jack shot the major in the back of the head. Startled, Eve pulled the trigger and killed the driver. Jack pushed the major out onto the pavement, and getting out over his body, walked around to the driver and pulled him out. He dragged the still-convulsing body around the front of the vehicle, up against the building, and dragged the major's body over beside the driver's. He told Eve to get into the passenger seat, which she did. She looked slightly dazed, but responded immediately, without speaking.

Jack walked around the building and surveyed the sewage lagoons. The moon was up now, and visibility wasn't bad, after the eyes adjusted. A paved, one-lane service road ran around beside the lagoons and dropped out of sight just beyond them. About a mile away in the same direction, across the open valley, a graded firebreak ran up over the mountain. On the farther hill was where they had left the Jeep Cherokee.

Jack climbed behind the wheel of the Hummer and followed the road around the building and down off the rise toward the lagoons. As they rounded the lagoons where the road had dipped out of sight, they found that it turned into a dirt track that led down to an open storage area where cannibalized equipment moldered on the ground. Old centrifugal pumps, motors, air-conditioner

parts, tires and miscellaneous junk graced the city's bone
yard.

The track ended, but the country flattened out as it
ranged out across the small, open valley toward the foot-
hills. Jack thought the Hummer could make it, and was
proved right. An hour later, they recovered the Cherokee. Jack hid the military vehicle in a brushy draw just
off the graded firebreak, near the foot of an electrical
power-line tower. The Pacific Gas and Electric Company's
line crossed the track at an angle, coming inland from
the coast and crossing the hills to the municipal substation
at Palo Alto. It made a convenient reference point if they
ever wanted to recover the vehicle.

That evening, back in camp, Eve was withdrawn and
quiet. Jack understood. When he tried to comfort her,
she became forcefully amorous, almost tearing his clothes
off, and making fierce, passionate love. She finally fell
asleep, physically spent, lying against his side, her face
on his chest, one leg lying across his. He held her, and
fell asleep shortly after she did.

Jack came awake, instantly alert, in the early afternoon,
and lay listening for whatever it was that had awakened
him. He heard Eve retching, somewhere outside. He
found his rumpled jeans among the bedding. Pulling them
on, he carried his shoes and socks to the mouth of the
pipe, where he sat down and put them on.

Eve was on her hands and knees, about twenty feet
away, near the slope of the reservoir. He pitied her. A
few months before, she was a career woman and wife,
living an ordered life, and violence was just something
that she heard about on the news, and occasionally
discussed philosophically on her show. Like so many
others now, she was experiencing the loss of innocence,
and it was an unimaginably cruel education. America was
having the last traces of its comfortable, safe, twentieth-
century heritage torn out by the roots. Gentle people
were being emotionally, as well as physically, maimed.
Jack deeply hated it, however inevitable it might be.

He wet a washcloth at the water cooler, and crouching down next to Eve, wiped her fevered face and neck. He gave her a cup of water to rinse her mouth with, then he held her against him, stroking her head and back, the two of them kneeling in the dust. When she was better, he walked her back to their sitting area and put water on the camp stove for coffee. He got her to eat a slice of bread, even though she didn't want it, and when the coffee was done, her stomach had settled.

"I guess I'm not as brave as I thought I was," she said.

"You're about as brave as anyone I've ever known," he said. "No one is born being used to ugliness and unspeakable acts. You have to learn it. I'm sorrier than ever for keeping you here. I don't want you to have to learn it. I want you to stay gentle and optimistic inside. You're not what's wrong. They're what's wrong," he thumbed over his shoulder, toward the town, indicating the occupation forces.

Eve looked past him, her gaze locking on the horizon. "Look," she pointed.

He turned, his gaze following hers, and noticed a black cloud above the intervening hills. He picked up the binoculars and climbed atop the reservoir embankment. A moment later, Eve climbed up beside him.

"That was the gymnasium. I hope the diversion worked, and they got Robertson out okay," he said. "They are going to be busy for a while, but I don't think they'll search this far afield. If they put it together and find the Hummer, there are still several hard-surfaced roads crossing between them and us. We could have gone anywhere.

"Honey, I've decided that until we know there is no other way, we're going to stay out of sight. I won't risk you again without good reason. If the weapon fails, we will leave the country. We stand a better chance of living free in a more primitive country. It will take them generations to gain control of all the little towns and villages everywhere. They will never control the entire land surface of the world; it would spread them too thin. It wouldn't be economical either.

"I haven't quite figured out where we'll go or how we'll get there, just yet. We might be able to steal a boat and drift down the coast toward South America, like we did in Florida. Overland is possible, but it will be hard. We will have to walk cross-country to avoid roadblocks and checkpoints. A boat has its risks, too. Out on open water, there is no place to hide if we're discovered. We would have to travel at night and hole up during the day."

"What would you do if you didn't have me?" she asked.

"If I lost you now, I wouldn't want to live," he said, looking into her face. "There is no world for me anymore, without you. I realized that tonight. I'm blundering around, confused, trying to fit things together. I can't continue to think or operate like I've done all my life. You are not a soldier, and I don't want you to be one. I have to find a place for us, somewhere where we can live in relative peace."

"I still want to know. What would you do, now, if you had never met me; what if you were alone?"

"If that thing up there doesn't work, I would do what Hector and Eddie are trying to do. I would travel back east, maybe even to Europe, and as the people responsible for all this surfaced, I would destroy as many of them as I could."

"Then that is what we will do," she said. "We wouldn't be happy whiling away our lives in a thatched hut in some remote jungle. That would destroy us just as effectively as the enemy would, and accomplish nothing. I may not be a soldier, and I'd rather not be one, but I'll learn if I have to. I'll be a good partner to you. Together, we can go places and accomplish things that you might not be able to do alone. If war is the world's destiny, then we will play our part in it."

XLIII

Fourteen weeks after the purported fall of Damocles, Benito Salvitore called for a council meeting in Italy. He had a villa on an expansive estate near Rome, high on a rocky mountain outcropping. The villa overlooked the Mediterranean Sea, and was furnished in classical Italian and Grecian styles. Bright, white stucco walls beautifully contrasted with red tile roofs, pillared arcades and steps with carved stone balustrades. Walled gardens of roses and hibiscus were bordered by sentinel cedars, and occasional examples of Hellenistic period statuary.

The only thing that detracted from the classic scene was the satellite communications dish outside the garden wall. The promontory commanded breathtaking mountain views in all directions. The opulent architecture and spacious design bespoke lavish wealth. The car garage was like a barn, designed to hold thirty cars.

The leaders of all the governing houses of the world, nearly two hundred in all, began arriving in Rome on the seventh of August. Many would stay on for a few days after the general meeting on the eighth. Among those arrivals was Professor Leland Somerset. He landed in Rome at 7:20 in the evening and was soon checked into a hotel.

Somerset was of slightly more than medium height, with dark hair, brown eyes and a somewhat stocky build. The crinkles in the corners of his eyes were those of a man who had once liked to laugh. During the past few years, his mien had turned somber though, and he had become quiet and introspective, often staring off into the distance and thinking.

Among his peers in the scientific community, he was liked and trusted. That was partly because he made people feel that he was interested in what they had to say, and partly because he did what he promised, and never lied. Partly it was because he refused to be drawn into campus politics, or take sides in specious arguments. He preferred to let people think as they liked, unless they asked him for advice. In that case, his opinions were freely given, and given in such a way that the recipient never felt that he owed Somerset anything.

Those who knew him well never questioned his science or his motives. He engendered faith in others. How it came about couldn't be described, exactly. Somerset was not conscious of it, he simply was himself. He believed in old-fashioned honor, and he practiced it, and it came through to others.

His career had taken some strange turnings. He had worked on the directed-energy weapons research at Lawrence-Livermore National Laboratory during the Reagan years, doing "Star Wars" research, as it has been labeled by the press. For the past several years, he had been installed at the J.J. Pickle Research Laboratory in Austin, Texas, an arm of the University of Texas.

His wife Judy had died six years before, and his only daughter was married to a Navy officer and living in Naples, Italy. He stopped off there for two days before flying on to Rome. He wanted a last time with her before the end. He hadn't told anyone, but he had come to Rome to die.

He settled into his room and took a refreshing shower. He sat at the window, looking out over the street at the people moving along the sidewalks. Later, he walked out, got a meal in a small restaurant, and walked the city streets awhile before returning to his hotel for the night.

The next morning, he ate breakfast, then went to see the Coliseum, the Forum and Vatican City with its famous

St. Peter's Basilica, the greatest church in Christendom. He studied the famous Dome of Michelangelo, and the splendid square and colonnade. He had always wanted to see some of the wonders of Europe, but had never had the time before.

He spent the bulk of the day seeing the sights of Rome, walking alone through the quieter side streets, sitting in cafes and drinking the small, rich coffees and meditating. At 4:00 P.M., he returned to his hotel and took a nap, rising at 6:00 P.M. to shower and dress.

At 8:00 P.M., he hired a car and driver to take him to Villa Salvitore. The security guard at the gate refused him entrance at first. Somerset gave the guard a letter of introduction addressed to Benito Salvitore, and waited with the security guard while another man took the letter in. In a few minutes, two men returned and searched Somerset. All he had on him was a wallet, pen and pencil, and what appeared to be a penlight. They gave him back his things and escorted him into the house, past the crowded reception hall and garden, and into a small library.

As they passed through the house, he heard several different languages being spoken by the guests who were standing in pairs and small groups, talking casually. Apparently the council meeting was over, and the business of the day was winding down. One would never guess that these quiet, well-behaved people had parceled out the world today. The basic division had already been done, but today's meetings had concluded a ratification of understanding, and the finer details of authority, latitude, operating plans and target goals.

Somerset had to hand it to them, they were efficient. If it had been a bunch of pre-Damocles politicians, they couldn't have arrived at a sound agreement within a year, much less a day.

As Hitler had shown the world in the 1940's, the most efficient form of government was an autocracy. The union of the high aristocracy was run like a business, with shareholders, a board of directors and a chairman of the board. Benito Salvitore was the elected chairman, and his authority was almost absolute. That authority trickled down to thousands of minor community dictators, but in this place, this night, were all the ancient titleholders, the heirs of Byzantium and Rome, the descendants of the ancient and obscure houses of Europe and Asia.

These were the puppet masters. They who had secretly ruled the world via anonymous control of politics, currencies and business, for ages. Their control had been subtle but firm over the centuries—not always winning the moment, but always prevailing in the end—guiding the world slowly but steadily toward their secret goals. They had steadily consolidated their wealth and power, and grown stronger with each passing decade. The long-awaited time was at hand. The technology and economics were finally at the point where that dream of ages, true world conquest, was possible. They believed that they now enjoyed a hold over mankind that could never again be broken.

The security guards left Somerset alone in the room, closing the door behind them. One of the men waited outside the door while the other went to see the master of the house. In a short while, the guard returned, and they escorted Somerset into a large, sumptuous ballroom with perhaps two hundred curious people, all standing quietly, waiting for him. A man in a dark-gray business suit sat with two women in evening gowns on one of three openly-arranged divans near the center of the room. Three men occupied the other two sofas.

Somerset was led before these people and left standing as the guards withdrew a few feet. Benito Salvitore was a dark-haired, middle-aged Italian of obvious sophistication and charm. His accent was cultured and his language crisp and precise—almost Victorian-era in phrasing. He held Somerset's letter, and it was he who motioned Somerset to the adjacent sofa. The man occupying it got up and moved to stand a few paces away.

"Dr. Leland Somerset, is it?" said Salvitore, as Somerset sat down. "You have a strange manner of gaining entrance to an exclusive affair. Your note says that you have come here to die with me. What purpose exactly does this melodramatic entrance achieve?"

"Other than being the simple truth, it was just a ploy to gain admission, Mr. Salvitore," Somerset answered. "Your security people would not have allowed me in otherwise."

"And why do you desire admittance, Dr. Somerset?" Salvitore asked, smiling. "Is it your plan to shoot me down, and to die yourself, in a hail of bullets? Something like that?"

Somerset smiled in return. "Under the circumstances, you may patronize me if you like, Mr. Salvitore. I'm quite serious, though. I represent your enemies—the enemies of all of you that are here tonight. I and my colleagues have fought you this past year, and have at last succeeded in drawing you out where we can destroy you. I controlled the orbital weapon platform that destroyed many of your holdings in the United States."

A sigh of comprehension passed through the raptly attentive audience. Salvitore's face took on a serious expression. He gave orders to his head of security to search the house and grounds. He and his other guests remained where they were, along with the two guards who had escorted Somerset in.

"You have gained our undivided attention, Dr. Somerset," said Salvitore, waiting. Salvitore motioned with his hand, and told the wine server to "pour the good Doctor a glass of wine." Somerset accepted, just as graciously.

"You see," said Somerset, "we couldn't risk waiting any longer, while you consolidated your control. By the way, before you knew of Damocles, when had you planned to establish autocratic rule? Did you have a date in mind?"

Salvitore shrugged noncommittally. "Nothing specific. We had planned to assume overt control in another five or ten years. Things were going the way we desired anyway. There was no pressing hurry. We had hoped to disarm the United States through gun control legislation first, and to execute a more gradual, less violent take-over. We would have liked to have accomplished it without open warfare."

"That's sooner than we thought," said Somerset. "We had estimated another ten or fifteen years."

Salvitore waved his hand dismissively. "It may have taken that long. What difference would it make?"

Somerset sipped the wine, "None, to you. At least not in the way you've envisioned things working out, but to us, it was imperative that we act while we still had the freedom to do the things necessary to put our weapons systems in place. We also had to wait for you to move in and begin taking overt actions. To have acted too early would have triggered a backlash in the American people. Until the Vanderbilt administration, many people still clung tenaciously to a misguided loyalty to those figureheads that you put in positions of authority, thinking they were being patriotic. We had to wait until a lot of people were openly disenchanted, almost the last possible moment. If we had waited much longer, though, we would not have had the freedom to construct the weapons and get them into orbit. Right now, your control is almost complete. Research programs are dead, government institutions in limbo. I doubt that we could manage it under today's conditions."

"I compliment you on your assessment, and your achievement," said Salvatore, casually lighting a cigarette. "What made you believe that you could precipitate our takeover?"

"We watched as you gained control of NATO and the United Nations, and the development of the hand-in-hand conspiracy between the World Bank, the International Monetary Fund, the European Economic Council, the Federal Open Market Committee and the Federal Reserve Board. It was obvious to all but the blind. The engineered collapse of most of the private banks and

lending institutions, followed by the assumption and sale
of assets to the bigger banks under the Federal Deposi-
tors Insurance Corporation, and finally, the rash of mergers of the larger banks and corporate holding companies
in America, the unprecedented bullish market—it all
seemed to point toward a final commitment on your part.
We assumed that if we fanned the flame of independence
for a little bit, then appeared to fail, that you would seize
the chance to get it over with once and for all. It appears
that we're batting a thousand, so far."

Salvitore stirred the air with his finger. "You say that
you intended to fail?"

"We intended for you to *think* we had failed. Otherwise, you would never have surfaced. Now, we know who
you are, those of you here, and the smaller fry that are
running things for you. Once you've all been taken or
destroyed, your holdings and your fortunes will finance
a new cooperative of independent governments without
hegemony. It will take some fine-tuning, no doubt, but
it will work."

Salvitore laughed. "Are you telling me that this
organization of yours has tricked us—that you are in
control? Your weapon is destroyed! We have armies in
every major city on the globe. What do you think you
can do—you and your band of renegades? Who are you,
anyway?"

"On the contrary," said Somerset, rolling the wine
glass between his hands, "Damocles is still very much
in existence. Two more weapon systems are also in orbit.
As we speak, Damocles is locking grid coordinates into
his fire-control computer. Your main troop contingents
are being recalled to their local bases and barracks. They
each think it's just a local thing, and they are not the
least bit alarmed. In a few moments, at 9:00 P.M., to be
exact, those armies will be as imaginary as your belief
in your cultural superiority.

"Speaking of culture, with your Greco-Roman heritage, you should appreciate the irony of the names we
gave to the weapon systems, the instruments that are

about to compass your defeat. We decided to retain the Grecian mythology theme. Damocles held the threat over your heads, forcing you to react in a predictable way. Ariadne was the Greek princess who gave Theseus a thread with which to find his way out of the Minotaur's labyrinth. She hangs above our heads now, doing the same thing that Damocles is doing over the American continent. We wanted our daughters to be able to identify in gender with one of them, you see.

"Apollo, god of the sun, music, medicine, prophecy and poetry, hangs over Asia. Actually, we had a bit of dissension there; some of our Asian members wanted to call him Rama, and of course, Buddha came up, along with Allah, Mohammed and several other deities and prophets. Apollo won out. It maintains the poetry, don't you see? Damocles to show humanity the threat; Ariadne to show us the way out; Apollo to heal us, and show us the beauty of the new day. If that isn't poetic justice, I don't know what is. I wish my friend Paul could hear that. He's always getting the last word. I don't think he could top me tonight."

"I appreciate your droll wit, Dr. Somerset," said Salvitore. "If what you say is true, what do you think you will accomplish? Man is man. They will just revert again. People do not change. Do you think you're going to divide up everything equally, and it will stay that way? The very day that your great utopia is founded, someone will bring forth a pack of cards or a pair of dice, and the reapportionment of wealth will begin anew. What will you have gained? Come, come, Dr. Somerset, surely you're not that naive or socialistic in your thinking. Would you overrun all good things with the common herd?"

"No, I'm not a socialist or communist. I believe that restrained capitalism is the best way. And, you are right about the darker nature of man. But it can, with effort, be controlled. It was you who were setting up a socialistic hierarchy—a return to feudalistic serfdom. You would have owned everything. The rest of humanity would have been equal only in their abject poverty and lack of say in their lives.

"I believe that all of humanity, as individuals, should enjoy the things that they earn through honest labor and personal ingenuity. That does not include the theft, coercion, fraud, rape, subjugation and murder that you practice. Those who make their living by those means are no better than savages and sewer rats, no matter how well they dress, or how modern the methods they employ." Somerset picked up his wine glass and held it toward Salvitore, in salute.

"Here's to mankind, Mr. Salvitore. To another chance for happiness. Maybe they will use it wisely, and maybe they won't, but they're going to get another stab at it. Here's to all of you," he swung his glass at the watching faces around the room, "in the hope that there is such a thing as divine justice." He lowered the glass, and his voice, looking inward for a moment. "Here's to the atonement of Leland Somerset; I just hope I don't have to spend eternity in the same hell as all of you."

"You haven't said who your organization is, Dr. Somerset," said Salvitore.

Somerset emptied his wine glass, considered it briefly, then set it aside. "Forgive me, Mr. Salvitore," he said, looking at his watch. "I'm afraid I tend toward verbosity once I get started. We are just a group of concerned scientists."

The city of Rome felt a small tremor during the evening of the eighth of August. People noted and forgot it. A seismologist at the University of Rome made a note of its direction and amplitude the following day, and assumed that some construction company was blasting nearby. It would be two days later that a delivery driver would discover that the Villa Salvitore, and the hilltop that it had occupied, were gone.

XLIV

It was early morning, on the tenth day after the excursion to Palo Alto. Jack and Eve Townsend had risen at 5:30 A.M., and Jack was squatting in front of the camp stove, near the mouth of the pipe, boiling water for coffee. Eve was under the camouflage canopy just outside, rummaging around in the back of the Cherokee for another can of coffee. The one Jack had was almost empty.

Suddenly, a tremor ran through the ground. They both froze for a moment. It happened again, closer and more energetic than before.

Jack stood up. "Honey, get out of there," he called. "C'mon, hurry up."

Eve complied, running to stand beside him. They were both looking around in all directions, searching for clues.

"Earthquake?" asked Eve.

"Maybe," he responded. "Let's go up on top and see if we can see anything."

They scrambled up the slope. Another closer tremor began before they reached the top, causing them to slip and falter, but they kept on going until they could look out over the long valley towards Mountain View.

A flickering at their backs made them turn, and to the distant south, a shaft of bluish light danced and flickered in a sky gone black and ominous. They could see minute flashes of lightning arcing sporadically in the distant, roiling cloud. The tremor rumbled again, and very faintly now, they could hear a crackling and popping noise, and an eerie singing drone, like someone blowing through a bamboo pipe.

"What the hell . . . ?" Jack murmured, watching the blue spear of light dance and flash back and forth across the horizon. As they stood watching, the tremors became continuous, and continued to increase in amplitude. The crackling and popping was gradually increasing in volume, also, and the background drone was now a deep thrumming that was becoming synchronized with the vibration in the ground. Realization dawned in Jack's mind.

"Get down! Hurry! Get inside the pipe," he shouted, dragging Eve down the slope after him. They fell and slid the last few yards down the dirt embankment. Jack scrambled to his feet, lifting and pulling Eve into the opening of the pipe. He moved them back to the tent and inside it before he stopped.

"It's the weapon," he said. "It's Damocles. Lay down and wrap the pillows and blankets around you. We're going to get shaken pretty hard, I think."

"Are we going to die?" she asked calmly, looking at him.

"I don't know, honey," he said, hugging her to him. "We're probably as safe here as anywhere. It's a choice between being inside this pipe if it collapses, or getting fried by radiation outside. We can only hope we don't get a direct hit. Cover up. Cover your eyes and ears as best you can."

It occurred to him that if the beam hit the reservoir, boiling water and super-heated steam would flow through the pipe. He didn't tell her.

The jarring vibration in the earth was being transmitted to the concrete pipe now, and Jack could feel the low-frequency sonic waves passing up the length of the pipe as it coupled weakly with some harmonic in the modulated beam. The thrumming drone was so loud now that they would have had to shout to be heard above it.

Jack could differentiate now between the crackling and popping as it grew louder, and could feel the shocks, as individual blows followed the louder pops more closely than the distant ones. Hope grew in him, even as the bouncing tent frame was slapped more and more violently against the concrete floor of the pipe. The beam was not being fired continuously, was not obliterating everything. It was selectively darting from target to target across a wide area as it advanced northward, hitting dozens of individual, pinpoint targets each second, sparing non-enemy real estate. If he was right, the reservoir might not be hit. Their main danger would be from the seismic shock.

Even as he thought it, a mighty bang almost deafened them, as a pulse of hellish energy vaporized the military encampment near San Jose, ten miles to the east. The pipe moaned like the bass pipe in a gigantic church organ.

Two seconds after the bolt hit San Jose, they were lifted almost to the ceiling of the pipe—tent, wooden pallets and all—and slammed against the concrete floor. The roof of the tent collapsed on top of them, pushed down by the ceiling of the pipe. Eve screamed. The breath was knocked from their bodies when they hit the floor. A spray of water hit them, but no flood came through because the pipe was no longer connected to the reservoir. It had jumped upward, through the ridge of covering earth that formed the rim of the reservoir, and separated into the twenty-foot sections of which it was composed.

Jack and Eve held grimly to each other, and he tried to pin her body between his and the pallet that they were clinging to, shielding her from the walls of the pipe as it spun around sickeningly, bounced and began to roll down the hill. There was a two-hundred-foot fall where the hill sloped steeply down into the canyon, and he knew they did not have a prayer of surviving it.

They were wrapped in blankets and he couldn't see anything, could only feel what was happening to them. He heard a grinding crunch, like a metal trash can being run over by a truck, and the pipe stopped rolling, rocked back and forth a couple of times and was still. The heavy thrumming vibration was gradually fading, and a minute later, bruised and hurting, they began to claw their way out of the wet, tangled bedding.

When they could see, they discovered that they lay in a section of pipe, open at both ends, with water flowing around and by them, running down the slope. Jack got shakily to his feet and hurriedly half-dragged, half-carried Eve out of the pipe and along the slope until they were out of line with the breach in the wall of the reservoir, and on dry ground. They collapsed together, then rolled up on their elbows and looked back. The section of piping they had occupied had rolled up on, and partially crushed, the Jeep Cherokee. The vehicle had formed a chock that held the pipe in place on the gentle slope, not fifty feet from the edge of the canyon.

As they watched, the water sluiced away the soil beneath the pipe and vehicle, and they shifted sideways. The section of pipe rolled slowly at first, gained momentum, then bounded over the lip of the canyon. A long moment later they heard it hit and shatter against the canyon bottom.

Jack and Eve looked at each other, gasping and bruised, not saying anything. Jack ran his hands over her legs, arms and ribs, then collapsed beside her, his head resting on her chest. Eve lay panting, looking up at the sky, now clearing above them.

After a while, she put her hand on his head, closed her eyes and smiled. They were alive.

XLV

Senator Isley banged his gavel. The mutter of conversation began to die out in the auditorium. It was a bright, sunny October day in Atlanta, and the university was the rich, dark green of late summer in the South.

The seating was at rows of long, narrow tables, set up like a Bingo hall. Possibly three hundred people were present—Congress, scientists, administrators, educators, businessmen, bankers, newspeople and the military. On the stage, Isley shared the long table with Hector Ortiz, Clarence Patterson, Gene Stickle, Able Johnson, Joseph Miller and Paul Haas. They comprised a panel that would answer some of the remaining questions these new leaders and the public had, concerning the past ten days of committee meetings. Joseph Miller, Acting President of the United States, opened the meeting.

"We have decided on a course of action that will surely be criticized by many, but we believe that it is vital to the emergence of a new public philosophy. The new International Union of Scientists will act as an oversight committee for the independent national governments. They have mapped out a twenty-year plan, complete with benchmarks and periodic assessments of policies and performance, for global democratization. Those countries that have never known democracy will need the time to learn how to live and work in a democratic environment. In many cases, it will scarcely be long enough.

"It will be organized as a controlled experiment, and adjusted as necessary. Grassroots feedback will be the principal yardstick used to assess effectiveness, so in a sense, it will be a democratic experiment in government—a scientific approach to what works best for a free society in education, commerce and law. I can tell you right now that the core tenet and law of political reform will be to tell students the truth, and only the truth. In commerce, we believe that American free enterprise proved itself for two hundred years to be superior to all other economic systems. In a free society, it is the only choice possible. Stocks and securities trading will be curtailed, and in future, done very differently. We need a method of obtaining investment capital, but it will no longer be a poker game for the wealthy. With regard to civil law, we will start by building a constitutional matrix against which every existing law, regulation, ordinance and policy must be tested. If a law fails the matrix, it will be deleted from all justice codes. To begin with, in the United States, it cannot conflict with the existing U.S. Constitution and Bill of Rights. Until amended by the people, that proven document, with its universal concepts, shall remain the basis for all our laws. Secondly, the law, rule, ordinance or whatever cannot be redundant. It is asinine and unnecessarily restrictive to make multiple laws to address one crime. The old legal system could make a jaywalker appear to be the most heinous of criminals, simply by the number of redundant laws he had broken. We want to clean the legal system up and make it the purposeful tool it is supposed to be in a society, rather than a burden imposed on the populace by grafters. The old state policy, that ignorance is no excuse, pretty much permitted any law—no matter how esoteric or hidden— to go unchallenged. You didn't know what laws you had broken until the judge told you.

"To summarize, the new legal architecture will be designed for the people it is supposed to serve, not for the benefit of lawyers and government control freaks.

"The industrialized nations will start off with a much greater latitude of self-determination, but they too, will need time to adjust to principles of true justice and ethical practice in government and business. Since the practice of those principles are rather rare in some societies, including our own, punishment for non-compliance will be severe at first. Make no mistake, the old ruling families and autocratic governments are gone. It will take time to decide how best to reapportion the wealth those regimes sequestered from the people they ruled, but it will be done, even if it comes down to just dividing it evenly and starting over from scratch.

"The tax ceiling will remain for now, and we've agreed it shall be a global practice. No citizen may be taxed more than twenty percent of her income, ever again, and whatever method of taxation is adopted by the various countries, the rate and method of enforcement must be the same for every citizen. It allows countries to differentiate based on their own regional assets, cultural preferences, and so on, but protects the citizen from uneven and excessive exploitation. Private property and privacy are two more common tenets already agreed upon as basic human rights that are not the purview of government.

"It will be a twenty-year, gradual, hopefully bump-free transition period. In America, free enterprise, affordable education and self-determination will be the cornerstones of this administration. It will also be an honorable government, an accountable government, without secrets, for the first time in at least a century. We must have and enforce those tenets above all else."

"We've heard rumors that all armies are to be disbanded. Is that true?" asked a reporter.

Miller motioned to Gene Stickle, who turned from those he was conversing with on stage, and came to the podium to stand beside Miller. "Not completely," responded Stickle. "We've agreed that each country will be permitted to retain an independent military, and to develop technological defense systems—excluding biological, chemical and radio-nuclides. Military expenditures may not exceed one percent of the country's GDP.

This really amounts to just local security forces. Anything excessive, such as a sudden massive buildup, will trigger a response from the machines, and censure from the world community. For America, it works out to be about a hundred-billion-dollar budget for the combined military services, about a fourth of what it was. We're still human—we have to be eased into the idea of *no armies, no wars*, and from a survival perspective, we can't afford not to develop and maintain both a national and global capacity for defense. Who knows when, or from where, a threat to human survival may come. It may eventually come from space. We have to continue learning and advancing technologically, even in weapons of destruction. From now on, though, the President will not have the authority to commit the military without a national vote. Neither will Congress. The only exception is when the United States is under immediate attack. Then, and only then, can the President act unilaterally. Even then, congressional and state controls come into play within twenty-four hours."

"What about all the military personnel that have spent their careers in the service? What happens to them?" asked a military man. "When the services are down-sized, there will be a lot of jobs lost."

"That's true," Stickle responded. "Right now, the public doesn't have a lot of sympathy for the military. About half the personnel strength is gone, anyway—dead or in camps. Nevertheless, the IUS has agreed to a fair draw-down and dispersion, over a two-year period. The military will be restructured. There will be an Air Force and a Navy. The Marines will remain as assault troops under the command of the Navy. The Army, as a separate service, will be no more. As you can see, our purpose is to eliminate the capability of any nation to form a large invasion or occupational force."

"There will be some demand for various military skills in the new United States Space Service," said Patterson, stepping forward. "The Air Force Space Command, for example, will be absorbed by NASA. There will be no military involvement in space anymore, except for operation of reconnaissance satellites.

"I've gotten involved in this thing so recently that I'm not up to speed yet on projects and programs, but we've had a lot of scientific projects waiting in the wings for years, overlooked for lack of funding, or deferred due to misguided priorities. We're dusting them off and reexamining them in light of new objectives. Earth and planetary sciences, and space exploration are worthy areas to apply all of that national investment in military training and equipment, and humanity will reap a remarkable harvest of advancements.

"We're going to develop commercial interests in space—orbital factories and research facilities. We will need engineering and manufacturing skills in propulsion systems, avionics, radar, communications, aerospace systems, microgravity construction and maintenance, as well as jobs in administration. We will begin constructing an orbital research station next year, and permanent manned bases on the moon and Mars as soon as we can get there.

"As for the infantry and similar support skills, they will have to seek jobs in private enterprise, retrain, reeducate themselves. Pensions will be prorated in some fashion, and if they choose, they can roll them over into private retirement funds or draw them out. We don't want to create another punished caste. We want to forget and go on with life in a better world. We've all earned the right to a new day, not just a new beginning of the same old world. This is a transition time in human history.

"Two teams of administrative and fiscal scientists are working out the economic and government fiscal parameters for the U.S. Without thirty percent of our national budget going into defense-related activities, we should have the funds to generate lots of productive jobs in health services, scientific agribusiness, scientific exploration, orbital space factories, alternative and renewable energy industries, green automobiles, etc.

"We have an ambitious agenda on the table, and we

welcome input. There are going to be lots of town-hall meetings and national interactive discussion of issues in the future. You might not think so now, but I think you will all come around, and truly like what is ahead for us. It's going to be exciting and productive times. We hope to have more specific answers shortly."

"What happens to all the prisoners you've taken?"

"They will be isolated from society on island work farms," Ortiz responded, ambling over to join the group at the podium. "They will produce their own food and clothing and shelter. They will have no rights or inter-actions with normal society, outside the boundaries of their farm communities. They will be allowed to trade, so as to diversify their lives. That's more than they had in mind for us. Internally, they may operate as they like, within limits. They may not leave their island. They shall not be supported. Excepting the initial tools, educational materials, medicines and supplies they need to get started, they will be on their own. They will work, and make their living, build their own society, or starve. All work farms will be located in moderate climates in the tropics. They will have a far better beginning, and a far better chance than our pioneer ancestors had."

"What if they have children?"

"The prisoners will be segregated by sex until they can be sterilized, then they will be put together so that they can have a semblance of normal life. Any existing children shall be removed into normal society. It wouldn't be right to punish them for their parents' sins.

"For the present, that's the best plan we've come up with. Their philosophy is not going to change, and they can't be allowed to raise another generation of potential tyrants. The chain must be broken. Their philosophy must die out with them. It's as humane as we can be, and still accomplish our purpose."

"Some people are concerned that we will all be lumped together, just as the Euro-American Alliance had planned. Is that what is planned?" asked the first reporter.

"No," said Miller. "The United States of America will

still be an independent nation, as will all other countries. We believe that nationalism is a *good* thing, that different customs, traditions and cultures are what make life interesting. If the world were forced into a polyglot culture, most of the beauty of the world would be lost. We don't have to have the same customs, or language, or religious beliefs in order to get along with one another. All we have to do is practice tolerance and honesty in our relations.

"In the past, the term 'diversity' was a cover for making everyone exactly the same, an ignorant robot reciting a politically-correct mantra. The subterfuges of government and international business are largely responsible for every war ever fought. When greed and lust for power are allowed to flourish, a commonness of slavery is always the natural end product. How can it be otherwise? Who wants uniformity, especially at that price? It is not the common people who start these things. It is the ambition and greed of those in power.

"To that end, the nations of the world have agreed to become a little isolationist. We will trade and travel freely, even undertake joint ventures, but we will no longer permit foreign investment or interference in each others' internal affairs, beyond the establishment of the basic human rights I've mentioned. When permitted, foreign influence is seldom in the interest of the penetrated nation. It becomes an influence that destroys cultures and makes enemies. Such activities shall be universally illegal. We think that the force of self-determination, by its very nature, can only propagate greater freedom and greater individual opportunity for everyone, no matter what other cultural traditions make up their society."

"The banking community and foreign investors are really going to hate that idea," said a businesswoman sitting in the front row. Several other voices echoed the sentiment.

Ortiz spoke up, "What we are trying to do is lay a common groundwork for a free society, based on principles that are common to humankind. To establish liberty throughout the world's peoples. Beyond that, we will not interfere in each other's affairs. The peoples of other nations can take the common substrate of freedom and shared knowledge, and build on it what they will. We want to elevate mankind as a whole. As an administrative body, we scientists agree that there are few political or commercial advantages consistent with universal liberty, that are derived from the capital investment of outside businesses in other countries. Investors want control of any resources they put money into. That foreign influence overruns local concerns and customs, and disenfranchises the natives. We want to live together on this planet, like brothers and sisters who live together in the same house, each with our own things and our own ways. We can find ways to communicate and work together in harmony, and to trade, and still retain our individuality. Only commercial greed and political ambition require the invasion of another's territory, or acquisition of his resources. The citizenry of each country must learn to control their would-be despots and monopolistic enterprises. They will be held accountable."

"What about the weapons?" another reporter asked. "Who controls them now that Dr. Somerset is gone?"

"They are controlled at present, by a five-member committee, and overseen by the IUS at large. Dr. Somerset programmed the weapons to operate automatically for a long period of time. At the end of that period, unless we interfere, they will self-destruct. All the committee can do is reset the program clocks every month. If anything happens to the committee, and the weapons are not reset, they will begin to destroy thousands of targets, all over the earth."

"What are the targets?"

"Only the weapons know. They are *smart* systems, capable of reprogramming themselves within limits. They can analyze every square meter of the earth's surface, monitor communications, compare global activities among themselves. If something is not right, they will override their reset instructions and fire. Only Leland Somerset knew their full capabilities. For a few decades though, no one had better try to raise an army. The machines won't tolerate it."

"What about news and entertainment programming? You've made it plain you don't like the media. What happens now?"

"What we don't like," said Ortiz, his eyes black with anger, "is manipulative lying. Only absolutely factual reporting will be tolerated in the future. No anti-liberty political propaganda, and no media bias will be permitted. No monopoly of attitude, and no constant barrage of one social viewpoint. The crime for violating a public trust is treason, and the punishment will be life on an island work farm. You reporters will be given a transcript of this meeting at its conclusion. Make certain you do not alter its meaning or edit any information out of it. You will regret it if you do."

XLVI

A Halloween party was in progress at the Townsends' house. Ortiz' faculty friends and a few people from Townsend's company had brought their families. Small children, costumed as witches, fairies, rock stars, ghosts, skeletons and various mythical creatures were bobbing for apples, drinking Kool-Aid and playing pin the tail on the donkey amid squeals and shouts. The few teenagers present were talking, drinking cider, and listening to "The Monster Mash" and other classical Halloween music on the radio. Adults were talking and drinking in casual groups.

The Townsends, Teller, Ortiz and Haas stood apart from the other guests for a few moments, sipping their drinks and watching the children play.

"Is everybody back from Chile, now?" Townsend asked.

"Yes," said Ortiz. "We had almost three hundred people in all. The last bunch came back through Mexico by train."

"How did they all take it? And how did you manage such a big camp without the government becoming suspicious?"

"Actually, everybody did quite well. Had fun, in fact. You and Eve should have come. We excavated a pre-Columbian tomb of at least moderate significance, and it was a lark for almost everyone. A few complained about living in tents and showering outside at first, but when news of the killing and plundering started coming in, they suddenly saw things in a different light.

"As for the government finding out, it's not that much out of the ordinary for universities to have summer camps. It would be impossible to track what all of the various institutions do, or where they go. They didn't consider us that important, anyway.

"That has been our single, greatest advantage throughout all of this. Universities are generally treated as being somehow apart from mainstream life. That's really the only reason we were able to accomplish what we did. The general public think of colleges as if they were on another planet that you send your kids to for four years. The government treats them as databanks that they consult occasionally, and not much more.

"Our camps in Alaska, Canada and the Caribbean seem to have enjoyed similar experiences. It was much more difficult for our European people. They've always had tighter controls, over there."

"Where did they hole up?" asked Townsend.

"In the Austrian Alps and the French Pyrenees," answered Teller. "They trickled into staging points by rail, bus and car over a period of several weeks, then guides took them on to camp. One group was at eleven thousand feet, in a glacial cave. Conrad had his hands full with logistics. He spent a year stockpiling canned rations, blankets and fuel at four different sites. Got to hand it to him, though. He did a first-rate job. Only one small group got caught, before they ever left town. An alpine patrolman found one site and had to be killed. Other than that, all the sites were remote, and didn't interact with the locals. With the world in a state of chaos, they were essentially forgotten. I guess you had it pretty bad here, huh buddy?"

Townsend hugged Eve to his side as he answered. "It was bad enough. San Francisco and L.A. really got the worst of it. The suburbs didn't put up as much resistance, so the retaliation wasn't what it was in the cities."

"Where were you and Eve?" asked Ortiz.

"We stayed in the hills above here, most of the time,"

said Townsend. "There's a water reservoir back over that hill." He pointed southward. "It's off the beaten path, and no one bothered. Inside two weeks, their subjugation of the local population was over. They herded everyone into school auditoriums and public parks, and laid down the rules.

"Eve and I holed up inside one of an array of big concrete pipes that form an overflow system for the water reservoir. We did a little sniping. We blew up a supply area in Palo Alto ten days before Damocles fired.

"After that, we formed citizens' groups armed with confiscated weapons. Those occupation forces left alive after Damocles fired were rounded up in short order. We have thirty-six holding compounds full of prisoners, being held by civilian guards. That's in addition to the jails. Almost ten thousand prisoners in all. We're preparing tent camps at Fort Irwin, near Barstow, to receive them. They don't have a lot of fight left in them, right now, but we've got to get them moved to places where they can be contained. After a while, they'll get restless, and we need to be prepared.

"They had a big encampment near San Jose that was destroyed, and all the major Army, Navy and Air Force strategic and tactical combat bases in California are gone, of course. I guess it's the same across the rest of the country, isn't it?"

"Pretty much so," said Ortiz. "Leland was thorough. He didn't want the government of any country to have the military capacity left to recover. All tactical and strategic bases were destroyed."

"I still don't see why Leland had to die," said Haas, his eyes tearing for his lost friend. "He didn't have to shoulder all the blame. We should admit to our share of the responsibility, Hector."

Haas and Ortiz had viewed a computer file the evening before—a file that Somerset had left for them. It contained Somerset's good-byes, the reset control codes for the weapons, and some final suggestions. For the most part, he tried to absolve them of any guilt for the destruction, and shouldered the responsibility for creating and firing Damocles and his siblings.

"I think that would be a grievous mistake," said Ortiz. "If all of us involved in the conspiracy were to come out of the closet and admit to the public that Leland wasn't alone, that there are several dozen people who cold-bloodedly planned the deaths of millions of people over a period of several years, we would be looked upon as war criminals. That's okay for you, if you are just so full of remorse that you need to be punished for your sins so that you can die at peace, but what about this new world we're trying to build? It will lose all its leadership just when it needs it the most. All the planning and dying will have been for nothing. No one will want to be led by, or want to follow the mapped-out plans of a bunch of mass murderers. They won't be able to admit that they had to be forced into action under a lash, and that their new leaders are the people who whipped them without mercy. It would drive them into festering resentment—not creativity and hope for the future.

"We've psychoanalyzed this to death, Paul. If we do what you suggest, in ten years little children will hate and distrust all scientists. There probably won't be any scientists left, and the earth will be covered by tiny, warring, bickering feudal states again, with no goals and no progress. It will set mankind back centuries. If we do what's best for the world, we'll see an advanced society in twenty or thirty years, with colonies on the moon and Mars, with great gains in scientific knowledge. We'll be on the threshold to the stars. Would you rob the world of that, and destroy the lives of billions? Would you rob Leland of that?"

"I guess I'm not thinking straight," said Haas. "I suppose I am being self-indulgent, and parading my guilt. I'm over it. I promise. Just tell me, Hector—how do you feel about what Leland did?"

Ortiz stared into the glass of beer he was holding, his forehead gathering in a frown. After a moment, "I don't know what I feel. Leland meant a lot to me. I can't go to the innocent dead, and justify to them why it was necessary for them to die. How does one *ever* justify such a thing, in any war, no matter how noble or righteous the reasons for the war. How do we justify the innocent children at Hiroshima and Nagasaki, or Berlin, or Viet Nam." He sighed, looking at Eve in a remote, introspective way. "I believe that what Leland did was necessary, in order to achieve all those important objectives I just mentioned. Someone else will have to say whether or not the objectives were worth all the innocent lives. It depends on the future, I guess—what eventually comes from it all. "From a personal perspective, I knew the boy—knew his heart. I can't think of him as a monster, anymore than I can believe I'm a monster. Maybe that's just my own human hypocrisy. It was war.

"I don't suppose it makes any difference, anyway, at least not now. He believed that he had to do what he did. For him, as horrible as the act was, there was no other way. He could not live with the billions of lives that would endure centuries of suffering if he did not act. He couldn't permit the loss of centuries of progress. It was a scientist's choice. You put aside your emotions and prejudices, and face facts. It was those lives, or the end of civilization, maybe forever."

Ortiz paused a moment, thinking. Finally, "I think he planned to die all along. It was his genius that made the weapons possible, no matter that others helped put them up. I think he knew that the nation couldn't heal, especially the relatives of those who died at his hands, until someone paid for those lives. I think he also knew that some sort of trial would have divided the country and set old animosities into new channels, and if we refused to try him, we would be viewed as just another bunch of tyrants, with a different set of standards for ourselves than those we forced upon the rest of humanity.

"I think Leland wanted to avoid all of that, and to give the country a fresh start. As excited as he was about the potential for a new, free and peaceful world, and as much as he dearly wanted to be a part of it, he thought that this was the only way. He taped a statement for the press, which will be aired in a few days, explaining everything, taking full responsibility, and passing control to us. Now, people can have a sense of closure."

"He consolidated the scientific community too," said Haas, "in a way that I would never have thought possible. That is his real legacy, and unfortunately, its importance will likely be lost on the general population. Thanks to him, we now have an open, international community for the first time ever. Humanity can progress as a whole. Everybody will share in the discoveries. Maybe future generations will have fewer fears and suspicions to divide them."

"I know it's self-centered, but I wish I could have played a bigger role," said Townsend. "I know why it had to be, but I still would like to have been in the thick of it."

Teller clapped him on the back. "Well, now that we know you're straight, you can be in on the next one," he said, laughing. "Seriously, Jimmy, there was just too much at stake. You said it yourself, this was probably the last chance we would get. If they had won, mankind might have been enslaved for centuries. Besides, you did more than you know. You saved the lives of a million people, maybe more, by discovering the plot to destroy L.A., and you crippled their ability by destroying Broderick and his international terrorist links. In that light, you did exactly what you were trained to do. You protected this sovereign nation. You upheld your oath and defended the Constitution. Thanks to you, and to the others who gathered intelligence and fought to save our country, we have another chance."

Townsend swatted Eve on the bottom, lightly, and smiled. "Another chance," he said.

She smiled and took his hand. "I love you," she said, looking dreamily into his eyes.

Teller rolled his eyes. "I gotta get another beer, or

I'm gonna cry. Maybe I'll take a leak while I'm at it," he said, ambling toward the bathroom.

Ortiz cast a meaningful look at Townsend. "If I were you," he said, "I'd make him go in the yard."

DAVID DRAKE
& S.M. STIRLING

–THE GENERAL–

A GREAT NEW MILITARY SF SERIES FROM THE TWO TOP WRITERS IN THE FIELD!

Military genius Raj Whitehall was given the daunting task of uniting his planet and dragging it up out of the black hole of history into which it had fallen. But the ancient battle computer in Raj's mind was God, and God was on his side....

"...a new series pairs two of military science fiction's most gifted authors with considerable success.... There is plenty of fast action, intelligently conceived tactics and weaponry, and a full-blown world with a lived-in quality. A treat for military science fiction buffs."
—Roland Green, *Booklist*

"...outstanding....a delight of Byzantine plots and counterplots set in a roughly 19th century technology civilization. Even the most jaded SF reader will enjoy this one."
—*Reading for Pleasure*

The Forge	72037-6 $5.99	☐
The Hammer	72105-4 $5.99	☐
The Anvil	72171-2 $5.99	☐
The Steel	72189-5 $5.99	☐
The Sword	87647-3 $5.99	☐

If not available from your local bookstore, fill out this coupon and send a check or money order for the cover price(s) to Baen Books, Dept. BA, P.O. Box 1403, Riverdale, NY 10471. Delivery can take up to ten weeks.

NAME: _____

ADDRESS: _____

_____

I have enclosed a check or money order in the amount of $_____

EXPLORE OUR WEB SITE

 BAEN.COM

*VISIT THE BAEN BOOKS
WEB SITE AT:*

http://www.baen.com
or just search for baen.com

Get information on the latest releases,
sample chapters of upcoming novels,
read about your favorite authors,
enter contests, and much more! ;)